ALSO BY PAUL KEARNEY

The Mark of Ran

The Way to Babylon

A Different Kingdom

Riding the Unicorn

Hawkwood's Voyage

The Heretic Kings

The Iron Wars

The Second Empire

Ships from the West

"Fantastic . . . a wonderful blend of *Treasure Island* and classic fantasy. It is the beginning of what looks to be an incredible voyage and presents a refreshing twist on the classic fantasy story. . . . So splice those mainsails, feel the wind in your hair, let the salt sea fill your nostrils and set a course for The Sea Beggars."

—*Outland* (UK) on *The Mark of Ran*

"Kearney's new novel marks a triumphant return for one of the very best British writers of hard-edged, visceral, gritty fantasy fiction. . . . Kearney has never been one to bow to the conventions and stereotypical tropes of fantasy fiction; he's always left the bog-standard kiddie-quest lying trampled in the dirt where it belongs and struck out in new directions [with] a focus on high-quality world-building and great strength of characterization. . . . He was writing the sort of gritty, hard-edged, visceral fantasy that speaks to those bored to tears by the horrifically overdone kiddie-quest even before Martin began his Song of Ice and Fire or Erikson embarked on his Malazan Books of the Fallen, and *The Mark of Ran* will certainly appeal to fans of both these series, as well as readers who enjoy the likes of David Gemmell or Glen Cook as well. . . . Kearney's prose is consistently and typically excellent . . . you are in for a treat."   —TheAlienOnline.com

"If there is a subgenre of naval fantasy, Paul Kearney is its master and commander. With provocative, complex characters and written in a language evoking the sea's own rhythm—a language that is, quite simply, beautiful. Kearney is to my mind one of the very best writers of fantasy around. And recognition of that is long overdue. His previous series, Monarchies of God, delivered a raw, uncompromising world and some of the most memorable characters in fantasy—memorable for their imperfections as much as their deeds, courageous and otherwise. As with Glen Cook's Black Company series, there's no romantic gloss to Kearney's fantasy worlds. He delivers a much-needed dose of reality to fantasy, and I eagerly await the next installment."   —Steven Erikson

"In this gritty fantasy swashbuckler... Kearney's crisp, often lyrical writing shines brightest when his characters take to the sea. Readers who fancy the creak of ship's timbers and the flash of live steel, the taint of dark magic and the lure of long-buried secrets, will gladly sail away with Kearney's latest novel." —*Publishers Weekly*

"Kearney injects an enthusiasm into his tale that makes it new and exciting. There are echoes of the best in other fantasists... and yet it's all Kearney's own delicious style... I can hardly wait for the next volume." —SFSite.com

"Think *Master and Commander* with added magic.... Kearney writes well, his prose roars along like a riptide, and he delivers plot broadsides with panache." —Jon Courtenay Grimwood, *Guardian*

"Gorgeous... about as three-dimensional as a fantasy world can be. You can taste the salt in the air of this barbaric, corrupt expanse, smell the blood.... An immersive joy in which you must bathe. Full gudgeons ahead!" —*SFX*

"Everything a fantasy reader could possibly want... Kearney's handling of this page-turning, atmospheric tale is never less than expert." —*Starburst*

"Finally, a fantasy novel that lives up to the billing... Kearney's novel is every bit as good as it promises to be ... a cracking story." —*Birmingham Post*

"Dark, compelling... bodes well for the next book." —*Interzone*

"One of the most exciting of fantasy storytellers returns with a suspenseful and well-crafted tale in a subgenre that could well be called nautical fantasy—if so, he is the admiral of the fleet.... There is a brilliant twist at the end... and you're left eagerly awaiting the next installment." —*Western Daily Press*

"Kearney constructs a solid plot that is awash with maritime detail [that] will certainly be appreciated by maritime fantasy fans." —*Booklist*

THIS FORSAKEN EARTH

BOOK TWO *of* THE SEA BEGGARS

Paul Kearney

BANTAM BOOKS

THIS FORSAKEN EARTH
A Bantam Spectra Book / December 2006
Originally published 2006 by Bantam Press,
a division of Transworld Publishers (UK)

Published by Bantam Dell
A Division of Random House, Inc.
New York, New York

Book design by Sarah Smith

Library of Congress Cataloging-in-Publication Data
Kearney, Paul.
This forsaken earth / Paul Kearney.
p. cm.
ISBN-10: 0-553-38363-9
ISBN-13: 978-0-553-38363-8
I. Title.
PR6061.E2156 T48 2006   2006047733
823/.914 22

Printed in the United States of America
Published simultaneously in Canada

www.bantamdell.com

BVG 10 9 8 7 6 5 4 3 2 1

For three friends:
John Wilkinson, Peter Talbot, and Darren Turpin

ACKNOWLEDGMENTS

To my parents, Mary and Seamus, always there for me. My brothers, James and Sean, who help keep me in the real world. John McLaughlin and Simon Taylor, who are not only great professionals but also, dare I say it, friends.

And Marie, of course, who makes it all worthwhile.

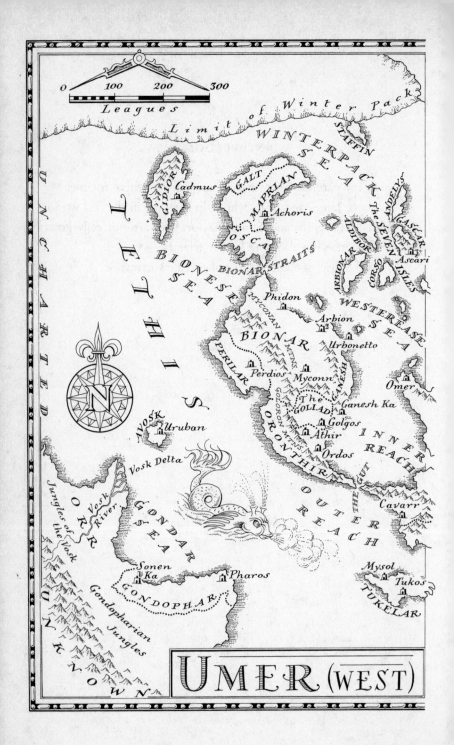

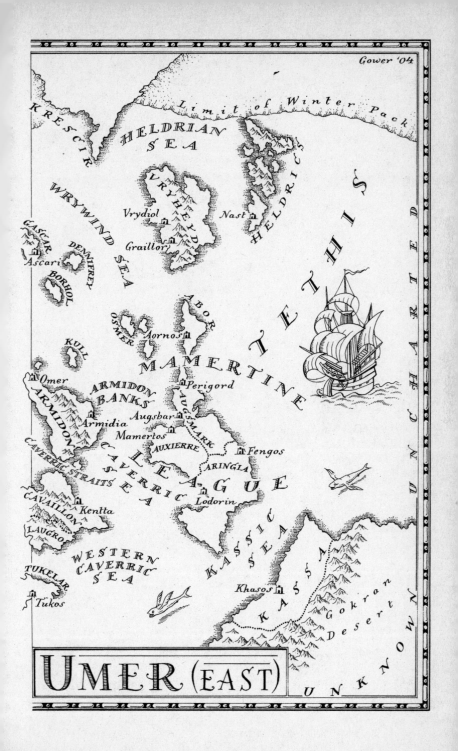

THIS FORSAKEN EARTH

PROLOGUE

In the end, man dies like any other animal: alone, and raging against the dark. I know this. I know there is no God, no trusty patchwork of angels to speak for us. We are but cages of flesh, waiting for the worm.

Some things endure. Love, hate. These can be passed down through the lives of many men. They can become more important than life itself.

Only to fools.

This love—this hate. It has endured within you. You think of her still.

I—I dream of her. At night—when the moon is a long broken gleam on the black waters of the sea—then she seems close. She was a thing of the night always. A creature of shadows.

Can you feel her?

Sometimes. It is like the flash of a star, which fades if one looks too close. She lives. She is alive—and she thinks of me yet.

She hates you. She would see you dead.

No. Perhaps. And yet she may love me too. That is the way she was made.

A pause.

Will I see her again?

Silence.

PART ONE

The DEEP DARK
of the SEA

One

SIMPLICITY ITSELF

IMAGINE FIVE HUNDRED GREAT TREES, EMBEDDED IN THE good earth of the world and watching some two centuries go by, in happiness and woe. War and peace, winter and summer, they are nothing but some thickening of the rings. And let us say these trees—a moderate wood—were cut down by men, and put aside for twenty-odd years, set on stilts to allow the air of another quarter-century to come at them. And after that, they were hewn, and sliced and steamed and nailed into something else. Something to last beyond the lives of the craftsmen who had wielded plane and adze and axe on their enduring flesh.

A man might say they were more than the sum of their parts.

The *Revenant* was a ship-rigged man-of-war of some three hundred tons—a vessel constructed to bear guns and the men who served them. Built out of black Kassic teak, she was broad in the beam, but with a fine, narrow entry that spoke of speed, and despite the fact that she was getting old now, even in the lives of ships, her timbers were still hard as iron, sound right through.

She had been afloat for the better part of eight decades. A thing of purity, of severe beauty, she had been built solely for the waging of war.

Such was the measure of her conception.

On her gun-deck were a dozen twelve-pound sakers, each nine feet long and a ton and a half in weight, whilst on her quarterdeck four two-pound swivel-guns protruded from her larboard and starboard bulwarks. To bear this mass of metal, she had been built with a pronounced tumblehome, which is to say that her hull widened as it approached the waterline, and in her hold there was room to provision her crew for a year or more.

That crew consisted of ninety-seven men, or things approximating men. Of those, over forty served the guns, some thirty the sails, and the rest were officers, warrant officers, and artisans of many trades. The *Revenant*'s needs were manifold. On board were carpenters, sailmakers, smiths, coopers, and a brace of ship's cooks. Some of this assorted company knew elements of navigation, others could point and load a great gun, and yet more could fashion brand-new masts and spars out of raw wood. The ship's company was a self-sufficient community in which every man had a place and a task to take his hand. A community that looked to one man alone for orders, and a direction in which to point this floating battery, this beautiful seaborne engine of destruction.

Elias Creed, second mate. A sturdily built man of medium height with a head and beard as brindled as that of a badger. One eyebrow was cloven by a skinned line, and more scars marked his wrists and ankles, the legacy of eleven years in the penal quarries of Keutta. A quiet man with dark, thoughtful eyes, his life had been spent as either pirate or convict. He stood now by the taffrail of the ship with an axe in his hand, ready to bring it down upon a taut cable, waiting for a word from his captain.

Peor Gallico, first mate. Nine feet tall, olive-green and long-fanged, the halftroll stood by his captain on the quarterdeck, fiddling with an earring. His legs were short, his immensely powerful torso long in compensation, the arms reaching to his knees and culminating in knotted fists as wide as shovels. In the deep-hollowed sockets below his bald forehead two jade-green eyes burned, the pupils lozenge-shaped, and when his tongue licked about the tusks protruding from his lips, it was black as that of a snake. Despite this, there was humor written across the halftroll's face, a willingness to be pleased with the world. Humanity, compassion—etched across the face of a monster.

And finally the lord of this little wooden world, dwarfed by his towering first mate, and yet a tall man in his own right. Captain Rol Cortishane, a broad-shouldered, fair-haired fellow whose eyes were as cold as a northern sea in midwinter. There was something in his chiseled, wind-burnt face more unsettling than anything in the fearsome countenance of the halftroll. Those eyes had known murder, and would know it again.

They closed now, as if the vivid afternoon sun was too much for them, and the face aged for a moment, becoming that of an older, careworn man. A leadsman was at work in the forechains, calling out the depth of the water beneath the *Revenant*'s keel with increasing urgency. It was a beautiful day, a stiff inshore breeze hastening the ship landward with steady ease.

Rol opened his eyes. Blinding bright, the sun bounced off the waves as they came jostling toward him. He blinked to ease their bitter light from his head and squeeze away the dregs of his thoughts. I sleep awake, he thought. More and more, I dream in daylight. What is it now, eight years? Enough. It must be enough.

Memory is the mind's assassin. It will lie quiet for months, years, then sidle up quietly on a sunny day to plunge its knife deep. And no armor is proof against it.

Memory is the enemy of happiness.

He bared his teeth in the effort to wipe his mind free from the smear of his past, and the quartermaster at the wheel spoke to him with outright nervousness.

"Three fathoms, sir. They called three fathoms."

"I heard the goddamned call, Morcam. Hold your course."

The *Revenant* cruised on implacably, the sea a hissing shimmer of sound as her beakhead cut through it. The Inner Reach, one of the ancient oceans of the world, deep and blue and wicked and entirely beautiful.

There was blood on Rol Cortishane's face. It had stiffened into a mask, and it soaked his clothes, made black scimitars under his nails. Looking along the crimson sheen of the deck, he saw a severed hand lying there forgotten, browning in the sun. Momentarily, the violence of the morning came back, bright and unbelievable. As he shifted, easing his shoulders out from under the memory, his boot-soles came off the soaked deck-planking with little sucking rips of sound that made his stomach turn. His face never changed. Far astern, a pack of gulls shrieked greedily as they feasted on the corpses.

"Two fathoms and a half!" shouted the leadsman in the starboard forechains.

"We'll scrape the arse out of her if we're not careful," Gallico said, his voice a deep burr.

Rol glanced aft, to where a tense group of seamen was standing with axes, ready to send the kedge plunging from the quarter and bring them to an undignified halt. Elias Creed stood amongst them, blood matting his brindled hair, and he nodded gravely as he caught Rol's eye.

"We'll rein her in quick enough, if it comes to that," Rol said. And he managed something like a smile for Gallico.

Forward of them, the men stood in the waist and upon the fo'c'sle like things frozen, listening for the yell of the leadsman or his mate as they swung out the tallow-bottomed lead and felt for the bottom, which was running under the keel of the ship at a good five knots. Shoal water—treacherous sandbank-riddled bad ground with the rocks they called the Assassins somewhere in its midst. And the tide was ebbing.

"Bring up the prisoners," Rol ordered.

The master-at-arms darted below. There were muffled shouts and oaths from belowdecks, a cry of pain.

"On deck there!" the lookout bellowed from the foretop. "There she lies, anchored behind the headland dead ahead!"

"Two fathom," the leadsman called. Twelve feet of water under their keel.

"All hands to take in sail," Rol said. "Gallico, prepare to back topsails."

"About bloody time."

They staggered as the ship touched ground under them, the keel grating on rock with a groan that reverberated through the very soles of their feet.

"Let go the kedge!" Rol shouted, and at once Elias and his party hacked through the cable suspending the anchor aft. The iron kedge fell from the taffrail and plunged into the clear water below with a spout of foam. Seconds later the ship slowed.

"Back topsails!" Gallico called, and the topmen braced the yards right round so that the wind was pressing on the forward face of the sail, pushing the *Revenant* backward. The ship came to a full stop. Again, that awful grinding under their feet as the keel touched submerged rock. The ship's company seemed to flinch at the sensation, like a man pricked with a needle.

"Set a spring to the kedge," Rol said calmly. "Bring us broadside-on to that ship."

"Deck there!" The lookout again. "She's unfurled Bionese colors."

"As if we needed to be told," Gallico growled, the green gleam of his eyes sharpening with malice. "Think she'll come out?"

"Probably. In any case, I intend to persuade her."

"Prisoners, sir," Quirion, the master-at-arms, said. He and his mates were shoving half a dozen bloodied men in the livery of Bionese marines toward the starboard gangway.

One of them held his head higher than the rest, and he had a ragged frill of lace at his throat. "What are you going to do with us?" he shouted up at the quarterdeck. "That's one of our vessels out there, a man-of-war. If you harm us it'll—"

"It'll do nothing," Elias Creed snapped at him, joining Rol and Gallico at the quarterdeck rail. "Except meet you in hell."

"Clear for action," Rol said quietly.

His command was a thing of habit. The *Revenant* was largely prepared for battle. The port-lids were open, tompions out, and the sakers still warm, but inboard. Now the gun-crews began hauling their massive charges up to the bulwark with a deafening thunder of groaning wood and squealing blocks. The ship tilted under their feet as her equilibrium shifted.

"Unfurl the Black Flag."

It snapped out from the maintopgallant backstay, a long, shot-torn streamer of sable without device. No quarter asked or given, it said. Few had the gall to fly such a flag in this day and age.

"Now lash the prisoners to the muzzles of the guns," Rol said, still in the same quiet tone.

Quirion and his mates looked blank. "Skipper?"

"You heard me, Quirion."

There was a short pause before discipline kicked in, but despite that, it took the prisoners a few moments to understand.

They did not begin to struggle until they were lowered over the ship's side by their bound wrists. Then they began to squeal and wriggle. The saker-crews reached through the gun-ports and attached lengths of cordage to the writhing men's waists, then pulled them taut so that the round muzzle of every twelve-pounder was snug against the spine of a kicking, screaming human being.

"Deck there!" the lookout called, high above the squalor of the sights below. "She's clearing for action, eight guns a side. They look like nine-pounders to me."

Gallico ripped his gaze away from the pinioned men who now lined the side of the ship. "We're in range," he said.

"All the better. Gun-crews! Wait for my command, and then fire from number one, a rippling broadside."

There was a moment of quiet when even the babbling of the prisoners died away. Rol caught the eye of a youngster tied to number four, in the waist on the starboard side. The saker bent his spine like a bow and there were tears and snot streaming down his face. He was fifteen years old if he was a day. All about his eyes there was a line of white.

"Fire!"

The six guns of the starboard broadside thundered out one after another; and as they did, a heavy white smoke spumed up, to be blown away to leeward. In the smoke were darker things, spat out of the muzzles of the sakers, and something like a fine warm spray drifted about the decks of the *Revenant*. Rol wiped his sticky face and peered landward to see the fall of shot. He saw splinters explode up out of the hull of the enemy man-of-war—good practice, at this range—and the ball from number six smashed plumb into the mizzen-top, bringing a clatter of rigging and timber down onto the enemy ship's quarterdeck.

"Fire as they bear!" he shouted. "Fire at will!"

The severed limbs of the unfortunate prisoners were cut loose and the gun-crews began to work their pieces in earnest.

When the recoil threw the sakers back from the bulwarks they sponged out the barrels to stop any burning remnants within from setting off the next charge prematurely, then rammed home cloth cartridges of black powder, followed by iron twelve-pound balls, and topped off with wads of cloth which would tamp down the explosion and make it more intense. The guns were hauled back up to the ship's side again and a spike was stabbed through each touch-hole to pierce the cartridge within the barrel. The touch-holes were then filled with loose small-grain powder. The gun was elevated and traversed with wooden wedges and iron crowbars according to the grunted word and gestures of the gun-captain, and when it bore on its target he slapped the touch-hole with a length of burning match. The powder there ignited, in turn setting off the cartridge in the base of the barrel. The explosion, confined by the heavy bronze, propelled the cannonball, wad and all, out of the saker's muzzle with incredible force—the fall of shot could be followed, a dark blur, no more, if one had quick eyes—and then the process began again. The Revenants were a veteran crew, and could get off three aimed broadsides in six minutes.

The enemy ship was firing back now. Some of her nine-pound balls fell wide, showering the side of the ship with spray. Others passed through the rigging with a low howl, slicing ropes, punching round holes in the sails. One struck the hull somewhere amidships, but with that caliber and at this range the *Revenant*'s timbers shrugged off the impact as a bull might twitch his hide under the bite of a gnat.

Six broadsides, with every shot aimed low into the hull of the enemy. Over four hundred pounds of iron hurled across a thousand yards of sea.

"She's slipped her anchor—she's making along the coast," one of the quartermasters shouted.

"Damn her. Keep firing," Rol spat.

The wind veered in a burgeoning wave of hot air off the land and the *Revenant* began to swing on her spring-cabled anchor. One moment her broadside was pointed squarely at the enemy vessel, and the next she had yawed under the press of air and was presenting her vulnerable stern, the soft spot of every ship.

"Gallico, get a party to haul on that goddamned spring! Bring us back round!"

"She's taken the wind," the lookout shouted, hoarse as a crow, "she's coming out. Deck there—"

A full broadside lashed up the length of the ship, dismembering men, smashing blocks and tackle to matchwood, slicing rigging, sending wicked chunks of wood flying, as deadly as iron. The carriage of the starboard number-three gun was blown to pieces, her crew scattered in a bloody mess as far aft as the ship's bell. The party working on the cable to the spring was shattered. Rol saw a forearm travel the length of the ship and disappear over the fo'c'sle. The wind of one ball jerked him aside as it missed him by a hair.

"A fair return," Gallico said, knuckling blood from his face and leaving it streaked bright as paint. "Come now, pull on this bloody cable—am I to do it all myself?" About him, his crew gathered to haul on the three-inch tarred rope once more, like men drunk or stunned.

Blood poured out of the scuppers of the enemy ship, a red foam in her wake as she picked up speed, the offshore breeze now on her larboard beam. Her staysails were unfurled, as the courses would hardly draw with this wind—they were having trouble with the mizzen. The *Revenant*'s guns must have shattered the yard.

A huge shadow fell over the *Revenant,* a choking fog that was the powder-smoke of the man-of-war's broadside, drifting on the wind like a curse. Rol could taste it acrid on his tongue. His eyes smarted.

Kier Eiserne, the ship's carpenter, hauled himself up the companionway and sketched a greeting in the air with one fist, his words drowned out by the thunder of the *Revenant*'s return broadside, largely impotent—the ebbing tide was working against Gallico and his two dozen straining at the spring. They were coming round, but slowly. The tide rushing out of the bay was pushing the ship clockwise, with the spring-anchor at her stern the pivot upon which she turned.

The powder-cloud passed over, and they were in brilliant sunshine again.

"...below the waterline, but we've plugs in place," Kier was saying. "I need men for the pumps." His wedge-shaped face twitched with worry for the ship's bowels.

"What's she making?" Rol demanded.

"Three foot in the well and gaining maybe a foot a glass. It's not the shot-holes—she must have been pierced when she touched the rocks."

"Can you get at the leak?"

"I need more men, to shift the water-casks. It's somewhere under the main hold."

"Damn the water-casks. Pump them out, or break them up if you have to, but get that leak, Kier. I'll give you more men when I can."

"Aye, sir."

Creed appeared at Rol's side. "That son of a bitch is changing course. He's going to come round east of the Assassins. He's coming out."

Rol considered. There was a momentary lull in the tremendous hammering of broadsides as both crews concentrated on the maneuvering of their vessels. He lifted his head—how blue the sky was—and felt the wind. It was still veering. Northeast, and soon to be east-nor'east. Once it came round the tail-end of the Assassins, the enemy ship would have it on the stern—and she would be upwind of the pinioned *Revenant*. She would have the weather-gage. Rol swore quietly.

"Slip that blasted cable, Elias, but buoy the anchor. We may come back for it."

"Aye, sir." Obviously relieved, Elias ran aft and began shouting at Gallico and the men hauling there.

The rope was cut. They would need a power of ship's stores to make up for today's profligacy—if they made it through today. The end of the cable had been attached to a longline and buoyed with a pair of pigs' bladders, which now bobbed astern in some derision. The *Revenant* took the wind at once. It was on the larboard quarter. "Gallico!" Rol called. "Mizzen-course and jibs. Elias, reload and run out the guns but hold your fire. Morcam, pass the word for the gunner."

Once again the beauty of the day struck him. The white spangle of the sunlight on the sea, the honey-colored stone of the Oronthir coast, now full astern. The sand-martins carving gleeful arcs out of the air.

Beneath Rol's feet, the *Revenant* came round at last, her fragile stern hidden from the enemy guns. Now, let's see your nine-pounders break these scantlings, Rol thought with a jet of hatred.

The gunner, John Imbro. A burly native of far-off Vryheyd, he had a full yellow beard and a pink-bald scalp. When drunk he would declare himself born with a head upside down. His face shone with sweat as if greased, except for the matt-black smudges in the sockets of his eyes.

"John, how are we for shot and powder?"

"Enough for another four broadsides, sir—"

"What? Ran's arse—"

"The leak below got into the powder store and has soaked all but two barrels of best white long-grain. It'll be a week's work ashore to dry out the rest."

"There's nothing else? What about the fine stuff?"

"Oh, it's still snug and dry—but it'll only be of use in swivels and sidearms. Cram it into a twelve-pounder and you may as well fart at yonder bastards."

"Do what you can, John."

The gunner stumped away unhappily.

Rol studied the enemy man-of-war. Some eight hundred yards away, it was now off the larboard quarter, upwind and running out its guns. They were slow to reload—the *Revenant*'s earlier broadsides must have thinned out the crew. Rol turned to the quartermasters at the wheel. "South-southeast, as sharp as you can."

The wheel spun, creaking, and the ship's beakhead made the turn to larboard as another broadside thundered out of the enemy vessel. One second, two, and then the nine-pound balls were whistling about their ears, chopping blocks out of the rigging, ripping through the courses. A loud *clang* as one clipped the bow anchor and whipped across the fo'c'sle. Someone screamed forward, a hoot more of outrage than of pain.

"Hold your fire!" Rol bellowed at the gun-crews in the waist. Four broadsides. What to do with them?

"We could make a run for it. No shame in that—it's been a bloody morning." This was Gallico, at Rol's side once more.

"No; that's to leave the job half done. And who's to say we mauled him badly enough to stop him following? No—we must fight it out, Gallico."

"We'll board, then."

Rol caught his first mate's eye, though he had to crane his neck to do so. He smiled bleakly. "That's the way of it. Best get the arms chests into the waist. All the pistols we have. And one more crew to help with the swivels." He paused. "What about our people?"

"Six dead, or will be before the day is out," the halftroll said tersely. "Another thirteen taken below."

"We must get ourselves a surgeon, one of these days."

"Aye. Giffon can take off a leg quick enough, but he's all thumbs when it comes to the fine work."

The two ships were on parallel courses now, their bows pointed toward the open sea. The wind had veered round to east-nor'east and was still freshening, as it did this time of year, pushed out to the ocean by warm masses of clouds forming inland. Rol estimated they were making a good six knots, though he was not going to check for sure; the ship's company was busy enough. Under Gallico, Creed, and Fell Amertaz, the bosun, they worked to splice and knot the loose-flying rigging, scatter the deck with more sand, replace the match-coils that had burned out, and bring up the last of the powder-cartridges from the powder-room, where Imbro and his mates were scooping and weighing the deadly stuff into the cloth bags which would be thrust down the gaping maws of the guns.

Four broadsides.

"He's packing on more sail, skipper," Morcam said from the wheel. Rol looked back over the shattered taffrail. Sure enough, their enemy was unfurling topsails, topgallants, even weather studding-sails. They would prove awkward if he had to fire his windward broadside.

"He's a bloody-minded bastard, I'll give him that."

"They're getting rid of their dead," said one of the swivel-gunners. The men on the quarterdeck went silent, watching. Rol counted twenty-six splashes in the pink wake of the enemy. "Morcam," he said. "Jig your steering. Put a few nicks in her wake, like we're having trouble with the rudder."

Morcam grinned. "Aye, sir."

"Gallico!"

"What now, damn it?"

"Make like a winged duck. Spill a little wind. Lose us a few knots. Elias, get the boarders out of sight in the waist. Four broadsides when I give the word, and then we board her in the smoke." Elias nodded.

They ran on, less swiftly now. The topmen were loosening the braces, letting the yards jink and swing in the wind. The sails cracked and boomed as the air behind them spilled round their slack leeches and clews.

Rol felt Fleam stir at his hip; she knew what was coming. He set his palm on the pommel of the scimitar and felt the trembling eagerness that ran right through the blade. As always, something of that bloodlust communicated itself to him, a momentary, dizzying mote of pleasure.

"She's coming up hand over fist, skipper," Morcam said. "Seems she has the same idea as us."

"Bionese," Gallico said, and spat over the bulwark.

The enemy had cleared away his chasers and now they were firing deliberately, first the larboard, then the starboard. He had altered course two, three points, and was barely two cables away. Rol could see the crowd of Bionese marines packed together on his fo'c'sle, armor winking in the sun. Bionari men-of-war carried large contingents of marines when they were not going far foreign; they trusted their soldiers more than their sailors.

"Morcam, when I give the word, hard a larboard. Gallico, at the same time, back topsails. Elias, wait for my command." The air seemed to crackle in the confines of the ship, a tenseness that showed in the whites of men's eyes. Rol breathed in deeply, watching his enemy, taking in the wind, the swell, the swaying statues arrayed about the remaining guns, the sweat glimmering in the pleats of their backbones. He saw fragments of timber and wreckage drift by the side of the *Revenant* and realized they had retraced their steps all the way out to the scene of the first battle of the morning. A troop-transport, shot to pieces even as its passengers came sculling in the ship's boats for the *Revenant* in a desperate attempt to take her hand-to-hand. A few bodies still littered the swells of the Inner Reach, though most had sunk like stones. What kind of vainglorious fool would wear steel armor aboard ship?

A second lot of vainglorious fools was almost upon them.

"Hard a larboard," he said to Morcam. A nod was enough for Gallico. The deck tilted inboard under their feet as the ship came round. They could hear the rudder groan and the tiller-ropes creak as they fought the pressure of the water beneath them. The enemy warship's beakhead was now pointed directly at their side. Gallico's topmen backed topsails and the wind took the ship back so dramatically that many of the crew were staggered. The yards complained and flexed, but nothing gave.

"Gun-crews—fire!" Rol shouted.

The five remaining sakers of the broadside bellowed out in one terrific roar, the knees of the ship groaning at the tons of iron blasted backward, only to be brought up short by the deep twang of the breeching.

"Reload, reload, reload," Rol was repeating childishly. He peered through the powder-smoke and saw the enemy ship bearing down on them like an appalled giant. She had begun to yaw, but then had fallen off. Her fo'c'sle was a slaughterhouse, scarlet remnants of her marines hanging from the very yards and smeared all over the forecourse.

The Revenants got in one more broadside at pistol-shot. Rol saw the Bionese ship's foremast stagger, then it came down over her chasers. One of her knightheads had been blasted clean away. She had slowed, but was still coming on.

"Gallico, weather gangway!" Rol shouted, drawing Fleam for the second time that day and leaping down from the quarterdeck into the mad fury of the gun-crews in the waist.

"Give her two more, lads—then join Gallico and me on the gangway. Point them low, into the hull. Rake the bastards!"

A hoarse cheer—or rather, a collective growl—went up. Rol

clapped Elias Creed on the shoulder, missed, and ended up slapping his face. Laughing, he ran up to the gangway, where he found his first mate and a dozen others who were firing pistols at the enemy bows, then ducking down to reload them with an absurdly childish air of mischief.

"Hold on now," Gallico said.

The Bionese ship struck amidship, and the *Revenant* shuddered at the impact. But it was not a wicked blow, more like a man whose shoulder has been jostled in the street. They were a taller, weightier ship than the enemy, and the *Revenant*'s tumblehome created a gap between the shot-splintered bows of the Bionese and her own bulwarks.

Two more broadsides, the swivels barking their two-pound loads of grapeshot and shrapnel—anything their gunners could find to cram into them. The snapping rattle of pistols fired gleefully at anything that moved. The enemy maintopmast came down, and then the mizzen—they must have been almost shot through earlier in the fight.

The sakers stopped firing. Their crews boiled up out of the waist onto the gangway, yelling, eyes red as cherries, faces smoke-black. Some seventy Revenants paused on the larboard gangway of their ship and stared down at the enemy man-of-war, treading on one another's toes and wincing at the jab of neighbors' cutlasses.

"Revenants! Follow me!" Rol shrieked, holding Fleam as upright as a banner. With a roar, the crowd of men scrambled over the side of their ship and down to the bows of the pitching enemy vessel. Gallico made fast a grapnel in the gammoning of her broken bowsprit. Men panted and shouted and gouged bloody slivers out of their hands as they climbed over the wrecked headrails, through gaping holes with fringes of sharp wood that tore the shirts from their backs. They swarmed over the fo'c'sle of the Bionese vessel like a plague, wide, bloodshot eyes starting out of their heads.

Nothing moved in all that tangled mass of wreckage and shredded cordage and shattered spars. All along the decks, flesh, wood, and iron had been beaten into one unholy, pulped mess from which trickled streams of blood that brightened the brown stains venting from the scuppers. The enemy vessel was a dead thing, which even the wind could no longer stir to life. The Revenants stared around themselves in heavy wonder, as if uncertain as to who could have brought such a thing to pass. A silence fell, broken only by the weary creak and groan of seaborne wood, the death rattle of a tall fighting ship. There was a moment almost of reverence.

"This," Rol said, "is victory."

Two

THE SLAVER

"IT IS SAID," GALLICO DECLARED, "THAT NO MAN HAS YET
sailed south of the Tropic of Mas Morgun, which girdles the
world eleven degrees south of Khasos."

"It's said the gods made the world round to confound the
ambitions of men," Creed retorted. "But then how does one
stand on the underside of a spinning sphere?"

"How else is it that we see topsails on the horizon before the
ship becomes hull-up?" Gallico asked reasonably. "Because
the earth curves under our feet. And it's the weightiness of
the stars that keeps everything on the surface of this globe
from floating off into the ether. The stars we steer by are nails
driven through the warp and weft of heaven to hold our world
in place, hammered in by God to fix us within space and the
unwinding clock of the universe."

"I have heard of the Tropic line," Rol broke in, speaking for
the first time that evening. "I've heard a dozen old men up and
down the length of the Westerease and the Reach talk of it—

usually after their bellies have been filled with beer. Who fixed it in place, Gallico? Not your God, I think. And no man has sailed so far south and come back to boast of it."

"The Ancients mapped out the world in millennia of exploration long before man was born," the halftroll said confidently. "They had every grain of sand numbered and gave the leaf of every tree a name. They counted the hairs on each man's head, and knew when a sparrow fell to earth."

"They had the wits of God, then," Rol sneered.

"Yes," Gallico said quietly, "they did."

"How do you know all this, Gallico?" Creed asked.

"He makes it up," Rol scoffed, punching the halftroll's granite bicep playfully. His eyes were cold, though.

"I used to read," Gallico admitted. "In the days before I fell in with bad company."

They fell silent. All about them in the fire-stitched darkness that bad company was cavorting and singing and snarling and laughing, as men will when drunk. The beach was a long gray blade with the bright moon-kindled silver of the sea before it and the darkness of the forest behind. Their campfires seemed an intrusion, a presumption in this tranquil wilderness. Strangely enough, only the black silhouette of the *Revenant,* at anchor a cable from the shore, seemed at one with the black and silver serenity of the night.

"How many were on that transport, you think?" Elias Creed asked no one in particular.

"A battalion maybe," Gallico rumbled. "Five hundred men."

"And on the warship?"

"Heavy crews, these Bionari cruisers. Some two hundred."

"Seven hundred men. Gods above us."

"What's your point, Elias?" Rol asked irritably.

"Just this: we're not mere privateers anymore. This is not piracy—it is warfare."

"It's been a rough week," Rol consoled him. "Have a drink. As soon as we've refitted we'll strike out east, or north or south. Anywhere that takes us away from this goddamned continent and its wars."

The others said nothing. They knew his words were empty.

A boat put off from the side of the *Revenant,* sculled by half a dozen of the harbor watch. The crew ran it up the beach in a flash of spray and trudged through the sand, exchanging banter with the men at the campfires as they came. They stopped before Rol, the firelight making uplit masks of their faces.

"Well, Kier, how goes it?" Rol asked, and handed his carpenter a round-bottomed bottle.

The cadaverous little man took a long swallow and passed it to his neighbor.

"The leak is plugged for now, skipper; a couple of planks started. There's not much else I can do with it, lessen we haul her down or get her back in dock. The stern will take another mort of work too; your cabin windows are gone, frames and all, and the stern-lanterns too."

"The rudder?"

"It took a glancing shot, nothing much."

Rol nodded. "So she'll float, then?"

"Oh, aye, we're seaworthy—or near as, damn it. She don't look so pretty, but by God she can take punishment."

"I saw nine-pound balls bounce off her sides at a thousand yards, like they was peas," John Imbro, the gunner, volunteered.

"Powder, John?"

"We took some six barrels out of the Bionese, skipper; enough for a dozen broadsides."

"We have teeth again," Gallico said with relish.

"That we do, 'Co. And there's those nine-pounders we salvaged before we burned her. They'll come in right handy back at the Ka."

"Who'd you leave on board, John?" Rol asked.

"Gill Whistram and Harry Dade. They're upright and sober; I checked myself."

"Good work. Go and get something to eat. There's fresh game doing the rounds; though what beast it is, I don't know."

"Right now, skipper, all I want is a rock to lay my head on; me and Kier both. There's a lot more to be done tomorrow." Rol nodded, and the carpenter, the gunner, and their mates left the firelight and staggered out into the darkness.

Gallico raised his savage head. In the moonlight it seemed sculpted out of stone, a gargoyled physiognomy. "Wind's backing at last," he said, his nostrils sniffing wide. "Be due north by morning, you see if it's not. And then we'll have a long and weary time of it beating back to Ganesh Ka."

Ganesh Ka, the Hidden City. For Rol and Elias it had once been a fable, nothing more. A city of pirates, its location unknown to the wider world—a tall tale for mariners all about the Twelve Seas. Now they knew it for what it was: a vast and ancient ruin, in which squatted a host of the outlawed and the dispossessed. Murderers, thieves, escaped slaves, or men who simply found the world too small for them; they congregated there on the strength of a legend.

"Not much of a trip," Rol said. "All blood and thunder, and damn-all to show for it but a pockmarked ship and half a dozen dead shipmates."

"Seven hundred less Bionari in the world," Gallico retorted. "There's treasure for you."

"You can't put a corpse in your pocket, or eat one either."

"I know some who've tried," and Gallico grinned horribly, making them all laugh.

Rol drank from another bottle; they lay all about the beach like flotsam.

"*Osprey* and *Skua* are back in fighting trim this long while. It's not like the Ka is undefended. What say you, Gallico, to a far-foreign cruise? Why not get this wind on our quarter and make for the Gut, and the Outer Reach? There's fat Mercanter ships there that would make us rich men in a month. We could try and find that Tropic-line of yours, and cut it with our keel."

"*Skua* and *Osprey* don't carry such heavy metal as we," Elias Creed said quietly. "Rol, you know we're the only ship the Ka has that can take on men-of-war."

Cortishane stood up, fist clenched around the neck of his bottle. He strode away from the fire—and as he did, a light began to shine in his eyes, cold as the edge of a sword.

"I know, I know. Where would I be, Elias, without you beside me to play mother hen?"

He made his way through the scattered clumps of mariners who were sprawled on the beach about their fires. Here and there he exchanged a word, a wave, a smile. The men respected their captain, esteemed him even. But he knew there was something in his eyes that prevented them from making that full, human connection.

And why not? Rol wondered. After all, I am not human.

He joined Giffon and his improbable infirmary. The company's wounded had been made comfortable with what slim facilities the ship possessed. For those in unbearable pain, this meant stupefying amounts of hard liquor. Kier Eiserne had run up a crude table for Giffon's heftier work, and this now stood in the sand with the raw wood of its top dark as mahogany, stained deep with blood. Giffon sat on it wiping his eyes with a filthy rag. At his side was a smeared bundle of tools more suited to carpentry than surgery.

"Giffon. How do they go?"

Giffon was a young, round-faced man with sandy hair and a snub nose. He seemed to be in his early teens, until one looked into his eyes and saw the memories there.

"Al-Hamn and Boravian will do well, I think. The stumps were clean, and I sewed flesh over the bone. Gran Tomasson died this evening."

"Damn. He was a good man, as good a gun-captain as I've ever seen."

"Half his ribs were gone. I'm amazed he lasted this long. As it is, all those who are still alive now will remain alive, if they can steer clear of fever."

Rol gestured to the dark stains of the table. "You were cutting again tonight?"

"I didn't like the smell of Morten's leg, so I resectioned it again."

Rol studied his youthful would-be surgeon closely. Giffon was exhausted. He had been looking after the wounded virtually single-handed for a week. Rol had sent seamen to lift and carry for him, and at times they had needed a half-dozen men to hold down some unfortunate when the pain of the saw was too much. But the bulk of the burden was Giffon's. There was something indomitable about him. Had he the requisite knowledge, this boy might be a real healer. He had that touch. But he was no more than a butcher's apprentice who had fled a harsh master and been picked up by slavers on the coast of Borhol. The usual abuse had followed, but somehow Giffon had escaped and made his way to the Ka. No one knew how, and the memories in those eyes stopped folk from asking. Like Elias Creed, he had buried his pain so deep there was no longer any way to go delving for it.

"It's hard, for those of us who live and die in ships," Rol said gently. "The blade, the shot, the surgeon's saw—"

"And the deep dark of the sea," Giffon said. "I know. We can put ships back together that are all but sunk, but when a man has a leg splintered, all we can do is take it off, and hope."

Rol offered the boy his bottle. "Get drunk, Giffon. That's an order."

Giffon's face twisted into a smile. "Can't stand the taste of the stuff, skipper. I'd sell someone's soul for a pint of cold buttermilk, though."

"There's wild goats in the hills. Grab ahold of one for long enough and we'll get Gallico to tug on its teats for you."

Giffon laughed, a short bark, no more. "I'll sleep, I think. Skipper?"

"Yes?"

"Are we going back in now? Back to the Ka, I mean. There's men here who ought to rest in beds ashore."

Rol sighed. "Yes, Giffon. We're going home."

The word was still echoing in his head as he left the lights of the beach behind him and struck out into the woods, the taste of the evening's rotgut sour in his mouth. The ground rose under the canopy of the trees, bare bones of stone thrusting up through the thin soil. Wild olive, juniper, pine, and cypress, and here and there a poplar, straight as a sentinel. As soon as the firelight had been left behind the night brightened in his sight, becoming clear as day. Part of it was the moonlight; part of it was the nature of the blood that beat through his heart.

He made his sure-footed way up one bald outcrop, and straightening there he found the vast, eldritch expanse of the Inner Reach spread out below him, the *Revenant* as tiny as a child's forgotten toy, the campfires mere golden buttons. If he looked east, there was nothing but open sea for two hundred and fifty leagues. Behind him, the bulk of the Goloron Mountains loomed up in long blunted ridges of shadow to claw at the stars.

And what stars. They swirled in sky-spanning horsetails and banners and speckled sweeps of sprinkled silver, here and there the brighter glimmer of something larger. The Mariner. Gabriel's Fist. Quintillian, the star his grandfather had once told him pointed to their home.

The only real home Rol had ever known was now a burnt-out shell on Dennifrey. His grandfather had died there with a crossbow bolt in his guts, murdered by a mob as his wife had been before him. Because of what ran in his blood.

You are not human, he had told his grandson. Almost his last words. Well, thank you, Grandfather. For raising me in ignorance, for telling me nothing of my heritage or history, until it was too late. You old bastard, long-winded in telling everything but the truth. And now here I am nursemaiding a city full of derelicts, doing the decent thing, keeping the wolf from the door. But what if I am the wolf?

The stars glittered down, everything below them a matter of cold irrelevance. Ganesh Ka had started to become home for him. He did not like that, but had no say in the process. You cannot choose the things you care for, he thought. If only you could.

He closed his eyes, a panoply of memories parading again before that tireless inner eye. And as always the last of them was the white, set face of a beautiful woman, her hair as dark as the wing of a raven. Rowen, the woman he had loved as a boy. His sister, now fighting to make herself a queen. The scalloped scar on the palm of his left hand tingled and he scratched it absently.

They stayed five more days in the sheltered cove, working on the ship, sending out foraging and watering parties, burying the latest of their dead. Elias took a work-party into the forests and came back with a pair of mature trees trimmed down to the trunk. They floated them out to the *Revenant* and hauled them aboard with tackles to the yardarms, then stowed them with infinite pains on the booms among the ship's boats. Kier Eiserne was particularly glad to have them aboard; the carpenter had always worried about their lack of spare topmasts.

They hunted game with ship's pistols, fished over the side, and caught birds inland with nets and quicklime—anything to vary the monotonous shipboard diet of biscuit and salted goat. After the first few days, Rol kept them at watch on watch, so that most of them had four hours of work followed by four hours of rest, around the clock. This was shipboard routine and they were used to it. The only exceptions were the so-called "idlers," men like the carpenter, the cooper, the blacksmith, the sailmaker, and their mates. These men were only expected to work daylight hours, but still put in sixteen-hour days. A thing as complex as a ship-of-war needed the continual attention of a whole host of specialists, even when she was riding at anchor.

The five days passed, and the efforts of eighty men began to put the *Revenant* to rights again. The heaviest work was the restowing of the stores in the hold which had been boated ashore to let the carpenter come at the leak. As it was, she would need to be careened or dry-docked to give Kier Eiserne complete peace of mind, but she was ready to face the sea nonetheless. They had been helped by the fact that the ship was not deep in stores; they were only eighty leagues from Ganesh Ka, their cruise cut short by the encounter with the Bionese troopship and her escort. Now it was time to steer north again.

Rol sat in the great cabin, staring landward through the new timber of the stern window-frames. No glass, of course, but Kier had done a beautiful job of replacing the blasted wood. The sun was coming up, and the yellow dawn-light sent the ship's shadow pouring onto the beach. The watch had been up on deck this last glass or so, making ready to weigh anchor. He could hear the quiet dawn-murmurs of the ship's company through the deck-head, and yawned, muscles in the sides of his face cracking. Under him, the *Revenant* was pitching and rolling with a cacophony of creaks and groans, like a horse eager for the off. The wind must have picked up.

A soft knock on the cabin door, and without further ado

Gallico twisted his huge form through the doorway. Rol grinned at him crouching there.

"Gods in heaven, Gallico, what in the world ever made you think you'd be comfortable on board a ship?"

The halftroll raised his paws helplessly. "Can I help it if all shipwrights are midgets?"

"How's the wind?"

"Blowing in our teeth like a cheap tart."

"Where from?"

"Due north, where else?"

Rol swore. "We need sea-room, then. No point in beating up the coast against it—if it veers it'll have us on the rocks. What say you to getting it on the larboard beam, making east? There's the southerly Trades that come up out of Cavaillon this time of year, off the mountains."

Gallico studied his captain closely. "There is that, I suppose. But they don't take hold until halfway out in the Reach. That's a hundred and fifty leagues of blue-water sailing, if it's an inch." He paused. "You have no wish to go back to the Ka anytime soon, have you, Rol?"

"I'm thinking of the ship, and her crew."

"Is it Artimion? He's not the man he once was."

Rol stood up. He, too, had to stoop under the deck-beams, and did so without conscious volition. "No, it's not Artimion. He and I have made our peace. It's Ganesh Ka itself, Gallico."

"What about it?"

"Just a feeling, a notion, nothing more."

"Spit it out before we grow old."

"Gallico, I have this feeling that Ganesh Ka is unlucky. I think it was unlucky for whoever built it all those centuries or millennia ago, and I think it is for us also."

Gallico's eyes blazed. "It has sheltered some of us well enough these thirty years and more."

More softly, Rol said, "It has sheltered me, too, Gallico.

Nevertheless, something in me believes it is doomed, and everyone who remains within it."

The halftroll's anger faded, but there was still a hot glare about his eyes. "These Bionari cruisers and troopships?"

"They have something to do with it, yes. We've been sending them to the bottom one after another for going on six months now, and still they keep coming. Sooner or later, one will get through. Either that, or our luck will run out, and one of them will send *us* to the bottom."

The halftroll considered this. "That's as may be, but they've always had traffic up and down this coast—to supply their bases south of here. Golgos has a big garrison."

"Had. We sank most of it in the Reach last spring."

"You think that's where they came from?"

"Where else? And now they're not going to stop sending troops south until they find out what happened to it."

"They're fighting a civil war. They'll give it up in the end—there are bigger fish in their pot."

"Perhaps. In the meantime, this one ship and crew cannot hold off the entire navy of a great power single-handed."

Gallico opened his mouth, but what he said was not what had been in his eyes. "Shall we weigh anchor, then?"

"Yes. And set a course due east. Get us out in blue water, Gallico."

"You're the captain," the halftroll said, and his huge frame disappeared through the doorway with startling swiftness.

Rol stared after him. I'm become like Grandfather, he thought. I can mix truth and lies and make them sound the same.

Due east they steered, the wind on the larboard bow and the yards braced round as sharp as they could haul them, a quilt of staysails keeping the courses company, and all bellied taut and drawing with creaks and groans as the wind continued to freshen into a blue-water blow. They made better than forty leagues a day for three days, and then the wind began to fail them. It backed round, became whimsical and inconstant, and both watches grew weary trying to guess its next move. Four more days of wallowing and twitching and cursing Ran under their breath for his capriciousness, and then the storm-god or his spouse grew tired of toying with them, and let go their bag of winds.

The true southerlies off Cavaillon began, no more than a zephyr at first, then growing in brashness until the air was washing through the rigging with a hiss of glee. They altered course to west-nor'west, took the wind on the quarter, and spread courses, topsails, topgallants, every stitch of canvas they could rig on the yards. They were four hundred long sea-miles from Ganesh Ka, but at this constant ten knots they would run it off in two days.

Or would have, if Ran had not decided otherwise. The splendid southerlies slackened a day later to a steady breeze, no more. Their speed came down, and soon they were cruising along sedately with the beakhead barely pitching. They resigned themselves to it, as mariners must if they are not to go mad, and the convalescing wounded, at least, were glad of the ship's easier pace. There was less banging of stumps or twisting of broken limbs, or bumping of burnt flesh.

Thirteen days and nights had passed since the battle with the Bionari. Though Kier Eiserne made a formal and lugubrious report to his captain every morning concerning the fragile state of the *Revenant*'s hull, the days of sailing were uneventful. They were well found in stores, fresh and preserved, and all of the more obvious damage to the ship had been repaired, even down to the replacing of starboard number three's gun carriage. Giffon was able to come on deck and sun his pallid, moon-shaped face more often as his charges healed, and Rol made a point of inviting him to dinner in the great cabin more than once.

The *Revenant*'s captain never dined alone. Gallico and Elias Creed were permanent fixtures—Gallico seated on a specially strengthened stool—and often the gunner or the bosun or the carpenter would be invited also. The youngest of the topmen would serve the food, one standing behind each diner, and they were compensated for their servitude by drinking glass for glass with the guests and joining in the conversation whenever the whim took them. Though the ship's company was in many ways a rigid hierarchy, it was not an oppressive one, and when dinner was over the diners would repair to the quarterdeck and join in the tale-telling and song-singing which usually sprang up in the waist with the last dogwatch.

A clear night sky, with skeins of cloud drifting ghostlike before the magnificent sweep of the stars. The moon was a wide-bladed sickle halfway back to the full, and the ship was coursing along at no more than four knots, the sails drawing without strain to the yards. Rol stood at the break of the quarterdeck and listened along with most of the crew as the bosun, Fell Amertaz, a man as hard and fearsome as any pirate in a landsman's imagination, sang a ballad of his native Augsmark, the tears trickling unashamedly into his iron-gray beard. The ship's company listened respectfully, for Amertaz, though given to sentimentality, was a hard-handed bastard to cross.

"It must be a fine thing," Elias Creed said quietly, "to be able to call one place home, one land your own, even if you never go back to it."

"Your father was an Islander, wasn't he, Elias? From Andelys?"

"So he was. But my mother was a ship's slave and I was born on board the *Barracuda*."

Rol smiled wryly. "Once I was told that I, too, had been born aboard a ship."

"Then we are brothers in that, Rol—men with no country to call our own."

Rol gestured to the ranks of privateers listening intently to Amertaz's song. "You imagine any of them think of themselves as citizens of here or there? We belong to the sea, Elias. As for our home, we stand upon it."

"Some of them think of Ganesh Ka as home."

"Ah, yes." Rol stared up at the towering intricacies of the mainmast as it loomed above them. All those tons of timber and canvas and cordage, balanced and designed to take the wind and with it move the little world that sustained them across this vast inimical wilderness that men named the sea.

"Sometimes it doesn't profit a man too much to know where his home lies. It's just one more thing that can be taken away from him," Rol said with some bitterness.

"A man must fight for something, or somewhere or someone, or else he is no more than an animal," Creed said quietly.

"We are worse than animals," Rol answered him. "We will fight for nothing, simply for the joy of fighting; and if our conscience pricks us afterward, some will give that joy a name, and call it patriotism. That's where it leads you, Elias, that possession of a home to call your own."

"A man may fight for many things," Creed countered. "What he thinks is right or wrong—"

"And who are we to judge what is right and what is wrong, Elias Creed, convict, pirate? Killer of men. Right and wrong is a matter of opinion—or of fashion."

"Are you trying to tell me—" Creed began with some heat.

"Do you smell that?" It was Gallico. He had joined them at the quarterdeck rail with that odd graceful speed it was so remarkable to see. He had lifted his head and was sniffing the wind.

"What is it?" Rol asked at once. They had learned long ago to trust Gallico's nose.

"I smell shit."

"We've been talking it this last glass and more." Creed grinned.

"No. It's coming down the wind. Human shit."

The smile slipped off Creed's face. "A slaver?"

"Must be. The stink can drift for miles with a good breeze."

Rol went to the taffrail and stared over the ship's wake, slightly phosphorescent under the sickle moon. Nothing on the horizon, not so much as a gull. The starlit night was vast and empty. Yet Gallico was seldom wrong.

Then Rol caught it himself. A land smell, heavy and alien to the cool freshness of the sea-breeze. "They're astern of us. Masthead there! Look aft. What do you see?"

The lookout was perched comfortably in the foretop. At Rol's hail, he started, and quickly swarmed up the shrouds to the cap of the foretopmast. "Nothing, sir!"

"He'll see damn-all from there, looking aft," Gallico muttered.

Rol turned to the quartermasters at the wheel, one of whom was old Morcam, a foul-smoking pipe clenched between his carious teeth.

"Starboard two points."

The wheel was spun without question or comment. The ship turned right through some twenty degrees. Watching the yards Rol saw the courses slacken and bulge and crack as the mizzen ate into their wind. He stepped forward. In the waist, Amertaz had stopped singing, and the ship's company was staring aloft, wondering. Then all eyes came to rest on their captain.

"Take in the mizzen-course," Rol said. He glanced aloft again, his mind working with the variables. "Take in topgallants. Douse all lights. Lookouts to all three mastheads. Imbro, fill cartridge for two broadsides. Quirion, arms chests to the waist." Then, slightly louder, "All hands. All hands on deck."

The crowds of men who a moment before had been sitting

listening, smoking, exchanging banter, broke up at once. The decks rumbled with the smothered thunder of their bare feet, and the mizzen topmen came scampering aft. Within a few seconds the ratlines were black with climbing figures, deck-lanterns had been blown out, and the gunner, the master-at-arms, and their mates had disappeared below. It never failed to give Rol pleasure to watch this—his crew going about their business with the purposeful efficiency of true professionals.

As soon as the mizzen lookout was up in the topgallant shrouds, Rol hailed him. "Generro, what do you see astern?"

Generro was a lithe, dark-haired young man with the eyes of a peregrine, the arms of a moderate ape, and an absurdly pretty face. "Vessel on the horizon, skipper, dead astern! She comes and goes, nowhere near hull-up yet."

"Odds are she won't have seen our lights. Damn that fool moon. Gallico, what do you know of slavers?"

The halftroll bared his fangs a little farther. "They're swift sailers; they have to be to get their cargoes to port alive—or half-alive, at any rate. I'd say this fellow is bound out of Cavaillon, one of the great markets there such as Astraro. And on this course he'll be making for ancient Omer, biggest auction-port of live flesh you'll find north of the Gut."

"Omer of the black walls. Yes, I know it."

"They're fore-and-aft-rigged for the most part, slavers, flush-decked and narrow in the beam. Everything for speed."

"They'd outrun us, then."

"Given anything like a fair wind, yes. But it's a southerly we've got here, a stern wind—not good for his lateens, if that's truly what he has shipped."

"How many would they carry?"

"Slaves? A vessel much the same size as us would reckon on cramming in some five hundred."

Rol whistled softly. "Five hundred! How do they carry stores for so many mouths?"

"They don't," Gallico said glumly. "A certain amount of wastage is acceptable."

"What kind of price do slaves bring on the block these days? We could be looking at a fortune here."

"You're joking, I know." Gallico looked positively dangerous.

Rol smiled without humor. "Of course. Now, how's about we figure a way to steal the weather-gage from this fellow?"

It was a dreamlike night, the sea hardly chopping up under the steady southerly, the ship gliding along like a ghost, orders issued by the ship's officers not in their usual bark, but in ridiculously low tones. Sound carried over the surface of the sea at night; a man's sneeze might be heard a mile away downwind. Rol took the *Revenant* ever more steadily out to the west, and unfurled almost everything from the topmasts down; the topgallants were too high to risk their prey catching a glimpse of them over the horizon. The lookouts reported the progress of the slaver in hoarse, furtive shouts. She came on northward, expecting nothing, and being a private ship and not a man-of-war, she had taken in a few reefs of sail for the night so as to reduce speed a little in the dark hours. Her crew had no inkling that out in the wastes of the sea close by there loomed a three-hundred-ton predator waiting for the moment to strike.

Rol moved in just before dawn, packing on every sail the *Revenant* possessed. They had the southerly on the starboard quarter by then, and were coming up on the slaver's larboard quarter. The sun rose up almost full in their faces, springing up out of the molten bosom of the ocean, and at the same moment the sleepy lookout on the slaver finally saw them, and the xebec—for such it was—came to startled life. Men hammered up her rigging like ants and began letting out the reefs in the big lateens. The slaver picked up speed at once, but the balance had already tipped against her. Rol had the guns run out and the crew of number-one starboard fired a twelve-pound ball across her bows that lashed her fo'c'sle with spray, so close did it skip to her hull. Men were running about the xebec's decks, shouting and pointing at the black ship that was powering down on them with the sun rising upon her yards and her guns run out like the grin of so many teeth. The *Revenant* ran in under the slaver's stern, stealing her wind, and there Rol backed topsails and lay-to with his broadside naked and leering at the xebec's vulnerable stern. The big lateens fell slack, and banged against the yards impotently. Rol clambered forward into the bowsprit and yelled across two hundred yards of sea, "Heave to, or I sink you!"

The Cavaillic ensign at the slaver's mizzen jerked, then came down in submission, though the Mercanter pennant remained snapping and twisting at her mainmast. Her crew ceased their frenzied running about and stood silent on her deck like men condemned. And about the two ships, predator and prey, a terrible stench arose, and from the hull of the wallowing xebec there came the wailing of hundreds of voices, a host of people in torment.

The *Revenant* possessed two eighteen-foot cutters, which sculled eight oars apiece. Getting these off the waist booms and into the sea by tackles from the yardarms took some time, however, and Rol went below to the great cabin while the ship's company manhandled the heavy sea-boats overboard. He came back on deck with his cross-staff and took a reading off the swift-rising sun, grunting with satisfaction at the result. "Gallico," he called. "Sidearms and swords to the cutter-crews. And Giffon is to come across also with whatever he thinks he might need. And get some water-casks out of the hold—whatever you think necessary." The heavy stench had enveloped both ships now, swamping even the powder-smell of the burning match in the tubs, and the wailing aboard the slaver would bring out a cold sweat on the most hardened of men. The Revenants were no faint-hearts, but even they looked uneasy.

"Elias," Rol said. "Keep them busy, will you?" The ex-convict nodded. Under his deep tan, the blood had left his face.

Eventually the two cutters put off for the xebec, filled to the gunwales with heavily armed men and all manner of stores. The slaver was low in the water, and the Revenants clambered over her sides with the agility of wharf-rats. Rol fought the urge to gag at the miasma of filth that shrouded the ship, and snapped at the petrified crew, "Where's the master?"

He came forward clutching his ship's papers and setting knuckle to forehead like a peasant greeting his lord. "Here, Captain. Grom Mindorin, master of the *Astraros.*"

"What's your cargo?"

"Three hundred and seventy-odd head, bound out of Astraro for Omer. Captain, we are a Mercanter ship."

"What of it?"

"I thought perhaps—"

"You thought wrong. Show me your hold. I wish to see the cargo."

They went below. The sun was climbing up a cloudless sky, and despite the lateness of the year the heat of it beat down on the decks. Rol felt sweat trickling down the small of his back. All the hatches had bolt-fastened gratings that let in almost no light or air. Mindorin, bobbing his head apologetically, led Rol first to the stern-cabin, where he lit a lantern, then he made his way forward along a gloomy companionway. The stench grew worse, if that was possible, though the wailing had given way to a low murmuring, punctuated by the odd sharp cry, like that of a rabbit taken by a stoat.

They went through a reinforced bulkhead—every door in the ship had bolts to it—and at once the flame in the lantern burned blue and guttered low. Mindorin raised it up, his face streaming with sweat. The close, fetid air was hard to breathe, the smell almost a physical presence, pressing about their faces.

"Gods of the world," Rol croaked.

The compartment ran almost the full length of the ship, some twenty-five yards. It had been divided up horizontally by a stout wooden platform, so that there were two decks in front of Rol, each less than a yard high. A thick carpet of bodies lay on both of these, chained by the ankles, feet to feet. Hundreds of people, turning feebly, twitching, moaning, sobbing, or lying inert. All caked in their own filth, bloodied by the chains that bound them. All in darkness. The lantern was of little use, but Rol's preternatural vision spared him none of the details. There were men, women, and children here, mixed indiscriminately, all of them naked and plastered in their own excreta, dull eyes sunken in their heads, skulls shaven down to the skin. Corpses lying amid them with maggots working busily about every orifice. Lice in clusters the size of marbles, and here and there a venturesome rat crawling over the dead and the living unmolested.

A wondering fury blazed up in Rol's heart. He understood Gallico better now. But he stood there for a long moment, mastering the rage, beating it down. When he turned to Mindorin again, his voice was quiet, even.

"You will unlock these chains, and get these people on deck."

The slaver's master shrank from the light of those eyes. "Aye, sir, at once. I'll get the keys. One minute, and I'll have them—"

"Get your crew down here, every last one of them. You will bring these people water and food. You will wash them."

"Anything, Captain, anything." Mindorin scuttled away, falling over backward in his haste.

Rol bent low and hunkered his way through the dense-packed morass of humanity, sometimes reduced by the lack of headroom to crawling on his hands and knees. Tar from the hot deckhead fell on his shoulders and his boots slipped and shifted in liquid filth. Here was a young woman, dead, staring. Between her legs the corpse of a baby, which had issued out of her long before full term. A clenched, gray, globular thing gnawed by rats and running with maggots. But Rol could still make out the tiny fingers closed in fists.

Here, two men had strangled each other with their chains and were locked in a last embrace. Here a child, a girl not more than five years old, with the flesh on her ankles eaten down to the bone by the shackles. Rol could feel the eyes of hundreds on him as he made his noisome way down the compartment. People called to him hoarsely in languages he did not understand. Some struggled to their bloody and yellow-scabbed elbows, then fell back again. Just as he thought he could bear it no more his gaze was caught by that of a young boy, ten years old maybe. His limbs were stick-thin and lice-tracks were raw and red all over his narrow chest. The boy was smiling emptily. Beside him was an older man, the oldest Rol had seen here. For some reason he had been allowed to retain a full, gray beard. His eyes were dark, and lively with intelligence. They regarded Rol with grave appraisal, as though weighing up the defects and deliberations of his soul. Rol tried to speak to him, but his throat had closed.

Back up on deck, he breathed in the clear, clean air deeply. He could feel the vermin of the slave-hold crawling over his skin, and began plucking at his clothes. "Quirion!"

"Aye, sir." The burly master-at-arms had a naked cutlass in his hand, and the point of it twitched as though it ached to be in use.

"The crew of this ship will unchain all the slaves and get them on deck. The slaves will be watered, fed, and hosed down. Then that crew will go below and clean out the slave-deck with swabs. On their hands and knees, Quirion."

"Hands and knees, sir."

Naked now, Rol sprang to the ship's rail. "Get rid of those rags," he said, and then dived overboard.

The cold plunge of the water, the clean salt bite of the sea. He dived deep, deep as he had ever gone, trying to leave behind the filth that coated his skin, the filth he felt to be within.

Three

HOMECOMING

11th Jurius, Year 32, Bar Asfal. Wind southerly, the Cavaillic Trades. Course WNW under all plain sail. With Dead Reckoning we are two leagues north of the latitude of Golgos, three leagues west of the Omer long-line. Overtook a slaver at the end of the middle watch, a flush-decked xebec of some two hundred tons, the Astraros. On board were twenty-six crew, three hundred and thirty-two slaves, and two score corpses. I made the crew of the slaver clean out the hold of their ship, then had them bound each to a corpse and threw them overboard. The slaves remain on the xebec, which Gallico now commands with a prize crew of thirty men. I have not seen before a more pitiful collection of people. Before I drowned him, the Astraros's master told me that many of them had already made a voyage before this—they are natives of every coast about the Inner Reach, some kidnapped from fishing villages, others taken in war. Gallico insists that all must be brought back to the Ka, and for once I agree with him.

For all her dirty trade, the Astraros is a fine ship, and I think her hull will bear the nine-pounders we took from the Bionese man-of-war earlier this month. She would be a useful consort for the Revenant, *keeping so close to the wind, though I think I may change her yards to square-rigged on the foremast.*

A knock on the cabin door, and Elias Creed put his head around it. "Ganesh Ka is in sight."

"Thanks, Elias. I'll be up on deck presently. Where does the *Astraros* stand?"

"Fine on the starboard bow, some half a league ahead. She's a flyer, all right. Gallico has reefed every sail she has, and still has the legs of us." Creed sounded almost resentful, as if the *Revenant*'s honor had been slighted.

"I'll wager she stinks of shit, all the same," Rol said, with a weak grin.

Ganesh Ka. From the sea it appeared to be nothing more than some huge geological anomaly, a freak of soaring stone. Cliffs between two and three hundred feet high ran sheer and mustard-pale for over a league along the shore, the sea smashing in white breakers about their foot. But above them there reared up black, unearthly towers of volcanic stone—basalt and granite in poplar-shaped buttresses and barbicans, as variegated as the trees in a wood, and yet existing in some half-guessed symmetry. With the eyes half closed and the light behind them, they might almost become the castles of some rock-hewing titan, in places as rough as nature and the wind could make them, in others as perfectly smoothed as a sculptor's dream. A man might marvel at the sight, without ever guessing that it had been built by artifice, and the imaginations of minds long dead.

There was an opening in the sea-cliffs, invisible from more than a few cables away. They ran the ships in through the hundred-yard gap with four men to each wheel, all sails furled but for a few scraps of canvas to give the vessels steerage-way. Above their heads the seabirds—skuas and gulls and blue-eyed gannets in their thousands—wheeled and soared and dived, heedless of any human. This late in the year they had been joined by skeins of long-necked, raucous geese, black and white and gray, immigrants from the far, frozen north. No one ever hunted these geese; they were seen as part of the Ka's luck.

The wall of cliffs opened out before them into a great circular bay, a sight that never failed to take the breath out of Rol's throat no matter how often he saw it. Before him the sea-cliffs on the landward side had been tunneled and crannied into a subterranean counterpart of the looming towers of stone above, and three tall ship-gates yawned black and cavernous in the sun-warmed rock of their faces, each massive enough to admit a fully rigged man-of-war.

"Tide's on the ebb," Elias Creed said.

"Only just. Let her glide in, Elias."

Creed smiled. He knew how his captain savored the majesty of this view.

There were light fishing smacks and dories dotted about the water of the bay, men and women hauling in skein nets and longlines beaded with the silver flash of herrin and amarack, staples of the city. They stood up in their bobbing cockleshells and cheered the sight of the two ships. The *Revenant* they knew well—she had become a sort of talisman for the inhabitants of the Ka. But the *Astraros* was new, exotic, and they pointed at her and shouted indecipherable catcalls to Gallico, who stood grinning and waving from her bows.

Darkness, startling after the gold and blue splendor of the day outside. At once the quality of sound itself changed, the chop of water and creak of the ships' working echoing back at them as they passed through the ship-gates into the vast cavern within which housed the docks and wharves of Ganesh Ka. Woodsmoke, ordure, rotten fish, tar—the heavy smells of the land crowding about noses more used to the clean air of the sea. Lightermen came sculling out in their narrow craft and took cables from the bows to tow the ships to dock.

"Take in all sail," Rol said. "Gangplank to the waist. Fenders there, ready in the bows."

A ragged and malodorous crowd had gathered about the wharves, and now shouts and good-natured catcalls went to and fro between their ranks and the busy sailors on board the *Revenant* and *Astraros*. The two ships tied up alongside each other, and the crowds on the docksides went quiet as they saw the wretched, stubble-headed throng of terrified figures that peopled the deck of the slave-ship. Many there had been slaves themselves, and knew what they were looking at. Others gave full vent to their curiosity, and Gallico had three enterprising youngsters thrown overboard into the slimy water of the docks after they had shinned up the mooring-ropes.

"Dry-dock, skipper—as soon as we're able. I won't rest until her poor bottom is seen to." This was Kier Eiserne, the carpenter, his narrow face earnest with worry.

"Don't worry, Kier. She'll not sink yet. We'll have her off-loaded first. Get some of those ragamuffins on the piers to help you empty the hold."

"The guns'll have to go, too, skipper—every damn thing that's not nailed down."

"I know that," Rol snapped. And in a softer tone, "Do whatever you have to, but get her seaworthy again with all speed. If you have any deficiencies, see me or Gallico."

"Aye, sir."

In all probability Kier was overworrying, but that was no bad thing in a ship's carpenter. Rol patted the quarterdeck rail. Where once it had been all black teak, now sections of it were of lighter wood, the results of repairs after many sea-fights. All about the ship, the Kassic teak that had been the original flesh of the *Revenant* was patchworked with softer wood—good timber, the best they could find—but still, nothing like as hardy as that used by her original shipwrights. In time, the very stuff a ship was made of changed under the feet of her company, but her essence, the concept for which she had been made, remained the same.

If only it were that way with men, Rol thought.

A year before, the *Revenant* had been a mastless hulk, quietly rotting in a flooded dry-dock here in Ganesh Ka. The carcass of a once-proud ship, she had belonged to the Bionese—a heavy dispatch-runner surprised and taken by a cloud of the Ka's vessels, surrounded and beaten like a bull brought to its knees by the hounds. Her captain, Rol thought, must have been a fool, to let such a ship be taken by the light privateers of the Ka.

Now she was reborn. Rol had rescued her, rebuilt her, and made of her a superb fighting ship, a man-of-war to match any the Bionese might send against her. He regarded her dark hull with the jealous love of a father, or a lover. His blood was in her very timbers.

"Cortishane!" a deep voice shouted from the wharves. Rol lifted his head from contemplation of his ship and found himself looking down on the face of Artimion, his eyes two shivers of blue glass in a shining black face. A scar rippled like a tree-root down his forehead. This was the master of Ganesh Ka, or as close as anyone could come to that.

"You're looking well, Artimion. Life ashore agrees with you."

The pale eyes grew colder. "Come to my quarters when you have a minute to call your own, you and your officers. We have things to discuss. What's the xebec?"

"A slaver. The *Astraros,* out of Astraro for Omer."

"Any other meetings?"

"The Bionari, as usual."

"Did you fight, or cut and run?" Artimion was looking the *Revenant* up and down for recent repairs, shot-damage. His question inferred no manner of moral judgment; it was a professional inquiry, but Rol bristled all the same.

"We exchanged a few broadsides, Artimion."

"You must tell me about it." The black man coughed suddenly, a hacking churn of liquid. He spat on the quay and then wiped his mouth with a rag, grimacing. "My quarters, as soon as you can, Cortishane." For a moment he seemed about to say more, then he strode away with the rolling walk of one used to shipboard, though he himself had not put to sea in many months. He was a long time recovering from the wounds he had received in the spring.

"I'll take over here, Rol," said Elias. He smiled. "Artimion is never one for the courtesies."

"Artimion can kiss my arse. As soon as the wounded are ashore, talk to Kier about what he needs done. He wants her stripped and hauled down in dry-dock to check out her hull."

"He's overzealous."

"No harm in it, not now anyway."

"What about them?" Elias pointed to the troops of unsteady, shaven-headed figures now being helped across the *Astraros*'s gangplanks.

"What about them? They're here, they're free, the rest is up to themselves."

"We should perhaps hunt up some food for them, and clothes."

"Not my problem, Elias. As soon as they hit dry land, they're Artimion's. Our job is to get the *Revenant* seaworthy again as soon as possible."

Elias frowned. "There is something to be said, Rol, for a little compassion."

"I've already shown them a little, Elias. Now someone else can show them a lot. Talk to Kier—and don't let the crew ashore until he's got what he wants. They're no good to him drunk."

"Aye aye, sir."

A man-of-war was a crowded machine. Those who saw some form of romance in a life at sea usually knew little of its realities. Men ate together in messes of eight, slept together in swaying rows of hammocks, each touching their neighbors'. They defecated together from the heads in the bow of their ship, and they fought and died together surrounded by the close wooden walls of their little floating world. There were no secrets on board ship; eventually every man's proclivities, secret or otherwise, became common knowledge. A man could not play a part and remain a member of that company; the realities of his soul became known to all over time.

Thus it was that Gallico and Creed were viewed by their shipmates with an uncomplicated mix of respect and affection, and Rol Cortishane was viewed with something more akin to awe. His men had seen what happened to him in the extremity of battle, and they knew there was something in him that was not remotely human. They accepted this; they did respect him, they feared him, and knew him to be a master-mariner, a canny tactician, and a hard but fair taskmaster. But they could not love him. Rol knew this, and the man he had become shrugged it off. But the boy who had once dreamed of the fellowship of a ship's company could not help but be wounded by it.

He had his friends, of course. Gallico and Creed were as close to him as brothers, despite their disagreements. They all owed one another their lives many times over, and that was a bond unbreakable. Oddly enough, young Giffon, too, was closer to his captain than to anyone else on board. Perhaps he sensed the bruised boy that Rol had been not so very long ago. Perhaps damaged souls drew together.

Back now in Ganesh Ka, the close, enforced companionship, the cheek-by-jowl living of a ship's company was diluted by space and the addition of hundreds, thousands of other people. Wives, children, parents even—all re-established their ties on men come from the sea, whose only family had been one another, who had committed the bodies of their brothers to the depths of the ocean, whose blood had soaked into the very fabric of their ship. They became embroiled in the intricacies of land-living again, and their lives became that much less simple.

Standing on the ancient stone of the wharves, Rol felt the long roll of breakers still moving under his feet. Men called out greetings; women smiled, some lewdly; children plucked at his clothing. It took a moment's mental effort to collect his thoughts. The ship-cavern, vast though it was, seemed close, the gutrock of millennia bearing down on him. He pinched the bridge of his nose and picked his way through the tatterdemalion crowds until he stood by the towering bulk of Gallico, who was supervising the procession of unsteady slaves which filed endlessly off the *Astraros*.

"How are they?" he asked his first mate.

The halftroll grimaced. "We lost twelve more over the last three days, but Giffon reckons the rest will pull through. Most look worse than they are; it was the second-voyagers who had it worst. Some of them had come from as far afield as Mysol, and had been in that filth for many weeks."

Strange, how the slaves seemed to have lost all definition of age or sex; they might have been some strange other species, dead-eyed and hollow-faced. One of them had a beard: an older man whose face retained some humanity. In his arms he carried a young boy; Rol remembered them from his descent into the slaver's hold. The boy's smile was singularly sweet, but there was no knowledge in his eyes. Moved by he knew not what, Rol stopped them.

"Where are you from?" he asked the man.

"We were taken off the coast near Golgos," the man answered. His voice was deep; he would be a fine singer. His brawny forearms were those of a man whose life had been earned with sweat, corded with muscle that age and circumstances had not yet withered away. He was not tall, but there was a solid presence about him, a sense of calm. The boy's slim arms encircled his neck.

"Your son?"

"Yes, Captain. My only child."

"What's your name?"

"I am called Aveh."

"Well, Aveh, you're welcome here." Something in the man's steady gaze made Rol uncomfortable. "I hope you find some peace here," he fumbled.

The man nodded. "Thank you, Captain." Then he continued on his way, the boy smiling over his shoulder as emptyheaded as a butterfly.

Miriam had arrived on the docks with a company of her musketeers, the only standing soldiery the Ka possessed. Her men were making lists, issuing orders, asking questions. Behind them, a horde of folk were setting up trestle tables and lading them with food, plates, jugs, and others were coming up to the slaves with oddments of clothing, blankets, homemade sandals.

"It takes poverty to make one truly generous," Gallico said, watching them. "It seems to me sometimes that only the poor are truly human."

"Make me rich, and I'll test that theory for you," Rol said, and Gallico chuckled.

Miriam stalked up to the pair, musket slung at her back. She was a tall, thin woman whose hair was a bright halo of red-gold and whose skin was white as ivory. "Well, gentlemen, you have been busy, it seems." A gap between her front teeth gave her speech a small, pleasing lisp. Her eyes smiled up at Gallico, then rested on Rol with cold dislike.

"Three-hundred-odd to be found a place to lay their heads, Miriam," Gallico said. "They're in poor shape, most of them, and some speak languages I've not heard in many a year."

"We'll open up another tower," Miriam said. "If you brought back ten thousand, we could still find them room. No, it's food I'm worried about. We need more in the way of sea-fishing craft, and more land cleared up in the woods; most of the fields we have are close to farmed out."

Rol's attention drifted. He heard the same things rehashed every time he came back from a voyage. These were not his problems. His problems were to do with timber, iron, gunpowder, sailcloth; the mechanics of men's mastery of the sea.

"I bore you, Cortishane?" Miriam asked.

"You have your problems, Miriam, I have mine," Rol said.

"I apologize for bringing the inconveniences of the little people to your attention."

"Apology accepted," Rol snapped. "Now, if you will allow me, I must speak to my first mate."

Miriam glared at him, then turned to Gallico. "There'll be a feast tonight, in the square, if you and the Revenants want to come along, Gallico. It's not every day the Ka gains itself a new ship. And *Albatross* came in two days ago loaded to the rails with the plunder of two fat Mercanters."

"Ben Oban got lucky at last, did he? We'll be there, Miriam."

Rol watched her go, the boyish hips with the musket slung in the crease of her buttocks, the hair bright as a flammifer.

"If she saw you looking at her like that, you might get yourself shot," Gallico told him.

"Men have died for stranger things. Listen, Gallico, I want the *Astraros* refitted as a man-of-war. She'll bear at least eight of the nine-pounders we took out of the Bionese. I reckon we'll square-rig her on the foremast too. What do you think?"

"I think it's a fine idea. The only problem is crew. We've mariners by the score here in the Ka, but we're short on artisans, carpenters, and the like. And who's to captain her?"

"You are."

The halftroll shook his head. "I'm right happy with where I am."

"Your own command, Gallico. Think on it."

"Maybe I'm not the commanding sort. It's easier taking orders than giving them, I've always found. No, Rol, you must find someone else."

"We'll see. Think on it, at any rate. You'll oversee the work on her, though?"

"Of course."

The population of Ganesh Ka was a mixture culled from every coast and sea-lane in the world. All they held in common was the fact that the Hidden City had become their sanctuary, and all who came to it, whether destitute or deranged, were to be made welcome. Apart from Miriam's musketeers, the only officialdom that the Ka possessed was the quartermasters, who looked after the city stores, whether maritime- or land-based. In subterranean caverns hewn out of the bedrock by the unimaginable labor of the Ancients, there was laid up a great mass of supplies. Timber, pig-iron, sailcloth, rope, pitch, and all the paraphernalia that attended the maintenance of ships. But barreled up also were hundreds of casks of salt beef and pork, smoked and dried fish, pickled vegetables, tuns of wine. Enough to feed—frugally—the thousands the Ka contained for several months.

There were no work-rotas, but everyone pitched in as and when they were needed, and if they did not, their fellows soon persuaded them. Some were inshore fishermen, others farmed the tiny plots that had been hewn out of Ganesh's illimitable forests up in the foothills of the Myconians. Yet more were herders of half-wild goat herds in the high slopes of those mountains, and these goats provided meat, milk, cheese, and hides for the city.

And yet to call this accumulation of effort, this conglomeration of people, a city was, Rol thought, misleading. Ganesh Ka might be a vast architectural marvel, but to the folk who lived there, it constituted little more than an enormous campsite, with limited organization and a system that worked because it was oiled with a vast amount of goodwill. That, and the knowledge that for these people there was nothing else. The rest of the world was closed to this host of the dispossessed. Rol thought that if the goodwill and desperation that glued the city together ever frayed, then Ganesh Ka would descend into anarchy. But perhaps that was true of every society, every place where men came together in some common resolve.

Artimion had a superlative view of the wide caldera that formed Ganesh Ka's harbor. By the time Rol made it to the black man's apartments, the sun was sliding down behind the Myconians in the west, and the fishing boats were all docked. The only vessel out in the bay now was the sixty-foot guard galley that patroled the entrance to the harbor, bristling with experienced oarsmen and musketeers. The mustard and honey hues of the sea-cliffs seemed almost luminous in the last light of the sun, and as the shadow fell the air turned colder—a reminder that even this far south, winter had taken hold of the world. The Ka was only some two hundred leagues north of Mas Llurin, the Great Line that men of science said marked the widest mark about the girdle of the earth. Though there was deep snow in the higher passes of the Myconians, here by the sea the warm air lingered most of the year. It grew dark sooner, and the mornings had a bite to them, but winter by the shores of the Inner Reach was as nothing compared to the gray storms and white gales of the Seven Isles, or Northern Bionar.

In the city, no lights were lit facing the sea, for fear of giving their location away to cruising men-of-war, but Artimion's chambers were sufficiently far down the cliffs to be hidden from the sight of anything on the Reach. So he had a fragrant fire of pine and olive logs burning in his hearth, and olive-oil lamps flickering in the air from the huge, glassless windows. Gallico, Elias, and Miriam were already perched on wall-benches with cups in their hands as Rol flicked aside the goatskin flap that served as a door.

Artimion stood with his back to them, and he did not move as he said, "You took your time."

"It was mine to take," Rol said.

The master of Ganesh Ka turned at that, and smiled. With the dying light from the window behind him all that could be seen in that ebony face were the glint of white teeth and two glass-gleams for eyes.

"Of course it is," Artimion said.

Rol had been looking in on Giffon and the wounded one last time, but there was no reason Artimion should know that. He was very tired, so tired he did not quite make sense of all the shape and silhouette in the room, the competing radiances of sunset and firelight.

"How is the wine?" he asked, and yawned.

"Wet. Pour yourself a cup. Pull up a chair. Make yourself at home, Cortishane."

"The boy has grown," a strange voice said. "Why, he's become quite a man, after all."

Fleam was out of her scabbard and whining in the air before

Rol had even registered the action. In a darkened corner of the room, a shadow sat upon a three-legged stool. Rol sensed amusement there. "Ah, I see at least some memory of your training has survived. That's good." The shadow stood up, became a burly man of medium height wrapped in a cloak. Eyes black as those of a snake, and yellow teeth split in a crooked grin.

"Come, Rol; has it been so long?"

Rol collected himself, the white cold of the shock leaving him. He lowered his scimitar, though Fleam quivered urgently in his fist, the point trying to come up again.

"Canker. It has been . . . a long time."

"Eight years, my boy, and much water under many bridges."

Once Canker had been King of Thieves in Ascari, on Gascar of the Seven Isles. He was a figure from Rol's boyhood, a figment of a half-remembered dream. It did not seem possible that he should be standing here in Ganesh Ka.

Artimion set a wine-cup in Rol's free hand. "Have a drink, Cortishane. You look as though you need it."

Rol sipped without tasting. Thick, thrush-brown wine from Oronthir, the vintage Artimion saved for special occasions. He relaxed minutely, though Fleam remained naked and gleaming in his hand. Canker's face unlocked a hail of memories that pelted past his mind's eye. Almost all of them bad. He had raped Rowen. He had murdered with Rowen. Now he served Rowen, or so Rol had been told.

The Thief-King watched him closely, that slot-smile hovering on his mouth. There was no reason why they should be enemies—once they had even been allies, of a sort—but something in Rol knew instinctively that Canker's presence in the Ka was not a good thing. The world had changed since last they had looked upon each other.

"Is this betrayal, Artimion?" Rol asked lightly.

"I don't know what you mean."

"You told me once before that this man had offered you a fortune for news of my whereabouts. Did you think to wonder why?"

Creed and Gallico rose to their feet. "What is this?" Gallico asked, a warning growl rasping the edge of his voice.

"Nothing you need worry about, Gallico. There is no treachery here, I swear." Artimion turned to Rol. "You were friends once, you and Canker."

"We were of use to each other. Not the same thing." A heartbeat throbbed in the blue length of Fleam's marvelous steel. The sword's voice crawled along Rol's brain, warning, nagging. "Why are you here?" he asked Canker.

"To visit our new ally, for one thing. Artimion has thrown Ganesh Ka's lot in with us, and from what I hear, he—and you—have been doing a fine job of whittling down the Bionese navy this last half year and more. While we have been fighting in the mountains, you have been guarding our flank. You have our gratitude, and that may be worth a great deal one day, when this war is over. Diplomacy requires my presence here, Rol—and if you wish to flatter yourself, then, yes, I am also here because of you. Because of who you are."

"I'm a captain of privateers, no more."

"I think there's more to it than that. I'll tell you about it, if you like. Sit down, Rol, for pity's sake, and put away that blade. We are all here on the same side."

Tension sizzled in the room. Miriam, Gallico, Creed, even Artimion, watched the two men transfixed, like an audience waiting for the curtain to rise.

Rol sheathed the scimitar, and felt her rage needle up from the hilt to jolt his arm. He drank more wine, the good warmth of it easing the chill of his innards, and strode over to the fire, feeling Canker's black gaze crawling up his back. The wine-cup clinked as he set it on the hot stone of the mantel. "I'll stand, thank you. Say your piece."

Canker remained in the shadows, where, Rol thought, he had always been most comfortable.

"Come now, boy, I'm not your enemy. Last time we met we were brothers-in-arms, as I recall, fighting side by side." He had not changed at all. In eight years not a single extra line had been added to his face.

"Time has been kind to you," Rol said sourly, remembering the last days of Ascari, the mobs running wild in the streets.

"I've been well looked after. Indulged even."

All at once, the desire to hear news of Rowen flamed up in Rol's heart. The pain of that last day reared up all raw and glistening again. He was a boy once more, a brokenhearted assassin watching the only thing he loved in the world walk away from him. But his face never changed. Psellos's training had been good enough for that, at least.

He turned to Artimion, who sat like a man watching a horse-race on which he has bet a fortune. "Why did you let him come here? You've thrown away the location of this Hidden City of yours. Do you even know who he is?"

Artimion shrugged. "As to his presence here, I had no say in it. He found this place of his own accord. And yes, I know him. I told you once before, we were Feathermen together in our youth, Canker and I."

"So there is honor amongst thieves, after all."

"Honor, and mutual need," Canker broke in. "I've been three months on the road, wandering the damned mountains and forests of this part of the world like a vagabond, worming my way here on a web of rumor and legend. I am alone, Rol. You could kill me out of hand."

"Do not think I would not, Canker. Do not make that mistake."

Canker did not flinch; the black eyes sized Rol up and down, missing nothing. "I believe you would." He threw aside his cloak. Rol moved in a blur; he was ten feet from the fireplace before any of their hearts had beat. Miriam's mouth gaped in astonishment.

Under the cloak, Canker wore a threadbare tunic and breeches out at both knees. He was weaponless. "I left my killing things at home."

Artimion raised a hand. "Enough. Cortishane, I make the decisions here; it is I who'll decide what is best for Ganesh Ka. At least hear the man out."

Perhaps Artimion was right. But Rol knew only that the shadow that had dogged his life had caught up with him once more. If the doom of Ganesh Ka had come closer with his own arrival, then surely it was now finally upon them, in ragged breeches and wearing a yellow-toothed grin.

He bowed, face wiped of all expression. "Forgive me, gentlemen. Canker, proceed."

The King of Thieves smiled. "Rowen sent me," he said.

Four

BAR HETHRUN'S CHILDREN

"THE CONTINENT OF BION HOUSES THE MOST ANCIENT of the Kingdoms of Men," Canker said. If he did not relish their rapt faces, he was disguising it well. "The legends are well known. In the Goliad, the navel of the world, men woke from their sleep under stone and wandered the green plains while the angels watched." He grinned, and caught Rol's eye. "Angels, demons, Weres—they have many names, but we all know what they mean. Those who were here before us. Those who built the city in which we sit.

"Bion was the first chieftain of these men. The ancient city of Golgos was still inhabited then, and he went there to be instructed by the Ancients in all manner of disciplines and lore. It is even said he bedded the daughter of one of their lords in secret. In any case, he was quite a fellow, this Bion. He organized the scattered tribes of his people, and ruled them with a stern but kindly hand." Canker flapped his own black-nailed appendage. "You all know the legends."

"Then why are we listening to them twice-baked?" Elias Creed asked quietly.

"Because there is a new chapter being written," Canker retorted, all geniality vanished.

"Go on, Canker," Artimion said.

The King of Thieves collected himself. "It got to be that Bion's son Golias resented his father's stern but kindly hand, and decided to bring forward his own accession to the throne, as it were. Some would have it that this Golias had the blood of the Ancients in his veins, and was the result of Bion's dallying with the Weren princess. The tribes split in civil war, but Golias won, in the end, and Bion fled north with a large host of refugees, across the Myconians. Other, smaller bands trekked west across the Golorons, or took to the Inner Reach in their canoes. Golias ruled the Goliad, hence the name, and Bion set up Bionar across the mountains. His second son, Mycos, who succeeded him, established Myconn itself, and later on the Bionari—or Bionese, as they are variously called—founded others of the great cities of the world. Phidon and Urbonetto, Arbion and Gallitras. Those who had fled the civil war set up other princedoms and cities across the continent. Perilar and Oronthir date from this time. Thus the world we know was set in train.

"But what of Golias? Well, it turns out that after his brief flash of ambition he was an indolent sort of fellow, after all. He created no cities, carved out no kingdoms. He and his people were content to be pastoral nomads roaming the wide plains of the Goliad, taking instruction from the dwindling Weres in Golgos, and generally living a quiet life. Until, that is, the Bionari decided that they must take back their ancestral homeland, and so began the series of invasions that reduced the Goliad to the parched desert it has become. The people of Golias were decimated, and became a hunted remnant, but even then the other kingdoms of the continent decided that they, too, had a right to the Goliad, and so made war across it—for if one is to attack Bionar by land, the only passes through the Myconians great enough to admit the passage of armies are in the northwest of the Goliad. And so for this reason also, the Goliad, that ancient paradise, became the battleground of the world."

Canker paused. He sipped wine. "What is this to do with the present? I see you all wonder. I was once told by a wise man that we lay the bricks of our lives upon the bones of the dead, even if we know it not.

"Over thirty years ago now, the heir to the throne of Bionar was a fine, upstanding man named Bar Hethrun. He had a half brother, Bar Asfal. Their father, Bar Haddon, was a bookish sort who was fascinated by the legends surrounding the Goliad, and the Weren relics of Golgos and other places. It is said he led armies there simply to potter about the ruins. In any case, unlike his forebears, he held the scattered nomads of the Goliad in respect, and collected their stories and myths and oral histories as other men collect butterflies, or coins. He took one of these nomad women as a concubine and companion in scholarship, and Bar Hethrun was their issue. Haddon loved the boy, but the King of Bionar must needs have a consort more distinguished than some desert nomad, and so he made a political marriage, taking to wife a princess of Armidia, Bionar's great rival for the sea-lanes of the Inner Reach. Their son was Bar Asfal, and he took after his mother—a conniving bitch, by all accounts. Nevertheless, Bar Hethrun was the official heir to the throne, though there were many of the Bionese nobility who muttered against it. He joined his father on the old King's archaeological and military expeditions to the Goliad, and there he met a woman called Amerie, a raven-haired sorceress of remarkable wit and beauty, with the Blood strong in her. He took her to wife.

"The old King's health failed, and he died. Bar Asfal seized the throne, usurping his elder half brother's claim with the approval of most of the court. Bar Hethrun and Amerie took to the high seas with a band of followers, and came . . . here. Amerie brought her husband to this secret place, and in the ruined Weren city of Ganesh Ka they established a refuge, a word-of-mouth sanctuary for those fleeing the excesses of Bionar. But they did not stay here. They took to the sea again, and after many adventures and mishaps, they were finally hunted down by agents of the Bionese Crown, and murdered." Once again Canker paused. His eyes were bead-bright and there was a thin sheen of sweat on his forehead. Beyond the windows night had come upon the world. The lamps had burned dry and the only light in the room now was provided by the fitful flare of the fire.

"Before they died, Bar Hethrun and Amerie had two children, a boy and a girl. The girl is my mistress, Rowen Bar Hethrun, now fighting to reclaim the throne that is rightfully hers." Canker licked his lips. "The boy was named Rol."

His words produced a stunned silence. Rol stood at the mantel with the firelight below him, his shadow streaming out long and black across the room. He was remembering another evening such as this, similar words. Michal Psellos telling him of what might have been his heritage. Rowen knew better; she had not told Canker the whole truth.

"Why *Cortishane*?" Artimion asked. He was staring at Rol, his eyes full of the firelight, like two hellish little windows.

"It was my grandfather's name," Rol said mildly. *Orr-Diseyn, Prince of Demons.*

The fire spat and cracked to itself. Faint and far away the sea rushed and roared on the sea-cliffs of the Ka, in that clear, dark world beyond the windows. At last Gallico spoke up. "Rol, you knew all this?"

"Yes."

"And to think we've pissed in the same pot!" Rol glanced up at the grinning halftroll, and in that moment he loved him. Creed's eyes said the same thing. *What of it? We are shipmates.*

Rol spoke to Canker. "You've loosed your little broadside. Now, what's the upshot of it all?"

"Your sister needs you, Rol."

"Sincerity sits ill on your face, Canker. Why not be honest? You might find the change refreshing."

"You must go to her. This war approaches a climax, and she would have her brother by her side to share in the final victory."

Her brother. "I'll write her a letter. *Dear sister, have fun running the world.* Will that suffice?"

Canker's face darkened. "You damn fool; do you know what it has cost me to get here?"

"What's wrong, Canker, the war effort tripping up a little? What need has Rowen of me when she can command armies?"

"She needs leaders, men she can trust. Do you think a woman like her—"

"Like what, Canker?" Rol advanced on the Thief-King, and as he left the hearth the light in his eyes quickened. His voice grew loud, ugly. "A woman who has prostituted herself to all and sundry—who fucks and murders her way through the world, whose carcass has been pimped out a thousand times. A woman like that? I can do without her favors—or her goodwill."

Canker looked up at him calmly. "You love her," he said.

Rol backed away as if he had been struck. Fleam leaped out of her scabbard and was in his fist like a flash of sea-lightning. The scimitar swept through the stool on which Canker had been sitting, cutting it in two and striking sparks from the stone floor below. The Thief-King had thrown himself aside almost as quickly as Rol's arm had moved. He rolled across the floor like a ball. Gallico and Creed stepped over him. "Rol, no!"

It was there—he was on the cusp of it, so easy now. Gods in heaven, how good it would feel to let go of it.

The others in the room watched, horrified, as a vile brightness spilled out of Rol's eyes. He seemed to rise up off the floor, and a clutch of luminous spears grew at his back, like the unfurling of great wings. The scimitar in his hand grew into a bar of unbearable bright light.

Gallico's fist punched back Rol's head, bursting open the lips on his maniac leer. The halftroll launched himself bodily at Rol and bore him against the far wall, crushing the air out of him.

For a moment Rol struggled. Fleam shrieked in his head, a woman's voice that clawed across his brain. Gallico's weight lay upon him like a hill, but the strength was in him to toss it aside, to rise up like . . . like . . .

And some form of sanity whispered in his ear, like the drunk's sodden realization of what lies in wait for the morning. He threw the scimitar away, and the blade scored a long, smoking furrow in the solid basalt of the floor.

"Hold him down!" Artimion was yelling, and Miriam was clicking back the hammer on her musket. Creed clapped his hand across the lock and wrenched free the flint, scattered the powder in the pan. The two of them fought over the weapon like children with a favorite toy.

Gallico's eyes, inhuman and yet compassionate, staring at him from six inches away. Rol fought for breath. The tears were trickling helplessly down the sides of his face, liquid fire. Within him, the white flame guttered, struggling against his will. For a moment, he thought he could see clear to the heart of it, and the room about him vanished, to be replaced by a fearsome landscape from another world. But it died before he could make sense of it.

His ribs creaked under Gallico's bulk. "Get off me, you big green bastard."

"That's better." The halftroll's weight lifted fractionally.

"It's all right, Gallico. I'm all right."

Gallico stared at him a few seconds more, studying his eyes, then he nodded and got to his feet. Rol clutched his bruised ribs, blood pouring down his chin. It was Canker, of all people, who finally helped him up.

"You are full of surprises, Master Cortishane," Artimion said.

"You have no idea," Rol gasped, spattering blood. He saw Fleam lying on the floor and bent to retrieve her, but Elias Creed set a hand on his arm.

"Maybe it's as better not," he murmured.

"It's a sword, Elias."

"No. There's more to it than that."

Rol bent regardless, and set Fleam back in her scabbard. The steel was dead and cold.

"This has happened before," Artimion said, looking at Gallico. The halftroll hesitated a second, then nodded.

Rol wiped blood from his chin and smiled bleakly. "My secret is out, it seems."

"Remind me not to goad you again, Cortishane," said Canker. Strangely, he seemed unfazed. In fact, he seemed more like a man satisfied with his work.

"You had some idea about this," Rol accused him.

The Thief-King seemed about to deny it, then shrugged.

"What plots are you and Rowen hatching, Canker? I want no part of them, but if you persist, I'll make it my business to put an end to them."

Miriam spoke to Artimion as though they were alone in the room. "Whatever this thing is, we should not have it in the Ka. It is dangerous."

"The thing has ears, Miriam," Rol said wearily. He felt like a bear in the ring, beset and bewildered.

"There has been enough talk for one night," Artimion said. "Cortishane, your friends will see you back to your chambers. Do me a courtesy and remain there until morning. Miriam, you will see Canker looked after. A room in one of the Towers, and two of your men at the door." He smiled at the Thief-King. "Merely to see that you come to no harm." Canker bowed.

"Nothing that has been said or seen in this room is to go beyond it."

"Who'd believe it anyway?" Elias Creed asked wryly. He hoisted one of his captain's arms over his shoulder, for Rol's knees were buckling, and he and Gallico half carried, half dragged him from the room.

It was not a darkness like that of sleep, but rather some womb of starless night, black as the end of the world. He fought through it like a man struggling through deep water, but without direction or sense of progress.

A quicksilver light grew about him, and at last there was up and down, left and right. There was weight and air and all the things that made existence a rational thing. He stood with his feet planted firmly in black soil, and a wind was in his hair. There was water in the wind, a rushing moistness, a smell of rich, writhing, striving life so intense he felt it had entered his lungs and punched them wider in his chest, shocked the slow beat of his heart into something faster, stronger. He stood on a gray nightscape, drenched in star-light. A rolling plain dotted with drumlin-hills, rising up to vast mountains, and then the starfields blazing and wheeling above.

A woman stood beside him, nude and pale with a magnificent mane of black hair which fell down over the lush curves of her breasts. She turned to him and smiled, and he saw that her eyeteeth were fangs of bright silver.

"Fleam," he said.

"That is what you have called me." And she linked one arm in his, her satin-soft skin producing a jolt of fierce pleasure as it met his own.

"What is this place?"

"Give it a name. Any one you like."

Rol looked at the walls of mountains about the horizon, the rolling grassland monochrome under the stars.

"It looks like—like the Goliad."

"Then that is what it is."

His bare toes dug into the moist black earth beneath him. "This is no desert."

"This is the Old World, Orr-Diseyn. This is the shadow cast by the world men have made."

"The world men have made." He smiled, but there was no mirth in it. "Do men make things like this, outside of dreams?"

He began walking, mostly to feel the soft earth beneath his feet, the mud balling up between his toes. The woman he had called Fleam followed, her feet barely imprinting the ground. He felt heavy and leaden in comparison; but all the same, there was that exhilarating sense of well-being, of strength. It was as though something in the air and in the ground was nourishing him, making him grow like a light-starved plant brought into the sun. He marveled at it, and brought a hand up in front of his face to stare at his own palm as though he had never seen it before. It was his scarred palm, the mark set there by what might have been a god. More than ever, he felt that the wormed lines in its paleness were some form of ideograph, a message he must decipher; but that did not seem important now.

"This *is* a dream," he said. It made things more understandable to say it.

"No, no, this is all real," Fleam contradicted him. Her smile was both alluring and vicious. "It is time you stopped thinking like a mere man, a mortal thing, Orr-Diseyn."

"I am a man."

"You are nothing like. That carcass you haul around is a vessel, nothing more, as inessential as is a ship to its company."

"Men at sea are wont to drown without their ship."

"They do not feel pain when the ship's hull is pierced. If it sinks, they will swim. They have a life beyond its wooden walls. Do you understand me? The body you inhabit will be cast off someday. You must prepare for that day."

"I have no idea what you're talking about."

She stopped before him, caressed his face. "You will, in time." She pressed herself against him, and he moaned as her mouth reached up for his. He could feel the fangs against his lips, felt her tongue come questing into his mouth. It was cold and dry, like that of a reptile, but the rest of her was a glory of soft flesh and smooth skin. He dug his fingers into her buttocks and pulled her closer.

But then she wrenched herself out of his grasp as though she had been burned. She screamed, high and shrill.

"That's enough," a quiet voice said. "Leave him."

And Fleam was gone. Rol fell to his knees, light-headed. Strong hands took his arms and lifted him to his feet again.

When the dizziness had passed, he found himself looking down into the face of an old man, dark-eyed and bearded, with broad peasant shoulders.

"You should be more careful of the company you keep," the man said lightly.

The mud was cold now under Rol's feet, the air chill. He looked up and saw that clouds had come across the stars and were building steadily over the mountains. The old man touched him lightly on his shoulder. On his other side, a small hand slipped into his and gripped it tightly. It belonged to a boy, not ten years old. There were tears coursing down his face.

"Why is he crying?" Rol asked the old man.

"He knows what is coming."

Five

A MATTER OF SHIPS

THE SEA-BREEZE, THE RUSH OF THE PATIENT WAVES—
these things calmed his spirit now as always. He stood on the
lip of the sea-cliffs and watched the long swell of the waters
roll in from the east, like the heralds of a different tomorrow.
The sun rising fast behind them.

"Quite a little show you put on last night."

Rol did not turn round. "I thought Miriam had her lads
guarding you."

Canker joined him on the edge of the cliff. Two hundred
feet below them the Inner Reach beat upon the stone in a
long belt of foam. The climbing sun was bright, but there was
a coolness in the air, borne off the white heights of the
Myconians in the west.

"I was not once a Thief-King for nothing."

They stood side by side and watched the sea, almost com-
panionably. There were three fishing yawls out close to the
horizon, performing the dual functions of gathering in their
catch for the Ka and keeping a lookout for Bionari cruisers.

"There may indeed be a freedom in the sea—for such as you, that is. On a morning like this I can almost fathom it."

"It's clean," Rol said. "It has no memory."

Canker seemed about to speak, then held his tongue. He smiled instead, the first genuine smile Rol had seen him make.

"What does she want with me, Canker?"

The smile left his companion's face. "I can rely on your discretion?"

"About as much as I can rely on yours."

"Rumor will out in the end, I suppose. We're losing, Rol."

Cortishane stared at him. "The war?"

"What else? Phidon had fallen to the loyalists before I left Myconn, and Myconn was on the point of falling back into their hands. We rebels are being driven back into the mountains."

"You've been on the road three months, you say. This is old news."

"Yes. Many things, both good and bad, may have happened since. Rowen was trying to regain diplomatic contact with Perilar and Oronthir—last summer they were on the point of granting her official recognition as Bionar's Queen."

"And now?"

"Now they hold their hand, waiting to see how the tide will turn. They may even invade on their own account, seeing opportunity in Bionar's chaos."

"How did she do it, Canker? One woman alone—how did she start such a storm?"

"She is extraordinary, Rol. You of all people should know that."

Rol stepped back from the cliff-edge, glimpsing as he did an odd look in Canker's black eyes. "So what is her plan, and why is she so keen for me to figure in it, after all this time?"

They strolled away from the sea, to where Ganesh Ka's ruins were strewn in cyclopean walls and arches about the feet of the soaring towers. On the forested slopes above them, work-parties were trudging uphill to the logging camps in the depths of the trees. Charcoal was created there in vast earthen kilns, to provide smokeless heat for the inhabitants of the city below. Faint over the wind, there came the hollow clanking of goat-bells, a dog barking.

"Even before our recent reverses, she was thinking of you," Canker said at last. "I have watched over her these last several years, and have seen the strain that bends her."

"Ambition will do that."

"Indeed. It does strange things to people. And hers is the highest ambition of all. She can afford to trust no one, and this has made her task almost insupportable. Phidon did not fall through battle and siege, but through treachery. Bar Asfal is suborning our generals with bribes and titles and amnesties."

"Artimion has always thought you will win, in the end."

"Artimion has a mind as sharp as a pine-needle, but he is not on the spot—he has not seen what I have. We are losing; and if we lose, Rowen's life will be forfeit."

Rol smiled, but there was bitterness in his voice. "Queen or corpse, is that it?"

"You know her, Rol. She could do nothing else."

"Oh, I knew her, Canker. Once. What is she to me now?"

"Your sister. The woman you loved—the woman I see that you love still."

Rol's breath sucked in sharply. When he exhaled again the words rushed out with it. "It was—it is—a thing of sickness, this love. I'd be better off without it. My soul would be that much the cleaner."

"We cannot choose who or what we care for. Your feelings for your sister do not rank that high in the list of this world's perversions. Believe me, I know."

Rol collected himself. His voice hardened. "Those feelings

were not enough for her eight years ago. She holds me cheap if she thinks she can play upon them now."

Canker laid a hand on Rol's arm, halting him in his tracks. "She is tired, Rol, and she's surrounded by traitors and fools and greedy men. I would not have her end her days on an impaler's stake."

"So she has set her charms about you, too, eh, Canker?"

The Thief-King frowned, and looked away.

"If you want my help, you'll have to be a damn sight more honest than this. Maybe I do still love her, but what of it? I am not some starstruck boy anymore, ready to uproot my life for the snap of her fingers."

"If I thought you were, I would not be here," Canker said with some asperity. "Do you have no interest in the world beyond this half-baked little kingdom of yours? You have a ship, yes, but you could command whole fleets. What are you here but some floating brigand, living from one day's plunder to the next? The blood that is in you deserves better."

"The blood that is in me. I wonder, Canker, has Rowen told you the whole story of our shared parentage? We came out of the same womb, that's true; but Psellos told us before he died that we had different sires. Your mistress is indeed the Lost Heir of Bionar, but my father was not hers. He was someone else entirely. Did she tell you that?"

Canker blinked, taken aback.

"So don't prate to me of blood. My mother was a witch out of the Goliad, my father someone known only to the gods. I have no stake in the future of Bionar, and no wish to marshal fleets and fight for the destiny of nations. All I have ever really wanted, I have."

"All except Rowen," Canker said, collecting himself.

"A man must learn to live with his disappointments, or else he is not much of a man."

"And what manner of man are you anyway, Cortishane? Did you see the looks on the faces of your friends last night, when the other thing came blazing out of your eyes? They wonder now what kind of creature they are sharing their precious little pirate camp with. Your welcome here is wearing thin, I fear."

"No thinner than yours." But Canker's gibe had hit home. "You were not surprised by it, were you? Not completely."

"They have a library in Myconn, the greatest in the world, it's said. Rowen has had scholars working for us there, in the Turmian, ferreting out secrets and lore, anything that might aid our cause. They have dug up quite a few bones, my boy."

"Explain."

"No. Rowen will tell you herself."

Rol laughed. "Gods in heaven, is that the sweetest you can make your pill? Psellos did the same, as I recall, dangling knowledge before me like it was a carrot for an ass."

"Laugh if you will," Canker said, smiling himself now. "But would you not like to know what is happening to you? These rages, the transformations, the visions of another world beyond our own . . ."

Rol turned to seize him, but the Thief-King was out of his reach, darting away like a dragonfly. "Well, now, have I touched a nerve?"

"I'll kill you," Rol choked.

"Aha, the starstruck boy is back. Use your head, Cortishane. Do you think you can sit here forever and play at being a pirate, while the world burns down around you? People are looking for you; it just so happens I found you first. If you do not come with me by choice, sooner or later you will be forced to go somewhere against your will."

"Lies."

"No, simple truth. It is not just the Bionese who are looking for this Hidden City of yours—there are a hundred ships scouring the Reach alone. Stay here and you are doomed."

"And your old friend Artimion—have you told him this?"

"No. I care not a damn for Artimion, or any of these other vagabonds. The truth is, I was sent here for you, pure and plain. Whatever you say about your father, or lack of one, I know that you and Rowen are connected, and together you will decide the fate of this continent. Now put aside your distrust, your anger. Come with me to the Imperial City. Face Rowen again. She needs you. She loves you yet, Cortishane, I know it. I swear it."

If Canker was not being honest now, then his dissembling had been raised to the level of art. Rol found that he had no other words to say. He walked past the Thief-King blindly, his feet picking their way between the stones, guided by the comforting rush of the sea.

On first coming to Ganesh Ka, Rol had laid claim to a series of rooms high up in one of the city's weird towers, close to the tunnel that led down to the docks. It was a stark eyrie, hewn out of solid rock, but he had softened its austere lines somewhat with the pickings of piracy, gathered over the course of a dozen cruises. When ashore, he was singularly indifferent to his surroundings, but when he had had occasion to bring a girl or two up here, they had one and all complained about the bare stone, the wind that hissed through the window-slits. So he had furnished the place, after a fashion. It had chairs and a table, hewn out of wood so fresh the resin still oozed out of them. There were bright rugs on the floor, woven in Aringia or Tukelar and brought out of the holds of captured merchantmen. An ancient, exquisite bronze lamp in the shape of a dancing girl with an enigmatic smile, and a rope-bottomed bed to support his mattress.

Creed had lit the fire again. He lived next door, Gallico close by. The three of them ate together most evenings, much

as they did at sea, and when they were gathered about the
sticky table, the fire blazing and the girl of the lamp smiling
her thousand-year-old smile, it seemed to Rol that he had
found a home at last, and two men he would gladly have
claimed as his brothers. For that reason alone, Ganesh Ka was
worth fighting for.

"There's a nip in the air," Elias Creed said, entering without
ceremony and dumping an armful of wood on the floor.

"You soak up heat like a lizard, Elias," Rol told him. He was
sat in an elbow chair, scanning a list of provisions which the
city quartermasters had grudgingly deigned to part with.
Canker's words were still running through his head, as insistent and annoying as a half-remembered song.

"Aye, well, we're not all cold-blooded as frogs. Gallico got
himself a haunch of venison off one of the hillmen, and is
roasting it down in the square. Will you eat there, or have it
brought up?"

Rol raised his head and looked round at the room, tawny
with firelight. "I'm not hungry."

"I'll have him bring it up, then. Some of the good wine
too . . . How's your face?"

Rol touched his mouth. "Still bearing the mark of Gallico's
knuckles, I fear."

"You saw Canker this morning?"

"Yes. He does love to talk."

Creed hesitated. He seemed about to comment, then
shrugged. "Well, if you want to come down to the square
tonight, there's many would be glad to see your face, knuckle-
marks or no."

"You think so, Elias?"

"Aye. And most of them are prettier than me."

"I'll bear it in mind."

It was in many ways the heart of the Ka, the square—or so
they called it. It was a place to gather around the cooking fires

and talk over the day's labor with friends and acquaintances. It was never empty, often crowded, and the woodsmoke that hung under its cavernous roof was a permanent fixture. The smoke smarted the eyes and soaked into clothing, and everything they ate was tainted with it. Rol found a place at one of the fires, people making way for him, nodding, staring. The *Revenant*'s captain was seldom seen here, except when drunk and looking for some nocturnal companionship. But he was stone-sober now, and withdrawn, and was handed venison and a wooden mug of birch-beer without comment. He sat cross-legged on the stone floor to enjoy them.

Easy to lose oneself here, in the close-packed crowds about the fires. The gabble of a hundred conversations and arguments, the leaping shadows, the jostling bodies; they were a fine curtain of anonymity to sit behind. Rol wiped grease from his lips, wincing at the scab there, and listened to the people milling around him as they talked through the minutiae of their lives. A more tattered, patched, and filthy crowd it would be hard to imagine, but under the grime there were people of all stations in life, from scholars to cutthroats, and they rubbed along surprisingly well with one another. There was a little recreational thievery, but no violence. In many ways, women, in particular, were safer here than walking the streets of Urbonetto, or Myconn itself. Another of the Ka's peculiarities. Was it unique, or could it be duplicated elsewhere?

"I'll have a sup of that beer, Captain, if you're to do nothing but stare into it," a voice said beside him.

He looked up. "You're welcome to it, Esmer."

The woman took a seat beside him, close enough for her elbow to nudge his ribs. She was a pretty thing, past the first flush of youth, with black hair and eyes to match. As she took the beer from Rol her shawl slipped to reveal a Kassic slave-brand on her left shoulder. He had kissed that brand in the past, and supposed he might well do so again. Esmer and he understood each other, in many ways.

"A short cruise, but profitable, I hear," she said.

"We picked up a slaver."

"Yes." Her jawline tightened. "What of its crew?"

"Threw them overboard."

She leaned into him, a smile lighting her face. "So? Then you have made the world a little better."

"With what, murder?"

"Justice."

Rol nuzzled her hair. It was musky as a cat's fur, and full of woodsmoke. "It's a fine line between them, Esmer."

She cupped his face. "Lonely tonight, my captain?" And she looked up at him with the firelight burning in her black eyes. Rol leaned and kissed her on the lips.

"Always lonely, Esmer. You know me."

In the morning he pulled back the deerskins from the windows and let the sunlight slot through them in long bars of honeyed warmth. Esmer stretched in the bed, her white limbs stark against the furs. "Can't you keep the morning out for a while longer?"

Rol kissed her absently. "I have things to do, ships to attend to."

"You and your ships," Esmer drawled. "The only woman men like you ever take to wife is that bitch widowmaker Ussa."

Rol walked downhill, a corkscrew progress into bowels of stone, the searching rays of the sun cut off. The *Revenant* was in the dry-dock where he had first encountered her almost a year before, propped up by a maze of timber frames and baulks, her topmasts lying on the quay amid a welter of stores and cordage and all manner of naval supplies. A mere abandoned carcass she had been back then; now she was aswarm with life. Working on her were most of the artisans that the Ka possessed: shipwrights, blacksmiths, caulkers, riggers, sailmakers; they swarmed over the Black Ship's hull like maggots taking apart a corpse.

Elias Creed stood on the quay consulting lists of work-rotas and supplies, and having a shouted argument with Gallico, who was invisible somewhere under the bulk of the *Revenant*'s hull.

"How goes it, Elias?"

"More heat than light, but we're getting there. Kier has replaced half a dozen of her bottom timbers, and a couple of her transom planks which had been battered loose." Creed had something of a smirk on his face. "You slept late?"

"I had a busy night. How long before she's ready for sea?"

"Have you a piece of string?"

"Answer me, damn it."

Elias raised an eyebrow, looking closely at his captain. "Kier thinks another three days of fine work."

"What kind of fine work?"

"Well, he has yet to glaze the stern-windows, and there's the headrails to look at."

"That's just prettying nonsense. Tell him to make her ready for sea and forget the other bullshit. Now, what of the *Astraros*?"

"She's still none too sweet-smelling, but we've ripped out the slave-deck and repainted her below. You said you wanted her foremast converted to square-rigged—"

"Forget about that too. Get those nine-pounders into her and rustle me up a crew. I want her ready to sail within a week."

"What's the sudden hurry, Rol? We only just got in."

"We must put back out to sea, Elias, as soon as we can. Now, see to it. And tell Gallico he's going to be master of the *Astraros* whether he likes it or not. She needs an experienced skipper, not some half-baked merchant pilot. That's an order—these are all orders."

"Aye aye, sir," Creed said quietly.

Rol paused. "Humor me, Elias," he said. He touched his

second mate on the shoulder, frowning. His frown deepened as his eyes traveled over the beached carcass of his ship.

"What's that old man doing working on the *Revenant*?"

"Who? Oh, Aveh. He's one of the slaves we freed. Turns out he's a carpenter, and a damned good one. Kier wants to take him on as carpenter's mate."

"Very well. But he has a son, a half-witted boy. There's no place for the child on a warship—you make that plain to him." Creed said nothing, but his gaze shifted to the crowded wharves beyond the dry-dock. Following his eyes, Rol saw a pack of the Ka's youngsters engaged in horseplay, running along the waterfront and hooting with laughter. One of their number was being herded up and down with brisk welts of a switch; they had put a goat-collar about his neck, and its bell clanked hollowly as the boy scrambled and stumbled in a middle of a jeering crowd of his peers. The boy with the goat-collar was Aveh's son, the half-wit. He was crying and holding his hands over his ears.

"He'll not do so well, if he stays here alone," Creed said.

"That's his father's problem," Rol retorted.

They worked twenty-hour days on the two ships, at Rol's insistence, and Gallico canvassed up and down every passage and tower in Ganesh Ka for volunteers to crew the *Astraros*. These were young, for the most part, bored with fishing or logging or herding goats. Most had seen service of one kind or another at sea, but some were landsmen who merely seemed willing and able and quick-witted enough to make some use of themselves. When Gallico had gathered some sixty altogether he set them to work alongside the Revenants, cutting gunports in the sides of the *Astraros* and setting up the tackles and ring-bolts that would hold the nine-pound cannon in place.

Rol saw nothing more of Canker for several days; the Thief-King seemed to have disappeared. But Miriam managed to have a party of her musketeers loitering about the dry-docks most hours of the day and night, ostensibly to keep an eye on the mountains of marine stores that were building up there (the Ka had its fair share of larceny), but in reality, Rol thought, to keep an eye on the apparition she had seen a few nights before.

They refloated the *Revenant* six days after their return to the Ka. The Black Ship was towed to the outer wharves and there moored fore and aft while the heavy but mundane work of restowing her hold got under way. Alongside her, the *Astraros* floated as trim as a lady's maid. She had been scrubbed and re-painted several times over, and the vile usage she had suffered was now but a memory. If the *Revenant* was a battle-scarred old destrier, the xebec was a racehorse. She would not take much punishment, Rol thought, but on the other hand, she would outrun most of her punishers.

"Two more days," Gallico said as he stood at Rol's side on the wharf and surveyed the two vessels with an air of vast satisfaction. "I never would have thought it possible. Kier and his new mate—what's his name—they've done wonders."

"Aveh. You're short a chips, Gallico, so Aveh will move into the *Astraros.* Let him—let him take his son aboard with him."

"The half-wit?"

"It's not much of a mouth to feed."

"His father will be happier, I suppose. Very well. I had to cuff half a dozen of the local scallywags off him this morning anyway. Evil little bastards, children."

"Aren't we all?"

They stood and watched their crews at work about the two ships. One hundred and fifty-odd men and women; the Revenants a tightly knit band who were in many ways the elite of Ganesh Ka, and knew it. The Astraroes, still raw, but keen to prove themselves, and happy to have Gallico as their captain.

"My own command," Gallico said. "Well, she's a flyer, and good-looking to boot, but I'll miss that old black bitch of ours. I've put my blood into her."

"The command of one's own ship, the company that sails her. That is the finest thing in this life, Gallico. Wait until you've been at sea in her a month or two, and you'll wonder how you ever took someone else's orders."

"You may have a point there. I'm itching to see what this filly can do, I must admit."

"The guns will take the fine edge off her speed."

"Exactly. And those lateens will be hard to get used to."

"Alter the sail plan if you like. She's yours now, Gallico, to do with as you please. As soon as we put to sea we'll—"

"Cortishane."

Rol turned. It was Miriam, and four of her musketeers. Her face was set and pale. "You're to come with me, Cortishane. Artimion wants to talk to you."

"Artimion knows where he can find me."

"A private word, he wants, in his chambers. Now."

Rol looked at the men behind her. Their muskets were all at half-cock, in their hands, not slung on their backs as usual.

"Are you arresting me, Miriam?" he asked lightly.

"No, but I'm not taking no for an answer either. You'll come with us, one way or another."

Rol shrugged. "Very well. Gallico, carry on here, but do me a favor." He smiled. "If I'm not back by tonight, start looking."

The halftroll nodded.

Artimion kept to his rooms more and more these days. Pierced by a Bionese bullet some seven months before, his lungs now fell prey to a series of infections and fevers which flared up sporadically, and just as quickly passed again. One of these lung-fevers was running its course through him as Miriam and her unsmiling comrades escorted Rol into his presence. Artimion was propped up in bed, his black face running with sweat, the whites of his eyes shot through with blood. He coughed into a sodden rag and gestured for Rol to sit by the bed, then waved a hand at Miriam. Face twisted with concern, the red-haired woman left, and the two men were alone.

"They get worse," Artimion rasped. "Rol, pass me that water, will you?" There was a jug and cup by the bed. Artimion slurped greedily, then cleared his throat. It sounded as though he were breathing through slime.

"You need a physician," Rol told him. "A real one, not some highland quacksalver."

"It'll pass. It always does. I've been too long on land, is the problem."

Rol nodded. "The land is a dirty place. You'd breathe freer if you were at sea again."

Artimion shot him a strange look. "Tell me about your ships—how goes the work? Miriam tells me you have your men working like things possessed."

They talked of things naval, the hard-edged, precise nomenclature of all things pertaining to ships and the sea. The light came back into Artimion's bloodshot eyes, and he straightened in the bed as if even talk of ships was a tonic for his fevered frame.

"The crew of the *Astraros*—how raw are they?"

"Oh, they're seamen of sorts, in the main. Small-craft sailors, inshore fishermen. Perhaps a dozen have blue-water experience. Gallico will soon knock them into shape of some sort. It's gunnery experience they're really lacking; I doubt more than half a dozen of them have ever pointed anything bigger than a swivel."

"How are you for powder and shot, provisions?"

"We've dried out the *Revenant*'s powder that got wet in the last fight. Nine-pounders take a much smaller charge. Kier Eiserne has made a powder-magazine in the hold, though it's not tin-lined. Fighting one side, she could give forty broadsides."

"Good, good." Artimion's attention trailed away. Rol saw there was blood in the balled-up rag he held in one fist.

"Rol, we have rubbed along together well enough, these last months. At one time, I wanted you gone from the Ka as soon as you had something that could float. But you have stayed, and had you not, this city might well be a smoking ruin by now. For that I thank you."

Rol watched Artimion warily. "Think nothing of it."

"But my misgivings remain—they are stronger, in fact, than they ever were. What are you, Cortishane? I know the Blood is in you—it is in me also, else I'd be dead by now. But what is this thing you have shown us? Be honest with me now. *What are you?*" Artimion's face glistened with sweat. Rol could not meet the appeal of those thread-veined eyes.

"I don't know, Artimion, truly. I wish I did."

Artimion slumped back in the bed. His fist kneaded a goatskin bolster. "I have been talking to Canker."

"I'm sure he's been a veritable fount of knowledge."

"He is that. I'm not a fool, Rol; I know he has a mission, a play of his own to stage in which I have merely a bit part. He has been digging up legends in Bionar, looking for I'm not sure what. He wants you for this so-called sister of yours. He believes he knows more about you than you do yourself."

"That is the impression he likes to give."

"He was always a good liar, it's true. But I sense truth in there now. He's afraid."

"Of what?"

"He is afraid of you."

"Good. May that fear speed him on his way back over the mountains."

Artimion's sigh turned into a cough. When he got his breath back he expended it again in a vicious series of curses. Rol knew that behind his back the skin flap that covered the doorway had twitched, but he did not turn round. Once, he would have been able to tell who it was that eavesdropped there, but Psellos's training was being slowly forgotten. His hand strayed to Fleam's hilt, and he felt the warmth there, the minute tremors in the steel.

"I want you to go with Canker to meet this Rowen Bar Hethrun, this rebel Queen," Artimion rasped. "Go by sea; it's quicker. Find out what it is she wants, with you and with us."

"The fever has boiled your brain, Artimion," Rol said icily.

"Canker is not the only person who is afraid of you. Your secret is leaking out even as we speak, Cortishane. I'd heard rumors these six months, as had everyone, but they were dismissed as the tall tales of your mariners. Now they have been confirmed."

"Indeed. And who's been spreading that night's glad news?"

"Miriam." Artimion raised a hand as Rol made as if to leave. "Don't blame her. She doesn't hate you, but she loves this place, and—"

"She loves you, Artimion," Rol said. "She always has."

"Perhaps." Artimion's brows furrowed. "In any case, she has warned all her musketeers about you. Another little incident like the last, and they'll do their best to kill you."

"Still, it's a comfort to know she doesn't hate me." Rol knew now who was outside the door. "Canker, I think you can make an appearance."

The King of Thieves ducked under the flap. "Impatience made me fidget. I must be getting old."

"So you have suborned Artimion, have you? What addled moonshine did you dream up to convince him I must be your ferryman?"

"I told him that he has too many enemies already to go making more." Canker's face was grave.

Rol spoke to Artimion without taking his eyes off the Thief-King. "Have you ever thought that we might do well by ourselves in handing this fellow over to the Bionese? There are two horses in this race, after all."

"That has occurred to me," Artimion admitted. "But our choices are not all you might think, Cortishane. Bar Asfal will never stop hunting for this place no matter what we do, if only because Ganesh Ka was his brother's foundling. And if he hears the rebel pretender has a brother, he will never stop hunting you either."

"And besides," Canker added, "Rowen will win, in the end. Especially if that brother is by her side."

"I see your minds are in accord," Rol said. "Canker gets me, whatever good that does him, and Artimion sees the back of me. Everyone's a winner."

"Take the *Astraros*," Artimion said. "She's the fastest vessel we have. Go with Canker." He paused. "You must leave the *Revenant* here to defend the Ka."

"Leave the *Revenant*. I see. And who will captain her?" Rol asked.

"I will. As you said, I need sea air in my lungs again."

Rol laughed. "Give up my ship, for you to sail? Never." He stood up.

"The *Revenant* must stay here," Artimion said. "Call it a loan. You will see her again."

"I refuse. What now?"

"Miriam has forty of her musketeers waiting in the passageways outside," Artimion said wearily. "If you leave this room without Canker at your side, they have orders to shoot you on sight."

Rol blinked. "You're bluffing."

"I'm too tired to bluff, Cortishane. Grow wings and light fire in your eyes if you will, but at least one of them will find a way to put a bullet in you."

For a moment, Rol actually tried. He closed his eyes and attempted to summon up the rage, the desperation, whatever it was that brought out the other thing in him, that fire in his blood. But nothing happened. Fleam was cold and unresponsive in her scabbard, as inanimate as steel should be.

He opened his eyes again. Artimion and Canker were staring at him as mice might eye a snake.

Psellos was right, he thought. They are all cattle, in the end.

He would see Rowen again. That was something. She and Canker might even possess in truth some of the secrets they dangled in front of his nose like bait. But to leave his ship behind, in another's hands . . .

"All right," he said at last. "Let's lift the curtain on this little performance, and see where it takes us."

It had been no bluff. The musketeers were there, in white-faced ranks. He walked through them as though he were a condemned man, Canker beside him like the jailer, which in a way he was. Miriam's handsome face was blazing with tension and dislike. Rol smiled at her. "I'll see you again, Miriam." She did not reply, but all around, her musket-bearing minions looked down the barrels of their weapons and followed the track of Rol's heart.

On the wharves, word had gone round that something was afoot. A great, silent crowd stood there in the ship-cavern and watched as Rol was escorted to the quaysides.

"Quite a send-off," Canker murmured.

Gallico and Elias Creed and most of the Revenants were there also, standing in a compact body with cutlasses and ship's pistols in their fists. They made a wall which brought Miriam and her cohort to a halt.

"What's this, Miriam?" Gallico called. "I don't believe I've ever seen so many of your lads in one place at one time."

It was Canker who answered. "We're to board the *Astraros,* bound for Bionar. Rol has agreed to come with me for the war there."

"And the *Revenant*?" Creed asked. His voice echoed off the cavern walls along with a gathering murmur, the muttered whisperings of the attentive crowd.

"The *Revenant* stays here, to defend the Ka," Canker said calmly, though sweat had come out on his brow.

"Why will the captain not speak for himself?" a woman's voice called out. It was Esmer, her face white and hostile.

"Who commands the *Revenant,* then?" demanded a one-eyed mariner who had once worked on the ship.

The murmurings rose, like a sea-storm seen off on the horizon that might presently draw close. "Talk to them," Canker hissed in an undertone.

More shouts, the crowd growing restive. The Revenants and Miriam's musketeers faced one another with growing hostility, while about them the temper of the multitude gathered form like a cloud.

"Cortishane." It was Miriam, at his shoulder. "Cortishane, say something. Do you want to see what will happen next? There will be blood on the ground—and who will be the winner then? Don't do this, do not destroy this place to get your own way."

Rol stared at her. Miriam had been a household slave, freed by Artimion some eleven years before. Ganesh Ka and its lord were her life, as this place was life for many thousands of others. Rol had never before seen such desperation written across that proud face of hers. At the same time, he knew that there was a loaded musket pointed at the small of his back. He smiled at Miriam, and then raised his voice to shout across to his ship's company.

"Revenants! Stack arms, and finish this foolishness. For shame, Gallico—did you think I walked down here like some kind of hostage? Make the *Astraros* ready for sea. We set sail on the evening tide. The Revenants will stay here for the time being, and will try to help Artimion remember how to steer a ship. Do you hear me there? Make a lane for us and stop standing about like a bunch of moonstruck sheep. Gallico, Creed, set these men back to work."

And it was done.

Six

BOATS IN THE MIST

UNKNOWN FACES. SIXTY MEN WHO HAD NEVER SAILED together before, and a ship that still carried a reek of suffering about her, for all her sleek lines. The *Astraros* had been a quick, lively, responsive vessel, but that was before they had chopped eight gunports in her sides and set ten tons of iron and timber on her deck; it was as though a thoroughbred had been harnessed to a farm-wagon. For the first few days, Rol, Gallico, and Creed were on deck day and night, assessing her capabilities and becoming accustomed to her foibles. They had a fitful breeze from the southeast to contend with, some vagary of the Cavaillic Trades, and they pointed the xebec's stem north-nor'east to keep it on the starboard quarter, trying to come to terms with the fore-and-aft rig, which seemed so odd to them after the square-rigged yards of the *Revenant*. The *Astraros* was flush-decked, and it seemed wholly strange to Rol to look forward from his station by the ship's wheel and see the unbroken sweep of her extend forward to the bowsprit. More strange still to look up and see the great lateen yards with their triangular sails looming above.

"This gull-winged lark is all very well if we're close-hauled, but I'll be damned to it when sailing large," Gallico said discontentedly. "We have to square-rig her on the foremast."

"Agreed," Rol said. His eyes were smarting with tiredness, but in his mind the wheels still turned within wheels. The anger smoldered. "We have some spare spars in the hold that might suit if we reshape them. Get Kier on it."

"Kier stayed with the *Revenant*," Creed said quietly. "It's Aveh now, the old slave."

"Damn. I hope he's up to it."

"You were quick enough to foist him on me," Gallico said, and his big paw took Rol at the back of the neck and shook him in good-natured admonishment.

"Of course. But it's my own valuable carcass we're talking about now—and Canker's, of course. How is our supercargo? Still puking?"

"Like a drunken schoolboy. It would seem that Feathermen do not always sailors make."

"He must be hungry. We should perhaps send him down some salt-goat and weeviled biscuit."

"If we did, they would soon be sent back up again."

"All right. Get this Aveh at work on the new yards, main and top, and rouse out the larboard watch to help. Gallico, who in hell is that up on the mainmast?"

They looked up to see a slight figure clambering about the shrouds of the maintopgallantmast high above their heads, hooting and laughing to himself and waving down at them.

"That'll be the boy, the half-wit," Creed said. "He seems to like it up there."

"He'll like it less when he's broken his blasted neck. Send up a good topman, Elias, and get him down."

"He's agile enough," Creed protested. "He can run the rigging along with the best of them—first time I've seen him laugh since he arrived at the Ka."

"Well, well, all right. But keep an eye on him. We don't want the carpenter to see his son go over the side."

The xebec was turtle-decked, to let the seas run off her into the scuppers, and the sharp overhang of her bow and stern meant she cut through the waves, as opposed to shouldering her way over them as a round-bowed ship might. The deck was thus continually running with water, and so her builders had rigged gratings clear across her beam to help keep the crew a little drier. This construction also meant that she was not a ship in which one could ride out a severe storm; a following sea would find it easy to swamp her, and the great breakers of the Westerease would sweep clear across her bows. But with a moderate sea, and the wind forward of her quarter, she would be one of the fastest ships in the Reach, and it was the seas of the Reach for which she had been built. Rol admired her spirit, but he could not find a match in her for the bluff courage of the *Revenant*.

She worked her crew harder, for one thing, the long lateen yards heavy to lift and brace, the sails massive and unwieldy to one used to the sensible courses of a square-rigger. For another, she seemed cramped below, the master's cabin lacking the graceful dimensions of that in the *Revenant*. But it was, if nothing else, a further education in the ways of the sea and the crafting of ships to make her go where he wanted, and to work out which way she liked best to be driven.

"Wind's dropping. It'll have faded away to nothing by nightfall, you mark my words," Gallico said gloomily.

"Whistle up another one, then. Elias, take a reading, will you? And bring it down to me. I'm going below."

All ships stank, by their very nature. In severe weather, seamen would sometimes sneak down into the hold to relieve themselves rather than squat in the heads at the bow of the ship. And then there were the combined smells of tar and stagnant seawater, damp timber, and the mud on the cables that were stowed forward, slime from fifty different harbors. But belowdecks in the *Astraros* was different. Here, there had been a foulness beyond anything in Rol's seagoing experience, and though much reduced by constant scrubbing and painting, the dregs of it remained. Use made master, of course, and in a few more days they would no longer notice it, but for now it was one more mark against the xebec, filed away in some private corner of Rol's mind. He wondered that Aveh had been willing to work on this ship, which had housed him in such degradation.

Unbidden, there came into Rol's mind a picture of Artimion on the quarterdeck of the *Revenant*. It was akin to a man imagining his home inhabited by strangers.

The great cabin was a triangle with a flattened point, that being the stern. The stern-windows were mean and narrow, but there were also scuttles to larboard and starboard, and a skylight through which Rol could see the mizzen, and the backs of the quartermasters at the wheel. He bent over his chart-table with a pair of dividers and with them pricked away in a series of steps the distance from Ganesh Ka to Arbion, their destination. As he did, he felt the way come off the ship slightly, the water gurgling past her sides taking on a lower tone. He tossed the dividers onto the chart in disgust just as Elias Creed knocked and entered, cross-staff under one arm.

"Well?"

Elias consulted his figures and pointed to a spot on the chart midway between the coasts of Ganesh and Armidon.

"Could be worse."

"Could be. Pull up a chair, Elias. Gallico's prognosticating is on the button, as usual."

"Yes; it's dropping fast. Do you want to make more sail?"

"No. The men are tired, and I'm not in that much of a hurry. I want to have the new yards ready and swayed up before we make landfall."

"The carpenter is a good man. Doesn't say much, but knows his trade."

"Have you ever known a carpenter who didn't?"

Elias shrugged. In the graying light from the skylight Rol caught a different aspect of him. He was tired—they all were—but age had bitten more deeply into Creed's face than those of his shipmates. He could pass for forty, though he was not much older than Rol himself. More of his beard had silvered, and the lines fanning out from the corners of his eyes and nose looked deep enough to have been carved with a knife.

"You should eat more," Rol admonished him, "fill out a bit. I've seen portlier scarecrows."

"I'd rather drink something, Mother." Rol tossed him a bottle from a wall-locker, and he gulped from the neck of it with his eyes closed. He sighed without opening his eyes, and said, "We'd have fought for you, there on the wharves. Not to keep the ship, but for you."

"I know."

"Do you think, Rol, that you're going to your death?" Creed opened his eyes now. They were black as sea-scoured slate, and almost as hard.

"I think . . . I think I am doing something inevitable. Rowen and I were always going to meet again, one way or another. The gods have a way of arranging these things." He rubbed at the scar on his palm.

"I admit, after all I've heard, I'm rather looking forward to meeting this woman myself."

"No. I won't get you and Gallico embroiled in all this. Canker and I will leave the ship, and you will take her back to Ganesh Ka."

"As my captain, you can feel free to order me to do many

things. As your friend, I feel free to ignore certain of your orders, and that is one of them." Creed tossed back the bottle, and stood up. "You bloody fool—you think you can get rid of us that easily? Think again." He left the cabin. Rol stared blindly at the tabletop before him, the bottle forgotten in one hand.

"I'll take a slug of that." It was Canker, whey-faced and gaunt, but with some of his old smugness already wrapped about him like a cloak.

"I should charge admission," Rol told him. "Most people knock."

"The door was ajar. Give us a drink, will you, and stop being so high and mighty."

Once again the bottle changed hands. "I suppose you heard all that," Rol said.

"The dropping of eaves is part of my trade. That's a good man you have there. You're lucky in your friends, Cortishane." Canker wiped his mouth and peered down at the chart on the table. "Where are we?" When Rol pointed, he raised his meager eyebrows. "We're running out of map."

"I've not had much call to sail this far north."

"Aha. Why have we stopped? Is something wrong with the ship?"

"Alas, yes. She's running out of wind. Perhaps I should plant you on the quarterdeck to aid our progress."

"What a wit you are, to be sure. How long before we arrive in Arbion?"

"If we had a fair wind, we could run it off in a week."

"A week! Excellent. And to think of the time it took me toiling over the mountains. Now here's—"

"Sail ho!"

Rol cocked his head at the shout, then pelted out of the cabin and up the companionway without further ceremony. "Where away?"

The lookout at the masthead shouted down again. "Fine on the starboard bow, a ship, topsails up."

All about the deck, men paused in their work. The wind had fallen entirely, and now the *Astraros* was the epicenter of a glass-calm ocean. Off to port black-headed terns were diving, and the oily ripples they produced circled out for hundreds of yards.

"Break out that Mercanter flag," Rol told Gallico. "Make all sail, and then prepare to lower the boats." He ran up the mainmast shrouds as though they were a set of stairs and joined the lookout at the maintopgallant cross-trees, some ninety feet above the deck. "Point her out to me. What's your name?"

"Phelim, sir."

"Well caught, Phelim. Point her out to me."

"Which it was the boy as saw her first, sir. He deserves the credit." Rol saw to his surprise that Aveh's son was above them, clinging to the maintopgallant backstay like a monkey and chortling. When he caught Rol's astonished eye he slid down the cable out of sight, like a bead on a string.

Three masts, limp topsails just nicking the horizon. The vessel was perhaps five leagues away, it was hard to tell. There was a haze thickening about the brim of the sky, and the light was going. No top-lanterns, which meant she was not a merchantman. A man-of-war, then, and in these waters almost certainly Bionese.

In the *Revenant,* with the crew he had formed and had come to trust and esteem, Rol would have felt keen anticipation, a kind of joy at the sight. In this ship, with this crew, his only thought was how to avoid any encounter. As he hung there above the placid sea, he cursed Artimion and Miriam and Canker with all the venom in his heart.

All about him, the yards were filling with men as the ship's company unfurled every sail they had. The canvas fell dead from the spars, however, with not so much as a zephyr to stir the reef-points.

"Keep an eye on her for as long as you can, Phelim," Rol told the lookout.

"Aye, sir." That would not be long. The thickening haze had turned to mist, and even as he watched, Rol saw the distant ship's topsails disappear into it. He looked up, and saw that the first stars were already out. There would be something of a moon tonight, but the mist would hide it.

"Could be worse," he told Gallico and Creed back on deck. "We'll tow her northwest, try and get her into a wind. I want both cutters in the water. We'll change crews every four glasses."

The Astraroes were not veterans, but most of them knew the sea in some way or other, and all of them had passed time in small boats. The two cutters were hoisted over the side with a minimum of fuss, and both Creed and Gallico picked their crews in little more than a murmur. Rol saw Giffon standing by the ship's rail, hoping to get picked, and called him aft.

"No rowing for you, lad. We need those hands of yours to be as dainty as a milkmaid's."

"I'll do my share," Giffon said stubbornly. Rol laid a hand on his arm.

"It may be you'll be sewing up a few of us tonight, or in the morning, Giffon. That's your share, and we all value you for it. Any fool can pull on an oar."

The boy hung his head. "If you want to do me a service," Rol told him, "get up to the foretopmast, and bring down the carpenter's son in one piece, and deliver him to his father."

Giffon looked up, and smiled. "He seems happy there."

"And I'll be happy when he's down on deck. Be careful, Giffon." The boy nodded. How old was he—sixteen, seventeen? What turns had his life taken to give him those eyes? He had come aboard the *Astraros* without a word, lugging a goatskin bag almost as large as himself, and had set up a little sickbay in the forepeak without order or invitation. But it had warmed Rol's heart to see him, like having some of the *Revenant*'s luck on board.

The cutter-crews sculled their craft past the bows and took on cables from the fo'c'sle. The *Astraros* had a good bosun in Thef Gaudo, a small, seal-dark man from Corso, but there was no gunner on board, and some of the topmen had never handled anything bigger than a large fishing ketch. Still, the operation proceeded with not much more than the usual profanity. Everyone was talking in undertones now, and the men in the boats had muffled their oars with wads of sheepskin. The mist was thickening; it felt cold on Rol's face, like a wet linen handkerchief laid across his forehead. Already, the *Astraros*'s upper yards had disappeared into blank vapor, and her bowsprit was a mere shadowed guess from the quarterdeck. One of the men at the wheel, attentive to the thinning sand in the hourglass, stepped forward and struck four bells, the end of the first dogwatch; the sixth hour after noon to a landsman.

"Belay that," Rol told him. "Wrap up the clapper."

"Aye, sir."

The *Astraros* began to move as the men in the cutters took the strain. Luckily, she was a light ship with a narrow floor, easier to pull than the three-hundred-ton, bluff-bowed *Revenant*. Almost her only point of superiority over the Black Ship, Rol thought sourly. But it was good to hear the water whispering past her sides again. Nothing more unsettling than to be aboard a ship of sail in a flat calm. It felt almost like a form of death.

The bosun came aft. "What do you think, sir, three knots?"

"About that. Keep them quiet, Thef. Every sound will carry tonight, and we don't know if yonder bastard saw us before the mist came down. See that the crews switch every two hours."

Rol walked forward. Fifteen paces, and he was on the fo'c'sle, where Aveh was busy trimming down the new foreyards with a few hands to help with the rough work. His son sat cross-legged beside him, watching the white curls of wood come shaving off the new spar with avid fascination. It was indeed a soothing thing to watch. The carpenter worked with a deft economy that was a pleasure to see, and his hands ran up and down the timber as though feeling out the best places to lay the edge of a tool.

"Aveh," Rol said softly. "How long before we can start getting them up on the mast?"

The old man raised his head. "The mainyard will be ready by the middle watch. The topyard will take until the morning. It's more slender, so there's more to take off."

"You've worked on ships before. You're no landsman."

They had lit a candle-lantern so the carpenter could see where his hands were going. Its flame was tall and thin as a willow-leaf around which the mist drifted in gauzy tendrils. But the light did not reach Aveh's face. "I have been to sea before, yes."

Almost, Rol asked him where, but the question died in his throat. As quiet and equable as the carpenter seemed, he gave the air of a man not to be trifled with. Rol ruffled his son's curly hair instead, straightened, and went forward to the prow of the xebec, from where two cables stretched out into gray nothingness. He could hear the plash of oars out there, but nothing else. The mist pressed close now, and somewhere beyond it the sun had set behind the continent of Bion. The world had become a dark, shrouded place within which the only reality was the vessel under their feet.

Canker came forward, wrapped in a cloak that was already beaded with moisture. As he spoke, his breath clouded about his face to merge with the mist.

"Damn, it's getting cold again. I had forgotten."

"Winter draws upon us," Rol told him. "North of Omer's latitude, and you begin to feel it, especially at night."

"You should see the Myconians this time of year—I suppose you will. A kingdom of snow, glaciers longer than rivers. Black nights where the frost crackles in a man's very lungs."

They stood in silence. The Inner Reach hissed past the cut-water below them; and all around, the *Astraros* creaked with a million minute shiftings of wood on wood. In his mind, Rol pictured a line traveling up the chart in his cabin at three sea-miles in every hour, a worm inching its blind way past the coast of Bionar and passing from the blue waters of the Reach to the wider, colder waters of the Westerease Sea. Windhaw Island lay nor'-nor'west of them, and southwest of that, the great Free City of Urbonetto with its thousand-ship harbor and miles of warehouses and great sea-walls. But it seemed like it must all be a dream. There was nothing but the black water below them, this house of mist that loomed all around, Aveh's candle-lantern the sole point of brightness and warmth in all that sodden darkness.

The bosun joined them, wiping moisture out of his black eyebrows. "Ran sleeps," he said. "Ussa has taken him to her bed."

"You know these waters, Thef?" Rol asked.

"Corso's almost due north of here, less than two hundred leagues. I know the sea-lanes between it and Urbonetto like they was written on the back of my hand."

For a second, something flashed through Rol's mind, an insight. He stared at his own scarred palm with the strange lines tracing their way across it. But his train of thought was broken as the bosun said, "Time to change crews."

The cutters came alongside again, the exhausted rowers hauling themselves up the side of the xebec. Elias Creed handed Rol the hand-compass, a cold weight of brass. The ex-convict was shivering. "A cold seat at the tiller," he said to Rol. "Best take a boat-cloak."

"Gallico, you have the con," Rol said to the halftroll. "Thef, you steer the blue cutter and I'll take the red. Come, lads. No one goes below, but you can lie down on deck. Gallico, get the cook to rouse out a few bottles." The halftroll nodded. In the dim light he looked like a thing made of stone. Rol paused, and then said, "Break out boarding-weapons, but no pistols, mind. I want every man armed, and that includes the men in the boats."

To Rol's surprise, Canker followed him down into the cutter. He sat beside him in the stern, muffled to the eyes. There was the inevitable clunking and swearing and fumbling of men in a small boat at night. The cutter rowed six oars a side, and it took a while to sort them out.

"Pull," Rol said quietly. Stroke oar pushed the boat away from the side of the *Astraros,* and the others let fall and leaned back as one. The cutter surged forward, trailing the heavy cable behind it.

Three strokes of the oars, and the mist swallowed them. The cable lifted out of the water and the men's oars dug deeper, creaking at the padded tholepins. Rol leaned on the tiller, the course clear in his mind. He called the stroke for a time, until the men were in the rhythm of it, and then there was only the plash and groan of the oars, the panting of the scullers.

"How long can we keep this up?" Canker asked through a fold of his cloak.

"We hope to tow her into a wind; a calm like this is unusual this time of year. It won't be long."

There was an hourglass and a slot-lantern at Rol's feet. He set the compass between them and every so often lifted the metal slide in the lantern to check the time and their course. He might have the night-sight of a cat, but it heartened him, all the same, to let slip that little wand of yellow light. One glass slid by, then two. The mist was thickening, if anything, and it sat like a dream of salt on their lips, trickled down their chilled faces.

"What happens when we reach Arbion?" Rol asked in a low voice. Canker started as if he had been half asleep, though his eyes were bright and clear.

"That depends on where the front lines are. We should still hold the line of the Embrun River. If Myconn has fallen, then Rowen will withdraw across it toward the north. Gallitras should hold out. Its governor, Moerus, is a good soldier, a man of his word. In any case, when we leave the ship we'll set off south. It should be easy traveling; once you get down from the mountains, Bionar is a pleasant enough kind of country, well tilled and watered, good roads, inns. Civilization!" And Canker's eyes smiled above his mask of oilskin. There was a lie in the smile.

"You've grown used to the finer things in life since I first saw you in a derelict warehouse in Ascari," Rol said.

The Thief-King shrugged. "I always had the finer things in life; I just chose not to flaunt them. Snigger if you will, Rol, but it so happens that I am a man of some station in Bionar now, chamberlain and chancellor to Queen Rowen herself, no less."

"And how do the Bionari feel about an Islander thief lording it over them?"

"They have learned to like it." And Canker's voice was as cold as the mist and the night that pressed in around them.

Rol bent again and let slip that shard of light from the lantern at his feet. The hourglass was out. He turned it, and the sand within began its journey once more. He was about to speak but something out in the darkness, a rumble of sound, stopped him.

"Easy oars." The boat-crew lifted the blades out of the water and leaned on the looms, breathing heavily and staring at him, twelve white faces.

"Do you hear that?"

Canker cocked his head, pulling his cloak from his face. "It sounds like thunder."

Again it came, more sustained now. A rolling growl of deep noise passing over the sea from the east.

"Those are broadsides," Rol said. His heart seemed to fill his chest as it beat and beat. He twisted at the tiller and looked over his right shoulder. "Silence fore and aft." The crew's muttering ceased.

Again. It was like some bad-tempered god turning in his sleep. Rol wiped the mist from his eyes irritably, and caught a glimpse of something far out in the fog: a light, a diffuse glow. "Can you see that, Canker?"

"Yes, yes, I see it. Looks like a bonfire or something."

"It's a ship on fire."

The men in the boat watched, straining on the thwarts. The light flared up briefly, and seconds later there came the dull roar of an explosion, louder than anything that had gone before. The light sank in darkness, and silence fell about them again.

"What happened?" Canker asked.

"The powder-magazine must have blown." Rol snapped out of his reverie. "Come lads, get her going. Another glass and we change round."

The men dipped their blades, and began sculling again. About them, the black, mist-bound night kept its secrets.

Seven

THE NECESSITIES OF WAR

THE WIND RETURNED WITH THE DAWN, AS THOUGH IT had been frightened of the dark. It came from due east, and shredded the mist in a matter of minutes, but bore on its wings a squall of rain which drenched the *Astraros* and her crew, numbing them to the bone. Nevertheless, the exhausted ship's company were at once sent aloft to take in sail, and reefed the lateens on main and mizzen while Gallico took the wheel and pointed the beakhead northwest, to make the channel between Windhaw Island and Urbonetto.

Rol did not allow the crew to rest even then. They had a moment's respite to stand and chew cold chunks of salt-beef and biscuit, and then were set to changing the yards on the foremast. Aveh had worked all night, and now the two spars were resting across the beam of the xebec. A series of lines to the capstan lifted first the foreyard, and then the foretopyard up in the air, to be eased through the rigging as though they were made of eggshell and then laid close to the foremast. Lifts were then attached to the mid-point, the parrel fastened about the mast itself, and all that paraphernalia of cable, the stirrups, the lifts and braces, were rigged on one by one. When that was done, more sails had to be bundled aloft and bent on the new square-rigged yards—all this in a brisk easterly that was already churning the Westerease into a hillscape of white horses and a wicked fathom-high swell. Only when all this had been accomplished did Rol allow one of the two watches to go below; two dozen shattered men who would not even change out of their dripping clothes before climbing into their hammocks.

The starboard watch, resigned to another four hours of keeping the deck, found themselves nooks and corners out of the wind and huddled together, nodding and dozing and talking in a desultory fashion while Rol, Creed, and Gallico stayed by the wheel, studying the motion of the ship, feeling the lift and fall of her on the choppy swells, sensing the forces at work on her hull and through her masts.

"She will do very well," Gallico said with a smile. Under a scudding sky, with the spindrift flying aft and the *Astraros* heaving under them like a willing lover, the fog-bound apprehension of the night before seemed far in the past.

A hand in the fo'c'sle threw the log into the sea foaming past and let the line run off the spool in his other fist. His mate shouted, "Nip!" as the sand in his tiny hourglass ran out, and they hauled the line back in, counting the knots in the rope.

"Six knots one fathom sir!" they shouted aft.

Rol bent over the binnacle and wrote in the running log. "If this keeps up, we'll run under the southern edge of Windhaw Island in three days."

The wind held true; it would seem that Ran had left his bed and was running up and down the seas of the world again. They passed Windhaw in the forenoon watch, giving themselves a clear five leagues of sea-room, and the grim island remained a shape on the horizon, ragged and forbidding, half hidden by distant showers.

"They say that on Windhaw, Gibniu himself has a smithy, and that is why smoke issues from the mountains there," Elias Creed said.

"Four-thousand-foot cliffs all the way around, over fifty leagues of them," Gallico said. "No man has ever set foot on it; not even seabirds will nest there."

Rol was looking in the other direction, southeast, to where the coast of Bionar was a long shadow on the horizon. Fifteen leagues to Urbonetto, greatest city of the world, a place he had never seen. He frowned and turned away.

"We hold this course through tonight, then put her about at the start of the forenoon watch—if the wind holds. The Wintethur Peninsula lies ahead. I want some comfortable lee-way, especially with this easterly on our tail. Once we're past the peninsula, we'll head due south, keep it on the beam, and see how these lateens really earn their money."

The lookout was kept on his toes all day, for the *Astraros* was now in some of the busiest sea-lanes of the world. They passed by a Mercanter convoy of fifty sail, with three mercenary brigs of Maprian as escort. One of the brigs edged closer to inspect the xebec, and see if a little piracy might be in order; but she sheered off as soon as Rol had the nine-pounders run out. It was a bluff, of course, but it worked.

"Greedy bastards," Gallico said, not without a kind of approval. "They get paid a king's ransom to escort Mercanters up and down the Westerease, and still they're on the lookout for an easy prize."

"The Mercanters know about this?" Creed asked.

"Of course. But they turn a blind eye as long as their convoy makes it to port in one piece. Look at that for a sight to glad-den a privateer's heart. Fifty fat merchantmen with barely a long gun between them but for those brigs. Had we the *Revenant,* we'd be in there like a goddamn wolf among sheep."

They passed skeins of sail on every horizon, but saw no men-of-war. Arbion and Phidon had been Bionar's two great naval bases, but one was now held by the rebels and the other had only lately fallen back into Bar Asfal's hands. When Canker came back up on deck he studied the passing ships as intently as the Astraroes did.

"We must have burned thirty men-of-war alongside the docks when we took Arbion," he said. "Some of it was accidental, what with the quantities of pitch and tar and timber on the wharves, but some was deliberate. A damned waste. The loyalists sank two big ships in the harbor-entrance to try and block it off, but it wasn't enough. There's still a channel open, right in the middle."

"What about the wall-guns?" Gallico asked. "Are they still in place?"

"Some. Many were spiked, many more toppled into the sea as the enemy retreated to their own ships. The harbor walls of Arbion used to mount two hundred cannon, but I doubt there's a dozen left now fit to fire."

"Is Rowen trying to take over Bionar, or destroy it?" Rol asked with a sneer.

"A certain amount of destruction is inevitable in war. Things happen that one might not sanction or approve of, but they cannot be helped. That is the nature of war itself."

"You speak like a politician, Canker."

"I am a politician, Rol."

Flurries of sleet came flocking in from the northeast, off the Seven Isles. The ship's company dug out what warm gear they possessed, but there were not enough oilskins to go around, and they were swapped about between the watches. The easterly remained with them, veering or backing now and again, but always coming back to due east. They rounded the Wintethur Peninsula eleven days after leaving Ganesh Ka, and it was as if they entered a different world. There was snow in the air now, fat flakes which accumulated on the deck and froze to the rigging. The swell eased as the peninsula took the brunt of the wind and the *Astraros* took what was left of it on the larboard beam as she turned south toward the wide bay of Arbion itself. On either side of her, the coasts stretched away black with pine forests, but the snow was already piling up on them. The sky was as blank as a dead man's eyes.

That night they dropped anchor in fifty fathoms. They had been unable to take a reading all day, and Rol's charts of the approach to the city were inadequate. The wind was dropping, and the snow continued to fall in an eerie silence. They could see the mast-lanterns of merchantmen out to sea, but the bay itself was empty of ships. They gathered in the stern-cabin—Rol, Creed, Gallico, and Canker—and sipped rough ship's wine without taking their seats.

"We take the red cutter in, the four of us," Rol said. "I'm not chancing the ship, what with Canker's wrecks scuttled in the channel and the fact that none of us but Gaudo have ever piloted in these waters before. Thef can navigate well enough; he'll take the *Astraros* back out to sea and cruise this latitude for a few weeks in case"—here Rol's mouth smiled—"in case we decide that Bionar is not for us. We leave tonight, with the turn of the tide. Any questions?"

"How far from the harbor are we?" Canker asked.

"About three leagues. We'll step a mast in the cutter—it shouldn't take us more than a couple of hours to get ashore." Canker nodded. He seemed remote, as if the proximity of land was already throwing some other mantle across his personality.

"To Bionar," he said, raising his glass. The others drank, but did not echo his toast.

*   *   *

The snow feathered their faces invisibly in the darkness. The cutter bumped and dented the side of the xebec, a sullen weight with umbilicals of ice-stiff cable. Rol took his place at the tiller, wrapped in a threadbare sea-cloak but shuddering with cold nonetheless. Only Gallico seemed unaffected by the bitterness of the night. Thef Gaudo hung from the main-chains, his lower body soaked with the chop and slap of water between the two vessels.

"Three weeks, Rol. No farther west than the Swynderbys, no farther east than Windhaw."

"And keep her out of trouble, Thef. Remember she has fine legs, but no teeth worth speaking of."

"Aye, sir." Rol saw the bosun's own teeth flash white in the gloom. He was cock-a-hoop at the prospect of his own command.

"And after three weeks with no word, I take her home. Good luck, Rol, Gallico, Elias. Good-bye."

They cast off the bow and stern lines and Gallico shoved off from the side of the *Astraros.* The mast was already stepped, and their scrap of lugsail took what was left of the wind and pulled the cutter with it. Rol let the wind take her until the *Astraros* had become a darker shadow on the face of the iron-dark sea, then brought her round to larboard. There were no stars, but slack water had come and gone and now the tide was on the flood, carrying them in toward the land. It was hard to tell, but Rol thought they might be making a good five knots, borne on the back of that great mass of moving water.

"Looks like we'll not have to row, after all," he told Canker. The Thief-King did not answer, but stared intently southward to where the coastlines on either side of them came together. As they converged, there was a glow, a thickening of lights almost dead ahead, some miles off yet. Arbion.

The snow continued to fall soundlessly. Rol could feel it on his eyebrows. The interior of the cutter brightened as it began to lie on the thwarts, but it kept down the swell and spindrift so that they remained fairly dry.

There was an exclamation in the bow of the cutter. Elias Creed gave a shout of surprise.

"What is it?"

"We have a stowaway, hid under the tarp. For the love of the gods, boy, what in hell do you think you're doing?"

"I'm coming with you." The voice was Giffon's, and he sounded remarkably composed.

"Gallico, take the tiller." Rol clambered forward and leaned on Creed's shoulder. Giffon's moon-face looked up at him, stubborn and set. He had his bag with him, and it clinked as the boat pitched.

"Giffon—"

"You might need sewn back up, if you start fighting in Bionar's wars. And they say a battlefield is the best place for a surgeon to learn his trade too. I will go where I please. I choose to come with you."

"We may not choose to have you," Rol said quietly.

It was as though some light in the boy's face went out. He ducked his head. "That's for you to decide. Throw me overboard, if you like; I'll swim to shore."

"You'll freeze first," Creed said grimly. The frost had turned his beard entirely white; he looked like some hoary prophet. "We'll have to get him back to the ship."

"I won't go," Giffon said, entirely calm.

"Gallico?" Rol called aft.

"We'd be all night beating back up against this wind. We're stuck with the little bugger."

"All right." Rol was glad of the darkness; he hoped it would hide his grin from the boy. For some reason, Giffon's presence heartened him. Something indefinable and absurd to do with his luck, perhaps. "One of these days, you'll have to stop this stowing-away lark," he said, as sternly as he could.

"I'll be no burden. The day I am no longer of use is the day you can wave me good-bye."

"I'd sooner kick you in the arse, you little idiot," Creed said, but his tone was softer than his words. Rol went aft again and took a seat on the snow-covered thwart beside Canker. Gallico was as good a helmsman as himself, and could likewise see in the dark.

They sailed on. The lights of the city grew close, separating out into ten thousand separate shards of fire. Candles at windows, street-lanterns, braziers, watchfires, bonfires. So many nurtured points of flame, and a story behind every one. But between many of them were wide stretches of empty darkness which even Rol's eyes could not penetrate.

"We're in the channel," Gallico said.

Two great flammifers of iron blazed high on towers either side of the cutter, and out from them the immense hulk of the harbor wall extended into the night, a faint flash of surf all about its foot. The sense of open water about them faded, and the current picked up as the tide surged through the sea gates. The walls passed, shadowed and flamelit and tossing back the echoes of the water chopping in their lee. They slid past the masts of a great ship, poking black and forlorn above the sea. The wind had dropped, but the tide still had them on its back, and it brought them into the docks at a slow walking pace, a silent craft full of snow, five bundled shapes within, silent as stone.

Arbion's waterfront stretched almost two miles, a city within a city of wharves and jetties and warehouses. Even at this time of night it should have been crowded with vessels, busy with longshoremen and lighter-crews and dockworkers, but as they broke out the oars to scull the last few yards to the quays, there was barely a sound. A tang of burning hung in the air, and the charred hulks of ships lay beached like broken whales in the shallower water, a veritable graveyard.

The cutter's prow thumped the stone of the wharf and Giffon clambered up to take a round turn about a stone bollard. They moored their craft fore and aft and then left her in puffing procession, their breaths clouding about their faces as they climbed up a sea-slimed ladder. They had moored by a dock built for bigger ships, because it was one of the few that did not have a jagged wreck moldering beside it. Forsaken though the dockland seemed, they had been ashore only a few minutes when a bent old man accosted them and declared himself the harbormaster. Six copper minims, it seemed, was the going rate for a day's mooring in this desolation. They gave him silver, enough for many weeks, and Gallico at his most menacing impressed upon him how important it was to his welfare that the cutter rest unmolested. Canker stood by and said nothing, his face hidden in his cloak.

It was getting on for a year since Rol had set foot in any city except Ganesh Ka. To pay the harbormaster in money—real coins—seemed a novelty. In the Ka most things were exchanged through barter, or the understanding of simple fellowship. People in need were often given things freely by others, in the knowledge that this would, in the end, help everyone. It was a system Michal Psellos would have found amusing to the point of hilarity, depending as it did on some innate philanthropy. The rest of the world did not operate that way. The rest of the world believed only that men should better themselves by any means that came to hand.

None of them save Canker knew Arbion, and the Thief-King, eager to be off, walked away whilst Gallico was still handing over coin to the harbormaster. Thus it was that the four of them—Rol, Gallico, Creed, and Giffon—followed Canker's sprightly progress through the streets like so many children trailing after an impatient parent. There was no time to stop and stare, but for all that, the scenes about them made them stretch their eyes.

All of them had seen violence firsthand. It was one of the constants in their lives. They had suffered it; they had dealt it out. But none of them had seen true warfare, waged with all the energy that a state, an entire people could muster. They saw some of its fruits now, as Canker brought them away from the margins of the sea.

Gallico, the reader, the hoarder of facts, had told them while still on board the *Astraros* that Arbion housed some third of a million people. It was shaped like a horseshoe, with the open end resting on the sea, and its walls were forty feet high and almost as thick, bastions of stone over three leagues long. There were public baths, theaters, racecourses, and three tall citadels built over each of the city's gates. One watched the Phidon Road, one the Gallitras Road, and one the paved highway to Urbonetto.

But now, in the chill winter dark, Arbion stood in ruin around them. Outer walls of tall houses reared up like incomplete skeletons on all sides, within them mounds of rubble, blackened timbers, oddments of furnishings and possessions. The streets had been swept clear, but broken stone and brick was piled up on either hand to the height of Gallico's head. Whole districts had been flattened in this manner, as though the Creator Himself had sauntered past with the hem of His robe trailing an apocalyptic wake.

"How did this happen?" Rol asked, extending his arms to the wilderness of broken stone that surrounded them.

Canker's face was closed. "We lost a lot of people here," he said tersely. "Bar Asfal ordered that it be held to the end. We had to blast them from every house, street by street."

The shattered city was not deserted. On every corner were clots of ragamuffin children with filthy faces and predatory eyes. Gangs of men and women, muffled against the cold, pushed endless convoys of handcarts up and down. Some were laden with stiffened corpses, others with whatever they could pick out of the ruins. Here and there a body of soldiers marched past in column of fours with firearms slung from their shoulders and short-bladed swords slapping at their thighs. If they wore a uniform, it was hidden by an eclectic assortment of furs and scarves and woolen cloaks. Their eyes glittered under their hoods and they wrapped their hands under their armpits, boots slapping the cobbles. Tramping inland, uphill in the ruin-scored night, Rol felt that he had put behind him one part of his life and was being presented with another, one that opened out before him in the desolation of Arbion like some dark and noisome flower.

Eight

THE ROAD SOUTH

THE GALLITRAS CITADEL TOWERED OVER ARBION'S RUINS like a grave-marker; two hundred feet of quarried granite, its summit marked with a line of blazing cressets. In the dark, it looked relatively undamaged, but Rol's eyes could pick out the pockmarks of artillery fire, the broken merlons and gapes in the curtain-wall. Down in its guts two stout barbicans guarded the entrance and egress of all traffic. Even at this hour of the night, these torchlit tunnels were crammed with convoys of vehicles and footsloggers. Heavily laden ox-wagons trundled south, and in their midst plodded half-starved-looking men and women with handcarts and barrows. A sullen traffic, clotted with wailing children and traversed by lean dogs, noses to the ground. Off to one side a group of soldiers warmed their hands at a glowing brazier and watched the procession with expressions of profound boredom. Occasionally some of them would break off to cuff and curse the lines into less sluggish progress. The wagon-wheels thumped and cracked on the pitted surface of the cobbles, and gangs of sweating, pop-eyed men fought to keep the vehicles out of the deeper shell-holes.

"The Gallitras Road," Canker said. He still kept his cloak about his face like the villain in a stage-play, though his breath had frosted it white. "I must seek news of the war. Stay here."

"We'll tag along, if it's all the same to you," Rol said. He felt he was adrift here, and whatever arrangements Canker chose to make, he wanted to witness them firsthand.

The Thief-King shrugged, and the five of them picked their way through the dismal concourse on the roadway to the band of soldiers warming themselves. Gallico brought traffic to a standstill, and there were exclamations, pointing fingers, the nervous shrieks of women. He clenched and unclenched his great fists as he walked, ignoring them all.

The soldiers stared, and some fumbled for weapons that were buried under layers of warm clothing. Canker dropped his cloak from his face, and Rol saw their officer stiffen, like a beaten dog that glimpses the stick.

"You know me, Lieutenant?"

"Yes, lord. I saw you at the Embrun River. I was in Bayard's Regiment."

"Excellent. Does Governor Hass still maintain his quarters here?"

"Yes, my lord. The eighth level. I will see that—"

"I know where it is. Carry on, Lieutenant." Canker walked on, leaving the soldiers standing awkwardly at attention. Rol and his companions followed, somewhat bemused.

The people in the roadway drew back from them as though they carried a disease. At first Rol thought it was alarm at Gallico's towering bulk, but as he studied the gaunt, fearful faces, he realized that they were staring at Canker. He summoned up some dregs of his training and sorted out their whispers from the clatter within the barbicans, read the stiff lips as they mumbled a name.

Through a postern in the gate-tunnel, and then a series of cramped rooms that had Gallico crouching and swearing and scraping his knuckles on the floor. Startled soldiers who leaped to their feet and stood at a loss until the more knowledgeable among them nudged their fellows and they snapped to attention with crisp salutes. The dreary squalor of a military barracks where spit and polish had gone to the wall under pressure of war. The atmosphere reminded Rol of certain taverns in Ascari, where the cheapness of the liquor and the women were all that mattered, and the customers cared nothing for the filth in which they drank and fornicated. He felt a pang of dismay. So this was Rowen's great crusade.

A cramped circular staircase. Gallico's profanity became worn down through sheer repetitive weariness. It seemed a long time since any of them had had their fill of sleep. Shipboard muscles ached at the endless steps. They passed level after level of dank stone, their eyes smarting with the smoke from guttering torches and rushlights, the thin reek of overused privies, stale food, damp plaster. Once there was a sudden, startling panorama of the broken city below them, as they passed a yawning hole in the exterior wall.

And at last they stood in a spacious hallway with wide doors, archaic arrow-slits through which a fearsome wind whistled, and two sentries who bore arquebuses with smoking match on the wheels. These were leveled squarely at Gallico, who growled ominously, his usual good humor abandoned several stories below.

"Names and purpose," one said, whilst the other whispered through a square hole in the wall. Seconds later, the heavy door swung open and six more men joined them, likewise armed.

"I wish to speak with the governor," Canker said calmly.

"He's asleep. Who are you? Names and purpose, if you please."

The Thief-King fumbled under his cloak and produced a

heavy ring with a scarlet gem glinting upon it. The sentry leader studied it with something approaching horror dawning on his face. He lowered his weapon, and bowed. "My apologies, lord. You may enter, of course. But the governor is still in his bed."

"Wake him up," Canker snapped. "And bring us some wine, for pity's sake."

They resurrected a half-dead fire from its ashes and piled on faggots of wood until it blazed up in the stone hearth and softened the worst of the chill.

"The stone holds the cold," Elias Creed said. "Ye gods, but this is a miserable place."

The room was impressive nonetheless, if one were interested in architecture. A cantilevered ceiling of beautifully finished sandstone blocks. More arrow-slits, like wedges sculpted out of walls some three feet thick—though these were disfigured by the rags and furs that had been jammed into the slits themselves to keep out the wind. A checked floor of black and white marble slabs worn smooth by centuries of use, and the huge fireplace with a black iron spit on a pivot. They could have roasted a sheep upon it.

They settled for gathering about the fire, the only light in the room, and sipping at clay mugs of army wine. Mule's Blood, soldiers called it, but there was heat in the vinegary liquid.

A door swung open, and two comely young women in hastily belted robes brought in candles and wooden platters heaped with food. They left without a word.

"I've been in cheerier prisons," Gallico said. He stumped over to the massive oak table and sniffed the fare on offer. "Horse-meat, and two-day-old bread. I hope the rest of your war is a more organized affair, Canker."

The door opened once more and a limping man entered. He was tall, thin, and bald but for a few sprigs of gray about his ears. He had a wide forehead, strong jaw, and nostrils as flared as those of a winded horse, but age had softened all these features somewhat. Only his eyes were notable: pale gray gimlets deep-set under hoary brows. He wore a long black robe of dyed wool trimmed with leather and he had stuffed his untied laces into the tongue of his boots.

"My lord, you honor us," he said. He bowed, rather awkwardly, and his eyes passed over Canker's companions in some surmise, resting on Gallico a second longer.

"Take a seat, Hass, and spare me the pleasantries," Canker said. "I've been away, as I am sure you know, and I need to be brought up-to-date."

Hass lowered himself into a chair, one leg remaining stiff and straight as he did so. "I heard you'd left Myconn, but that was months ago."

"Fifteen weeks, give or take." Canker leaned forward in his chair. "What's been happening?"

"We're a long way from the front here, lord. Things have been exceedingly . . . fluid." Hass rubbed his poker-straight leg absently. "We do know that the loyalists have assaulted Myconn three times in the last six weeks."

"We still hold the capital!"

"Yes—for what it's worth. But enemy reinforcements are being shipped in from Phidon, and are attacking Gallitras. That city will soon be beleaguered, and if it is, the southern supply line, or what remains of it, will be cut. My lord, the Imperial City is now under siege, and the Queen has refused to leave it. She sent many regiments north to keep the Gallitras Road open—too many, some think. She and Gideon Mirkady have fewer than eight thousand men to defend the capital, and Bar Asfal himself has taken to the field there, to be in at the kill."

Canker straightened, and took a sip of his wine. His black eyes glinted. "What of Moerus? Is he just sitting on his hands?"

"He has over three hundred miles of supply line to keep open, as well as the defense of his own city. My lord, we simply do not have the men, not since the losses at the Embrun River last summer. I hope I do not speak out of turn when I say that the general consensus is that Myconn must be abandoned. The Queen must pull back to a more defensible line, or our front is liable to collapse."

"We lose Myconn, and we lose all pretense of legitimacy, and are back where we started three years ago," Canker said somberly. "The Queen knows this; it is why she is hanging on."

Hass raised his hands, veins blue at the back of them. "The city can be retaken at a more propitious time."

"There will be no more propitious times, Hass. We are near the end of our little venture. This next campaign must be decisive, one way or the other. You must raise more men."

"There are no more to be had, my lord. The barrel is scraped clean."

Oddly, Canker turned here to look Rol in the eye. "Perhaps. Perhaps not." He stood up, and stretched. "In any case, we will go south in the morning, but we'd appreciate some rest first."

"Of course. I shall see to it."

"Bring pallets. We'll sleep here, in the warmth. I've seen the guest chambers in this damn place."

"I was at your side when you took it," Hass said, smiling a little.

"Yes, you were. I can be plain with you, Hass, I know that. It is why I am here."

Hass nodded, but once more his gaze traveled over Canker's silent companions. The questions burned in his eyes.

There were still two or three hours until dawn. Weary to the depth of his bones, Rol was awake nonetheless. Canker joined him at the fire whilst Gallico, Creed, and Giffon lay on straw pallets three yards away. Gallico lay on his back, and his snores were loud enough to drown out cockcrow.

"Your war is running out of steam," Rol said quietly.

"On the contrary; our war is running full-tilt. I meant what I said to that old fool; I mean this campaign to be the end of it."

"One way or another."

"Bar Asfal has stuck his head back out of his hole; we've been waiting for that a long time. We will go to Gallitras, pick up troops, and relieve Myconn. Bar Asfal will die before its walls. One way or another."

"When did you become a general, Canker? What did she do to make that out of you?"

The Thief-King laughed. "We live in a wicked world, Rol. A thief may make a better general than you think."

"I still do not see what is my role in the midst of these heroics."

"Ask your sister, when you see her."

If anything, Arbion was even uglier in daylight: a sea of serried ruins, gray as a woodlouse's back and mirrored by a lowering winter sky which was already spitting sleet. With the morning, they could see that there was reconstruction work going on here and there, but it seemed pitifully inadequate compared to the scale of the destruction.

Hass had wanted to provide them with an escort for the road, but Canker demurred. He accepted horses and provisions instead, and spent half an hour closeted with the governor whilst Rol, Creed, and Giffon outfitted their mounts, and Gallico looked on, grinning. "How many of you old sea-salts have ever ridden one of these damned things anyway?"

Rol swung himself up into the saddle of a restive bay

gelding. It was eight years since he had ridden a horse, but he found that it came back to him easily enough. Creed and Giffon had never sat on a beast's back in their lives, and they regarded their steeds with a mixture of dismay and suspicion.

"Gallico," Creed said, staring at some undefined space between his horse's ears, "if this son of a bitch takes off on me, I want you to punch it in the head."

"Just yank on the rein; I've heard that's like backing topsails."

Canker joined them. He had found means to change into a leather cuirass and canvas breeches. A shabby-looking short sword hung at one hip, balanced by a long knife on the other. Over all he had thrown a heavy fur-lined cloak fastened with a brooch of niello-worked silver. He patted it in some complacency. "All happy? Then let's be off!"

Hidden by cloud, the sun did little but brighten several shades of gray in the sky above them. Canker pressed the pace to a swift trot, and it took a while for Creed and Giffon to learn to stand up in the long stirrups instead of bouncing like sacks in the saddle. Gallico jogged alongside them tirelessly, his keen eyes missing nothing. Travelers on the road stood aside and let the little cavalcade pass in rapt astonishment, and oxen rolled wild eyes while their drovers stared.

It was a wide, flat country of dark earth and green grass, with tall hedges whose bases had been thickened with laid courses of stone. Most of it seemed under pasture, though there was little livestock in the fields, and often they saw farmers plowing with their children and womenfolk serving as draft-animals. The people they passed were a good-looking, dark-haired folk, pale-faced and gray-eyed. Like Rowen, Rol realized with a start.

"So these are the Imperials," Giffon said. He had picked up the essentials of horse-riding more quickly than Elias and now had time to look about himself. His wide, pallid face was tired but happy. It was still an adventure to him. "They look ordinary enough to me."

"The eldest nation of men," Canker told him. "That's what they call themselves. That notion has set them at war with half the kingdoms on Umer at one time or another."

"And with us," Elias Creed added. "I hope we've been sending the right side to their graves of late. Bionari all look the same to me."

They halted at a fine, stone-built inn for lunch, and though the fare was frugal and the beer watered, they admired the place for the grave courtesy of its proprietors and the beauty of their daughters. Many of the local people came and went as they sat there nursing their aching thighs, and Rol noticed several of them making the sign to avert evil behind Gallico's back.

Saddling up again, they pushed hard all afternoon, while above them the clouds knuckled in slate thunderheads and snow began to fall, fine and thin and stinging in their faces as the wind picked up. They had covered perhaps six leagues since dawn.

"How long until Myconn?" Rol asked Canker.

"From Arbion, Royal messengers with fresh horses at the posting stops have been known to do it in four days. But that's a killing pace, even in time of peace. The road is not what it was, especially as one goes farther south. If we can make Gallitras in five days, I'll be pleased. Forminon, over the Embrun River, is as far again, and Myconn itself is thirty leagues beyond the river."

"Between two and three weeks, then."

"Depending on how many enemy armies there are in between," Canker said dryly.

"Tell me, Canker, how did you come to get here? Last time I saw you, you were on your way to reclaim Ascari." Rol was irritated with himself for asking; he felt like a callow youth begging stories off a veteran, but he had to know. It had been gnawing at him.

The Thief-King did not answer at once. He slowed their pace to a brisk walk, the horses' sides steaming, their breath a frosted cloud about their muzzles. The cobbles of the road had become flea-bitten with fine snow under them.

"I sought Rowen out," Canker said at last. "Ascari was lost to me, the Feathermen split, mercenaries brought in to restore order, the creatures on the Council dividing the city up like it was a cake. For almost two years I wandered the face of Umer like a vagabond. Going back to my roots, you might say. While you were sailing the seas, I was cutting throats in alleyways. Armidon, Cavaillon, Oronthir—I became useful to many powerful men, and moved on before they started to resent that usefulness.

"There are guilds of Feathermen all over the world, but one cannot simply walk in among them and demand a place by the fire. It was hard graft. I relearned many old skills. Finally, I heard of strange happenings in Bionar, talk of the Lost Heir, rumbles of strife about the throne. When I found out that this pretender was a woman, a famed beauty who was nonetheless an accomplished killer, I made my way to the Imperial cities, and looked up my old colleague."

He smiled. "Once more, I made myself of use. I became Rowen's knife in the dark—for as she grew in importance she could no longer undertake certain tasks herself. It took three years of intrigue and secret murder before she was ready to declare open war. And now we are in our third year of that war. We hold the east and south, Bar Asfal the north and west. We hold the mines, he the farms. Thus our troops are well armed, but hungry and dwindling in numbers, whilst he has the grain-fields and farmlands of Canossa and Palestrinon and Flamigrie with their big populations. His generals have been throwing lines of farm-boys into the mouths of our guns for over two years now, and the weapons we turn out from our manufactories have been cutting them down, campaign after campaign."

"Has every city you've taken gone the way of Arbion? Is that how you do it, Canker, blasting them all into submission?"

"Yes, Rol. That is how we do it. A necessity of war. When Bar Asfal fled the capital, he managed to take the Treasury with him. His money buys what his armies cannot take. Now that Phidon has gone over to him, we are pushed back to the east of the Embrun River, and hold the towns along it in force; any attempt at a large-scale crossing would likely result in a massacre. But Myconn is outside the loop of the river in the south, and is more vulnerable. Asfal knows this. Raiding parties cross the river regularly to try to disrupt our supply lines, but the main assault will come on the capital."

"Then why is Rowen sending troops away from it?"

Canker smiled. "Your sister is making a gamble, I think. For almost a year now, Bar Asfal has stayed largely out of sight, for fear of assassination. If he dies, it is all over—the war is won. Now as he gains in confidence he raises his head above the parapet again. Rowen has drawn him out."

Four days passed, and as the party traveled farther south, the weather grew colder and the aspect of the land changed around them. On their left the Eastern Myconians reared up white and forbidding. Fifteen thousand feet high, they ran down the entire seaboard of Southeast Bionar without a pass or a cleft. Deemed impassable until they reached the latitude of the Goliad, they were one of the reasons Urbonetto, on their far side, had been able to declare its independence from Bionar in centuries past, and they contributed to the mystery of Ganesh Ka's location.

The travelers passed endless convoys of army wagons drawn

by famished oxen and piled high with rations and ammunition. Broken versions of these vehicles littered the roadside, though they were little more than skeletons. Rol saw children with little hatchets chopping them up for firewood.

The country was as rich as before, at least to one used to the ocher, dust-blown fields of the south, but there were scars across it; burnt and blasted villages silent as cemeteries in the newly fallen snow. Roofless farmsteads, abandoned inns, and where several roads came together in one spot the party rode over strange undulations in the ground, hollows and bumps and holes.

"Shellfire," Canker said briefly. "We fought our way up this road on our advance to the capital, and the scars remain."

The land began to rise in a wide plateau winnowed by a bitter blast off the mountains. The snow thickened, powdered and blowing like smoke across the road, filling every crevice in their clothing, clogging the ears and eyes and nostrils of their patient horses. They pulled their cloaks over their heads, their feet numbing in the stirrups, and plodded on.

They rode on in the dark for as long as they could because the days were short, quick to finish and slow to begin. Sometimes nightfall would see them in the relative warmth of a roadside inn, and sometimes they would camp in a ruined house or under the bare limbs of a snow-bound wood. Winter became an adversary, an enemy to be held at bay by any shifts necessary.

"How can you campaign at this time of year?" Elias Creed asked Canker one evening as they huddled about an inadequate fire, their horses crowded around them, caked white with snow.

"It's miserable, I know," Canker said, and he grinned, black eyes glittering like those of a cocksure rodent. "It used to be that war stopped for harvest, and started again after the first spring sowing. One of the reasons we have made what progress we have in this struggle is the willingness to break those rules. Day and night now, winter and summer, the war goes on."

"Your fields are empty," Gallico rumbled. "It seems to me that your war is eating the people of this country as it goes. Without sowing and harvest, your armies will starve."

"Yes, they will," Canker admitted. "They have been starving this last year and more—but you would be surprised how little a man can subsist on. It cannot go on forever, of course, but there is a year or two left in them yet. Enough to see the thing to a close."

"I wonder they fight for you at all," Giffon told the Thief-King. His wide-boned face was drained of color, and his eyelashes were frozen white. He spoke through the jump and quiver of clattering teeth.

"The Bionari are a disciplined people; they do as their superiors say."

"More fool them," Creed muttered.

On the morning of the sixth day's travel they woke to a white, windless world. They threw off their blankets, and with them a good half foot of snow which had fallen in the night. The air was cold and still and clear, the sky as blue as a cornflower. Giffon's mount had died in the dark hours, and lay a white, contorted heap in the midst of its fellows. The boy knelt by the dead animal's head and wiped snow from the eyes, scowling. The others straightened like old men, shuddering and beating life into their limbs and staring about themselves at the changed world, a blank desert in which all features and landmarks had disappeared and all sounds had been tamped down.

Almost all. As they saw to the surviving horses, there came from the south a staccato rattle of crackling noise, punctuated by louder booms. It went on as they packed their gear and rubbed down their half-frozen animals and Giffon cut choice gobbets out of his own dead mount.

"Gallitras," Canker said. "The city is only a few miles away now; they must be fighting at the river. The Embrun curves east ahead of us in a great salient, and with this weather it sometimes freezes over."

Fireless and breakfastless, they mounted up, Gallico lifting Giffon onto his shoulders as easily as if the boy were a newborn. The road was still discernible between its low-hummocked hedges, and they plowed doggedly along it. In places the snow had drifted so that it was above the horses' knees, and there was a brittle surface crust which soon bloodied the poor beasts' legs.

They saw no human being that morning, though there were crows aplenty perched black in the trees by the side of the road. The ground continued to rise ahead of them in a low, blunt-shouldered ridge, and from the other side the sounds of battle came and went. For long periods there would be only a few isolated shots, and then a fusillade would rattle out, like a tremendous cart-wheel rolling across gravel.

When they finally crested the ridge around noon, they found themselves looking down into an immense, shallow valley. A sword-gray river curled out of the west and then ran north for many miles, before disappearing westward again. East of the river a city stood, neatly confined by walls. It covered perhaps eight or ten square miles, a darker blot on a searingly white world. Such was the flatness of the country below them that even from their relatively low eminence they could see for twenty leagues in the glass-clear air.

West of the city a smaller settlement, a large village or small town, stood astride the river, the two halves of it connected by a pair of bridges. Thick ribands of smoke rose from this place, straight as spears in the still air, and both Rol and Gallico could make out formations of men in the streets and marching across the snow-bound fields around it. More columns were forging along the road from the city itself, and farther off on the western bank of the river there was what seemed to be a vast, tented camp overhung by a haze of woodsmoke. Everywhere across the snow-covered countryside, knots of men were running to and fro, those west of the river carrying the saffron and black fighting flag of Bionar, those in the east carrying banners of deep scarlet.

"Gallitras," Canker said again. He pointed. "There at the river is the town of Ruthe, and the Ruthe bridges."

"We seem to have stumbled upon a battle," Gallico said.

"Bar Asfal's man in this region is Marshal Surion, a capable and intrepid commander. He's trying to take the crossing."

Now, faint over the still air, there came the hoarse, faraway roar of men in the extremity of close combat, a vast crowd of them. They teemed on both banks of the river and seemed irresistibly drawn by the lure of the two stone bridges. These were crammed with struggling mobs of tiny figures, overhung by smoke and battle-flags. Volley-fire ripped out in a crackling line from the riverbanks, and powder-smoke rose up like a fog to drift in limp skeins across the water.

"It must be very like hell down there," Giffon said, awestruck.

"There is no hell," Canker said briskly. "There is only the here and now. Gentlemen, let us go down. Time to join the war."

Nine

THE EMBRUN RIVER

THE SENSATIONS OF BATTLE OPENED UP AROUND THEM.
First came the smell: the drifting fetor of gun-smoke. It
seemed to have soaked into the very snow, catching at the back
of the throat and making the eyes smart and water as it con-
gealed closer to the river. Then the noise. Isolated shots
seemed sharper to the ear, and then they grew more frequent,
overlapping, rolling through the air until they were a continu-
ous tumult which hammered at the senses. And below that,
the terrible, full-throated roar of the men fighting on the
bridges, spiked now and again with high shrieks that carried
over all.

The horses bucked and fought their bits. Creed was thrown
just as the party entered the northernmost streets of Ruthe,
while Rol's and Canker's mounts danced under them, white-
eyed and blowing foam. They dismounted and hobbled the
terrified creatures in the ruins of a house, then continued on
foot. Squads of men in crudely made scarlet livery ran past

them toward the river and a steady stream of broken bodies was dragged or stretchered in the opposite direction. The streets were littered with shattered roof-tiles, clumps of burning thatch, and shoals of broken brick. Smoke hung low in motionless clouds, and soldiers ran in and out of it like actors on the stage.

Rol bent close to Canker's ear and shouted over the mad cacophony that now beat upon them, "What are you doing?"

"I must see the bridges, talk to these men's commander. This is no raid—it's a major assault."

Rol felt like bidding him good luck and turning around, but something kept him at Canker's side. Curiosity, perhaps, and the determination to appear as unmoved by this mayhem as Canker seemed to be. He had known warfare of a sort before, on the decks of ships, but the epic confusion, the scale of this thing confronting him, was something else entirely. How could any commander impose order on such chaos?

The town of Ruthe was a town no more; it was a mere husk of smashed stone and burning timber within which thousands of men were struggling to kill their fellows while remaining alive themselves. In the choked, smoke-filled streets it seemed impossible that Canker should be able to find his way, but the Thief-King led his doubtful companions unerringly toward the river, the epicenter of the storm that shook the air about them.

Here and there they passed decimated companies re-forming in the shelter of the ruins, their officers haranguing them in barely heard shrieks. In less choked stretches of roadway gunners were manhandling artillery pieces yard by fearsome yard toward the river. Ambulance-wagons heaped high with the maimed and the dying were drawn eastward by groups of exhausted men. Horses lay dead in harness, or kicked and whinnied in the slick ropes of their own entrails. Parts of bodies were plastered across walls or ground under the boots of advancing battalions. Blood, smoke, and stone stirred in a vast cauldron and put to the boil.

"The Embrun is up ahead," Canker shouted, clapping Rol on the shoulder. "Don't worry; this is not the first time this has happened. They'll never make it across the river."

A series of shells landed on the battered houses of the street, spraying masonry and clay tiles and knocking men down right and left. Those who could picked themselves up. Others lay motionless, faces set in dulled surprise, and yet more grasped at broken places in their bodies and screamed and screamed. Giffon knelt beside one of these unfortunates and began ripping up his own cloak to bind the man's wounds. Gallico lifted him by the scruff of the neck, as though he were a recalcitrant pup, and dragged him away. He and Giffon shouted at each other; though they were but ten feet away, Rol could not make out what they were saying.

They were only a cable or two from the bridges now. There was a broad street that still had the stumps of shell-blasted trees lining it. Once, it would have been a pleasant place to pass a shaded afternoon, but now it was narrowed by the collapsed frontages of the houses that lined it.

A tide of men came running down the choked roadway with wild eyes and blackened faces. "They've taken the south bridge!" one yelled. "They're across the river!" His words spurred on those around him. Hundreds of men were now streaming eastward in complete disorder, some throwing down their weapons as they ran.

"Help me!" Canker bellowed to his companions. He was halting individual men, punching them in the chest, shoving them backwards, haranguing them with a scarlet face. He whipped out his sword and beat them with the flat of it, set its keen point at their breasts when they tried to push him aside.

"What's this—are we provost marshals now?" Elias Creed

demanded, but he drew his cutlass all the same and set about
blocking the path of the fleeing soldiers at Canker's side. One
swung his gun-butt at him, but the ex-convict snapped his
head back and struck the man a wicked blow on the temple
with the guard of his sword.

Gallico stood like a rock in the middle of the street and
roared, the olive-green skin of his face deepening to the hue of
seaweed. The mob quailed from that sight. "Stand fast or I'll
break your fucking necks, you worms. Stand fast, I say!"

The rout's momentum was broken. Dozens of men stood
appalled as the halftroll raged at them. A few arquebuses were
raised; Rol slapped one down. Canker was moving through the
men now, speaking swiftly, clapping them on the bicep or on
the back, shaking them. Elias Creed held at least a dozen at bay
with the mere glint of his gray eyes and the bright point of his
cutlass. The men in the mob became soldiers again, and stood
there panting, willing to be told what to do.

They were very near the eastern bank. Up ahead, slender
twin spires marked the eastern foot of the bridge, and there
was movement there in the smoke, a banner sailing above it
like the head of a snake.

"Quickly now," Canker shouted. "Three ranks. All weapons
loaded. Those without firearms to the front rank. You there—
Sergeant—get those men in line."

The companies filed obediently across the street and presented a barrier of flesh and bone and iron. Rol found himself
in the front rank with his friends about him, the soldiers seem-
ing to draw strength from Gallico's fearsome bulk.

"Front rank, kneel," Canker called, waving his sword in the
rear. "Second rank, level your weapons."

A ragged line of red flashes in the smoke ahead, and split
seconds later the cracks of gunfire. Men toppled out of the
line, crumpling at the feet of their comrades.

"Steady!" Canker bawled.

Two bullets thudded into Gallico with the wet slap of metal meeting raw meat. The halftroll grunted and fell to one knee.

A harsh baying from the bridge, and then trooping out of the smoke came a company of soldiers in a livery of saffron stripes upon black-dyed linen. They checked for one second at the grim sight of Gallico trying to struggle to his feet, and then marched on, yelling, their leader a short, dark-haired man in half armor who waved a rapier.

"Second rank, fire!" Canker screamed.

Rol's right ear was scorched as the man behind him fired close to his head. A high hissing sound filled his skull. The street disappeared in the volley of fire and fume.

"Giffon, run," Rol said to the terrified boy at his side.

"No, I'll—"

"Get the fuck out of here, now!" He drew Fleam as Giffon took off and shared a look with Elias Creed. The dark man nodded and grasped Gallico's arm, helping him stand.

"I'm all right," the halftroll said, but he swayed, and out of his chest the blood bubbled in a pink foam.

More bullets cracking past their ears. The men about them were edging backwards, some firing, some reloading. They looked over their shoulders. Canker's three ordered lines were disintegrating again. The enemy appeared out of the reek, still in disciplined ranks. Canker tugged at Rol's sleeve.

"Come on. Time to go."

The enemy officer raised his sword and bellowed wordlessly; about him his men raised a dry cheer, and charged.

"Help Gallico, you bastard!" And without a coherent thought in his mind, Rol raised the scimitar two-handed and stormed full-tilt into the approaching horde.

Those before him gave way as will sheep before a wolf, flinching from the light in his eyes. But to right and left their comrades were thundering down the street to encircle him.

Somewhere in the rear, Gallico's deep voice was raised in a bellow of garbled fury.

Rol's world closed down to the few feet of space before him, the hedge of contorted faces, the sharp-edged weapons that were seeking out his flesh. Fleam was no longer made of metal; she was a feather of fine wire in his grasp. This kind of fighting she understood. The sword arced left, then came up in a sharp curve to carve a figure eight in the air, a blur of brightness no more. But men were cut cleanly in two by that swift hissing steel. They collapsed about Rol in steaming pieces, their warm blood spraying his face. He stepped forward until he was right in the middle of the enemy, and out of some forgotten recess in his brain Psellos's and Rowen's training emerged and took hold of his limbs. He moved as lightly as a dancer, aware of every face about him, each indrawn breath, sudden wideness of eye, tilting of balance. He ducked under a blade, jabbed out with Fleam's point to pierce a skull, caught a wrist and snapped it cleanly, swung his free elbow into a man's face to crush the nose, swept the scimitar at an exposed neck, taking off the head with its stunned eyes.

He was not as quick as he once might have been. Swords nicked him here and there, slashing his clothing, slicing the skin beneath. Blood was running down inside his shirt, but he knew that nothing consequential had yet bitten his flesh. There was no pain or fear, just the deadly joy of the blade in his hand, the all-consuming delineation of his foes' movements. It was at once a supreme discipline and an animal delight in his own strength, the frailty of his assailants, the slaughter he was inflicting.

He pushed forward, and the knots of men about him opened out, recoiling from this murderous engine in their midst. Confusion gave way to fear, and the killing became easier. Rol had shattered their lines, smashed the momentum of their advance. It was enough to bring their entire company to a halt. In the smoke and chaos, they no doubt thought that Canker's men had counterattacked.

The short, dark-haired officer met Rol blade to blade, eyes flashing above his sword. Fleam cut through the inferior steel, lopped the man's arm off at the shoulder. He went down with a shocked wail, and Rol's boot sent him flying backwards into his compatriots.

They broke. Tripping over one another, lashing out blindly, shouting, screaming; their circle opened, and all at once Rol was staring at their backs. Three- or fourscore men were running away from him in brazen panic. A thing not unlike laughter rose in his throat. He leaped forward in pursuit, cutting them down with slashes at the backs of their knees, their necks. He felled half a dozen more before the first bullet snapped past his ear. Fetching up short, he found himself almost at the lip of the bridge itself. Fifty feet wide, it was a massive construction of hewn and mortared stone, and there were hundreds of men upon it still, and more boiling on the western side of the river. Running soldiers were being halted and cajoled into some form of order, and a line of soldiers were leveling their firearms. Rol threw himself to the ground just as the volley cracked out. One ball struck Fleam square on the blade and almost spun her out of his grasp. Another splintered a stone cobble and sent fragments of stone tearing across his face. A third nicked his thigh, blasting away a divot of muscle.

He rolled in beaten gray snow, and as he did the killer elation evaporated. Pain racked his torso now; the snow where he lay was blushing with his blood. His mouth was dry and foul with smoke. He crawled crabwise into the lee of a tumbled house at the riverbank, hands shaking. His mind was fogging up like a steamed window. Fleam slipped out of his fingers; the bullet-strike had numbed them to the knuckles. He lay there blinking hard and trying to bring some order to his thoughts.

A rising clamor of gunfire and shouted commands outside. Fresh companies were arriving on the eastern bank and kneeling in ordered lines. Rol grasped the scimitar again in one nerveless fist and crawled deeper into the ruins like a hurt animal going to ground. The noise beat upon his head. He poked through the lacerated rags of his tunic and found a flap of his own flesh hanging free of his shoulder. Pressing his fingers to the hole, he felt them touch upon bone. He began to shudder, and clenched his teeth until blood started from the gums. Artillery had begun to boom outside, and the ground flinched under him every time a shell fell to earth. Cascades of dust and grit poured down on his head and stuck to the blood that plastered him.

Psellos would laugh if he could see him now. What had happened to all that training—Rowen's training? Rol closed his eyes and tried to recall her face, the heat of her as their bodies had fought and joined in the darkness under Psellos's Tower. He remembered the glorious softness of her breasts, incongruous in all that tautness of muscle. The memory calmed him somehow. Recalling her face, her quiet, priceless smile, he knew that he loved her still. He would love her until the last beat of his heart. It was why he was here, in the eye of this madness—to perhaps glimpse that smile once more. He would do anything to be with her again, anything.

At last he mustered the strength to rise to a crouch. His feet squelched in the gore that had filled his boots. Gummed-up nicks and cuts reopened all over him as he moved, staggering with the pain in his injured thigh. Several of the houses here had been blasted into one long series of mangled ruins, cast in gloom by what was left of their roofs. He tottered through them, his mind slowly clearing.

Gallico. Creed. The thought of them sped his feet, and he bared his teeth as the pain came and went in sickening waves. Fleam steadied in his hand, and insane though it might seem, he thought he sensed a kind of amusement thrumming out of the sword, a smugness. He stuffed the bloody scimitar back into her scabbard, not caring that she was caked with hair and viscera and shreds of men's innards. He staggered on, keeping to the maze within the ruins, glimpsing scraps of the battle here and there through holed walls and empty windows. He did not care who was winning; all he wanted was to find his friends alive.

Creed saw him first. The ex-convict was quartering the ruins with a cutlass in one hand and a cocked pistol in the other. When he saw a tall figure dressed in brown and scarlet shreds who was weaving amid the rubble like a man drunk, he ran up to his captain with furious concern burning out of his eyes, and steadied him as the taller man's body tilted toward a fall.

"Elias." Rol smiled. "Still alive?"

"Still alive."

The smile disappeared. "Gallico?"

"We got him to a dressing station in the rear, with Giffon. It'll take more than a couple of musket-balls to shut his big mouth."

"Thank God."

"Let's get you back there to join him." Creed took Rol's arm and pulled it over his shoulders. The two limped along, oblivious to the musketry and gunnery that flashed and foamed behind them.

"Canker is wild with worry," Creed said.

"Is he indeed? Well, I'll be damned."

"His people retook the bridge. Your one-man assault on the entire Bionese army paid off, it seems."

"They're all Bionese, Elias. Those we've been fighting, those whose side we're supposed to be on. All the same."

"Yes, I know. A man could grow confused. He might

wonder what in the hell we're doing here in the middle of someone else's war."

"The thought had crossed my mind."

A line of cottages near the eastern edge of the town had been knocked through into one long corridorlike space. There was a charnel-house within. Several hundred men lay on rough straw palliasses or on bare earth whilst half a dozen physicians and surgeons, almost demented with the scale of their task, went from man to man, assisted by some of the local women who had volunteered to stay behind. They sewed up gaping wounds, extracted arquebus-balls with fine-nosed forceps, applied tourniquets, and where the bone had been splintered, they amputated upon a series of red-slimed tables, the patients held immobile by their friends and biting down upon wooden gags until the teeth cracked in their heads.

Giffon was there in the midst of the bloody work, arms scarlet to the elbows. Gallico sat propped up in a corner with bandages crisscrossing his chest to keep blood-soaked pads of linen in place. Rol collapsed beside him. The halftroll smiled and laid a hand upon Rol's head like a father. "There he is; the hero of the hour, or most of him. There is more blood on you than in you, Rol."

"I can believe that." Creed left and brought back Giffon and one of the harried nurses, a young girl with brown hair scraped back in a bun and eyes as old as a matron's. They cut off what was left of Rol's clothing and began to mop and stitch. Rol felt the needle popping in and out of his skin, but the pain was little more than an irritation. He stared out at the writhing carpet of broken humanity that covered the ground before him.

"It would seem we joined Canker's war," Gallico said.

"Where is he?"

"Looking for transport, I think. He took off like a scalded cat when those fellows crossed the bridge, but, to give him

credit, he came back shortly after with a whole bloody battalion at his back. Good for us he did. Creed and I were getting
tired. He's looking for you too. Worried your appetite for glory
may have been your undoing."

"It damn near was."

Rol tried to raise his hand to see if it still shook, but Giffon
slapped it down. "Be still. It's like trying to sew the tail back on
a pig." The boy's tone was bantering, but there was a hurt shine
to his eyes.

"I'm sorry, Giffon."

"Nothing to be sorry for, skipper. Hold still now."

Rol turned to Creed. "Elias, I need fresh clothing. The
horses?"

"All dead, blown to bits. I'll see what I can pick up. There
must be a few long-limbed corpses lying around." He winked
at Rol and left, picking his way through the bodies.

The fighting sank down as the day drew on into an early-
winter dusk, and a thin veil of snow began floating down upon
the tortured earth of the battlefield. The bridges remained in
rebel hands, the loyalists withdrew to their camps west of the
river, and the wounded were hauled off to hospitals in
Gallitras in open wagons whose every jolt produced a litany of
screams from the unfortunates within. Rol and Gallico were
luckier; Canker procured a covered carriage for them and an
escort of dragoons. Their well-sprung vehicle covered the
league or so to Gallitras in less than an hour, taking to the
frozen earth off the road when the highway itself was too
choked with military traffic to proceed.

It was dark as they clopped in through the massive barbican
of the city and made a slow progress through the dense-packed
cobbled streets within. There was destruction here, but nothing on the scale to match Arbion. Rol, Creed, and Giffon hung

their heads out of the carriage window and studied the passing city like gawping tourists. Gallico was perched on the roof like some monstrous figurehead. The sight was enough to halt pedestrians in their tracks.

"How come you didn't have to blast this one stone from stone?" Creed asked Canker, who had reverted to his face-in-cloak mode.

The Thief-King shrugged. "Gallitras fell to a subtler assault. Her governor was assassinated by persons unknown and his replacement proved a venal man."

"A pity more of these fellows were not so amenable," Gallico snorted above them. "You might have a kingdom left with one stone upon another."

Canker did not reply. His eyes glittered. He was watching Rol.

Their carriage pulled up in front of a grand, colonnaded mansion with large windows that had light streaming out of them. Footmen opened the carriage doors, but stepped back as Gallico leaped down from the roof, letting the vehicle bounce up on its springs as his weight left it. He staggered as he hit the ground and stood for a moment with head bowed, eyes tight shut in pain.

The five of them were met in the grand hallway by the sound of music—strings and pipes bubbling in sedate merriment. Candles burned by the score all about them and in a massive chandelier above their heads. A knot of darkly garbed men stood waiting. Canker dropped his cloak from his face and his entire manner changed. He became brisk, commanding. He shook someone's hand.

"We need beds, maids, clothing, food, and wine. It is late, and my fellow travelers are wounded and exhausted. We will talk tomorrow."

"My lord Chancellor," someone said, and everyone bowed low. Canker caught Rol's eye and he gave a rueful grin that had yet something defiant about it, as though daring him to be amused.

"But first, Governor Moerus, let me introduce to you the Queen's brother, Rol Cortishane." There were audible gasps, widened eyes. Standing there with the blood still seeping from his hastily stitched wounds, Rol shot the Thief-King an irritated glare, but said nothing. It was all he could do to keep his feet.

Moerus bowed. "We had heard rumors, of course, but it seemed too much to hope that it should be true. You are very welcome, my lord."

He was a spare, well-knit man of medium height in a wine-colored coat. A narrow face, and an eagle nose that lent it both ugliness and distinction. His eyes were brown as the neck of a thrush. They took in Rol, Gallico, Creed, and Giffon in one swift sweep, giving away nothing except concern and dutiful interest, but one of his hands was working as though it played an invisible pipe.

A period of talk and bustle, and then stairs that seemed to go on forever. A winsome young housemaid propped up Rol's elbow. She smelled so clean and felt so good that he leaned more weight on her than he had need to, and hazily wondered how long it had been since he had dirtied up a sweet-smelling young woman.

Clean sheets, a wide bed like an expanse of pale desert. The maid stripped him naked and he was too tired to care. He lay back in the bed and stared at a fire burning in the brick and marble hearth close by, and staring into the heart of those flames, he drifted down deep, deep into darkness.

In the dream, or what passed for a dream, his wounds were healed but their scars remained. He stood as he had before, and stared out across a moonlit expanse of silver-gray hills to the savage heights of the Myconian Mountains in the distance. They seemed to ring every horizon, and nowhere could he find any glimpse of the sea, or any smell of salt. He was lost, buried in a ring of snow-girt stone.

Fleam stood beside him again, but something about her had changed. She was still a statuesque beauty, white-skinned and black-haired, but now she wore the loose ocher robes of a desert traveler, the keffiyeh thrown back on her shoulders. She looked older; there were lines at the corners of her eyes and a hint of dark hollows under them. Her resemblance to Rowen was startling. She did not turn when Rol spoke her name, but studied the mountains in the distance as though some secret was hidden in the shape of the peaks.

"Cross these eastward, and in time you will come to the edge of the Inner Reach," Fleam said. "On the shores of that ancient sea is a ruined city whose true name has been forgotten. It was a place of refuge once. It is where I was made, forged in blood and iron and rage by one whom I had betrayed." She smiled, and there was a humanity in her eyes that Rol had not seen before. She seemed to realize this; the smile curdled.

"In the beginning, I had no name. I was a shape, a snarling shadow of the Old World that slipped into this existence. An old man who was not a man, not anything like a man, gave me this form, and in it I walked the earth. I became a woman who loved, and lost, who betrayed and was betrayed in her turn. Little of that woman remains; the shadow swamps what soul he gave me. What is left is a mere ghost in the blade, and the other thing feeds upon the blood the metal spills."

Now Fleam turned her head and looked Rol in the face. Her eyes were the color of burnished steel. "The woman died, murdered. The sword is all that remains—and the ghost within the blade. I am but an echo of who she once was." A change came over Fleam's face. The lines smoothed out.

"My name was Amerie."

Ten

GHOSTS OF MEMORY

ROL WOKE THIRSTY. THERE WAS A PITCHER BY THE BED, and he pulled it to his mouth, gulping back cold water until it spilled down his neck and chest and soaked the bedclothes. He swung his legs onto the floor and stood up. The fire was dead, and there was a gray light in the room; it was still some time before dawn, but dawn came late these days. The air in the place was chill enough to beget a white cloud out of his breath, raise goose pimples on his skin. He scratched at the wound on his shoulder; it itched damnably. Then it struck him. He peeled off Giffon's neatly bound dressings and as he did they came away crusted with dried blood, and stuck in it a tangle of short black threads. His stitches, he realized; they had all come out.

His wounds were closed, pink with new flesh. He was as hale and healed as if he had slept a month away in the night.

He stretched and flexed his limbs experimentally, fear fighting wonder in his mind. A round roseate dimple was all that remained of the bullet-wound in his thigh. The more minor wounds had entirely disappeared, as if they had been inflicted in a dream.

Is this it now? he wondered. Is this how it will be from now on?

The sight of his new scars frightened him. He realized that there was some process at work within him that he had no control over, no inkling of rhyme or reason.

"I am not human," he said aloud to the empty room. He had known that; what he had not suspected was that he would grow even less human as he grew older. When would it stop, and what would he become?

There was another stone in his mind's shoe: a memory of visions in the night. If they were dreams, he had not remembered them, but retained the aftertaste. He began to shiver, the stone floor numbing the soles of his feet. Human enough for that, at any rate. Looking about him, he saw that fresh clothes had been laid out for him on a chair. A linen shirt, leather jerkin and bronze-buckled belt, woolen breeches and hose, and well-made half boots. On top of them lay Fleam in her scabbard. He picked up the scimitar; the leather of her sheath had been sliced open halfway down its length so that the pale shine of the blade peeped through. He drew it forth and studied the edge closely. Not a nick or scratch to be seen. Fleam never needed sharpening, never tarnished, and the gore that had clotted her had disappeared, though her scabbard was still stained with it. Rol kissed the blade, and it was warm under his lips. He had the strangest urge to run the edge of the scimitar across his face, and imagined that marvelous steel sinking into his own flesh with an inexplicable thrill of pleasure.

He set the sword down again, and had to stand still a moment to clear his mind. He dressed himself—everything fitted perfectly—and strode to a curtained alcove. When he drew back the drapes he found that they concealed a pair of windowed doors,

which in turn led out onto a balcony—the tiny draft had beckoned him. He opened the doors and stood looking out on a sea
of snow-covered roofs that was the city of Gallitras. He was high
up here; not only several stories off the ground, but on a low hill
that nonetheless afforded a fine view of the vast river-valley beyond the city walls. Always, the nobility built their homes on the
higher ground—it was a basic of human nature that the rulers
must look down on those they rule.

He was looking west, toward the still-smoking ruins of
Ruthe and its bridges. The Embrun River itself was a dark rib-
bon across the land, cutting through the matt paleness of the
snow-plain; beyond it, the fires of the loyalist encampment
were beginning to light in their hundreds in a drear country
that the slow-rising winter sun had not yet touched. On the
Inner Reach that sun would already be kindling to jewels the
broken facets of the waves, but the tall bulk of the Myconians
still hedged the kingdom of Bionar in shadow.

"Winter lies long here, and the sun begrudges the journey
over the mountains."

Rol spun on his heel, his hand automatically slapping the
hip where Fleam should have been, but she was still on the
chair by the bed. The speaker was an old, withered man in a
shapeless robe that must once have been fine, judging by the
heavy embroidery, but which was now grimy and faded. The
man had an inquisitive, triangular visage with prominent front
teeth and bright black eyes. He looked like Canker's grandfather. He leaned on a knobbed blackthorn stick, and age had
brought the joints of his fingers out in bony lumps. "So you are
Rowen's long-lost brother, eh?"

"You're quiet on your feet," Rol said. He went back to the
side of the bed and buckled Fleam's scabbard to his belt.

By way of reply the old man lifted his stick and pulled back
another set of drapes behind him. A black archway loomed

beyond, and dank air eddied out of it. "Set there so that the household slaves would not wake up the occupant in their nightly comings and goings. You slept like one of the dead, my friend."

"Who are you?"

"A friend of Canker's. A scholar. My name is Phrynius. I see you have no more need of your dressings."

"It would seem so."

"Fascinating. Come with me, my young friend. My rooms are not far from here, and I have warmed wine and fresh bread for to break your fast." The old man's face was bright and friendly. He stooped over his stick, but had he straightened he would have been as tall as Rol.

"I'd sooner look in on my friends first."

"They're mere yards away, and all sleeping like babes, despite the halftroll's snores. Come, now. The house is still abed; we're the only folk awake. The best time to talk with discretion."

"What's to talk about, old man?"

"Michal Psellos, for one thing."

There was a fire burning, which was something. Rol stood before it warming himself, wondering if his time in the south had rendered him more susceptible to northern winters. The backs of his hands were faintly blue, as if his blood were cramped out at the wrists. Phrynius had a little spirit-stove on which he heated a copper pan of wine and added cloves, cinnamon, and other spices Rol did not recognize. The heady scent of them filled the cramped room, along with that of newly baked bread.

"There is a bakery in the basement," Phrynius explained. "There's not much in the way of flour to be had these days, though; we eke it out with ground chickpeas, and it answers well enough, if you have a pat of butter to melt on it." He stirred the wine.

"You like books," Rol said, scanning the room. Every wall was lined with them. They were piled up in pillars on the floor and lay perilously close to the hearth. There were two tables, but one was hidden in papers. The other supported the little brass stove and a slatternly collection of unwashed clay plates and bowls, one of which housed a sleeping dormouse.

"They are my life," Phrynius said equably. "And my friends. One is never alone if one possesses a book."

Rol selected one at random, a slim, leather-bound affair. *The Roots of Cantrimy.* He flicked through it, but it seemed gibberish.

> *... and when one is assured that the hagrolithic interstices in the blood are in fact closely bound enough to occlude the introduced substances, then it can be said with some certainty that upon the death of the subject a hagrolithic transformation is possible. How much this transformation is a result of the subject's conscious volition, and how much it is an irrefragable physical process has yet to be fully determined. With the paucity of research, and the inevitable dearth of subjects willing to—*

"Here we are," Phrynius said. "Warm wine on a winter morning—just the thing." He poured the steaming, fragrant liquid into two clay mugs and set down the pan with a clang, his knob-knuckled old hands trembling with the effort. There were two badly stuffed armchairs before the fire, and he and Rol sat in these sipping their wine and staring into the flames. From a small window above them a gray gleam of light seeped into the room as the sun began to top the mountains in the world outside.

Phrynius raised his pointed nose and sniffed the air. "It'll snow again today. Bah! I can smell it, and I feel it in my poor swollen bones. Let us hope those fools will leave their guns alone for a day and let us breakfast in peace. I prefer the night hours—less coming and going, and servants snooping with laundry and chamber-pots—and meals, the gods preserve us. Ah, this wine is rubbish, of course, as is all Bionese that is bottled east of the Embrun, but what is the matter when one adds all manner of stuff to it and boils it over a stove, eh?"

"You spoke of Michal Psellos," Rol said patiently. He was half convinced the little man was not quite right in the head, but that name held him fixed here, drinking the hot, execrable wine and half listening for the sounds of renewed battle from the river.

"An unpleasant man, though an apt pupil. Old Ardisan trusted him too much, but then he was his father, and oftentimes fathers are blind to the faults of their sons."

Rol leaned forward. "You knew my grandfather?"

"We were, you might say, contemporaries, fellow scholars and wanderers—until Bar Asfal's usurpation, of course. He dropped out of sight after that, buried himself in bucolic bliss, no doubt." The old man's eyes sharpened. "And you are the grandson. Well, the world is small, after all."

Rol studied the purple, trembling face of his wine. He did not know where to begin; he did not know what to ask first. He was almost afraid to open his mouth.

Phrynius's little rodent eyes were fixed on him like two beads of jet; like Canker's eyes, they gave away nothing more than they could afford. And yet the old man seemed inoffensive enough, and frail as a wind-borne leaf.

"It seems I have now met the entire family," Phrynius went on. His satisfaction was somehow unsettling, like that of a wine-drinker who rounds out his cellar with a final crowning vintage.

"Tell me of them," Rol said quietly. "Tell me everything you know—about Psellos, about Amerie and Bar Hethrun, about Ardisan and Emilia. I have lived my life being fed drips and riddles, and now I am here in Bionar because of a woman some say is my sister, walking into a war I do not understand and have no stake in." He raised his head, and out of his eyes there came a light colder than the glint of the winter dawn. "Tell me everything you know. And make it the truth, for if I hear one word of a lie, I swear that I will kill you."

Phrynius's old parchment face went gray. He spilled his wine, and winced as the hot liquid scalded his fingers, but kept his gaze fixed, fascinated, on Rol's livid face.

"There is no need to get testy," he said. His voice quavered. "Some of what I know is conjecture at best." But he did not seem entirely afraid; in fact, there was eagerness burning across his face, that of a man desperate to make a confession.

"I don't care. Everything you know."

"I was told as a boy," Phrynius said, having emptied his wine-cup in a rattling gurgle, "that I had some of the Blood in me. My people were from Perilar, near Geberran in the foothills of the Western Myconians. There were many in the towns and villages, and among the goat-herding peoples in that part of the world, who claimed the same. Your friend the halftroll; I grew up seeing things like him now and again. They were kept away from the settlements for the most part, hidden in remote crofts and bothies by their families—that is, if they were not strangled at birth, as many were. But the Mountain Folk were simple people, and they cherished their children in the main, no matter how grotesque they were when they issued scream-ing from the womb.

"My father's name was Pherion. He was a healer, of sorts, a wise man in a world where few could read and fewer still knew anything of their land's history beyond the lives of their grandparents. If he bequeathed any of the Blood to me, then it was very little; I am eighty-two years old, and I feel every single one of those years.

"But I digress. The Bionese invaded Perilar, seventy years ago now. They came by sea and took our great harbor at Onastir, then raided inland. Our town fell to a band of their marauding cavalry. They killed my father and many others, and took me as a slave. At night they used me like a girl, and in the day I gathered firewood and fodder and groomed their horses for them. I was taken back to Bionar in chains and sold there on the auction block at Palestrinon. A slave's lot in Bionar is not a happy one. My first master treated me as the soldiers had. I ran away, was caught and flogged, ran away again. I was sold inland, and in time my voice broke, I grew a little, and I was no longer abused in—in that particular way. In time, when I was almost out of my teens, I found myself sold to a good master, a man of learning who lived in Myconn itself. I could read and write, thanks to my father, and he loved books, this man, and delighted in sharing his knowledge of them, even with a household slave. His name was Magre Psellos."

Phrynius paused, his eyes far away. "He was a good man, a kind man. He became like a second father to me. When his death drew near he set me free, and bequeathed me a small sum of gold, and the beginnings of a library." Phrynius smiled, remembering. "That was more than sixty years ago, but to this day, every time I open a new book, I think of him.

"Magre was a supporter of Bar Hethrun, rightful heir to the throne of Bionar. He would host dinners at which Bar Hethrun—a young man then—and his friends would sit and discuss the great matters of the kingdom, and I as house steward would see to it that all the usual things were taken care of, and would stand in the shadow beyond the lamplight, and listen as these great men talked over their wine. It was at one of these occasions I first saw Amerie Bar Hethrun, the nomad witch out of the Goliad that Bar Hethrun had married, to the scandal of Bionese society and to his own eventual ruin." Phrynius stared at Rol, nodded. "There is something of her in you, as there is in Rowen. She was a remarkable beauty, and there was a sense of peril about her that both frightened and attracted every man who met her. Bar Hethrun was a strong man, but she held him enthralled. I confess that I did not like her—there was something raw about her eyes." Phrynius gulped. "Not that—I mean—"

"Go on," Rol said.

"There was something *bad*."

"For a scholar, you speak in simplistic terms."

"Sometimes language is at its best when it is simple. Amerie's parents were different from her. *Different,* you understand. Well, to me, at least. After Magre's death I set myself up as a pedagogue, teaching the young, tutoring the nobility's sons in history and languages. Ardisan and Emilia visited me often, while they were still tolerated in Myconn. Ardisan and I shared many interests, and Emilia, she was simply a joy to be around. She warmed every room she was in." Phrynius shook his head. Looking at him, Rol had an instant's picture of a gangling young man, all long nose and legs. Good eyes and a deep-burning fire of ambition.

"I fell a little in love with her, I think, and I was not the only one. She and Ardisan had a son, much younger than Amerie, named Michal. I say younger, but all these folk were of the blood of the Elder Race, and their lives are not counted like those of lesser men. Michal was older than I, but to all purposes he seemed a young man. He was a little wild, even then, and he dived into the intrigue and finery of the Bionese Court as though born to it. He garnered a name as a rake and a spendthrift, and the younger nobles associated with him because of his capacity for raising hell. But there was more to him than that. He hungered after knowledge, of all kinds. He was a glutton for it. I taught him all I knew, which is precious little in the great scheme of things. He grew impatient with his father's strictures and disciplines, and struck off on his own, leaving Bionar and his family, to hunt the world alone for answers to his questions. He stole two things from me when he left. My library, such as it was, and the name Magre had given me. An old Bionese name; perhaps he thought it would ease his way in the world."

"He's dead," Rol said. "Rowen and I killed him."

"I have heard this. Canker told me. There was bad blood in Michal Psellos, and I cannot think where it came from, for his parents were good people, untainted by the strain of the Fallen that infects so many folk of the Blood. In any case, you gave him the end he deserved."

Rol remembered a horrific night, eight years ago now, when he and Rowen and Canker had murdered Michal Psellos, pushing his grinning face into the coals of a fire while he kicked and screamed in their grasp. And yes, that death had been well deserved.

"Bar Asfal took the throne, and Bar Hethrun, Amerie, Ardisan, and Emilia fled the country, taking ship for I know not where. That was more than thirty years ago now. They are all dead, those formidable people, and here I remain, holding only their memories. But their children have survived. Rowen, the image of her father, is here trying to make herself Queen. And now you are sat with me listening to this old man's rambles as the sun rises over the mountains and winter lies white upon the world."

"What about after they left Bionar?" Rol demanded. "Do you know what happened to them then?"

"I know only what is common knowledge—though it's fast becoming legend. Amerie and Bar Hethrun took to the sea along with many of their followers, and lived as privateers, operating out of a hidden pirate city on the Ganesh coast. But a storm came one day, and their ship was wrecked. The ship's company was scattered in small boats, separated by the whim of Ran. Amerie was lost for years, and when she returned she had a son, who sits here before me."

"Who were they, my grandparents?"

"Nomads from the Goliad, the Birthplace of Man. That is all I know."

Rol's wine was tepid now, but he drank it back without a thought.

"Your family's name was Orr-Diseyn," Phrynius said gently. "In old Waric it is not a proper name, but merely a phrase meaning *the folk of Orr.* Do you know that name?"

"I've heard of it."

"Then you know that Cambrius Orr was the greatest of the Elder Race, and the land he named for himself is still reputed to exist, somewhere out in the unexplored regions of the world. There are those who think that the nomads of the Goliad are not truly Men at all, but are the last remnants of the people of Orr. The last of the Weren, who once knew the face of God."

"I thought Cambrius Orr's people were all twisted monsters; it's why he fled to Orr in the first place."

Phrynius opened his hands like a man releasing a bird. "I have heard that also. There are many legends and myths, and not all of them agree with one another. I will tell you this, for what it is worth: I have met Rowen, and now I have met you. The blood of Bion runs in your sister; it's plain for any man to see—but in you there's something else, something unfathomable. I don't believe your parentage is what you think it to be."

Rol smiled. He stood up. "You never told Canker that."

"I am only sure of it now I have seen into your eyes." Phrynius looked Rol up and down as though registering his features.

"You have a strange name—your first name, that is. Your sister Rowen—"

"I know. Psellos told me. In Waric her name means *queen*."

Phrynius cocked his head on one side. His eyes gleamed. "It could mean that, I suppose. It comes of two roots. *Ro*, signifying *high, masterful*, and *wren*, meaning *woman*."

"And my name means *king*."

"No. It does not. Properly speaking, your name is *Ro-uil*. You have the same *ro*-element, but in Waric the root *-uil* has been added, meaning . . ." He trailed off and dropped his gaze. "It signifies a spirit, a thing not of this world. In its very earliest forms it denoted a thing akin to God."

Rol smiled. "I am a god, then? Your brains are addled, Phrynius. You've been breathing the dust of the past for too long."

"Not a god, but something connected to the One God, the Creator who forsook this world. Or something sent by Him."

Rol shrugged. "What's in a name, after all?"

"There is power in a name. In the Elder times they were not given lightly." Phrynius raised his head. The genial old scholar had disappeared, and his face seemed that of a younger man with certainty shining out of his eyes.

"Below the Turmian Library in Myconn there are caves, deep under the rock of the foundations. That place was a shrine once, back in the times when men toiled with flint and did not yet know the names of any gods. In that darkness, the early men painted pictures upon the stone of the cave walls. One of those pictures would, I think, be worth your seeing."

"Why?"

"It is of you."

PART TWO

KING *of* THIEVES

Eleven

COLDER THAN KEUTTA

THEY LED BETTER THAN FIVE THOUSAND MEN OUT OF Gallitras, and pointed them south across the bitter snowbound countryside toward the siege-lines about Myconn, almost two hundred miles away. Their campfires were left burning, the tents left standing, and the army sidled out of its lines along the river in the dead hours of the night, the hooves of the horses wrapped in sacking and the wagons manhandled inch by creaking inch through frost-sharp snow that cracked and shattered under the metal-rimmed wheels. Canker was leaving a skeleton garrison to man the Ruthe crossings, gambling that the costly failed assault of days before would keep the loyalists in camp for a while. That, and the increasingly bitter weather.

Five thousand men, most of them infantry, trudging in column of fours along the broken stones of the Myconn Road. Along with the wagons of the baggage train, they formed a column over a mile long. Rol rode near the head of the army, beside Canker. Gallico was still confined to a wagon by his wounds, and Giffon and Creed had chosen to keep him company rather than chance the back of a horse again.

The Council of War the night before had not deserved the name. Canker gave orders, and they were obeyed. Moerus, governor of Gallitras, had raised a few murmuring objections to being stripped of half his command, but all in all it would seem that the Thief-King's word was not to be gainsaid in this part of the world. Rol had still not become accustomed to Canker's lofty status. He remembered the derelict filth of the Guildhouse in Ascari which had been Canker's headquarters when last he knew him, and could not equate it with this current man of power, this politician, this general who marshaled armies and gave orders to thousands on a whim.

"What is it?" Rol asked his companion. "Chamberlain or chancellor? I have heard you called both."

"That is because I am both," Canker told him gaily. The sun was breaking through gaps in the sullen slate cloud overhead, lighting up the morning snow on the fields around them, and spreading a little cheer along the thousands who sweated upon the road. Once again, the Thief-King had changed his wardrobe. His leather cuirass was now swamped by a scarlet cloak, and a feather protruded jauntily from his headgear.

"The chamberlain is the master of the Queen's Court, and the chancellor is the keeper of the Treasury—such as it is—and the Queen's right hand, as it were, in any capacity she sees fit for him to undertake. I am a jack-of-all-trades, Rol, always have been." And Canker laughed. It was mid-morning by now, and they were five miles out of Gallitras, leaving behind them the scorched and bloody battlefield of the Ruthe crossings. The Thief-King seemed glad to be on the move again, and so was Rol. Never in his life had he been so far from the sea. He felt that he was remote from his natural element, and the changing horizons of a journey made that knowledge easier to bear, left him less time to dwell on things.

I am sick of dwelling on things, Rol thought. Give me back my *Revenant* and my ship's company, and I would be well content.

It was not entirely true, but he would not bring himself to admit it.

"You met Phrynius," Canker said casually.

"He met me first. Did you tell him to seek me out?"

"Yes. He was interested, of course, but it took a prod to get him away from his damn books. I'm glad. He's a good man, though not long for this world. I don't suppose you thought to . . ." Canker hesitated, an odd thing for him. "No, I suppose not."

"What?"

"As I said, he's not long for this world. A few swallows of your blood would have given him another five or ten years of being a bookworm." And Canker laughed unpleasantly.

Rol stared at the backs of the troops ahead, their breath and heat misting up the frigid air above them. "It never occurred to me."

"I thought as much. It may become more important when we reach Myconn. It is the ultimate in incentives, you might say; the best bribe in the world."

"It's how Rowen first gained support, isn't it?"

"Partly, yes. She bleeds herself each week, and it goes out to all the brave, the loyal, the best of the army. A man will do much for an extra decade or two of life. Look at me!"

Rol did. "It had struck me that you've changed little with the years." He felt a growing disgust, but kept it out of his face. Canker knew, though.

"I got my first taste in Ascari, as you should remember. A gift from Psellos," Canker said. His voice was not so jovial now. "If a loyalist bullet does not find me before my time, I'll see out a century with ease. Now, there's power for you, Rol—the ability to give that to a man. Not all the gold in the world can match it."

"And yet Bar Asfal is bribing your cities away from you."

A small puncture in the balloon of Canker's smugness.

"Not everyone can have it for the asking; they must prove themselves worthy first. Some are too impatient to wait, and some fools reject the whole idea, preferring to keep their blood their own. And besides," he added irritably, "there's not enough of the damn stuff to go around."

Rol smiled. "Is that why I'm here, Canker, another cow to be milked dry?"

Canker tugged at the brim of his hat. He looked annoyed with himself. "That's certainly part of it, yes. Don't look so outraged, boy! This is the way the world works."

Rol did not look outraged; he was perfectly composed. "It's a smaller world than we give it credit for, it's true. You and I, Phrynius, Psellos, Rowen. I sometimes wonder if there is more than chance to all these many meetings."

"If there were still a God to direct the world, perhaps there might be. But it's more likely to be humdrum coincidence." Canker cocked his head at Rol. The brim of his extravagant headgear cast one bright eye in shadow. "Then again, we live in interesting times. Phrynius certainly thinks there's more to the tale of your life than meets the eye."

"He's lived too long with books for his only company. He reads things between the lines that are not there."

"Well. Well, we shall see, I suppose. Rowen has become something of a reader lately also—hardly surprising when she has the greatest library in the world within her grasp."

"Let me guess; she has secrets to tell me. You need a new line of patter, Canker."

The Thief-King, chamberlain and chancellor of Eastern Bionar, guffawed. He doffed his feathered hat to Rol with elaborate courtesy. "You may be right at that."

*   *   *

The column made four leagues that day, slowed by the grinding progress of the baggage train. So pitted and frost-broken were the roads that a whole regiment of infantry had to be assigned to keeping the heavy-axled wagons on the move.

The Embrun River was on their right, hidden in a line of snow-clad trees scarcely a mile away. On their left the Myconians glowered, their peaks hidden in cloud. Still a hundred miles away, the mountains dominated the horizon all the same, like sullen titans brought to earth. Their lower slopes were tinted pink as the sun set in the west and kindled the gray waters of the Embrun into a glorious few minutes of molten light. Tentless and fireless—for campfires were forbidden this close to Gallitras—the men of the army rolled themselves in their blankets and lay in the snow as the sun died in a glowing bar of flame-limned cloud. As darkness fell the sky cleared, and above them the welkin blazed with frost-bright constellations, and shooting stars streaked in showers. Five thousand men lying silent in that starlit desolation, their weapons beside them under the blankets to keep them from the frost, the patient horses standing in hobbled lines with their heads drooping. The cold night air tightened the rims of the wagon-wheels so that the vehicles creaked and groaned like tired beasts all night long.

Gallico, Creed, and Giffon had found themselves a quiet hollow on the fringe of the camp, and huddled together there like a mother hen and her chicks. The halftroll was coughing: loud, savage barks that rent the quiet clarity of the night and set nearby horses to neighing.

"I heal slower in the cold," he explained to Rol. "Damned air gets in the chest and lies there like a chilled knife."

"Giffon?" Rol asked.

The boy's face was pallid and blue-lipped. He spoke through shivers. "His wounds are closed already, but there's an infection in the lung, or else the lung has cleaved to a rib as it healed. I've seen it before, only I've never seen the process work so quick."

"I'll be fine," Gallico grated. He was breathing in harsh, shallow pants and his eyes glittered dangerously. "I've lived through worse."

"Can anything be done?" Rol asked Giffon.

"He needs to be in the warm, and out of this snow."

"Don't we all," Elias Creed muttered. The dark man's beard was white with frost and he had a doubled blanket wrapped about his shoulders like a shawl. "It reminds me of nights in the damned stone-quarries, but at least there it warmed up during the day, and the ground under my arse was dry."

Rol looked at him quickly. It was the most information Elias had ever volunteered about his years in Keutta.

"Canker says that we should reach the lines about Myconn in less than a fortnight. And tomorrow night we can light fires again."

"What are you now, Canker's errand-boy?" Gallico asked. When Rol glared at him, the halftroll smiled, two long fangs poking from his lower lip. "The more I see of Canker and his war, Rol, the more I think you are merely here to be used in some way."

"Fuck Canker and his Queen and their bloody empire," Elias growled. "I'm with Gallico. Let's take off for the coast and get back to the ship. We don't belong here; we're just little cogs in their machine."

"What is this?" Rol asked softly. "A mutiny?"

Giffon stared at him wide-eyed as a startled rabbit.

"This is your friends telling you not to walk blindfolded into trouble," Elias snapped. He rubbed a hand over his crackling beard. "We're with you to the end—you know that. But the end may not be what you think. Be careful, Rol. Canker is not a good man."

"We are none of us good men, Elias. We agreed on that once before."

"We've done our share of killing, I grant you, but we've not made an industry out of it. Will Bionar be a better place with Canker and this Queen in charge? The ordinary folk will have a new landlord, is all."

"I don't care who rules Bionar either, but it may be that with Canker and Rowen in power, Ganesh Ka will be left alone at last, whereas with Bar Asfal on the throne, Bionese ships will never stop hunting us. We're in it together now, all of us, whether we like it or not. You can thank Artimion's politicking for that. If Rowen wins, we secure the Ka's future, and are the ally of a great power. There's one thing at least that will be for the better."

"You may be right," Gallico conceded. The four of them sat in silence for a while, and the starlight silvered the snow about them and raised a billion lesser stars from its crisp carpet. Rol felt a helpless sense of loss. Something was fraying among them, some kind of brotherhood. These three were the people he loved best in all the world (*Rowen,* his heart added, cackling), and he realized he was losing them.

No, *he* was drawing away.

Gallico's helpless coughing broke the quiet at last. They had sewn four blankets together and he hitched these higher over his shoulders. "I should feel at home here anyway," he puffed. "I was born in the mountains, the Northern Golorons. My people were herders in the high pastures of Perilar, but it's been a century or more since I was last this far from the sea."

The sea. At once, Rol had an overwhelming desire to gaze once more upon it, to feel salt in the air and taste it in his mouth, to hear the hiss of the waves moving in his head. The sea was freedom, refuge. The sea was home.

"You'll stand upon a ship's deck again, Gallico, that I swear. We all will."

But looking at his friends' faces as they turned toward him in the night, Rol could see that they did not believe him.

* * *

They passed through the town of Corbie five days later, though it was little more than a tattered, teeming encampment in the midst of a wilderness of rubble. They picked up three batteries of artillery there, appropriated by Canker with his usual aplomb. Eighteen heavy culverins drawn by long teams of bad-tempered mules, the three hundred–odd men who crewed them looking as though they would rather have been left where they were. Apart from soldiers and the teamsters and muleteers and others who serviced the needs of the army, the countryside seemed deserted of all ordinary, unregimented humanity.

"I thought you said Bionar was a rich, settled country," Rol told Canker as they trooped out of Corbie and passed the endless lines of supply wagons being loaded and unloaded for garrisons to the north and south.

"It was," the Thief-King responded. "But it's taken a bit of a battering of late. Most of the civilian population has fled either to Myconn itself or to the towns nearer the coast. No point squatting in the middle of a battlefield, especially when your crops have been trampled and your house put to the torch. It's better this way. The men no longer worry about fighting with their own people in the line of fire. Southeast Bionar has become a vast, brightly lit stage upon which we act out our play without need or desire for an audience." He held up a gloved hand and panned it like an actor expressing a theatrical point, grinning.

Rol watched Canker and remembered him fighting Psellos. When it came to skill in pure murder, he did not believe the Thief-King was a match for Rowen, and at one time he himself had been close to besting her—but that was a long time ago. He was not sure he would be able to kill Canker if the need arose, not unless the thing within him decided to come roaring out at the world again at just the right moment. His own training had been too brief, and it was too long ago. He did not doubt that both Canker and Rowen kept their skills perfectly honed, but his own were mere cobwebbed memories—despite his prowess on the bridge at Ruthe.

He recalled Psellos's contempt for the ordinary run of humanity. Cattle, he had called them, as though folk of the Blood were the only rational creatures in the world. He had tried to inculcate that attitude in Rol, too, and though he had largely failed, it still reared its ugly little head at times. But Rol did not truly believe it. Deep down, he knew that he craved acceptance and respect—and yes, love—from those he sometimes affected to despise. He hated himself for craving it, and he hated himself for his contempt of them. That was part of Psellos's legacy which had sunk deep.

"When you talk," he told Canker, "you remind me of Michal Psellos."

"Perhaps I will take that as a compliment."

"You can take it any way you like."

"Psellos was a mighty man, though not, strictly speaking, a man at all. He was a colleague of mine in many ventures on Gascar—as you know. He betrayed me, or tried to, and yet I bear his memory no ill will. Make of that what you like."

"A man who does not resent betrayal will not find it far to stoop to become a betrayer in his turn."

"Possibly. I will do whatever is necessary to survive in this life, without evasion or contrition. All else is hypocrisy. We are animals, Rol, and in the end, all we care about is the worthless carcass in which our spirit finds itself imprisoned." Canker turned in the saddle to bring the full regard of his rat-bright eyes to bear. "Life is cheap—the lives of men. There is nothing cheaper or more tawdry. I am at bottom an ordinary man myself, so I should know. But if it is in you to refashion these lives by the thousand—by the hundreds of thousands—then there is some meaning there. The only meaning in a world abandoned by God." His attention drifted. He stared out over his horse's ears, frowning. Then, collecting himself, he made a smile; a false note.

"Thus, I serve Rowen, and I will do anything she deems necessary to put her at the head of the greatest nation on earth. Why? Because I believe she is worthy of that position, and I am not. I also believe that you have a place there beside her. I believe—truly, Rol—that you and she are greater than I, in the very essence of your humanity—or in your lack of it. So don't lose sleep at night, worrying about betrayal. It is not part of this man's plans."

"What in hell are you, then, Canker; have you become converted to the worship of the goddess Rowen?"

"I am willing to acknowledge reality," Canker said, gazing off into the distance again. "A man needs some kind of truth at the foundation of his life. I have found that I am a formidable man." He smiled wryly. "But it would seem I am not the stuff of which kings are made. Kings of Thieves perhaps, but not kings who make a mark on history."

Something in Canker's voice, his words, made the blood run cold about Rol's heart. "Canker, what has Rowen become?"

The Thief-King shrugged. "Give it a few days, my lad. A few days and a little carnage, and you shall find out."

The days were relatively few indeed, but they seemed long. Endless days of marching along the same road, watching the column of men and mules and guns proceed south with a kind of sullen stubbornness. Nights of freezing cold, where the campfires petered out long before the dawn through lack of firewood, the countryside around them picked clean as a desert carcass and forsaken by anyone who did not bear arms, or who did not in some way service those who did.

There was the odd, isolated inn still doing business and

serving as a waystation for messengers of Canker and Rowen's new empire. Usually it was the only inhabited building within a skew of ruined streets, though sometimes enterprising folk set up bordellos in the less broken houses nearby; and tired though the troops were, when the army halted for the night in the vicinity of these establishments there was a steady trickle of grimy men willing to spend their money there and have their needs seen to by a motley crowd of sad-eyed girls.

A week after leaving Gallitras, they found the Embrun River arcing round across their line of march again, flowing southeast to northwest. It was a narrower water here, and faster flowing, but still enough of an obstacle that the bridges over it were important militarily. Another smashed town, this one named Forminon, and another host of many thousands dug in along the banks and in the ruined houses, artillery emplaced in gabion-walled revetments, and the land all around them cratered and shell-scabbed under its merciful covering of snow. The army entrenched at Forminon was huge—to Rol's eyes, at least. Its tented city, butting onto the river, covered many acres, and the streets between the encampments had roads of corduroyed logs to keep the ubiquitous supply-wains from plunging axle-deep in the mud below. Fifteen thousand men, Canker said, garrisoned Forminon—for this was now more or less the front line. The land beyond was contested by both sides right up to the siege-lines about Myconn itself.

Once again, Canker requisitioned troops right and left, though this time the local commander protested with more spine than Moerus had shown at Gallitras. They stayed in Forminon two days, mostly to rest the animals of the baggage train and refill the wagons they drew. When they set off again they were more than ten thousand strong, and one of the new regiments was mounted: a thousand armored men on tall, half-starved horses. It took the better part of a day to merely clear the bridges, and once on the southern bank the army sent out flanking companies, whilst the cavalry rode ahead some half a league of the main body, sniffing for trouble. Ahead of them, the mountains loomed up closer than ever, and the ground rose steadily under their feet. They thought they had become accustomed to the cold, but now it deepened around them, a raw, dry chill that no blanket or campfire could keep out of their marrow.

Hitherto, Rol had viewed the army as a kind of snake. The column it made was defined by the road upon which it traveled. But now that changed. The snake grew legs, antennae. The formations opened up, and spread out over the blasted land, undulating with the rise and fall of the terrain, clotting at ruined farmsteads, trickling over drystone walls like lines of ants. In the rear of each company fire-bearers carried thick-walled clay pots that housed the embers of the nightly fires, so that their comrades would quickly be able to light the match of the arquebuses if the enemy should hove into view. When Rol remarked on the multiplicity of formations, Canker only grinned, doffing his feathered hat. "March divided, fight concentrated," he said. "I got that out of a book."

When they were ten leagues from Myconn the order was passed down the line that there would be no more campfires, no cooking of food. They would chew on raw salt-beef and biscuit, and shiver in their inadequate blankets through the long, frost-sharp nights. By day the army spread out still farther. Only the wheeled traffic kept to the roads, the wagons and the guns. The infantry advanced over the empty, low-hedged fields in broad-fronted field-columns. These moved in shadowed masses upon the white vividness of the snow, except when a gleam of sunlight passed over them and set all the thousands of metal accoutrements the soldiers carried to winking brilliance.

And still, there was no sign of the enemy. The countryside about them was as unpeopled as a wilderness. They were marching across the Vale of Myconn, which Rol had heard of in stories and songs all his life. It had been a densely populated, fertile, well-watered and well-tilled region, but now it was a snow-blasted waste.

Gallico had been here before. Rol joined him on the wagon, along with Giffon and Creed, and the quartet watched the world creep by around them as the army drew ever closer to Bionar's capital. The halftroll's skin was a paler shade of green now, and flesh had melted from his huge frame so that the bones were more pronounced, but the awful rasp and wheeze of his breathing had subsided. His eyes had regained some of their old mischief. He stared about himself with acute interest as the mountains came closer.

"See that gray smudge off to the northwest? That's Widnell, or what's left of it. I worked there for a while in a traveling carnival, lifting and breaking things and snarling like a maniac for crowds of farmers. There's roads under this snow, besides the one we're traveling on, but the blizzards have covered them and no one must be using them anymore. Those ruins? That's a town as well; I forget the name now. The mill still has a sail on it. It's maybe fifteen decades since I was in this part of the world, and nothing but the mountains looks the same."

They listened to him talk, glad to hear him sound like his old self again. That night they shared a skin of army wine and traded stories and memories all had heard recited a dozen times before. Many of the Bionese soldiers drifted over to them, bringing their own wine and losing some of their habitual reticence. One sang a song, and they joined in though they did not know the words. The soldiers were hard-bitten men, veterans of many battles who had followed their officers and leaders up and down an increasingly devastated country getting on for three years now. Though they had traveled together all this time, Rol had never had so much as a conversation with one of them.

Gray-eyed and dark-haired for the most part, they were a grave, stolid bunch who listened more than they spoke. Perhaps it was the proximity of the capital, and the inevitability of the battle they would be fighting before it, but they traded jokes and anecdotes now with the easiness of men who have been laboring together through a long day's toil. Only when Canker arrived did the soldiers' faces close again. They stood up as one, saluted him with real respect, and trooped off to their lines without another word, taking their wineskins with them. The Thief-King nodded at them with a crooked smile upon his face, and then gathering his cloak he turned away again, but gestured Rol to follow him.

Elias Creed came, too, weaving a little from the wine, and the three of them trudged up a low rise beyond the bivouacs of the army. There were clouds scudding across the face of the stars, and a sliver of a new moon. The mountains hung like phantom gods on the horizon, and under their feet the snow crunched like glass in the aching cold.

"I hope this is worth it." Creed hiccuped, and Rol steadied him with one arm. They stood on the brow of the hill sharing each other's warmth while Canker stood a little apart, smothered in his scarlet cloak, which hung black in the starlight.

"Canker—" Rol began irritably.

"Hush." Canker held up a gloved hand. "Do you hear that? Listen."

They did so. The snow creaked under their feet, a sound very like that a ship's rigging made when under sail. Somewhere in the woods beyond the road an owl hooted, as forlorn a sound as could be imagined below the frozen emptiness of that black sky. But there was something else also.

Rol caught it first. A faint rumbling off at the edge of

the world. Thunder, or the sound of an avalanche in the mountains—though they were still too distant for it to be that.

"Do you hear it?" Canker asked, rapt. "That sound?"

"What is it?" Creed asked, frowning.

"The guns of Myconn."

Twelve

CLIMBING A WALL

THE CAVALRY CAME BACK AT DUSK, THE HORSES BLOWN and stumbling, their riders hollow-eyed in the saddle. Their commander at once reported to Canker whilst his men unsaddled their mounts and rubbed them down, a haze of steam rising up from that vast overworked mass of muscle and bone. The rest of the army was still extending its flanks, and some of the more distant regiments were almost out of sight in the failing light. Four ranks deep, an (understrength) infantry regiment of a thousand men, with gaps for runners and the like, took up a frontage of three hundred yards—or a cable and a half, if one was nautically minded. Canker had nine of these regiments, plus the cavalry, plus three batteries of artillery, and a cloud of teamsters and cooks and smiths and stretcher-bearers and various other artisans who stayed back with the wagons. An impressive force; with three regiments held in reserve it still had a frontage of some half a league. Looking at it, Rol felt that armies such as this might change the very nature of the ground they walked upon. And, of course, they had.

The sound of the distant artillery was no longer notable; they had been hearing it for hours, ever since they had broken camp that morning and begun inching their way south, the regiments fanning out into lines, the gunners cursing and beating their mules to try to keep cannons and limbers from falling behind, the ox-drawn wagons of the supply train plodding doggedly in the rear. Now they had deployed across a rolling expanse of low hills, the regimental formations kinking here and there where companies followed the lines of hedges and stone walls, or bent out to occupy roofless farmhouses, or curved to follow the bend of a half-frozen stream. Men took these things into account when they picked a place to make their stand. They chose small rises in the ground, sunken lanes. A copse of trees assumed new significance when soldiers made it the center of their formation; it became part of the architecture of their morale.

Canker beckoned Rol over, and Rol nudged his horse into a stiff-limbed trot toward the Thief-King, where his scarlet cloak stood out among the drab, badly dyed livery of his officers. Once scarlet themselves, the surcoats of the men were fading to a dingy pink mottled with brown and darkened with sweat and melted snow.

Canker had unrolled a scroll of parchment upon which was a black-inked diagram. He bade one of the officers bend over and used the man's back as a desk, writing and drawing with a clipped quill which he refreshed from an inkwell in his button-hole.

"Myconn," he said. "It's over the hill, gentlemen, barely five miles away. Adlar's scouts got to within a mile of the siege-lines—without being spotted, he assures me. Bar Asfal is over-confident, and his men are none too keen to leave the comfort of their tents, and the security of their trenches. This is the lie of the land at present."

The officers craned their necks to look as Canker's brown-skinned fingers deftly scored quill across parchment.

"See, Bar Asfal has drawn his lines up to within a half mile of the city walls, but he's only dug them out from the Palestrinan Hills to the Corbians, an arc of some eight miles. The hills themselves are too rough for wheeled traffic or guns, and he patrols them with bodies of light infantry; sword and buckler men and peltasts. There are three main camps. One, the closest, guards the Gallitran Road; one in the west, the Palestrinan Road; and in the east, a small one between the Destrir River and the Corbian Hills. Asfal's standard is in the middle camp, on the Gallitran Road." Canker paused. "Adlar reckons the enemy strength at some thirty-five thousand."

Murmurs at this. The Bionese officers looked at one another. Significant nods, silent acknowledgments.

"We need to get word to the Queen that we are here. We need to coordinate our attack with a sortie from the city itself. We will have them between two fires." Canker smiled, rolled up his map, and clapped the shoulder of his living desk. The man straightened, face impassive.

"Rol here will enter the city tonight, under cover of darkness, and take tidings of our arrival and deployment to the Queen in person."

Rol met Canker's eyes coolly, though his heart had begun to hammer in his chest. Something told him this had been Canker's plan all along. Perhaps Rowen's too.

"Very well," he said. "But I don't know Myconn. I'll need a better idea of it than what's given in that scrawl of yours."

"You shall have it," Canker said.

"If the man is a stranger to the city, how can he be expected to find his way in and then get to the palace?" one of the officers demanded.

"Don't you worry yourself, Colonel," Canker retorted, and his eyes marked down the man's face for future reference.

"Young Rol here is rather adept at finding his way in the dark."

*   *   *

And dark it was. There was a half-moon that night, but the clouds rolled in to obscure it as if by arrangement. Canker had his men build a shack of brushwood spread with oilskin tarps to the rear of the battle-line, and within it was able to light a lantern while all the rest of the army lay in their thousands outside in the black, penetrating cold. There, he briefed Rol about his mission in rather more detail.

"A better map, this, though a little out-of-date." He spread the tattered vellum on the ground, avoiding the slush spreading by the base of the hissing lantern. "See, Myconn in all its glory. Half a million lived here, in better days, and as many more in the suburbs and outlying villages. But it's different now. The suburbs were razed to the ground to create fields of fire, and the villages are gone the same way. But the basic geography remains the same." His finger touched points lightly on the map.

"Here, the Destrir River, not much of an obstacle, but it runs right through the city and is bridged in three places before leaving the walls at East Culvert and heading north to join the Embrun. Here, the Palestrinan Gate, looking out to the west; here, the Forminon Gate, and the main barbican. Men call it the Warder. Bar Asfal has his main force opposite. Myconn stands within a sickle of high ground. To the west the Flamigrie Hills, to the south the Fornivan, to the east the Corbian. Only in the north is there an approach over clear terrain which can be used by heavy guns and wagons." Canker paused a second, as though considering. "You would be unlikely to succeed in any attempt to infiltrate from the north."

"I'll take to the rough ground," Rol said quietly. "The east, for preference. I'll enter the city there. What about the walls?"

"Sixty feet high, and as thick at the base. They've been much battered by artillery, mind. You should have no problem finding a way over them. The main difficulty will be not getting yourself shot by our own people."

"What do I do when I get over the walls? Who shall I reveal myself to?"

"The Bar Madivar Palace is here, plumb in the center of the city. Its walls overlook the river, and there's a bridge on its northwest quarter which leads onto a vast open space, Barbion Square. When last I saw it, that's where a great rabble of refugees had been allowed to throw up shacks and tents, but things may have changed. Rowen has taken up residence in the palace, in the North Wing, closest to the river and the bridge. Get in there, and her apartments are on the top floor of the complex, facing north." Canker rubbed his hand over his unshaven chin. "The commander of the Palace Guard, mainstay of Myconn's defense is—or was—Gideon Mirkady. He's fanatically attached to Rowen—they've been lovers in the past. He will be the man to convince."

A flicker in Rol's eyes, though his face was stone-still. "Convince?"

"That you're not a spy. His men are good, the best we have, and they're sworn to protect her. That may make them more inclined to shoot first and do some thinking afterward."

"Excellent," Rol said dryly.

"Don't worry, my lad; I won't send you naked into that den of desperation. Here." Canker held out his ruby-bright ring of office. It was heavy as Rol took it, warm from Canker's flesh.

"Show them that, and they should become fairly amenable."

"And Rowen. What do I tell her?"

"I'm writing no dispatch; safer that way. You must give it to her verbally. Now, listen well." Canker sounded off a series of points, folding back the outstretched fingers of a hand one by one as he did so. Rol took in the words and stored them safely away at the back of his mind, but mostly he was staring at the vellum map on the ground, and picturing Rowen in her palace,

surrounded by her guards, governing a half-ruined city and a
broken kingdom. She was the only reason for him to be here,
but now that it had come to it, he was almost afraid at the
thought of seeing her face again.

It was snowing outside, fat silent flakes that were felt rather
than seen in the darkness. They kissed Rol's eyelashes as he
stared up at the black sky, the invisible mountains, the moon
and stars cloaked by cloud. He did not know where it was he
called his home, but at that moment he had never felt farther
from it.

"Rol?"

Standing there before him were Gallico, Creed, and Giffon,
a mismatched trio of shapes whose presence abruptly warmed
his heart.

"Tonight, Elias. I go tonight."

"Then so do we all," Gallico rumbled.

"I go alone, Gallico. This calls for stealth."

"This calls for someone to watch your back, my friend.
We've come this far; we're not about to bugger off now.
Besides, it's black as a witch's tit tonight. As long as we keep it
quiet, we could troop in there by the hundred."

It was not a good idea; but then, nothing had seemed like a
good idea in weeks. "All right, then, but we'll have to be fast on
our feet to begin with. Myconn is still five miles away, and I'm
taking no horses. We'll run it."

Five miles. There were six hours until midnight, and another
seven hours of darkness after that, so they had a fair amount of
time to play with, but none to waste. They set off at a steady
jog, quickly leaving behind the prone lines of Canker's army
and striking east, then south. There were no stars to navigate

by, but Gallico had what seemed to be an internal compass, and his huge taloned paw touched Rol on the left or right shoulder as they jogged along, keeping them on course. After the first mile they were up over the bulk of the ridge, and Myconn came into view in the distance, a carpet of lights across the hills, extending for miles across the lightless face of the earth. But it was surrounded by a line of more lights, a thin string of them leagues long, punctuated by more concentrated clumps here and there, and rivaled in one place by a great concentration: the camps of the enemy, and the siege-lines they maintained.

"Left," Rol panted, and they struck off eastward once more.

Up into the broken gullies and scree slopes of the Corbian Hills, stones sliding under the snow as they set their feet upon them, the all-pervading cold sinking into their bones as their pace slowed on the treacherous ground. A wind picked up from the mountains, and blew snow in powdered clouds across the hills. They took a wide dogleg east, and then south, and then west to try and avoid the siege-lines, but they were close enough all the same for Rol's vision to pick out the black zigzagged furrows of trenches notched in the snow, and the sprawling tent-lines a quarter-mile in their rear. Campfires burned amid the tents, guttering motes of light struggling against the wind, but the trenches looked entirely empty—until one looked long enough, and glimpsed the shadows patroling up and down.

"Most of them are in their tents tonight," he whispered to Gallico as the pair lay in the blowing snow on their bellies, peering west.

"Sensible chaps," the halftroll muttered. "You know, Rol, if we could make it across those trenches here, we'd cut out a great loop of bad ground. I don't know about you, but I don't much fancy stumbling through these damn hills all night."

Rol looked quickly at his companion. Gallico's face seemed shrunken, and his eyes had retreated into his head.

"You're not right yet, Gallico."

"It's the damn cold. Gets into my chest and gurgles there like a spit-filled pipe."

Rol considered. His feet were numb in his boots and the snow felt fine as sand as it blew into the back of his neck.

"All right. To hell with it, we'll cross their trenches. We could be half the night finding a way through the hills. Let's get back to the others."

Creed and Giffon were huddled together like dogs, curled up against the wind. The boy still had his bag of surgical tools over his shoulder, and he gripped a heavy catling in one half-frozen fist.

"We're going through their lines," Rol told them, and they seemed both alarmed and relieved.

Fleam warmed his hand as he drew her. They approached the loyalist lines in single file, Rol out ahead, Gallico bringing up the rear. For Rol, the dark of the night did not exist; he saw no color, but every detail was plain and sharp, a monochrome world bright amid the blowing snow.

He padded up to the lip of the trench with no more noise than a stalking cat. It was neck-deep, lined with Hessian sandbags and wooden duckboards in the bottom that glistened with frost.

The first sentry died quietly, the scimitar entering the side of his neck and reappearing black and steaming out of his windpipe. He sagged, and Rol caught him in his arms, lowered him to the ground with great gentleness. Fleam slid free, the hot blood still smoking off her steel. Setting her down, Rol rolled the corpse into a corner of deeper shadow in the bottom of the trench. All quiet. He waved at Gallico, and the halftroll brought Creed and Giffon forward, their eyes wide as owls' as they tried to pierce a night that to them was black as cold pitch.

"Up over the side," Rol hissed. "There's another line about fifty yards ahead. This is just a reserve trench. Quickly now."

Giffon stumbled, and Gallico caught him by the nape, actually lifting him free of the ground for a moment. The halftroll's breath was sawing in his throat. "Take your time, lad. We've all bloody night, after all."

They felt horribly exposed as they dashed across the white, open ground between the two trenches, though in reality the starless night and blowing shroud of ice covered them from all but the most alert of watchers.

The second sentry turned around to see a bright-eyed shadow rushing at him. He had time to raise an instinctive arm before Fleam's glittering edge came down. The arm came off at the elbow-joint and the preternatural blade swept on, into the man's rib cage. Not so clean this time. He choked and twisted and thrashed his way to death, while Rol stood on top of him, crushing out what breath remained in his lacerated lungs. A hard death. Rol closed the man's eyes; for some reason he did not like the way they looked at him.

The four of them were now lining part of the forward trench. Before them were three cables at least of open ground, much shattered by shell-fire. Beyond that, the walls of Myconn loomed up black and forbidding.

"Two runs," Rol said, breathing evenly. "Halfway across we stop, listen, then go on again. Gallico, look after Giffon. Elias, you stay with me, and try not to fall on your arse."

"Lend me your eyes and I'll promise not to," Creed said tartly. Rol grinned in the darkness.

"Wind's dropping," Gallico said, raising his head. "Best make it quick."

"You first, then—and don't look back."

They swarmed up over the lip of the trench, Giffon dragged like a doll when he stumbled. The halftroll picked the boy up bodily and slung him under one arm. He was not so swift as he once had been, but still astonishingly fast on his feet. The pair of them disappeared two hundred yards ahead as Gallico dived into a shell-hole.

"Don't you be trying to stick me under your bloody arm," Creed murmured.

"Then keep up, Elias." Voices down the trench, and a flag of torchlight that seemed bright as a cannon-blast in Rol's night vision.

"Go, Elias. Go on ahead."

The dark man scrambled up over the trench and took off into the darkness. Fleam trembled in Rol's fist. He swore silently, and followed in Creed's wake, walking. A squad of men was coming up the trench.

Snow crunched under his feet. He saw Creed slip and fall, and immediately regain his feet and stumble on. Behind him, there was an outcry. The enemy had found their murdered comrade. Rol began to run.

Gallico had found a shell-hole to crouch in, a crater half a yard deep and five times as wide. The halftroll's eyes glinted green and luminous in the dark. Giffon looked both terrified and excited.

"Up, lads. No time to hang about."

The four of them charged onward toward Myconn's great walls. Behind them someone blew on a horn, and more lights were kindled in the loyalist lines. The crack of an arquebus, followed by a ragged volley fired in hopeful rage into the darkness.

Their ragged sprint was brought to a halt by towering buttresses of stone. They had reached the walls. Creed slapped the icy masonry with the palm of one hand. "Excellent. Now what?"

"Give me a leg up, Gallico."

Gallico gripped Rol's thighs and lifted him clear of the ground. Sheathing Fleam, Rol let his hands run across the stone, feeling for cracks and handholds. Everything was covered in ice; his fingers probed at it in vain. More gunfire from the trenches behind them, and now someone was beating frenziedly on an alarm triangle atop the walls themselves.

"Let me down."

He hit the ground hard. Gallico was bent over, fighting for breath and spitting dark liquid into the snow. A spent bullet snapped into the wall above their heads and sprayed them with glass-hard ice.

"No good; a fucking spider couldn't get up there. We'll head left, look for a better place."

Gallico shoved aside Creed's helping hand, and the foursome pelted along the base of the walls, panting hard. Broken masonry here; Giffon tripped and went headlong with a sharp cry. Rol picked him up, heart hammering, cursing Canker's insouciance and his own overconfidence.

"Here," Creed spat. He was a little ahead. "Broken blocks all over the place. Looks like a breach, or something similar."

"Keep your yapping down," Gallico growled. They clustered about Creed, stubbing their toes on shards of shattered stone. There was a stripe of blood below Giffon's nose, and the boy breathed as though he had a heavy cold.

Yes, the rampart was battered here, the outer courses of masonry blasted away so that the old brick of the wall interior was exposed. Slick, perilous, but a way up nonetheless.

"I'll go first. Gallico at the rear. It's sixty feet, remember. Take your time."

Heavy exchanges of fire were cracking along the top of the walls and out of the trenches behind them. A startling boom as someone let loose with a heavy gun, an eighteen-pounder by the sound of it.

"Looks like we woke up the neighbors," Gallico observed, wiping Giffon's bloody nose like a patient mother.

Rol jabbed his numb toes at the broken brickwork and felt

frantically for handholds. There was no shortage of them, but all were slimy with ice. His breath steamed in a wet cloud in front of his face. He gained two fathoms, three, then halted, foiled by the slipperiness of the wall.

"Go left after three fathoms," he whispered to Creed over his shoulder, and began edging sideways along a tiny ledge that gave purchase to the toes of his boots. It was easier here. He went up again, the wall leaning in from vertical under him, like a steep set of tiny stairs. Then there was a huge block of outer-facing stone which he had to haul himself over. He looked down and saw Creed's face, teeth bared.

"Take my hand, Elias."

"I can't see my own bloody hand, let alone yours."

He tapped the convict on the head, and at once Creed's chill fingers grasped his own. He pulled Elias up onto the wide block that supported him and they sat a second or two, puffing.

"Gallico?" Rol hissed.

"Keep going, you damn fools," the halftroll said. "I've Giffon on my back. It's all right; claws are better than fingers."

Volleys of arquebus-fire were now tearing out from the parapet above their heads, and the heavy wall-guns were bark-ing. A smell of powder-smoke eddying in the failing breeze, but at least the damn snow had stopped blowing in their teeth.

"We pop up in front of yonder fellows, and we're likely to get shot," Creed said, jerking his head toward the top of the wall.

"I know." There was torchlight up there now, men shouting. The walls of Myconn had come to irascible life, and were spit-ting fire and lead out into the dark.

"I'll give it a go, all the same. We can't cling here like house-martins all night."

"Don't get your head shot off," Creed said.

"You have a talent for the stating of the obvious, Elias."

He began climbing again. It was easier here, and the rubble of the walls leaned farther inward. It took only a few minutes to get his head below the parapet itself, or where the parapet should have been. This section of wall had been badly smashed up by artillery fire. He drew in a slow lungful of air, wondering a little at the strange turns his life had taken of late. Then with one fluid twist of his arms and torso, he was standing atop the wall itself.

A terrified soldier fired his arquebus from the hip, squawking with fear. The bullet plucked at Rol's side. Enraged, Rol whipped forward, a mere blur of shadow, and knocked the unlucky man clear off his feet. "Hold your fire, you damned fool! I'm a friend."

A massed crowd of other armed men was pouring down the wall with firearms in their fists. Rol swallowed his rage, and lifted his arms in the air, palms out. "Hold your fire! Messenger from Canker, the chancellor!"

Some other idiot discharged his weapon. The torchlight coming forward ruined Rol's night vision. The crowd of men paused; two dozen at least stood there with poised weapons, that wide-eyed flight-or-fight look on their faces. Rol glared at them. "I'm a friendly, on your side. I come from Canker. I came through the enemy lines."

An officer shouldered his way through the press in livery of black and scarlet. "Name and rank!" he snapped crisply. He bore a heavy rapier, and held a cocked pistol whose muzzle seemed black and enormous as it looked Rol in the eye.

"Rol Cortishane. Canker is here with a relieving army, just over the ridge. I have information for—for the Queen. There are three companions with me, still climbing up the wall below."

"Oh, indeed? Now, there's a novel way to make an entrance. Throw down your sword."

Rol stiffened. His arms drooped, and as they did a dozen firearms were raised higher.

"You have my word; I am what I say."

"I'll take your word, and your sword too. And tell these fellow wallflowers of yours to get up here or we'll shoot them off our defenses. Quickly!"

Rol raised an eyebrow. It had been a long time since anyone had spoken to him with that tone. He tugged Fleam out of her scabbard and tossed her at the officer's feet, then slowly leaned over and shouted into the darkness below.

"Elias, Gallico, Giffon! Get up here."

When he straightened again the officer was only one pace away. The man had a small, tight smile on his face. He smashed the butt of his pistol into Rol's temple, and in the bright, bitter light of the blow, Rol had not even an instant to curse his own ineptitude.

Thirteen

THE QUEEN OF BIONAR

"FISHEYE," SHE SAID, AND SMILED. IT WAS NOT THE SMILE
he had loved, like a gift of secret grace. It was something else,
something new she had learned in the years since last they had
met.

He tried to speak, but the effort merely sent the dry breath
clicking in his throat. The sight of her, after all this time, smote
his heart still.

"You have grown up," she told him softly. And the voice was
the same.

He tried to sit up, and she pushed him back in the bed. At
that, they both started, remembering.

She was the same, and yet not. There were threads of silver
in the raven hair, fine fans of lines at the corners of her eyes,
and deeper shadows under them. But the eyes themselves
were still the color of burnished steel, as striking as those of a
black-maned angel. And the line of her neck and jaw was as elegant as it had ever been. Her beauty was a thing of wonder to
him. All the pretty girls in all the ports of the world dissolved

from memory as he stared upon her once again. It could be she was more finely drawn now, and her skin was so white the veins stood out blue in her neck. Not age, but the tear and wear of the choices she had made. Those eyes, that face; they had broken his heart, and as he lay now seeing them again it was as though the years of murder and seafaring were taken back, and he was a mere boy once more, hammering in fear at a strange door.

He grasped her hand, his bruised head throbbing in time with his heart. All the hard-won knowledge and experience of his venturesome life seemed stripped away, and for a moment he was again that callow boy, a youngster willing to lay that life at her feet.

She touched his head. "They gave you a fine bump, but nothing worse, I think. Best not to eat for a while; you'll only throw it up again."

With that she rose from the bed and left him. She was dressed in a simple black gown with jet beads sewn on. They glittered and spangled like little iridescent beetle-wings in the light of the fire. Her hair had been piled up behind her head and was held in place with pearl-topped pins.

Rol swung his legs off the bed. Her bed? he wondered. They had taken off his boots and tunic but otherwise he was still in the travel-stained clothes he had worn into Myconn. The pain in his head made his eyes water.

He told himself it was the pain in his head. He did not take his eyes off her for one second. She stood in front of the fire and poured white wine into tall flutes, then turned back to him with the flames behind her, the fireplace huge as a wardrobe, the heat shouting out of it. She was a lean shadow, no more, a shapely demon standing before the open gates of some wondrous hell.

She was the woman he had loved his whole life. She was his sister, the Queen of Bionar. She was—

"Rowen," he said aloud, as though getting used to the sound of the name again.

She raised her glass to him, and sipped from it. "Fisheye," she said again, the old nickname he had always hated.

Rol stood up and padded over to her in his bare feet. It seemed strange to be so much taller than her; it did not feel right that she should have to raise her head so to meet his gaze.

"You grew tall," she said. "I knew you would. And broad-shouldered as a bear. But what made you plant that thing on your chin?" She tugged at his beard with her white fingers.

"Shaving at sea is no simple matter."

"Ah, yes. You are a mariner now, a man of ships. I heard that, a long time ago." A shade of sadness passed over her face. She turned away, finished the pale wine in her glass, and picked up the other.

"Will you join me, Rol?"

"You remember my true name, after all, it seems." He took the flute in his brawny fist; it was like holding a wand of glass.

"Your true name. Yes, I suppose so. There's a power in names, I've been told."

She strode away, and sat in an armless wooden chair close by the bed. Leaning forward, she set her elbows on her knees as a man might, and stared at the floor.

"Now, quickly, tell me of Canker."

A moment of bewildered silence, and then his voice came out harsh, loud as a crow's.

"He's five miles to the north with ten thousand men and eighteen guns. He intends to assault the main camp of the loyalists from the rear, as soon as you have made a sortie from the Forminon Gate to pin them in place. Bar Asfal is in that camp, on the Gallitran Road. He must fall in the attack. If you can kill him, and the main body of enemy nobles around him, then the war is won. The rest will capitulate. You must pick a date and a time for this combined assault, and you must take out

every able-bodied man you have in order to convince Bar
Asfal that this is a tactic of desperation. You must take the
field personally, and it must be soon. Canker cannot keep the
presence of his army a secret forever." Rol's voice had become
mechanical, a man reciting a meaningless list that meant nothing to him. Rowen raised her head and stared at him.

"Very good. Canker did well."

"He is a capable man," Rol said tonelessly. He drank back
the wine in his glass without tasting it.

"And a persuasive one. I was not sure he would be able to
convince you to come here."

Rol met her gaze squarely. "Yes, you were."

For a long moment they held each other's eyes. It was partly
a contest of wills, partly a naked search for what was in the
other. Rowen dropped her stare first. "There is murder in your
eyes now. It was not there before."

"As you said, I've grown."

There was a discreet knock on the door. "Your Majesty?" A
man's voice.

"Not now, Gideon."

"I'll be outside, should you—"

"Very well. I am not to be disturbed."

A pause, then footsteps retreating along a stone passageway
beyond.

"One of your acolytes?" Rol asked lightly.

"Gideon Mirkady, commander of my Guard. It was he who
gave you your bump. A good man, in his own way."

"Does he know who I am?"

"Oh, yes; why else do you think he struck you?"

"Well, it's something to be popular." Rol took a seat on a
stool by the fire. The heat could not stymie the ice gathering
heavy about his heart.

"You also have grown, Rowen."

"Indeed? I am the same size I always was."

She watched him with an air almost of amusement. Rol cocked one eye at her. If his presence here was important to her, she hid it well. He did not know how to say it, but he felt she had become more at ease with herself, and in doing so had lost something he had treasured about her.

"It would seem you are now one of the great people of the world, a matter for history to ponder. I wonder that you should even remember me, the boy you once knew."

"The boy I once knew." Rowen leaned back, arms crossed on her knees. Her face was unreadable, and on her mouth there curved that meaningless smile. He did not remember her ever smiling like that before. It reminded him somewhat of Canker.

"This man you are now, Rol, he is what interests me, not cobwebbed memories," Rowen said. "The past is over, finished. I have proposals for the future, on the other hand, that may interest you."

"Why am I here?"

She pulled a sad face. "Is it not enough that you see me again?"

"Coquetry does not become you."

"It is something I have had to learn; another skill, like killing."

"To be here, I gave up my ship and her company. I tramped halfway across a continent. Now I have seen you, and I ask again: Why am I here?" The blood rose in Rol's face as he spoke, and in his eyes there grew a light wholly unlike that from the fire. There was within it a wintry chill that held no hope of spring. Rowen nodded, watching.

"I wanted my brother here, to be—"

"Spare me the bullshit; Canker has already been down that road."

She was silent, white and still as something carved out of porphyry. She had once exuded sadness like a perfume; now it had turned into something rank.

"I wanted my brother here," she repeated with dangerous softness. "I wanted someone I valued to be by my side in this great undertaking of mine. Someone I trusted."

"Canker you can trust, and that fool outside. They would slit their own throats if they thought you wished to see the color of blood."

"Yes, I have many people about me who would do anything I wanted, but none of them would be willing to say the things you have said. I want—" She stopped and lowered her head again, though her face was coldly angry now, remote and perilous. More like the woman he had known.

"I'm not here to kill for you," Rol said. There were so many things whirling about in his brain. He took bitterness, because it was convenient, and flung it at her.

"I don't need any more killers," she retorted. "They're outside in their thousands."

They glared at each other. Once again, this seemed somehow fitting. It reminded them of past intimacies, and the ice melted a little.

"What would you say if I told you I need a friend?" Rowen asked, her voice hard as a plane and her slim fists clenched white. So slim, so fine, and he had seen them take men's lives with the consummate ease of a true professional. He craved the feel of them on his skin.

"I don't want to be your friend. I have enough of those already."

She rose in one fluid motion, like water pouring in reverse, and walked over to him, stood by his side so close he could smell her. Lavender; she had always stored her clothes with it. The smell hurled him back into the fogged alleyways and mysteries of his past. The black, bead-strewn velvet of her taut belly was a foot from his face.

"I have none," she said.

She ran her hands into his hair, and he encircled her slim

waist, pulled her close, and buried his face in her warmth. He could feel the toned muscle of her back through the stuff of her dress. Beads popped off under his fingers and ticked onto the floor. He rose, his face nosing between her breasts, up to her collarbones, the small of her neck, her ear. Their eyelashes butterflied together. He set his mouth on hers and felt it come to life under his lips. The tips of their tongues circled each other, their body's water mingling.

She drew back. A low moan in the air between them, and neither knew who had uttered it.

"No," she said, and her voice was thickened and raw. "We can't do this. Have you forgotten, Fisheye, who and what we are?"

"I don't give a fuck," Rol snarled. "People may think what they like. Even now, we could be happy, Rowen. Alone in all the world, we are the only people who could make each other content."

"No," she said softly, and turned away. Her feet crunched the jet beads underfoot to tiny shards of broken glass. "I must go now; there's a lot to be done. We'll talk later."

"Rowen!"

But she left the room without looking back.

Some time later—a long time, it seemed—the door of the room opened and a maid peeped her head round it. "Sir, it is past morning, and if you will break fast now, I have things here for you, and a valet awaits also."

Rol did not reply. He was sitting staring into the dead depths of the fire and picking a stick apart with his fingers, feeding it splinter by splinter into the last flame. The maid rustled into the room with a tray, wide-eyed as a mouse. There was a table, which she set for one, laying out food and drink with clicks and small clatters and the glug of good wine hitting the bottom of a glass. Rol raised his red-eyed face. Rage and grief had carved it into something not quite human. "What's your name?"

"Eben, sir." She clutched the wine decanter to her bosom as though it were a protective talisman. Rol stood up and cast aside his gutted stick. He pried the decanter from her warm fingers and looked her up and down dispassionately. She was a short, black-haired girl with fine green eyes and plump breasts that peered over the rim of her bodice. Rol took one of those breasts in his hand, staring down in her face. Her mouth opened, and he bent, kissed it shut again, his teeth biting down on her lips. His other hand seized her rump through the folds of her dress and kneaded it. She made piteous little squeaking sounds. He grasped her white throat, his tanned skin dark as leather about her windpipe. She moaned in fear, tears gathering thickly at the corners of her eyes.

"Get out," he said, and slapped her on the buttocks. "Send in your damned valet." He drank back a tall, bulbous goblet of red wine and felt it warm the black passageways of his innards. Ah, Psellos, he thought with bitter amusement, would you not be proud of me now.

"Sir, the Queen has requested that your wardrobe be refreshed in a manner fitting your station." This from a tall, thin, whey-faced fellow whose nose and Adam's apple vied for prominence in an otherwise forgettable face.

The *Queen.* I had almost forgotten.

"Indeed; well, show me your wares." Rol sat down and began wolfing chunks of roast chicken, wedging slices of ham between slabs of bread and spreading all liberally with mustard. He was starved; he did not know if it was night or day outside, but his stomach had not eaten its fill in longer than he could remember. He bit into the food as though it had somehow slighted him, and washed it down with throat-aching swallows of wine. Damn you, he was thinking. Damn you. Damn ambition and the stupidity of people's pride and the fucked-up fantasies of all damaged souls.

The valet stood perspiring, his Adam's apple bobbing up and down like a fisherman's float. Rol finally wiped his mouth and rose from the wreckage of the table. His head swam, and his stomach performed a greasy, interminable roll. "Let's see what you've got."

Court clothes, stuff that looked well enough in a warm hall but which would be sodden rags within half a day if worn out in the elements. Rol picked through it in disgust. A shirt with a ruffled front as proud as the breast of a pouting pigeon. A wide scarlet sash more suited to opera than practical wear. He could not bring himself to pick anything else, but donned once more his travel-worn breeches and filthy boots, which had been piled beside the bed.

"What is this room?" he asked the valet, hauling on his damp footwear. He knew now it was not Rowen's chamber. It had been touchingly absurd of him to even hope it.

"We're in the East Wing, on the upper side, sir," the valet said diffidently. "The Guest Wing."

"Where are my friends?"

"Sir?"

"I should have been brought here with three others, one of them a halftroll."

The valet's brow cleared. "They have rooms in the Old Wing, near the ground." He gave a significant look which passed Rol by. He simply nodded, and stamped his toes into the end of his boots. "And where is my sword?"

"I know of no sword, sir. You had best broach that matter with the commander of the Guard. It was his men who brought you to this room. You had no weapon on you that I could see."

Rol smiled grimly. "I see. Thank you . . ."

"Harkenn, sir. Abel Harkenn. I am to be your bodyservant."

"There's a first for everything, I suppose. Right now, Harkenn, I want you to find me a bucket, because I believe breakfast is about to reappear."

Rol had never walked the corridors of a palace before. Upon leaving his room, feeling a little hollow but no longer queasy, he was joined without invitation or fanfare by two sturdy fellows in well-made black livery that was trimmed in scarlet. They bore long poniards and a pair of pistols each, and as he caught their eye they nodded like men who have kept an appointment.

"What's this, an escort?"

"Orders of the Queen herself, sir."

"Why? To keep me from getting lost?"

They stared at him woodenly. Rol rubbed his forehead. "All right, then. Tell me, where can I find this Gideon Mirkady?"

"The commander of the Guard?"

"The very man. Take me to him, if you please."

The two soldiers looked at each other. One shrugged fractionally. Preceded by one and followed by another, Rol made his way through a series of narrow and bewildering passageways, all built out of well-plastered and painted stone and lit by swarms of oil-fed lamps which flickered above head height. Passing them, there came in motley succession a traffic of maids, manservants, palace guards, who acknowledged Rol's escorts with minute nods, no more, and much grander men and women who made walking into a processional and would have looked down their noses at Rol had they been tall enough to do so.

He realized that with his mismatched court finery and ragamuffin traveling clothes, he looked like nothing so much as a gypsy thief, and that thought gave him a little pleasure as he winked at noblemen and leered at their daughters. More than anything else at this moment, he would have liked one of them to take offense and seek redress in some time-honored manner that would result in the spilling of blood. He would never fit in here, and did not ever intend to, so he would play the part of boor. Why not? Much of his education and inclination lay that way.

Below all of these merriments there burned the blackened embers of a dream he had not even admitted to having, all these years. Whatever it was—and he did not care to examine it too closely—he knew that Rowen did not share it. He knew now that none of this would end happily.

Down they went, descending marble and granite stairways on which coaches could have passed without touching axles. The palace, or this wing of it, opened out. It seemed to have been built as a series of vast reception rooms interconnected by a bewildering series of passages and corridors and serviced by kitchens, storerooms, and servants' quarters all tucked neatly in convenient but largely unseen orbits about these huge central spaces. Once, Rol found his way to a long avenue of windows as tall as Gallico, and he looked out of them upon a city that was not the greatest in the world, but which had certainly been the epicenter of the world's greatest power. The winter-dark beyond the glass defied his efforts to decipher what time of day it was, and he had to ask one of his escorting soldiers. The man looked at him strangely.

"It's late afternoon, sir."

He had been unconscious longer than he had thought. This Mirkady packed a shrewd blow. And now he had Fleam, it seemed. Well, that would have to change.

The business of the palace seemed little affected by the fact that Myconn was under siege, and if anything it seemed to be mustering a surfeit of revelry. Rol passed packed ballrooms where dancing and masquerades were in full swing, and legions of waiters stood by with silver trays amid the hoot of woodwind and whine of strings. Admittedly, there seemed little enough upon those trays. More liquor than food, it seemed. Perhaps that added to the frenzied nature of the gaiety. He passed one gorgeously caparisoned masked couple fornicating in a less than discreet alcove, the lady's skirts hitched up high over her silken thighs, the man pumping into her with clenched teeth, as though he were performing a noble but necessary chore. Rol turned to one of his taciturn escorts. "How many levels are there to this palace?"

"I don't know, sir. Many. More than I have ever counted."

"Is it all in one block?"

"The main part is, sir. It's like a tower, hex-shaped. It rises high over the river, just by the Palace Bridge."

"And who built it? How old is it?"

But the man clamped his mouth shut at a glare from his companion. After that they strode along in not-so-companionable silence, except for grunts from the soldiers to indicate the way. Rol's head began to swim again, and he had to halt and be sick in the pot of some tall standing plant. Not much left to come up but bile. He fingered the black bump on the side of his head and staggered on.

Lower down, the stonework was more massive, and obviously older. Whereas the upper levels had been built for the pleasures of the nobility, it seemed that these parts were more akin to a fortress. And they had seen recent fighting. Rol could see blackened spots in the walls where shells had impacted, holes with the dull gray fragments of lead bullets still embedded. He guessed they dated from Rowen's seizure of the palace from its former owner. There were more men in the livery of the guard here also, dour-faced bastards for the most part; they reminded him somehow of Miriam's musketeers, obviously wedded to their duty and missing a sense of humor.

"Here," his own particular dour-faced bastard said, pointing to tall double-doors of black bronze-bound oak. These, too, were pitted with bullet-holes, but the evidence of battle seemed merely to make them seem more indestructible. The wood of their making reminded Rol of the *Revenant*'s hull, and he realized that they were not oak, after all, but black Kassic teak, the same as that which comprised his ship's timbers. He patted the doors affectionately as he passed through them. It was like the glimpse of an old friend in a strange place.

The legendary arrogance of the Bionari was reflected in their architecture. They were drawn to high, vaulted ceilings and broad pillars, platforms and daises that sought to embody authority in the relative heights of men's eyes. Thus it was that Rol found Gideon Mirkady staring down at him from behind a long black desk of teak which looked almost as old as the door outside. This was set on a four-foot dais, and coming and going from its black height were dozens of guardsmen with messages and the like. Rol wondered how many were here to stride self-importantly about the palace, and how many were out in the snow and shrapnel of the city defenses, facing Bar Asfal's army.

Mirkady was a good-looking fellow with economically padded bones and black ringleted hair which fell past his collar. He stared down at Rol and raised one eyebrow with just the right mixture of boredom and disdain.

"We meet again. Cortishane, is it not? I trust your quarters are adequate."

"You have something of mine," Rol said, and in the corners of the grand lobby about the dais, guardsmen paused discreetly to listen.

"What might that be?"

"A sword. I'll have it back, thank you."

Mirkady blinked. With a flash of his old training, Rol realized that he was weighing how far he could go. This man had been Rowen's lover, and obviously was besotted by her. The arrival of a brother, a rival for her affections and her patronage, had goaded him into a single act of viciousness, and he was wondering if he had already overplayed his hand.

"By all means," Mirkady said frostily. "A mere oversight. It should have been sent on to your quarters." He leaned aside and spoke to a guardsman standing next to him with a pregnant bundle of papers. The man nodded, hurried off.

Rol stepped up to the dais; he did not appreciate being looked down on by a man like Mirkady. "How goes the siege?" he asked.

"As well as can be expected."

"I'd have thought these popinjays of yours would be better employed out on the walls than running about in here conveying paperwork."

Mirkady flushed, but give him credit, he managed a civil smile through the hatred in his eyes.

"We all do stints on the walls, but the business of a great city must go on, even in times such as these."

Rol looked around the imposing chamber. It was hung with meaningless heraldic tapestries and antique weapons. The place was unheated, and cold as a tomb. The only windows were louvered openings high up on one wall, and through their slits he could see the dark blue of a winter's afternoon nosing down into dusk. Oil lamps burned on the dais and in sockets on the walls, but by their smell, they were fueled more by tallow than anything else. Perhaps the siege was having an effect, after all.

"How far is it to the walls from here?"

"Just under a league. You're quite safe, I assure you." Rol and Gideon smiled at each other. A moment of complete understanding, almost a kind of respect. Here, Rol knew, was a man he would likely one day have to kill. He did not even question why.

The guardsman came back with Fleam, still in her scabbard.

He handed the scimitar to Rol and wiped his hands down his breeches after, as though he had been touching something unclean. Some tense tightness about Rol's chest loosened as he buckled the weapon at his waist. The sword felt warm against his thigh, and he patted it as a man might the head of a faithful hound. Mirkady's eyes blazed up in brief, unalloyed interest.

"That's a fine weapon."

Rol did not reply, but turned and stepped down from the dais, walking away. He could almost smell the anger he left in his wake, and it made him smile.

Fourteen

PICTURES IN THE DARK

THE QUARTERS ASSIGNED TO GALLICO, CREED, AND GIFFON looked to have been those of palace servants at one time. They were warm enough, situated next to the kitchens, but lightless, poky places. The trio hardly cared, being content to have eaten their fill along with the kitchen-staff, regale goggle-eyed maids with tall tales of derring-do, and then stretch out like logs to sleep without dream or fear of cockcrow. When Rol found them, they were back at the long refectory table in the kitchen; the immense cooking hearths to their rear were banked down to sulking coals, and they were supping on heavily watered, steaming oatmeal leavened with salt and a little barley spirit. Around them the night shift was turning up for duty, yawning and stretching and stirring the fires and consulting lists.

Rol stood in the doorway of the place, felt the welcome heat of it soak into his bones, and sucked in the smells, savoring them. This beat any palace. In places such as this, he felt he could almost be himself, and leave behind the sneering little doppelganger of Michal Psellos, which sat on his shoulder ever more often these days.

"If you two are going to stay here, then you'd best sit down and loosen those tight collars," Rol told his escorts. Sweat was trickling down their faces already. One shrugged, and they did as he suggested. They were served bowls of food without comment, and tucked in with a will, supping the watery porridge with horn spoons.

Looking around at the growing bustle of the kitchens, the low, buttressed ceilings, the hanging hams and onion-strings, Rol wondered that his friends had been accommodated down here, treated like folk of a lower order than himself, but he decided not to dwell on it.

"Oatmeal gruel, is that all we have for supper?" he asked Gallico. The halftroll sat cross-legged on the floor but his eyes were still on a level with the maids'. They seemed unabashed by his appearance and flirted outrageously with Creed and Giffon as they prepared food around them; more results of the siege perhaps. Creed was grinning but Giffon had his nose almost in his gruel, and his ears were scarlet.

"We had a decent feed earlier, but most of the good stuff goes upstairs, it seems," Gallico told him, wiping his mouth. "Almost four months they've been blockaded, but the cooks tell me that a great deal of foodstuff still makes its way in through the hills on pack-mules by night. Merchants from the west pay Bar Asfal's soldiers to look the other way, and are recompensed by the great and the good here in Myconn, in gold, silver, family heirlooms, whatever they'll take. You can pay a silver minim for a chicken, they tell me. The poor, they live on lentils and oatmeal and horsemeat. They'll be skinning cats soon."

"We've eaten worse," Rol said. Like most mariners, he was fairly indifferent to what he put in his mouth as long as it did not poison him. He joined his shipmates and the two guardsmen at the table and leaned his elbows on the smooth wood. A knot of the kitchen staff gathered in the corner and whispered and peered at him, and whispered again. He still felt too sick to eat, and pushed away the steaming bowl that was set down in front of him, but smiled at the girl who set it there. She looked like a rabbit made to wait on a fox. Rol sighed, and rubbed his face with the palms of his hands, squeezing bursting patterns of amorphous light behind his eyelids. The heat of the long room was soporific, tempting him to lay his head down on the table.

"Still some sleep to catch up on, I see," the voice said, and he jerked open his eyes to see Rowen seated in front of him. The two guardsmen had risen to their feet in wooden alarm, but all the rest of the folk in the kitchen, Rol's friends included, seemed wholly unfazed.

Rowen took Rol's untested porridge and began to eat it with every appearance of appetite. She jerked her head at the guardsmen. "Off you go, back to Mirkady. Cortishane has no further need of you." The men bowed deep and left, tugging close their loosened collars and smoothing down their tunics as they went. Rowen went on eating her porridge composedly. She was dressed in dun-colored peasant clothes, and her long hair hung free down her back, a raven mane that shone in the firelight. A slim throwing knife hung from her waist in a wooden scabbard. She looked very young.

Rol leaned back on his long bench. Creed glanced at him. "What's up—you seen a ghost?"

"Elias, this lady here—"

"She served us our food last night, after we got in," Creed interrupted. He winked at Rowen. "A handsome lass. But girl, you could do with a little more meat on your bones."

"I'll bear that in mind," Rowen said dryly.

"Do you often slum it down here with the lower orders?" Rol asked her.

"I like it here," she said. "The staff are used to seeing me. I like the heat, the smell. I always did like kitchens. You should know that, Rol."

"I remember."

"What's this?" Gallico said archly. "You know this wench, Rol—what is she, an old flame?"

"In a manner of speaking." A smile went between their eyes as Rol and Rowen stared at each other. She set her hand on the tabletop, and he placed his own down next to it so that their fingers touched. A moment, no more.

"This is Rowen Bar Hethrun, Gallico. Some call her Queen of Bionar."

"And I'm the Queen of the May. Don't let him mock you, lass."

"I won't," Rowen said. "And if he lacks the manners of his friends, I will not hold it against him. Some folk are not so well brought up as others."

"Aye." Gallico grinned. "You must watch this one. He'll have you on your back given half a chance, and then walk away afterward with nothing more than a wink and a fare-thee-well."

"See? Now you've been warned," Rol told Rowen.

"I will keep it in mind," she said. She stood up, and seemed to hesitate a second. Then, leaning over the table, she took Rol's face in her cold hands and kissed him, a feather touch, no more. "I must go. They want me upstairs."

Giffon was staring at her in open adoration, porridge dripping from his forgotten spoon. Rol knew now why she had billeted his friends down here. It was a place she felt comfortable.

"They will want to talk to you later," she said. The weariness was slipping back into her face now.

"Who?"

"The nobles. My officers. I'm sending couriers to Canker through the hills. In two days, we make our move."

Rol's momentary happiness was snuffed out. He wanted her

to stay there in the busy warmth of the kitchens, and exchange banter with his friends, and be an ordinary woman who touched his fingers with her own.

"Until later, then."

"I see you got your sword back," Rowen said, and with that she left. No fanfare, no roll of drums. Just another serving-maid.

Gallico was sucking his teeth thoughtfully. "She was, wasn't she?"

"Yes, Gallico, she was. Elias, you just told the Queen of Bionar she needs fattening up."

Creed picked soggy oatmeal out of his beard. "Well, she does."

It was late, but Abel Harkenn was an insistent man, and Rol was too tired to argue with his deeply held conviction that a fellow invited to the Queen's Council Chamber must look the part. So when the breathless page-boy came to fetch him, he found a tall man with pale eyes and a neatly trimmed beard, dressed in sable doublet and hose and bearing a light scimitar on a baldric of black leather. Buckled halfboots completed the attire. The clothes were a little musty from long storage, but the doublet had panels of dyed leather stitched in the shoulders and back, which supported Rol's torso agreeably as he made his way through the bewildering passageways and corridors of the Bar Madivar Palace, steadily gaining height by way of staircase after staircase, until he stood before towering teak double-doors. Two guardsmen with silver-pointed halberds asked him his name and his business. The Queen of the May, he almost answered, here to steal away a serving-maid. But he took his tongue out of his cheek and told them.

He had a couple of copper minims for the page-boy, who

scampered off brim-full of gossip and bursting to spread it, and the doors opened before him on soundless hinges, though they must have weighed a half ton apiece.

Imperial Bionar, eldest of the Kingdoms of Men. Well, here it was, in all the pomp and finery it could muster.

Tall windows, looking out onto darkness. Some were broken and boarded up, but enough remained to give a sense of the night looming beyond the glass. The snow was falling again, in the blue dark, and down at the walls men would still be trying to kill one another across a shell-holed purgatory of beaten ground.

In here, the high ceiling was corniced and painted and hung with three tremendous chandeliers, fifty candles burning in each and reflecting off an infinity of faceted crystal. Three large fireplaces covered the length of the room. The fragrant tang of the flames within them caught at Rol's memory. Peat, like that he had once burned in a cottage on Dennifrey. He had not known there were peat-bogs around Myconn.

There was a long table, as long as the one he had sat at in the kitchens, but finer, and instead of benches there were twoscore gilt chairs with scarlet leather upholstery and a coat of arms painted on the back of every one. More candles, set at random in a forest of candelabras, and sheaves of paper, light-catching decanters, brass dividers, maps, inkwells of cut glass with silver rims, quills, and the knives for trimming them. The stuff of committees, of decision-making, of discussion. He wondered how much of it all was really necessary.

The nobility of Bionar. Some two dozen men sat the length of the table, their eyes turning toward him as he entered. Rowen sat at the head. The serving-maid had disappeared, and in her place there was a severely elegant woman all in black, no ornament save a silver fillet in her hair. He knew now the reason for his new wardrobe; it matched Rowen's perfectly. They were an exercise in sable.

"Beside me, Rol," she said, and patted the chair to her left. Rol took his seat, and found Gideon Mirkady's handsome face opposite him. The Guard commander smiled and inclined his head slightly. Rol did likewise. He felt he had just walked onstage, and the curtain had risen.

"Continue, gentlemen," Rowen said. "Introductions can wait. In any case, you all know this man is my brother, Rol Cortishane. Lord Brage, you had the table."

A florid-faced man with a heavy nose, Lord Brage looked like a soldier who had fallen in love with the bottle. His stare outdid courtesy. For a naked moment, Rol sat at the end of the endless table, and the great men of this old, broken empire feasted the greed of their eyes upon him without shame.

Collecting himself, Brage peered at a leaf of paper before him, eyes watering.

"Yes, Majesty. To continue, I must report that we lost thirty-eight men today, fourteen of those killed and only half a dozen of the remainder ever likely to fight again. That leaves our current strength at just over six and a half thousand, all told." He looked up the table at Rowen. "The dysentery that plagued the sections around the Palestrinon Gate has been contained, for now. We filled in two wells, which seems to have done the trick."

"Very good, my lord. Gideon, how many of the garrison would you recommend we could take out without exposing the city completely?"

Mirkady's face was bleak. "We can barely maintain a defense of the circuit as it is, Majesty." His hand flapped helplessly on the table. "If we left a bare minimum—a dangerous minimum— to man the barbicans and, say, one in four of the wall-guns, then we could sortie with some four and a half to five thousand."

The table murmured at this. Rowen's face was unmoved. Her steel-gray eyes looked them up and down, and the murmuring ceased instantly.

"Very good. We shall take out five thousand. Cavalry?"

"Two hundred at most, Majesty. We've lost heavily in horses these last months."

"Ammunition?"

"No shortage of that, or arquebuses either. We'll outfit every man of the sortie with half armor and fifty rounds."

"Field artillery?"

"Plenty of demi-culverins, twelve-pounders, but nothing to haul them with, Majesty. The wall-guns will support us."

"Very well; we will do without. As you say, the wall—"

"Men can draw guns," Rol said. Up and down the table, the assembled officers stared at him in astonishment. Because he had interrupted Rowen.

The Queen's eyes were cold as glass. "Explain."

"A dozen men can move a twelve-pounder as fast as any mule-team, if it's over broken ground—and that ground beyond the walls is shot up all to hell. Charge them with canister, park them hub to hub, and you could stand off an army."

There was a somewhat chilly silence.

"My men are not draft animals," Mirkady said with a curl of his lip.

"They are not," Rowen said softly. "They are soldiers, and as such will obey orders. You will ready as many batteries as you see fit, Gideon, and assign men to move them as well as crew them."

Mirkady bowed his head in answer.

"Your Majesty," another man said, a broad, blue-jawed fellow with a broken nose and the look of one who would whip his dogs, "how many men does Lord Canker have with him?"

"He has enough, Blayloc, and all of them veterans from the northern commands, hard fighters who have held the line of the Embrun these six months. What's more, he will have surprise on his side, and a thousand cavalry to guard our flanks. Bar Asfal's host in the Gallitran camps numbers some eighteen thousand. If we can break them before his forces in the Destrir and Palestrinon encampments can come up, then the battle will be already won. Gentlemen, these next few days will see the culmination of all our efforts. I mean to make this the end of it; Bionar has suffered enough."

A silence met this last remark. The assembled officers lowered their eyes, or in a few cases exchanged discreet glances with one another. Looking up and down the table, Rol realized that Rowen's hold on these men was fraying. If this adventure failed, they would desert her, seek terms with the loyalists. If she did not die in battle, these men would be among her executioners.

He caught her eye with this knowledge still in his own, and she nodded fractionally. She knew also.

"What about timings?" Blayloc asked.

It was Mirkady who spoke up. "We take out the army at dawn, two days from now. Blayloc, your regiments will be in the van. Cassidus, your brigade will follow. Remion, yours will bring up the rear. We sally forth from the Warder, at the double, and do not begin to deploy until halfway to the enemy lines."

"Their guns will tear up our columns before we've even shaken into line," someone protested.

"We need to cover that ground quickly, Remius; and more importantly, all regiments must clear the gate as swiftly as possible. We stay in column for the first quarter-mile." Mirkady looked somewhat dogged as he said this. Rol guessed that he was of two minds about it himself.

"If we do haul out artillery with us, it shall be at the rear." Mirkady looked at Rowen, and she inclined her head.

"Canker's men had best be on time," Blayloc said savagely. "Or we shall all die there, in column or line or whatever way their guns find us."

"Canker knows his duty," Rowen said coldly. "As do we all.

Gentlemen, this meeting is adjourned. Go to your commands. Quartermaster Affrick, you will fulfill any and all requests for supplies and equipment that are presented to you. No man shall leave Myconn's gates who is not fully kitted out and carrying as much ammunition as he can bear. That is all, my lords."

The long lines of men stood up, Rol included. Two dozen formidable, ambitious, pride-filled lords of men, and every one there aware that the best of them was not a man at all. They bowed to her as one, then trooped out without speaking another word.

Rowen shook her head at Rol, waved on Mirkady when he hesitated. The Queen and her brother sat on as the nobles and officers of her last army left the room, and the great doors banged hollow at their backs.

"You have a wolf by the ears," Rol told her, helping himself to brandy from a shining decanter.

"And what would you know about it?" She stood up, energy crackling out of her. "Do not presume to interrupt me in front of my officers, Fisheye, ever again. We are not sat here playing at pirates. If you have some homespun wisdom to impart, make sure you do so with the proper deference."

Rol's fingers creaked about his glass. "What will you do, Rowen, take me out and have me whipped?"

"If necessary, yes." That cold light in her eyes, akin to his own. He knew if he pressed her that they would be at each other's throats, here, now, in the very Council Chamber of Myconn. The training clicked in, and he found himself automatically mapping the way she stood, how she stood poised there on the balls of her feet like a dancer. There were throwing stars holstered along her ribs; he saw the tiny lined bulge under the dress for the first time.

Rowen's white, taut face relaxed a little. Her hands sank to her sides.

"Do not forget where you are," she said in a low voice.

"I came here because of you, and you alone."

"You came here because of a memory. Things cannot ever be the way they were, Rol. You are my brother." Her voice cracked.

"That does not matter to me."

"It matters to *me*."

There was a knock on the discreet side door. "Enter," Rowen said without shifting her gaze from Rol's face.

In came a small, bent man with a wisp of beard and a silver basin. He bowed without meeting their eyes, and padding over to Rowen, he set down the basin and began unwrapping a silken bundle he held in the palm of his hand. "It is time, Majesty."

The tension left Rowen's body. She sagged, looking instantly ten years older.

"Already?"

"Yes, Majesty. Forgive me. Your own orders . . ." The little man was plainly frightened.

Rowen tugged her sleeve up over her forearm to the elbow. With a start, Rol saw that the inside of her arm was covered in tiny little crescent-shaped scabs and older scars, all following the line of the blue vein that coursed through her pale skin.

"The usual amount?" the old, bent man asked. From his silken bundle he had taken a blade, a whetstone, and a needle threaded with white silk.

"Yes, but be quick, Marmius. I have things to do."

Rol watched with a kind of grim fascination as Marmius deftly sliced open the vein, and as the scarlet ichor within began to pour out, he set Rowen's arm over the basin and watched it fill with an unpleasant kind of satisfaction. Rowen pumped her fist open and closed to keep the blood trickling. All at once, Rol was back in Psellos's Tower, and the blood was his, his monthly payment. He turned away, tossing back the brandy in his glass, feeling sick with ebbing adrenaline, and a kind of grief.

It did not take long. When the process was over, Marmius left the way he had come, holding the silver basin as though it were made of eggshell. Rowen poured herself a tall glass of wine from a decanter and drank it off without a blink.

"What was it Psellos used to call it?" she asked. "Room and board. Well, here it buys armies, or the men who lead them, at least."

"Is it worth it, Rowen?"

"I intend that it shall be. One day, it shall be." She drank more wine. Her face was white as paper. He knew now there was nothing he could say to help her, no words that would re-call the woman he had once known. Her face was that of a stranger, not the dream he had carried in his heart all these years. And yet, and yet . . .

"You have not seen the Turmian yet, have you, Rol?"

He smiled vacantly. "I've not seen anything beyond the walls of this palace."

"We must fix that. We have time. There will be a ball the night before we take the troops out, but until then, the nobles will be busy with their regiments. We have some time. Would you care to ride out with the Queen?"

A closed carriage took them through the gates of the Bar Madivar Palace. It was a beautifully sprung vehicle, and the road passed smoothly under them. Apart from a trio of armed footmen, they were unescorted, their vehicle unmarked by livery of any kind. They passed without comment, and Rol peered out at the world through a chink in the curtained window. It was dark again—it seemed always to be dark here—and now that they were beyond the mighty confines of the palace, he could hear the artillery rumbling down at the walls, over a mile and a half away.

Myconn seemed crowded, and the streets were choked with traffic where they were not choked with rubble. Construction here had been going on in a grand scale for centuries, and on all sides monumental buildings reared up in waves of stone, though many had broken glass in their windows, and more lacked complete roofs.

"This is where it began," Rowen said. "In Myconn itself." She pulled her heavy black cloak more tightly about herself, stifling a shiver. "Mirkady was the first to come over, and then Blayloc and Brage. Their troops garrisoned the city, and were happy enough to change allegiances, given the right incentives."

"Blood," Rol said somberly. "Sex. Money. All three perhaps?"

Rowen's eyes sparkled with anger. "All three indeed. Canker and I approached from the north, even as Bar Asfal has done, while Mirkady and the others raised hell within the city itself. Bar Hethrun—my father—was a popular man, and legend had made him more so. Bar Asfal is a greedy, small-minded wretch, and people were quite willing for the Lost Heir to return, even if she was a woman. Once he heard the boom of our artillery, Bar Asfal fled. Some of his folk made a stand in and around the palace, but by and large, Myconn remained intact. Only now it has been battered relentlessly for some four months of siege, and the walls are crumbling, as is the resolve of its defenders. The thing is nearly finished."

"You may beat him in battle, but unless you kill Bar Asfal himself, the thing will never be finished," Rol said. "If there's one thing I've learned in the past few weeks, it's that these Bionari are stubborn bastards; give them a flag to follow and they'll march behind it through blood and slaughter. As long as the loyalists have a figurehead, they'll never give up."

"Quite true," Rowen said quietly. "That is why we must be sure Bar Asfal does not live through the coming battle." Her eyes were fixed on his. There was almost a kind of pleading in them, but she turned her head away without saying anything more.

"You want me to kill him for you," Rol said tautly. Rowen did not reply. "I don't do knives in the dark anymore, Rowen; I leave that to you and Canker."

"Not in the dark," she said. "It must be public, in battle, at the height of the fight."

Rol laughed. "Don't you have an army at your back? What need have you of me to do your dirty work?"

"I know you can do it, if anyone can." A bleak smile. "I trust you to do it, if you say you will."

"I'll fight for you, Rowen, but that's all. Don't count on any special favors."

They said nothing more. The little candle-lamp in the carriage threw Rowen's face into cruel relief. It was thinner than Rol had ever seen it, and her eyes were sunken. She did not look as though she relished what lay ahead. More than anything, Rol wanted to take her in his arms and kiss shut those tired eyes, but he knew he could not.

The carriage came to a halt and the driver opened a small hatch in the roof and spoke quietly. "The Turmian Library, my lady."

"Very good, Badir. Wait here. We go in alone, my brother and I."

Rol took her hand as she stepped down from the carriage, and she leaned her slim weight on it, swaying a little as her feet met the cobbles. "You're draining yourself dry," Rol said with a jet of concern he could not conceal.

"I'll be all right. Help me up these damn steps."

A towering portico loomed up in the wintry night, its pillars two fathoms wide at the base. They were in the higher streets to the south of the palace, and the sound of the guns was a dull flickering thunder off at the edge of the world. Myconn sprawled out below them, a sea of stone and slate teeming with half the refugees of a kingdom. Rol could pick out the outline of the palace over a mile away by the many lights in its windows. It seemed impossibly tall.

Rowen produced a key and a small lantern from the folds of her cloak. The Turmian's doors were three times the height of a man, bound with bronze that had greened with age, but near their base there was a postern. The key turned smoothly, and Rowen pushed in the little door, then gestured to Rol with a small, cold smile. "After you, brother."

There was a sense of echoing space, of moving air. It took a moment for Rol's eyes to adjust to the utter, impenetrable blackness, and just when his unnatural sight was beginning to assert itself, Rowen struck a light and set it to the wick of her oil lantern, dropping the glass with a snap. At once, the half-guessed outlines of the building around them retreated into the golden confines of the lantern-light.

"Can you still see in the dark?" Rowen asked innocently.

"Now and then. This place is black as the inside of a tomb."

"It stays locked at night, for fear of looters. During the day, only a few select scholars are admitted. Once, it was open to any citizen who had a mind to open a book, but times change. People are not so interested in reading anymore; they're more interested in finding something to fill their bellies."

"Who can blame them?" Rol asked.

Their footsteps echoed and the lantern-light sent their shadows capering up the walls. They were in a kind of foyer whose walls reared up into black shadow. There were tableaux carved in bas-relief into the stone, soldiers and horses and kings with expressionless faces, a long strip of chiseled stories, and writing that Rol could not read. Rowen raised the lantern higher.

"Old Bionese. Not many can read it now; they say it was

related to Waric, the tongue of the Weres." Her breath
steamed out white as smoke.

"Come, this way."

The foyer was long and empty, without furnishing. The only
ornaments were on the walls. Below the line of bas-reliefs
were a series of gilt-framed paintings, each taller than Rol.
Within them, stern, pale faces gazed out from below a cracked
glaze of varnish; men in archaic armor with crowns on their
heads, dressed in regal robes and holding weapons too ornate
to be of practical use.

"Who are these fellows?" Rol asked, gazing up.

"The Kings of Bionar—or the most recent ones, at any rate.
In ancient times they lined this chamber as statues, but that
stopped a century or so ago with the coming of the genius
painter Ordivalle from Urbonetto. After that, the fashion was
for portraiture, and the old statues were stripped out. They
still dot the palace here and there." Rowen stopped before one
of the last paintings and held the lantern as high as she could.
"See here; this is the man who began all the trouble. My father,
Bar Hethrun."

"I'll be damned." She was in his face. Bar Hethrun had been
a man of great beauty, with features both delicate and hard.
There was perhaps a weakness about the chin which had no
place on Rowen's face, and the color of the eyes was entirely
different, but the resemblance was striking all the same.

"I am my father's daughter, I've been told," Rowen said. She
moved on a few paces and raised the lantern again. "And here
is the last of the line."

In this painting, the sitter was in half armor of marvelous
workmanship, and he stared down at them with none of the
regal detachment of Bar Hethrun. A stockier man, if the artist
had caught him rightly, he looked like someone who continually found fault with the world. He had a small, black beard
and his eyes were dark as Laugran olives. A hint of jowl; he

would flesh out as he grew older, though in the painting he looked to be in his early thirties.

"Bar Asfal," Rowen said. "The man we fight."

"He would be older now."

"Yes, almost fifty. He has filled out and gone grayer since this was painted, but he is not so different."

"You know him personally?"

"I was his courtesan for a year, back at the beginning. It's as good a way into Court as any." Rol stared at her.

"Come; we'd best move on. There's still a ways to go." She led Rol past Bar Asfal's dark eyes, and the light went with her. For a long moment, Rol stood motionless in the dark as her footsteps went on ahead, then finally he followed.

Another tall door, another postern opened with a turn of the same key. Beyond it, the sound fell softer on their ears, soaked up by something other than stone. Lines of massive pillars trooped off into the darkness, and in between them were enormous shelved bookcases, scores of them, all piled high with scrolls and books and loose-leaved manuscripts, ten thousand years of reading all in one room.

"The main reading room," Rowen said. "See? There are desks here for those who wish to browse. Only in Myconn could a man or woman sit down and read anything they had a mind to take off a shelf. It is part of this kingdom's greatness. Psellos came here, many times. But this is only part of the whole. Under our feet, the hill has been tunneled out in centuries of labor, and there are whole libraries underground, more specialized knowledge, rarer books. Some are so fragile they can no longer be read. Some are written in languages no longer spoken. The Kings of Bionar were collectors of knowledge. Every time they fought a war, conquered a country, they brought that place's heritage back here to line the walls of their library."

"The most harmful kind of plundering I can think of," Rol

said. "It wasn't enough to defeat a nation, they would steal its identity and bring it back here to molder in the dark."

"They made a storehouse of knowledge that was open to all," Rowen said crisply. "They preserved."

"They raped," Rol said.

"That is a matter of opinion."

They found a steep set of stairs, and at their base yet another locked door. It opened on a deeper chill, and the dust-smell of dry paper. Rol sneezed. He felt he was descending deeper into the maw of a grave. Rowen's face was set in white resolve, though she staggered slightly when they reached the foot of the stairs. Rol put his arm about her waist, slipping it under the thick cloak. She seemed lean as whipcord, with no warmth to her flesh. One moment, she leaned into him, then she drew away.

"The Formian Level," she said. "Once, this was above-ground. Myconn has grown up around it. It was a scriptorium at one point. There are vellum books here older than the empire itself, but no one can read them. Psellos once searched ten years for a key to their alphabet, but in vain."

Rol said nothing. All about him, the cavernous walls of the chamber echoed up out of the light. They were rougher here, and there was no mortar between their huge blocks. Instead of bookcases, shelved platforms of solid stone ran like lines of sarcophagi along the dust-strewn floor, and on them books and scrolls with rotted wooden spindles were piled up with no discernable rhyme or reason. The thoughts of men long dead committed to crumbling paper and parchment, and now rotting away quietly here in the dark. A tomb of books.

"You must help me with this one," Rowen said. This time it took a different key, and the door was tiny, solid bronze. The key turned with an unwilling grate of metal, and Rol had to put his shoulder to the door itself and butt it open inch by inch. It opened on a set of narrow, crooked stairs going steeply down.

"What have you brought me here for, Rowen?" he asked, panting.

"There's something you have to see."

Phrynius's words were coming back to him now. He did not want to go down those stairs and see what she meant to show him. He felt it would be turning a corner with the unknown waiting beyond it.

Rowen went ahead, the lantern-light shining off the silver fillet in her hair, the bones stark in the back of her hand as she held the light above her head. Under her feet, the stairs were half a fathom wide, pitted and uneven and untrustworthy in the dark. Rol touched Fleam's hilt, but the sword was cold and aloof. He followed his sister down into the dark.

The stairs corkscrewed and wound first this way and then that. The passage narrowed further, until it was scraping at Rol's shoulders, and he had to duck his head to avoid being brained by bristling excrescences of stone, fangs of rough rock. There was no architecture here; this was a natural fissure in the foundations of the Turmian. And this was no longer the Turmian. They had gone below it, every foot taking them back another thousand years. They were in a cave system now, and the air grew damper, the stone slippery underfoot, freezing drips of water falling on their heads and trickling down the back of their necks.

"The Turmian, it's said, was built on the site of a shrine, a place of worship in times immemorial," Rowen informed him. "We come to it now. Very few people know of this place. Psellos had read of it, and mentioned it to me one night, a long time ago. Canker knew also, though I don't know how. It is not a place to visit on some whim."

The stairs ended, and they shuffled along a level tunnel.

There was dirt under their feet, black and muddy. Rol did not look down to watch for footprints. A growing sense of claustrophobia was rising in his throat, and it was all he could do not to turn and bolt back the way they had come.

The light Rowen held suddenly blossomed out. Rol saw stalactites far above his head, and there was the sound of running water. His breathing eased at the sense of space. They were in a large cave, and at the far wall, some ten fathoms away, a small underground stream cackled to itself and glittered in the glow of the lantern. Rowen raised the wick, and the light strengthened about them, sought out shadows and sent them reeling. She held the lantern high above her head, and her voice echoed as the cavern walls threw it back at her.

"This place has been here since God made the world," she said. "The First Men found it when there was nothing above us but a green hill, and the Elder Race still walked the earth. Other things walked the surface of the world also in that lost time, and men worshipped them. Come."

She took Rol's hand and led him over to one wall. "They drew pictures of the things they saw, Rol."

The wall was covered in images, all bright and brash with astonishing colors. Here was a bison delineated in half a dozen beautifully eloquent strokes. Here a gazelle running from the stick-figures of men with spears. There a huge, tusked beast with a serpentine nose that trampled the stick-figures underfoot and tossed them over its shoulders. And there were other things also.

Man-shapes, but taller than the others, and with what seemed to be flowing robes that plumped out the lines of their limbs. These shapes had bright, green blazing eyes, and they carried what could only be swords and shields. Rays of yellow pigment were spanning out from them like sunbursts, and behind them a great black wall spiked with blade-shaped towers reared up with banners or flags twisting from the battlements.

But the center of the picture was dominated by a single image. This was a huge thing, a shape manlike and yet not a man at all. The thing seemed to be floating in the air, looming over all the others like a cloud. In its head two eyes burned in streaks of yellow and scarlet, like stabs of flame, and the creature had wings, long snaking tendrils of light bursting from its back in feathers of flame. As it hovered in the air, the figures of the men below cowered either in fear or worship.

But it was the face that stole the breath out of Rol's mouth. Bearded, long-nosed, it was recognizably that of a man. Beneath those terrible eyes, the face smiled, and there was still a glimpse of humanity in the expression.

"Your face," Rowen said, looking from Rol to the painting and back again.

"It could be anyone," Rol spat, voice shaking. "A coincidence."

"And the light in the eyes, the great wings? Is that you, Rol? Has that ever been you?"

Rol glared at her. "What do you know?"

"I heard tell of a beast that slaughtered a crowd of people in Ascari as they were looting Psellos's Tower. Or an angel, a bright-winged thing that had death in its eyes. And there are tales up and down the seas of a Black Ship whose captain can transform into a murderous demon at will. What are these, Rol, legends?"

"Tall tales."

"Canker has a friend called Phrynius, a scholar who once worked in the Turmian."

"I know him."

Rowen paused. "I see." She gestured up at the painting on the wall. "He has been down here, before the war. He's made a study of this picture. Do you know what he believes this image to represent?"

Rol was mute.

"It is a depiction of the Final Judgment, a time when the Creator will return to the world and test mankind once again. And if they fail the test, then they will face His servant, a being that will exact His retribution on the face of the earth." Rowen stared up at the wall, eyes wide. "This thing here, with your face on it, is the Angel of Death."

Fifteen

THE DANCE BEFORE DAWN

WEARY BEYOND SLEEP, ROL LAY IN BED THAT NIGHT AND watched the firelight paint shadowed pictures on the ceiling of his quarters. He had opened his window, and flakes of snow were blowing in over the sill, and faint in the darkness beyond he could hear the unending staccato thunder of the artillery exchanges down on the walls. When morning came—or was it morning already?—he was to be fitted out in armor, something he had never worn before. Then that night there would be a grand ball in the palace, for which feverish preparations were already under way and had been throughout the black hours. And afterward, they would take their places with the waiting regiments by the gates, and march out to meet the enemy. And they would fight valiantly, and Rol would kill Bar Asfal, if he was able, and Rowen would have her empire, what was left of it.

And then he would say good-bye to Bionar, to wars and plotting and dungeons in the dark. He would take Gallico and Creed and Giffon, and together they would return to the coast and make their way back upon the waves of the sea, where they belonged. And Ganesh Ka would be there for them every time they wearied of the waves, a place where they could rest in peace between adventures.

That was the only life Rol wanted now. He loved Rowen— he would always love her. But they would never be together in the way he wanted. And in any case, she was no longer the woman he had known.

He would not stay; he did not want to spin out the rest of his long life here in the mountains, amid these cities of stone, no matter what titles and privileges were piled upon him. He had never wanted a sister, or to be brother to a queen. All he wanted now was his Black Ship, and the fellowship of the men who sailed her. The rest could go to hell.

"Well," he said aloud to the empty room, "at least I have a plan."

Abel Harkenn woke him by slamming the window shut on the snow. The stuff had piled up inches deep on the sill, and the air in the room was glacial. A maid was resurrecting the fire from its gray bones.

"The Queen has requested that you breakfast with her, sir," Harkenn said mildly.

"Tell the Queen— Well, all right. Where are my damned clothes? Lend a hand, there." Rol dressed in a daze, only half awake. It seemed he was destined never to get a thorough night's sleep in Myconn, and the toll was beginning to tell. He splashed water on his face from the ewer by the bed, stifling a cry as the freezing stuff struck his eyeballs. There was ice in it. Then he stood like a mannikin as Harkenn helped him on with yet another change of clothes, this time in a blue so deep it was almost black. Rowen must have had a platoon of seamstresses working round the clock to churn out a different outfit every day.

"Lead on," he told Abel Harkenn, yawning stupidly.

The kitchens again. He might have known. Rol took a seat at the long table, between Gallico and Creed, relishing the close warmth of the place, the fine toothsome smells coming from the spits. The kitchens were unusually crowded, and to-day there were no flirtations; the staff were preparing for the grand ball that was to take place that evening, and it was as good as a play to watch them busy at their work. The rest of the city might yet be down to skinning cats, as Gallico had said, but here in the palace the last storerooms had been routed out and a feast fit for a queen was being prepared. Rol piled him-self a plate of thick-cut cured ham and black bread and tapped the ale-cask in the corner for a foaming tankard-full. Creed, Gallico, and Giffon were already way ahead of him, their plates covered in nothing but crumbs.

Rowen the serving-maid joined them without ceremony, sitting opposite but eating nothing. The four of them stared at her, and Gallico said, "Girl, you don't look well."

Creed nudged the halftroll. "She's the Queen, idiot."

"I know who she is. She looks like she needs a square meal and a week of sleep."

Rowen smiled tightly. "I'll sleep soon enough. Gentlemen, I have had clothing suitable for the ball run up for each one of you, and our armorers have also been setting out some war-harness in case you mean to take the field tomorrow morning. It awaits you in the Guards' quarters."

"I've never been to a ball," Elias Creed said. He smiled at Rowen with something approaching shyness. Rol stared his three friends up and down, and realized that each and every one of them was a little besotted with her, and her fragile airs. He scowled into his beer. Jealousy? Surely not; it was a little late in the day for that.

"A word, Rol," Rowen said, and rose from the table. Creed's eyes followed her like those of a dog watching its master.

The noise in the kitchens covered them, a clamoring curtain. They spoke in a corner with no fear of eavesdroppers.

"A messenger has come in from Canker," Rowen said. "He will move his army up in the night, and then go to ground a mile from the Gallitran encampments. As soon as we have pinned the enemy in their trenches, he will assault them from the rear." Rol nodded impatiently. It was largely the plan Canker had expounded to him a few days before. But there was a strain on Rowen's face that outdid any he had yet seen.

"What's happened?" he asked.

"Moerus has gone over to the enemy. Gallitras has fallen, and the Ruthe bridges."

Rol whistled soundlessly.

"All communications with the coast have been severed. The supply lines have ceased to exist. Canker also is cut off now. If any of us are to survive, we must not only win the field tomorrow, but Bar Asfal *must* die. Do you understand me, Rol?"

"I understand," he said harshly. It was not even a question of emotional blackmail anymore. His hide also was in the balance, and those of his friends.

"We are all in the same boat," he said with a wry smile.

"Yes. We will all go down together, if it comes to that." She paused. "I'm sorry. The board is being swept far quicker than I had imagined."

She did not look sorry; she had a light in her eyes he had almost forgotten. That killing-light, bright at the prospect of battle.

"Rowen, if I can find Bar Asfal, I will kill him for you, but a battlefield is a crowded place. Someone may get to him before me."

"He'll be under the Bionese Fighting Flag, saffron and black, the Oriflammer. It's a huge banner, reserved for the King's use alone. It can't be mistaken. His face you have seen already, or a decent likeness of it."

Rol touched her chin. "Then he is a dead man."

Rowen drew him to one side, to a shadowed alcove beyond reach of candle or firelight. There she pressed herself full length against him and kissed his lips, her tongue slipping in over his teeth. When he tried to bring his arms up around her, she grasped his wrists and pinioned him. Her nails dug into his flesh, hard enough to draw blood.

"Thank you," she said, releasing him again, leaving him winded. Then she left without another word.

Rol stood there with her spit still on his lip, his mind a storm of bitterness and regret. He could taste her flesh in his mouth, and from his fingers there dripped slow tears of blood. Despite everything he knew about her, she could still dance a minuet on his nerves, pluck on his feelings as though they were strings. He knew this was what she was doing, and was not sure he even cared.

Later that morning Rol, Gallico, Creed, and Giffon stood in the reception chambers of the commander of the Guard, and picked over a dazzling array of garments and armor and weaponry that had been laid out before them on linen-hung tables like some militaristic fetishist's dream come true. Watched by a trio of palace servitors, a couple of senior guardsmen, and Gideon Mirkady himself, they rooted through the stuff like bargain-hunters at a market. Mirkady laid on wine, and took a cup himself, leaning by the door and watching them with a mixture of amusement and appraisal. Gallico lifted a war-hammer with a head as big as a watermelon and a shaft six feet long, and tested its heft with bloodthirsty relish. "I could do some damage with this."

"You're likely to damage whoever's standing next to you," Creed retorted. The ex-convict had selected a small iron-bound targe and a heavy-bladed cutlass with a basket hilt.

There were plenty of pistols and powder-flasks to go around also, modern flintlocks with brass and steel fittings, some with folding blades beneath the barrel.

But it was the armor that fascinated them most. Solid plate, most of it. It clicked and clanked under their eager fingers. Breastplates, vambraces, gorgets, pauldrons, gauntlets, and greaves, and visored helms with absurd crests.

"How does a man fight with an ironmongery stall on his back?" Creed demanded with raised eyebrows.

Mirkady sauntered forward. "You may be glad of some of that ironmongery when the blades begin to fly," he said.

"Will it keep out a bullet?" Rol asked.

The Guard commander picked out a breastplate and pointed to a hemispherical dent in one corner. "They're tested at fifty yards with an arquebus. You'll get bruised, but that's better than having your guts torn out."

"And if we're closer than fifty yards?" Giffon asked. Alone of the four privateers, he did not seem to relish the display.

"Then, boy, you're at it sword to sword, and you have other things to worry about." Mirkady slapped Giffon on the shoulder with a hearty hail-fellow-well-met air which fooled none of them.

"I've not yet seen armor that can halt a twelve-pound cannonball," Gallico said with a grin. "What might the dent of that look like on one of these pretty plates?"

The day edged round, and activities in and about the palace bifurcated. On the one hand, the streets had become rivers of men; regiments of infantry in column were leaving their posts to a skeleton remnant and were gathering in the squares and ruins behind the Forminon Gate. There, in the shadow of the formidable double-barbican known as the Warder, they

stacked arms and made ready to pass a cold night. Firewood
was brought to them by the wagonload, and casks of beer so
that they might toast their betters before following them out
of the gates in the morning.

Together with these martial preparations, there was more
frivolous work afoot. A small army of servants were turning
the palace of Bar Madivar upside down in readiness for the
ball that night; and in Barbion Square below the palace, the
hungry and hopeful of the city's inhabitants loitered in chattering crowds, to await their share of the largesse.

In the evening, Rol and his three shipmates, dressed in
their new finery, found a way up onto the battlements of the
palace and managed to evade guardsmen, servants, and sundry
hangers-on so that for the first time in what seemed many
days they could speak openly to one another. They stared out
over the city to where brief flashes and rumbles marked the interminable struggle of guns out on the walls. A fresh breach
had been made that afternoon, it was said, and fierce fighting
had raged until dark, the loyalists cut to pieces as they withdrew across the open ground to their trenches. If they had
pressed their assault a few hours later they would have found
little more than a corporal's guard manning the walls; one of
war's little ironies.

It was still snowing—there was almost a foot of it on the
ground, and now many of the crowds in Barbion Square had
gone back indoors. The campfires of the enemy could be seen
as a vague glow far off in the dark hills of the north.

"The year has turned," Gallico said, sniffing the air, as was
his wont. "It does not seem like it here, in these mountains,
but lower down the air will soon start to warm again, and the
sun will make its return."

"Still a long way to go until spring," Giffon said. He was
shivering, and Gallico laid one huge arm on the boy's shoulder.

He looked at Rol, and both knew what the other was thinking. It had been a mistake not to send Giffon back. He was no fighter, though he had a fine heart.

"When we go out tomorrow, I want you three to stick together," Rol said. "Look out for one another, and try not to be too heroic."

"I take it that's your job," Creed said dryly.

"Stay near the Queen; she'll be well protected."

"Even if it means staying in earshot of that prick Mirkady?" Gallico asked.

"Even then. None of us have ever fought in a battle like this before."

"What about Gallitras?" Creed asked. "Seemed like a battle to me."

"This is in the open. It'll be fast-moving, and there will be a lot of artillery and nowhere to hide from it. Until we reach their trenches, they'll be pounding the life out of us with their siege guns, mortars, field-culverins, anything they can stick a lump of iron in. Until Canker hits them in the rear, it will be rough."

"When did you become mother hen?" Gallico asked. "I thought that was Elias's job."

"By the way, if you ever meet your grandmother, let me know if she needs taught how to suck on an egg," Creed added.

Rol smiled. "It may be I'll have to break off and disappear in the middle of it. There's something I have to do. But you are not to follow, none of you. Do you understand me?"

They looked at him, all humor gone. "What is it, some royal errand?" Gallico asked.

"You could say that. I'm to bring down this Bar Asfal fellow. When he's gone, the rest of them should fold like a tinker's shack."

"That's a hell of an errand," Creed said.

"I know. I'll be all right, though."

"Was this the Queen's idea?" Gallico asked with a glint in his eye.

"I suppose so, yes."

The halftroll shook his head. "She is your sister, you say, and it's clear to my eyes, at least, that she has real feeling for you. But she's still a clever woman, used to getting what she wants. Be careful, Rol. These people with titles ahead of their names, they don't think the way we do. They can convince themselves to believe whatever they like."

"Rowen needs me to do this thing, Gallico. She would not have asked me else."

"Perhaps. She may be a fine woman, at heart. It's just that she has been ruined by her ambitions. You know that, don't you, Rol?"

"I know it. Yes." He had known it from the moment he had first set eyes on her again, but he did not like to hear Gallico say it.

They garlanded the ballroom with the limbs of evergreens, and great bunches of shining holly with berries red as wounds. The heat of the candles brought out a fine resinous scent from the decorations—a smell much improved by the tang of mulled wine and cider which sat in wide silver punch-bowls at the ends of the room. Some two hundred of Myconn's finest and fairest had been invited to the ball, but that took no account of the thousands more who crammed into the palace to take advantage of the free food and drink that was being distributed without thought for the morrow. If the rebels were finally going to lose their war in the morning, they would at least do so on a full belly.

This night, the Bar Madivar Palace was packed to the gills with a host of people who were intent on blotting out the frozen night beyond and the shell-fire down at the walls. There were clots of musicians on every floor with piled plates under their seats and bottles by their toes, and the palace servants had thrown off any sense of formality and were entering into frantic liaisons with any comely stranger who caught their eye. Why not? The dawn would bring a new set of worries, or an end to all of them. For this one night, the palace was given over to anyone who still had an appetite for life in their belly.

The chief generals were all there: Mirkady, Blayloc, Brage, Cassidus, and Remion. The last three of these five had wives on their arms, and small coteries of hangers-on to banish the lull from any conversation. They were all drinking heavily; but then, so was every man and woman in the room who had a mouth, and an arm capable of raising a glass. Except Rowen.

She sat at the far end of the ballroom upon a delicate chair of ebony wood inlaid with mother-of-pearl. She wore black, as always, but her dress was a plunging affair that revealed more of her white flesh than Rol had ever seen in public. With her hair piled up behind her head, and a white-gold crown resting upon it, she looked every inch the Queen, albeit a somewhat ethereal one. The revealing lines of her gown promised much, but the look in her eyes was enough to deter anything but the most formal of gallantries. Mirkady stood behind her like an old man jealous of a young wife, and Rol saw him set a hand once briefly on her bare shoulder. She raised up her own fingers to return the touch. At the sight, Rol felt an odd and ungainly flicker in his chest, a kind of pain, and he poured his wine-filled flute into his mouth until the pale, sparkling stuff trickled into his beard.

"Yon fellow aims higher than commanding the Guard," Creed said, his eyes following Rol's, and something of the same expression within them.

"It's as good a way as any to get on in the world," Rol said with a mirthless smile. He burped up an acidic bubble of the wine and grimaced. "Damn fizzy piss; don't they have any real drink in this place, something that hasn't been heated up or filled with air?"

Gallico was the center of a curious crowd, who were evidently drinking down a few of his taller tales. He had half a dozen glass flutes held in one fist like the barrels of so many guns, and would pour their contents into his gaping maw every so often, to the delight of his listeners. Performing for a crowd in Bionar again. He saw Rol and Elias and winked one lambent eye at them. It was almost as bright as it had always been. His wounds were closed at last and he was intent on enjoying this night to the full, as a privateer should.

Giffon stood nearby in the fragrant throng, exchanging quiet words with a serving-maid who looked no older than he. As Rol watched, she touched his face, but so flushed were his cheeks with the heat and the wine that it was impossible to tell if he blushed or not.

Abel Harkenn was at Rol's elbow, wax-skinned and gawky as a young heron. "Sirs, I thought you'd rather enjoy this." He proffered a tray on which squatted two wide-necked mugs of rum, the liquid tawny as a hare's back. Rol and Creed snapped them up.

"Ship's rum!" Elias exclaimed. "Ran's Road, man, but that's welcome. Where'd you get it?"

"Smuggled in from Arbion, not a week ago, sir. I thought you'd appreciate it." Harkenn beamed at their incredulous faces, and without another word, he turned and was off again, quickly swallowed by the swirling crowd.

"Enterprising fellow; he'd make a good ship's steward," Creed said. Rol sipped his rum reflectively. After the bubbling wine it felt like a punch to the throat.

Music was gathering into a pattern in the hall; there was danger of a dance. He did not relish the thought of prancing about in line, and tugged Creed's arm until they both stood well back from the middle of the floor, which was clearing rapidly.

"What's o'clock, Elias?"

"We're halfway through the first watch, I should think. The night is hardly begun." The rum was coloring Creed's face. With his brindled hair and heavy beard, he looked like a gate-crashing vagrant in this smooth-chinned company, though his clothes were as fine as any. The shackle-scars on his wrist were revealed every time he lifted his arm to drink, and Rol saw nearby ladies and noblemen staring at them in some dismay.

The music gathered form, after the interminable screeching of one untuned viola. The hubbub sank down into something near quiet. It seemed insufferably hot in the room, and candlewax from the chandeliers was dripping here and there upon ladies' coiffures and the polished wood of the floor. The Queen rose, those around her dipping their heads, the ladies curtseying demurely. She strode down the empty dance floor with that mannish stride that not even the most feminine of gowns could conceal, and she stopped before Rol.

"Cortishane, will you join me for the first dance?"

Not even Rol could summon up the churlishness to refuse her. He gave his mug to Creed, bowed slightly, and took Rowen's fingers in his own. The pair took a stately course out into the wide wooden wastes of the dance floor, and Rol whispered out of the corner of his mouth.

"I've not danced since Psellos's lessons, gods know how many years ago."

"It'll come back to you."

They stood still, facing each other, and as the music picked up and became a proper tune, it did come back to him. They drew together, his right thigh touching her left, his left hand in the naked small of her back, the touch of her skin a shock to him even now. Rol's feet found the floor of their own accord, and they stepped off together into the path of the music.

Rowen moved easily in the compass of his arms, and a perfume of lavender rose from her white throat.

Mirkady's gaze was fixed on them, two dark eyes watching the way their bodies swayed and bent and gave. Two by two, other couples joined in the dance, until the floor became crowded and people were moving in and out of each other's orbit with momentary contacts, caresses, grazes. The stateliness of the music belied the heat between the dancers. Hidden safely amid the throng, Rol pressed close against Rowen, his thigh at the crux of her legs. He slid his hand down her back by increments, until his fingers were under the low-cut line of her dress and he was able to stroke the silky crease at the very base of her spine. She leaned away from his touch. He bent his neck so that their foreheads were almost touching, but she turned her face aside. More than anything in the world he wanted to crush that slim body in his arms, and bite down on those dark lips. But though their flesh was pressed together, she would not meet his eyes. They moved through the evolutions of the dance with a perfection of grace that had no fire about it at all. Brother and sister.

The music ended. The dancers drew apart and applauded. Rol and Rowen looked at each other. There was color in her cheeks and he could feel sweat trickling in the small of his back.

"I told you it would come back to you," the Queen said coldly.

Rol bowed to her, the blood thundering in his head. Something indefinable went across Rowen's face—sorrow?

Then she turned on her heel and walked away.

The music began again, tinkly stuff Rol did not much care for, but it went down well enough with those on the floor. The

scores of partners broke up, reassembled, moved to the new
rhythm with the same intent, appraising looks on their faces.
Rowen remained on the floor, as slim and upright as a black
sapling. She danced with Mirkady next, and then General
Blayloc, and then faces Rol did not know. He stood beside
Elias Creed at the rear wall of the ballroom and sipped at his
rum, watching, turning away, watching again.

"For God's sake, Rol," Creed said, "take one of those
serving-maids outside and scratch that bloody itch."

"Am I so transparent, Elias?"

"I thought for a moment you were going to start in on her in
the middle of the dance. There was folk watching who didn't
know whether to shit or go blind."

"All right, damn it. Where's Gallico?"

"Over by the punch-bowls, where else? How that fellow can
talk. It's a wonder his guts don't tumble out his mouth."

"Giffon?"

"No idea. I'm hoping he's found himself a warm spot."

"You're a real romantic, Elias."

"We could all be dead this time tomorrow. Even these noble
fillies here feel it. No one ever died wishing he had fornicated
less."

"But not with his sister."

Creed regarded Rol mutely.

Rol laughed. Clapping Creed on the shoulder, he went off
in search of more rum. At least, that was what he told himself
he was searching for. He found himself missing Fleam's weight
at his hip—no one carried weapons to a ball. Abel Harkenn
had disappeared.

He made do with the fizzy Court stuff instead, and belched
as he tossed back glass after glass of the stuff, snatching them
off passing trays and dropping the empties in the potted plants
that lined the end of the ballroom. In the corner of his vision,

Rowen's dark shape seemed to flicker and dart like a mote stuck in his eye.

"Rol Cortishane," a woman's voice said, and he halted in his tracks, swaying a little.

"That is your name, my lord, is it not?"

"That's my name." A knot of ladies stood before him like a clutch of butterflies. All well dressed—but then, who here was not? All young, personable, and all slightly drunk.

"Queen Rowen's brother, it is said. Can this be true?"

"Half brother." Rol scanned their faces, reading possibilities. He was in no mood for flirting. As Elias had said, he simply wanted the itch scratched.

The girl who had spoken to him was a little painted blond thing not out of her teens and he dismissed her out of hand. But there was one other who caught his eye: tall, dark-haired—of course she must be dark-haired—and less simpleminded-looking. There was a coolness about the way she met his eyes that Rol responded to at once. I am nothing if not consistent, he thought.

The little blond girl was chattering away, demure and lascivious at the same time. Most of her friends giggled and nudged her elbows and bleated at her raillery, but Rol ignored her. "Why aren't you dancing?" he asked the dark-haired girl. She was somehow outside the little feminine fellowship that faced him.

"I never much cared for it."

"Rafa has big feet," one of the other ladies giggled, and the girl Rafa looked down.

Rol took her by the hand. "Come with me," he said.

Momentary alarm, then an impish smile. He led her away, abandoning her companions to drop-jawed outrage and perhaps, the gods knew, some envy. He liked the warmth of the girl's hand. When it threatened to slip out of his fingers in the press of the crowd, it was she who took a firmer grip, no non-sense about it.

"I need to get some air," he said to her, and meant it.

"I have a window in my room. It opens," she said, tossing her head.

"Where's your room?"

"Down by the kitchens. But it's not a bad place."

Rol looked her up and down. "You're a kitchen maid?" he asked in astonishment. She looked frightened and embarrassed at the same time.

"A chambermaid. Our mistress gave us these gowns for the night, out of her own wardrobe, and said we might join in the ball. She wanted more young ladies on the floor, she said."

"Who's your mistress?"

"I serve the Queen." Rol's stare was disconcerting her. "My name is Rafa. I'm from Oronthir. I was a slave once, but—"

"Take me to this room of yours," Rol said.

When he opened the window, the blessed chill of the night air swooped in like something hungry for heat. He stood in the draft and felt tiny hard flakes of snow smite his face, fine as sand. He was kneeling on Rafa's narrow iron-framed bed, as it was tucked just below the thick windowsill, whilst behind him she worked to raise a flame in her tiny fireplace, her skirts gathered up over her knees to keep them out of the ash. Turning round, Rol admired her white legs and feet—she had kicked off her cheap shoes upon entering the room—and savored the freezing night air as it flooded around him.

"Let me do it." The girl was making a meal out of striking fire, and as she rose, still holding the hem of her fine gown—Rowen's gown—Rol knelt beside her and brushed ash from her shapely knees, making her start, wide-eyed. She dropped the gown's hem, covering her legs.

"It's all right; I won't eat you." She sat on the bed behind him as he struck flint and steel, coaxing sparks into a nest of fine-shaved tinder, then blowing on it and transferring the rising flame to the kindling in the hearth. There was peat by the fireplace, in black, hairy bricks, and he set these on the fire one by one, taking pleasure in the simple exercise, the sureness of it. When he straightened he found to his surprise that Rafa was in bed, blankets pulled up to her chin, her fine gown a bouffant pile on a chair. She had closed the window, but the air in the room was still cool, not yet taking warmth from the peat. Rol sat on the bed and touched the girl's long black tresses where they lay unbound on the pillow. The stifling, raucous crowds of the ballroom seemed very far away now, though their noise, and that of all the other revelers throughout the palace, could be felt as much as heard, a low vibration in the air.

"You said you were a slave," Rol said.

"I was born of slaves, and so that made me one, too, but the Queen, years ago, she freed all the slaves in the palace on the condition they serve her seven years."

"That was charitable of her," Rol said.

"I have five years left to serve, and then I can go where I like."

"Where will you go?"

Rafa frowned. She had an endearing frown that pursed up her mouth. Rol bent and kissed it before she could answer. Her lips moved under his. She looked at him with no trace of coyness remaining. "Come into my bed. It's cold."

He shed his clothes, glad to be rid of the peacock finery, and slipped under the blanket, his flesh meeting hers the length of their bodies, forced together by the narrowness of the bed they shared. Rafa was wide-hipped, long in the leg, with round breasts and a strong serving-girl's back. Rol tugged her close to him, and for a while there were no words, only silent explorations, delighted and hungry. They kicked the coverings off the bed as they discovered how to fit together, and beat its iron frame against the wall with their eagerness.

When they were done they lay like spoons in a drawer, facing the fire, and Rol traced with one finger the shadows the flame-light painted up and down Rafa's naked skin.

"Are you really the Queen's brother?" she asked. Before he could reply she added, "You look nothing like her."

"Different fathers, different lives. I'm a mariner. I have a ship of my own and a crew to sail her." I will have, he thought. By the gods, I will.

"Are you going out to fight in the morning?"

"Yes."

Rafa took his hand and set it on her breast, cupping her own over it. "Be careful, then."

Rol kissed her shoulder, marveling that moments of such sweetness could still be found in the foul mess of this world.

"I will."

Sixteen

A GAUNTLET OF GUNS

IT HAD STOPPED SNOWING, AND NOW THE BLACK SKY WAS becoming blue with dawn, the moon hanging halfway to the full, reluctant to quit the world. In the vast, cobbled courtyard of the Warder, five thousand men stood waiting in patient ranks, their breaths pluming out into the frigid gloom. Here and there an officer's horse stamped and blew, but there was no wind, and the regimental flags hung limp and heavy, their heraldry hidden.

Rol stood some third of the way to the rear among the assembled regiments. He was on foot, as were his friends—half-decent horsemanship did not a cavalryman make. Behind them were Rowen, Mirkady, and two hundred mounted guardsmen, the personal bodyguard of the Queen. Rowen's horse was so close that sometimes, out of a spirit of mischief perhaps, it nosed Rol in the back.

He was in armor—even Gallico had been set up with a hastily cobbled set of carmine-lathered half plate—and in addition to Fleam, he bore three pistols tucked into a scarlet sash about the middle of his cuirass. No helmet, though; he did not like staring out at the world through an iron-slit.

Rol turned and looked at Elias Creed. The dark man stood with one hand on Giffon's shoulder. He and Rol nodded wordlessly to each other. Giffon's eyes were calm; he peered up at the brightening sky with something of a smile, remembering the joys of the night before perhaps. They both looked strangely unfamiliar in their breastplates and chain mail.

Gallico leaned his knotted fists on the head of the long warhammer he bore and stared up at the sky also. "The sun will shine today," he said. "I wonder how the wind is, out on the Reach." And almost to himself: "I hope Thef got the *Astraros* home."

A sharp horn-blast from the hulking gate-towers before them, and the thousands of men in the courtyard seemed to stiffen, like hounds that have seen the fox. There was a grinding noise, felt through the soles of the feet as much as heard, and the tall gates of the barbican began to open.

Rowen nudged her horse forward. The Queen of Bionar had donned mail so fine it seemed not to be made of metal at all, and her head was bare but for a silver circlet. She reined in at Rol's side and one black-gloved hand was set on the nape of his neck. He did not turn, but his own hand found her ankle in its stirruped boot and gripped it a moment, no more.

The files in front began moving. There were a few rasped orders, muffled curses, the clink and clank of metal. The fire-bearers lifted the lid of their pots and blew on the embers within. Arquebusiers wound lengths of match about their fists and checked the charges that hung from their shoulder-belts. The horsemen spoke quietly to their mounts but not to one another. Flagstaffs were shouldered, and the military files became a simple mass of queuing men, bumping, jostling, and cursing as someone stepped on their heels. Back at the tail of the host, there was a clattering sound as a dozen twelve-pound culverins were manhandled forward.

Through the barbican, the day was lightening moment by moment. Blayloc's brigade, in the van, was already outside the walls. Black against the snow, his troops began extending from column into a three-deep line. Sixteen hundred strong, they would take up a frontage of over five hundred yards.

Now Rol was outside the gates, Rowen's bodyguard behind him. The thunderous rumble of the cavalry brought up the hairs on the back of his neck; but still, there seemed to be no hurry. Now and again the infantry broke into a jog to keep ahead of the horses, but for the most part they kept to a fast walk. The armor bore down on Rol's shoulders, and he felt a sudden shaft of pity for the Bionese marines he had sent over the side of so many ships with all that iron strapped to their backs.

He looked back. Cassidus's brigade was moving up on the left and Remion's was still coming through the barbican. Men had begun to shout now, sergeants venting their impatience, men swearing, all of them openmouthed and panting the hot breath from their mouths.

There was a single distant boom, and a globe of smoke blossomed at the loyalist trenches some half a mile away to the north. A courier went galloping past Rol from the cluster that followed Rowen like the tail of a kite. He was off to Blayloc.

Horns were blowing up ahead, faint but insistent. An alarm triangle was beaten. Rol could see hordes of figures running without apparent order from the tented city of the enemy down to the trenches. Someone in the ranks ahead laughed. "Caught the bastards at breakfast!"

The army had shaken out now: three brigades in line abreast, almost a mile of men in three ranks, Rowen and her cavalry in the center-rear, and Rol and his shipmates somewhere in the middle. The artillery was lagging behind despite the fact that some two hundred men were sweating over the heavy wheeled pieces and their limbers.

"Sound General Advance!" Mirkady cried. He had dressed for the occasion, a magnificent surcoat of sable and scarlet silk over his armor. Rol wondered if it was a present from the Queen. His own and those of his friends were ill-fitting relics from army stores.

Horns sounded up and down the red-clad lines. The regimental flags dipped once, then came up again. And with that, the army began to advance. Slow strides, the men looking to right and left, sergeants shouting at them to keep their dressing, and the fire-bearers running up and down the line lighting the match, so that now the acrid burning of it came eddying about the field.

The regiments and companies hit old snow-filled shell-holes. The line fractured, was re-formed. Officers were shouting at the men to double up, to slow down, to wait for the men on their left, on their right. And now several field pieces were booming out ahead, but so far the shells were overshooting, detonating in spumes of earth and ice hundreds of yards to their rear.

"Gods in heaven, can they get any slower? We'd be better off on our hands and knees." This was Gallico, who was marched steadily along with the shaft of his hammer on one shoulder. His free hand rubbed absentmindedly at the iron covering his old wounds, as if they throbbed now in anticipation of another bullet.

"I say the hell with these pretty lines," Creed said. "We'd be better off running at those trenches like a bunch of maniacs, shouting our heads off. Yonder bastards are sighting their guns. We'll catch it in a minute, and the pretty lines will not look so neat then."

The advance speeded up, the ranks converging and drawing apart again as men dashed through old craters and negotiated the remnants of stone walls. They were halfway to the enemy trenches when the sun burst over the mountains to their right, and the white plain of snow before them grew dazzlingly bright. At almost the same moment, the guns opened up in earnest.

A line of smoke exploded all across their front, followed heartbeats later by the stuttering thunder of the retorts. The marching soldiers did not pause, but lowered their heads and hunched their shoulders, like men walking through heavy rain. The shells came on in a shrieking cloud, a volley of blurs that burst in and through the line. Fountains of soil were thrown up by the solid shot, but the loyalists were using hollow explosive also, and when these detonated in the ranks they could tear half a dozen men to pieces.

Rol saw one cannonball behead three soldiers like dandelions under a child's switch. Shrapnel from the hollow rounds went spinning red-hot through the ranks, ripping chunks of flesh out of men's bodies, spearing them with slivers of hot iron, taking off limbs, skewering eyes, disemboweling.

"Close your ranks!" rose the shout. "Close those gaps!" And the men did so, coming shoulder to shoulder over the corpses of their comrades, marching on. The roar of the barrage swelled, so that individual guns could no longer be heard, just a soaring madness of sound that shook the very air in their lungs. Behind the army, their own guns were now barking out to join in the spectacle, firing at maximum elevation to pass over the friendly lines. Rol looked back.

"Lazy bastards. Those guns should be moving up along with us, not sitting out in the open back there."

Elias Creed followed his eyes. "They'll be moving soon enough, once the enemy guns find them."

The army stumbled onward. The ridge behind the enemy trenches, upon which Bar Asfal's tented city sprawled, had disappeared in a towering bank of smoke, and now the very light of the winter sun seemed dimmed and choked by that fuming reek. Shells landed amid the horses behind Rol, and they shrieked and plunged and bucked under their riders.

"That bastard Canker had best make his move soon!" Gallico bellowed. He was streaming blood from a gash under his ear and his eyes glowed like green coals. Giffon was leaning in against him like a child clinging to its mother in a rainstorm.

"I thought these fellows weren't supposed to have much in the way of artillery," Creed complained. Then he staggered against Rol with a grunt.

"Elias!"

"I'm all right." There was a dent in his breastplate and a ragged piece of iron hissed in the snow at his feet. Creed looked down at it in some wonderment. "We must get some of this stuff for the ship's guns."

"We'd sink everything we fired at." Rol set him on his feet. "Come on, Elias, keep walking. The sooner we reach those guns, the sooner we spike them."

They staggered on in a rising storm. All lines and ranks had disintegrated under the ferocity of the enemy barrage. Rol had never seen so many cannon firing at one time. With ship-board battle, you took a broadside, and then had a pause as the other fellow reloaded. But this was unrelenting. It was madness. It was murder.

Two hundred yards. They were running now, thousands of men desperate to get out from under that tempest of killing metal. A shell burst to Rol's right and spun him off his feet, the smoke-stained sky wheeling in his sight. He saw a man tottering along with his lower jaw shot away, his tongue hanging down bright and red. A riderless horse with no hind legs, screaming on its side. Men congregating in shell-holes, heads down, their officers kicking them up again, shrieking like lunatics.

Gallico picked him up and pulled him onward, dragging

him through a deepening mire of bloody muck that slithered with nameless things underfoot. He lost one of his pistols and scrambled for it on his hands and knees, then found his feet and stared around himself, white-eyed.

The enemy trenches were scant yards away, and the rebels were rushing them in knots and broken clusters of men. All order had disappeared. Rowen was nowhere to be seen, though there seemed to be dying horses everywhere. The guns were firing point-blank now, canister rounds filled with musket-balls by the thousand that disintegrated whole squads and filled the shuddering air with the coppery reek of blood, a fine red fog in the smoke, a rain of steaming things falling out of it. And lines of arquebusiers were crackling out volleys from the lip of the trenches, the heavy bullets snapping and whizzing past Rol's head, throwing up clods of earth at his feet, thudding into bodies with a slap of meat.

I will die today, Rol thought, and that knowledge was curiously calming. The looming panic left him. He sucked a breath into his starved lungs and drew Fleam. The scimitar gleamed bright as moonlight, a cold smile of steel. Gallico, Creed, and Giffon crouched nearby, and with them perhaps two dozen rebel soldiers, their arquebuses unfired.

"With me—come on!" And Rol set off at a sprint for the loyalist trench without looking back.

A bullet dinged off his breastplate, but did not slow him. He felt a curious feather of laughter flap in his throat, but when it came it blossomed into a maniac screech. He jumped high in the air, and as he did the light in his eyes ignited and caught fire, and when he came down again in the trench, Fleam had kindled like a torch and was burning white and cold, pale smoke rolling off her. He thrust the blazing sword into one man's face, and broke open his skull as he wrenched it free again. They were flailing at him with swords and the butts of their guns, but he did not feel the blows. He did not feel the

ground under his feet, and the roaring cacophony about him
no longer troubled his brain. He poured up the trench, cutting
to pieces every human being in his path, and when he reached
a gun-battery it was a simple thing to slice through the
wooden carriages and let the hot two-ton barrels crash to the
earth, broken engines of slaughter.

Someone stabbed him at the base of his backplate, just beside his spine. His legs buckled, but he did not go down. He
spun on the man's frenzied face and thrust his fingers deep
into the eye-sockets, popping the soft orbs within. Then he
ripped free the bone surround and the man collapsed, still
alive, an awful abject howling coming out of that red ruin.

More men running at him. A bullet blew off the tip of his
ear, burst the eardrum. Fleam was a mere flicker of white
flame. Men fell cut in two, headless, limbs lopped cleanly free
of their bodies. Rol fell to one knee, used Fleam as a staff to
lever himself upright again. A volley spattered around him,
clanging off his armor. The tip of one finger was blasted away
at the joint. He lurched forward again, killed a shouting officer, and laid in scarlet ruin the men he had gathered about
him. Then Rol went to his knees again in a puddle of his own
blood. The battle roared full-tilt all around, a titanic storm
that laughed at his insignificance. Anger flared up in him. A
bracing coldness veined through his flesh. He stood up. His
feet moved under him, though he could not feel the press of
his boots on the earth.

Gallico and Giffon had reached him, and a score of others.
The rebel soldiers hung back at the sight of his eyes, but
Gallico cursed and cuffed them onward.

"Down the trench—take the trench! Giffon, go to Rol, for
the love of God—do something."

Rol felt Giffon's hands working at the straps of his armor
and slapped them away. He looked up and found a gap in the

smoke of war overhead—how blue the sky was—and as he did, some portion of humanity returned to him.

"Where is Rowen?" he asked Gallico.

"Mired in blood, out on the plain with her bodyguard dead about her. They were trying to bring on the artillery, but the guns have all been destroyed. Rol, this has all gone wrong."

"Take the trench, Gallico. Get them together. We hold here until Canker comes up."

"Where is Canker? Where is that bastard, tell me that?" Gallico roared back at him, veins bulging in sudden fury.

"I'll find out. I have things to do."

"You're bleeding to death!" This was Giffon. His black and bloody face had white lines cut from eyes to chin.

Rol smiled at him. "You just keep your head down, lad. Where's Elias?"

"Off looking for your bloody Queen!"

At that, Rol's smile disappeared. His mouth widened in a rictus. "Gallico, you will fight here. You will make them fight, do you hear me? Silence their fucking guns!"

The halftroll nodded, fury still bright about his eyes. "What are you going to do?"

Rol hesitated. More than anything, he wanted to run back the way they had come, to seek out Rowen and get her into safety, to know she was alive. *See?* he would say to her. *This is where your ambition has taken you.*

But they were walled in by a fog of war; there was nothing to be seen beyond a hundred yards in every direction but half-glimpsed groups of men fighting one another with the un-thinking ferocity of beasts. Hand-to-hand now, all down the line, or what parts of it he could make out.

"I'm going to try and turn this thing around," he said. A fresh concussion of guns broke out to left and right. The other brigades must be in the trenches, too, by now. The tumult of their agonized roaring rose up to challenge even the bellow of the guns.

So this was war—this murderous stupidity, this stunning waste. Why was it that part of him was laughing, sucking down these sensations like a drunkard guzzling wine?

He did not care. He looked at Fleam's blade, and saw blood bubbling and steaming upon it, and knew he had rage enough left to do what he had to.

He climbed up out of the battery trench and set off at a gliding run, north to the loyalist encampment. On his face, the inhuman grin broke out and widened and the light came smoking from his eyes.

I am among you, and you know it not.

Seventeen

THE DARK HORSE

HE RIPPED OFF HIS RAGS OF SCARLET LIVERY AND EX-
changed them for the saffron and black surcoat of a loyalist
corpse, another man's blood mingling with his own as it
flapped wetly against his thighs. Uphill, the ground rising
blasted and broken under his feet, dotted with the broken car-
casses of men, shattered gun-carriages, blasted wagons, and
dead horses. Streams of limping wounded were trickling out of
the trenches below, appearing out of the smoke and then swallowed by it again like demented ghosts. Rol's mouth was
parched. He bent and gathered a fistful of the filthy snow and
crammed it over his lips, chewing the foul-tasting ice into water, swallowing grit. He closed his eyes, letting the stuff cool
his head. In his fists, Fleam's trembling eagerness subsided to a
thrumming vibration, no more. The fire in him was banked
down a little.

"Where is Aldahir?" a man shouted at him, an officer bearing a pistol and rapier, who did not look quite sane. "Get back
down that hill and find the colonel. Tell him—"

Rol cut his throat, took the pistol, and thrust it in his sash. Then he continued on his way.

The enemy encampment was ahead, and the smoke was thinner here. Files of loyalist soldiers were running downhill, into the maw of the holocaust, and laboring lines of others were manhandling boxes of shells and casks of powder in their wake. Rol grabbed one gesticulating sergeant by the arm.

"I've a message for the King. Where lies the Royal Standard?"

"Don't know. Farther up, a few hundred yards maybe, the big yellow tent. How goes the battle?"

"We're winning," Rol snarled, and ran on.

The tents ran in streeted lines and the earth roads between them had been corduroyed with thousands of logs. Here, the snow had been trodden down into a brown muck by the passage of countless regiments. Rol passed a huge supply dump, crated and casked foodstuffs piled higher than his head and extending over several acres. The tall yellow tent was just ahead, looking over a squared-off open space like a courtyard, but there was no standard flying from it. There were men on horseback here with clean uniforms and shining half-armor. They stopped him at the point of a lance.

"Stay! Name and purpose."

They were all alike, these Bionari. Rol swallowed his impatience. "Message for the King, from the front line."

"From which commander? Whose regiment are you with?" The speaker kicked his horse forward, and the lance-point drove Rol backwards, clicking off his breastplate.

"None of your damn business. Where is the King?"

"Observing from up the ridge. But that is not your concern. You are no courier. What is this message?"

Rol grasped the lance and with one wild jerk he yanked it out of the horseman's hands. Then he sent the butt of it smashing back at the middle of the man's face. The fellow half raised his hands to his head, then toppled out of the saddle.

Dropping the lance, Rol grasped his rearing mount's bridle and swung himself up on the animal's back without pausing to put his foot in the stirrup—something he had not done since Rowen had taught him as a boy.

The horse, angry and alarmed at this stranger on his back, pirouetted under him, hooves stamping, eyes rolling. The other lancers were jabbing their weapons at Rol, shouting. One clanged off his backplate. Another dug a chunk of flesh out of his horse's rump. That made the animal squeal and leap forward, only to collide with another lancer's mount. Rol drew one of his pistols, cocked it, and shot the other animal just behind its eye. It collapsed, rider and all, and he kicked his own steed savagely and beat it about the ribs with his pistol-barrel. The terrified creature took a huge leap over the dead horse and its shouting rider, almost unseating Rol. He took the reins, beat his horse some more, and was finally into a fast canter uphill, the horse's hooves sliding on the mud-smeared logs underfoot.

The remaining lancers took after him, shouting, blowing a horn and all that nonsense. Rol checked his sash. He still had two loaded pistols. Turning in the saddle, he threw the empty one at the face of the lancer nearest to him and it struck the front of his helm. The man staggered in the saddle, pulling un-thinking on the reins. His horse half reared, skidded on the mucky wooden road, back feet flying sideways under it. It went down hard, and the two behind it plowed into the unfortunate animal full-tilt, with a snapping of lances and bones.

Passing lines of soldiers paused to stare at the scene, and a shot snapped past Rol's head so close it whipped hair from his temple. His right eye watered and blurred, but he kicked his injured horse ferociously. No one else tried to stop him and he rode at a labored canter ever more steeply uphill, thumping the gelding's shoulder in his impatience and passing line after line of the eight-man section tents that housed Bar Asfal's in-fantry.

The camp came to an end at last with a symbolic flagpole and a pair of negligent sentries whose match was not even lit. They shouted ineffectually at Rol as he galloped past them. There was blue sky ahead, the summit of the ridge rising steep and blinding white in the sunlight some half mile above him, and closer to, a group of riders with a tall standard flapping in their midst. The King of Bionar watched the carnage in the valley below from the perfect viewpoint, to the rear of every man in his army.

Rol slowed his horse. It fought the reins, a mettlesome black-haired beast with an evil eye. It struggled against the strange rider despite the savage wolf-bit stabbing its mouth, blood foaming from its jaws. Rol drew another pistol and beat the barrel of it down between the animal's ears. It quietened a little. He reined in. The sun was high and clear, and up here on the summit of the hill there was no smoke, the snow was featureless and clean, and the storm of noise that was the fighting remained at one remove. He chanced a look back down into the fuming chaos of the valley, and saw there only a long soot-gray series of boiling clouds, and in them the sparkling red spits of arquebus-fire, here and there lines and clusters of men tiny with distance, dying in anonymity. What was Bar Asfal doing this far from the front? Could one command from this distance?

The guns were booming out from Myconn's walls, but their range did not extend this far. Now, in daylight, Rol saw the true extent of the city defenses and the siege-lines about them. The walls were a rusty ocher where the outer facing had been shot away to reveal the brick filling within—a patched gray and tawny snake with a sea of roofs beyond it. The great tower of the Warder, and farther back, the looming massiveness of the palace. Looking at it from this distance, Rol realized at last that the Bar Madivar Palace was a Weren Tower, like Michal Psellos's, but on a vaster scale.

Closer to, in the west and east, fresh formations of the enemy were coming up, regiment upon regiment. They were still some miles away, but an hour would see them close in to complete the destruction of Rowen's army, and of Rowen herself. Where were Canker and his troops?

Rol turned back to the gaggle of riders before him. Thirty or forty gorgeously caparisoned horsemen replete with flapping banners and flags, and above them all, the saffron and black fighting flag of Bionar. He had found his man.

He kicked the sullen horse forward, liking the animal for its dogged hatred of him. They trotted forward unchallenged; clearly the King felt no threat here, so far from the battle-lines below.

One hundred yards. One of the King's aides raised a gauntleted hand to point at Rol, a bloodied man on a bloody horse, trotting toward them with a strange light to his eyes and a face that was a mask of gore. There was a strange sound in the air, a thrumming in the very earth which Rol could not place. Not the battle; it came from over the skyline.

He leaned over in the saddle like a man badly wounded, and eased a pistol out of his sash with his left hand, clicking back the hammer. His hair fell forward, lank and sticky. He laid his forehead against the mane of his horse, and for a second closed his eyes, fighting the dizziness that beset him. He reined in just in front of the King of Bionar. No trace left now of the otherworldly light, the puissant killing-machine. His wounds were killing him with their pain, and the weakness leaked into him as his blood trickled steadily forth. One side of his head seemed filled with a high hissing emptiness where his eardrum had gone. His missing fingertip—it was the ring-finger of his right hand—had begun to clot over, a stump of hardening blood with a gleam of bone-tip in the middle of it. That hand was swelling fast, puffing out into uselessness. And it was his sword-hand.

With an immense effort he straightened in his saddle. Two of the King's aides drew closer on their gleaming horses. That damned sound over the brow of the ridge, coming closer. If he were even at the height of a ship's maintop he would be able to look over the other side of the hill and see what it was. It was important, he felt.

His mind was clouding over, as confused as the shaking thunder of the battlefield behind him; but one tunnel of resolve remained, light at the end of it. This thing must be done.

He found the King's face. Even on the battlefield, this man wore a crown, a golden, scrolling thing with a great ruby in the middle. Their eyes met, and the King's mouth began to form a word. He was the man in Rowen's picture, though portlier, his face more florid and the eyes underhung with dark pouches of flesh—a libertine's face, petulant and arrogant. A man who needed killing. Rol pointed his pistol.

The King's eyes widened and he raised an arm as if to fend off a blow. At the same moment there clicked into Rol's dazed mind a realization of what the sound was, over the ridge.

Marching men, thousands of them.

They came into view at the very top of the ridge, a ragged, endless line of them in rank on rank. Arquebusiers with their match still lit, their regimental flags unfurled. Before them came a man on a horse, a dark-eyed, cloak-wrapped fellow with a yellow grin.

"Canker," Rol croaked, and he smiled.

The King looked back, jaw agape. "Canker!" he shouted.

Rol's finger tightened on the trigger in the same second, and the pistol went off with a faint fizzing, no more; the powder in the pan had failed. He threw it down. The moment of stillness was shattered. Canker's men broke into a run as the Thief-King stood up in his stirrups and hallooed and waved a short sword so that the bright winter sun glittered off it. The King's aides charged their horses bodily into Rol's black gelding and bowled it backwards, the horse screaming with rage. Rol drew Fleam and hacked clumsily first at one, and then the other. The aides parried his blows. One sank his sword into the neck of Rol's horse and it jerked sideways in a great spray of stinking blood. The movement saved Rol's life, as the sword of the other clanked down on his breastplate instead of cleaving his skull. Fleam came up in Rol's swollen fist like the leap of a sunlit salmon. Her point took the aide in the armpit, cut through the chain mail as though it were wool, then pulled free again. The man bent over, hugging his arm to his side, sword spinning away. The black gelding bounced under Rol, a creature of blood and fury. He wheeled it round, knocked the other aide's horse off balance, and of its own volition the beast reared under him and brought its iron-shod hooves down on the remaining rider's head even as he raised his sword to disembowel it.

The black crashed onto its side, a long slash opened along its ribs—the girth had deflected the point of the blade. The frenzied animal kicked madly. Rol rolled clear. Fleam struck him in the face as he tumbled, slicing his cheekbone open, a hot kiss he barely felt. He found his feet, and with them his strength came back, and his mind cleared. Perhaps it was Fleam's kiss, but all at once he felt as whole and hale as he had marching out the gate that morning. He sprinted forward. The clot of riders about the King were milling and shouting, and behind them several thousand men in long ranks were pouring over the head of the ridge toward them, Canker trotting at their head.

Rol went in low, slashing at the legs of the horses. Fleam whipped and sang in his hands as he cut through sinew and hacked bone. The animals became unmanageable, bucking and rearing and trying to bring their hooves crashing down on their enemy, as they had been trained. He rolled under the belly of one, stabbed upward and came out from under as the thing's insides collapsed onto the snow and it sank to its haunches, shrieking. He pulled the rider down and stabbed him in the throat, severing the windpipe.

"Canker!" the King was yelling. He had drawn his sword but had lost his reins. His horse circled under him in angry terror. Rol sprang up onto the beast's hindquarters and it kicked out under him. He pushed Fleam into the King's side, just where the backplate and breastplate met. Bar Asfal gurgled, his sword-blade flailing, his free hand scrabbling for Rol's eyes. The crown he wore tore a hole in Rol's scalp before it fell off, to lie in the trampled and bloody snow.

Canker had halted before them. He sat his horse and watched as Fleam sank deep, deep into the King of Bionar's body. The man's florid face darkened. His eyes bulged, his frantically working arms fell limp at his sides. Rol held him in the saddle as though he were embracing an old lover he had caught by surprise. He looked in Canker's face, and saw that the Thief-King had a triumphant smile spread across his face, and he knew that something was wrong, horribly wrong.

Bar Asfal slid from the horse's back and the beast kicked Rol off its rump so that he crashed to the snow himself, dragging Fleam free. So swollen was his injured fist about her hilt that it seemed the scimitar had become part of his engorged flesh. He sprawled there, his legs entangled with those of Bar Asfal's corpse. The sun was in his eyes. Canker nudged his horse forward a few strides until his shadow fell over Rol. He was no longer smiling. All about them both, men were streaming past, down to join the battle in the valley below. Thousands of men, a great horde of eager fighters with bright eyes and bared teeth and smoking guns. They wore no livery of any kind, but nearly all of them had a white feather tucked in their helms, or pinned to their shoulders. They ran past, regiment by regiment, but a company of several dozen gathered about the Thief-King with drawn swords. One of them Rol recognized; he sat on a fine horse, a brown-eyed man with an eagle nose.

Moerus of Gallitras, the man who had supposedly surrendered his city to the enemy. Rol kicked himself free of Bar Asfal's corpse and stood up.

"You look all-in, my young friend," Canker said. "You have done me a great service today; you deserve a rest."

Rol looked about himself, at the feather tucked in every man's helmet. He breathed in deeply. His body was near collapse, but he had been taught how to husband even the last dregs of his strength for moments such as this. And in this moment he blessed Michal Psellos for his training, and looking at Canker, he felt he understood them both.

"It was not enough to be chancellor, was it, Canker?"

"No, Rol, it was not enough. If you are happy coming second, then there is no point to running in the race."

Here Moerus dismounted. Bending, he retrieved Bar Asfal's buckled and bloody crown from the snow and handed it to Canker. The Thief-King stared at it a moment, face expressionless.

"What of Rowen?" Rol asked him.

"She will die today, if she is not already dead. Bionar is a tired and broken place. Rowen had her chance to take it, but failed. The war ends here. Today."

"And then hail King Canker, the greatest thief of all."

Canker nodded. There was no malice in his gaze; there was even a kind of regret. To the men who stood around him, he said quietly, "Kill him."

Rol turned and ran.

Fleam snicked out left, right. A clash of steel, the buffet of a sword-hilt on the side of his ringing head, and he was sprinting down the hill.

"Kill him!" Canker shouted.

The black gelding stood in his path as though awaiting him.

He vaulted into the saddle of the poor, wounded beast and kicked its bloody ribs. The horse took off at a gallop, shouldering running soldiers aside and leaving them sprawling. Gunfire crackled about them both and the horse groaned as a bullet found its flank, but galloped on, tongue lolling out of its mouth like a raw fillet of meat.

Downhill he went, along with Canker's regiments, a great river of hell-bent humanity intent on plunging into the cauldron below. Rol ripped off his surcoat as he rode, the reins dangling free on the black horse's neck, the beast plunging and slipping on the icy muck of the wooden road, but somehow always finding its feet again. Downhill, through the huge tented camp, many of the tents flattened now. Men made way for the big horse and its rider, the pair of them a bloody apparition, an avatar of war.

Downhill at a full, lurching gallop, the horse's blood spattering Rol's face as it sprayed from the animal's injuries. The smoke and fume and roar of the battle enveloped them again, a grainy fog lit with flashes of sudden red and yellow light, and in the middle of it men squirming in the snow and the mud, killing one another any way they could, with anything that came to hand.

The gelding stumbled and fell at the very lip of the reserve trenches. Rol leaped from its back as the animal rolled, crushing the pommel of the saddle flat. It kicked its hind legs as though convinced it were still erect, then lay spent, barrel chest heaving. Rol crouched by the animal's tortured carcass a few seconds and stared into the liquid eye. He patted the gelding's neck once, then rose and began to run.

He leaped over trenches filled with struggling bodies. Bar Asfal's men—they would become Canker's men now, he supposed—were fighting with the knowledge of victory in their eyes, but Rowen's people, outnumbered many times over, were resisting them with the valor of despair. Rol ran along the ground between the forward and reserve trenches, booting soldiers out of his way, slashing at those who tried to stop him, friend and foe alike.

Gallico. The halftroll's bellowing was unmistakable, even over the clamor of battle. He loomed up like some myth-made monster in the smoke, swinging his war-hammer and knocking men down like skittles. At his side were Creed and Giffon, both fighting furiously, and with them a dozen of Rowen's bodyguard, on foot now, their heavy armor streaked with blood. Gideon Mirkady's ringlets were plastered all across his face, giving him the look of a demented poet. And behind him was Rowen, pale as a lily and as calm, giving orders to a gaggle of junior officers. In the wider circle around them the survivors of the regiments who had marched out of Myconn that morning were gathering in ones and twos and broken squads, rallying to the Queen for a last stand.

Rol stumbled in his relief, going to his knees. He looked back up the hill but could see nothing through the smoke. Canker's army had not yet reached them. There might be time.

Fleam cleaved a path for him, the sword an intelligence unto itself. Rol felt he was merely propelling it forward while the marvelous blade did the fighting for him, a thing unwearied and unwounded, growing palpably stronger with each life it ended. Gallico shouted gladly in recognition as Rol joined their ranks. Once again his legs went out from under him. His precious blood was nearly drained dry. Giffon tossed down his sword and began searching through his satchel for dressings. For a little while, Rol drifted away.

He came back to himself with cold hands about his face, and Rowen was staring down at him.

"You are cut to pieces, Fisheye. You should take more care."

He grasped her fingers, striving to make his voice heard over the surrounding tumult.

"Canker has betrayed you. He means to take the crown for himself. Bar Asfal is dead. The field is lost, Rowen. You must get clear."

She blinked. "Canker?"

"His men are joining the battle as we speak—against us. He means to kill you. It's over, Rowen. We must get out of here."

"The bastard." This was Gideon Mirkady, wild-eyed behind his mask of bloody hair.

"I'm not going anywhere," Rowen said, her voice so low he had to read the words from her lips.

"It's death to stay here," Rol told her.

Giffon was pressing grubby linen into his wounds. "Heave him up," he said, and as they did he stuffed cloth into the gash in Rol's back. He tried to lever Fleam out of Rol's swollen fist.

"No. Leave it."

The world was graying. This could not be—not now, not here. He fought to keep their swimming faces clear in his head. He could have howled in despair.

Rowen leaned in close, and for a moment the battlefield disappeared. "It is you who must go, Rol. This is not your fight. I'm sorry I brought you to it."

"I stay with you," he groaned.

"No. You must live." She smiled, the true smile he had always treasured. She stroked his bloody face.

"We can run. We could be happy yet, Rowen, if you would leave all this behind you."

"No, Rol. You and I were not brought upon this earth to have happy lives." She kissed him on the lips, her flesh as cold as one already dead. "I stay. I can do no other."

"I love you," he whispered.

"I know." Her eyes filled. She straightened. "Gallico, Elias, take him. Get him out of here." She raised her voice until it carried about the men who were gathering around her.

"All who wish to can try to make their way back to the city, and seek whatever terms Canker chooses to offer. I am Bar Hethrun's daughter, last of the line of Bion, rightful Queen of this kingdom. I mean to stay here and fight on in this place. It's as good as any other."

Men stared at her in fear and awe and a kind of love. The ranks did not shift. Gideon Mirkady knelt at her feet with a smile on his face.

"I serve the Queen of Bionar, to the last of my strength."

She set a hand on his head.

A space, a gap; a gray intermission. When the world came back to him, Rol was hanging upside down and being pounded in the stomach. Six feet away, the shattered ground retreated at a great pace. He was across Gallico's shoulder, and the halftroll was running.

He squirmed. "No." And more loudly, "No—put me down."

The halftroll halted, and brought him down from his shoulder into his arms. He was wheezing like a punctured bellows. "Rol, we have no time."

"Turn me around, Gallico. Let me see."

They were under the walls of Myconn again, and about them the roar of the battle had receded somewhat. Creed and Giffon stood gasping, leaning on each other. Rol turned his head to the north, and stared back into that fuming cauldron, that storm. The arquebus-fire was dwindling to a crackle of isolated shots, and the artillery barked sporadically, as if in bad temper. Dots of scarlet came and went in the smoke, struggling with streaming crowds of figures in saffron and black. Here, even here, their shouting could be heard.

A cluster of scarlet stood out from the smoke for a few moments; a back-to-back group of two or three dozen, no more.

"Gallico," Rol said. "What do you see?"

The halftroll's arms tightened about him. "They are surrounded. I see that fellow Mirkady. I see—" He went silent.

They watched. The smoke came and went. Rol's world grayed in and out. Finally, Gallico gave a low groan.

"It is over."

The scarlet dots had all disappeared, and it was as though the earth had swallowed them. Gallico bent his head. And silence began to drift down over the battlefield.

Eighteen

THE MOUNTAIN ROAD

IT HAD BEGUN TO SNOW AGAIN. THE COLD BLED DEEP into Rol's wounds and seemed to be seeking what warm spaces there were left about his heart. Under him, the handcart rattled and jumped over the rocky ground, and he was aware of people laboring all around, an exhausted mass of humanity. But it was all at one remove. In his mind there burned a memory of Rowen's face. His poor sister, dead now, lying stark as a cut flower in the muck and mire of that stinking battlefield. At the end she had become a queen in truth, something larger than herself. Men had laid down their lives for her willingly, men who hardly knew her. And now he, who had loved her above all others—or so he had told himself—here he was, fleeing the scene of that crime.

A thing that had been Michal Psellos had once told him that he would never give away more of himself than he could afford. And that thing had been right. No matter how he might mourn his valiant, dead sister, he was glad not be lying next to her on that lost field, glad to be running with his tail between his legs. Glad to be alive.

It was a dream brought me here, he thought. A boy's infatuation. Well, it is done now, and I saw it out to very near the end.

They were in the Fornivan Hills south of Myconn, that much he knew. If he sat up, he would be able to look down on the Imperial City, its walls scarcely a league away. Canker had taken possession of it after only the briefest of struggles at the Forminon Gate; the massive fortifications had proved irrelevant when there were no men willing to man them. Of their own passage through the city, Rol retained only an impression of chaos and screaming crowds, Gallico's animal roar clearing a path for them as they trekked south through the city streets, accreting hangers-on as they went.

Canker had a fearsome reputation in Bionar, and though his heralds had ridden up to the city walls offering amnesties for all who threw down their arms, he was not entirely believed. Stark fear propelled a panicked horde out of Myconn into the hills, and many of those refugees had followed Gallico because he stood out, he had purpose, and perhaps also there was simply something reassuring about his blunt physicality. So now they were part of a streaming host of people: soldiers, commoners, nobles, criminals. Something for everyone, Rol thought muzzily.

In the back part of his mind the anger smoldered steadily. The promise that, one day, Canker would die under his hands.

Giffon was fidgeting with him again. It was dark—what had happened to the daylight?—and now the night was stitched with flapping campfires. A blanket had been pulled up to his chin and his breath had frosted it white. He tried to prop himself up on one elbow but the sharp pain that sent shooting through his arm stole the breath from his mouth. He fumbled with his right hand and found it swathed in neatly knotted linen. The rest of his body was cold, shivering, but under that mass of cloth something was radiating a putrid heat. His hand, or what was left of it.

"I had to cut off the rest of the finger," Giffon said. The boy was kneeling beside him with a steaming bowl. "You were senseless at the time. There's a fever building. If the rest of the hand goes bad I'll have to take the arm off at the elbow. Skipper, can you hear me?"

"I hear you." His mouth was dry. Giffon spooned watery lukewarm soup over his lips. Rol tasted wild thyme, some kind of game.

"Skipper, you must try to heal yourself." Giffon's attention never wavered. He wiped soup out of Rol's rime-frosted beard. His moon-shaped face was drawn now; it seemed narrower. Rol had a glimpse of what Giffon would look like as a middle-aged man—if he ever made it that far.

"Like after Gallitras, when your wounds healed in a night. You must do that again, skipper, or you'll die. Do you hear me?"

He heard him, but already Rol was drifting past the words and the meaning. One thing hauled him back to earth.

"Fleam," he said.

"It's beside you, on your left side."

He touched the familiar hilt, and smiled at the warmth in it.

"Skipper," Giffon was saying, tears coursing down his face. But Rol was already far away.

"I see you still carry that sword," Rowen said.

"Fleam? Yes. She's a fine weapon."

"She?"

Rol shrugged. "All things are she to a man. Ships, cities, even kingdoms."

Rowen knelt by the fire and stirred the logs with the iron poker. "Fleam, you call it. Not the most poetic of names."

"She was made for the letting of blood." Rol smiled and stood looking down on his sister, watching the firelight shine out a dark blood-brown from the lighter glints in her hair.

"I wielded it once," Rowen said.

"I wonder you were willing to give her up. Or did Psellos take her away from you?"

Rowen looked up quickly. "The sword hated me."

It took a few seconds to digest this. Then Rol asked, "Why?"

"I don't know. I was not meant to have it, I think. Nor was Psellos, or else he'd have kept such a weapon for himself. There's something alive in that blade, Rol, something trapped there that's been waiting a long time."

"Waiting for what?"

"For you."

Another place, the years whipping backward like the leaves of a book. Michal Psellos cradling a glass of wine between both hands, the white fingers vivid against the scarlet, he sniffing the fragrance of the liquid and smiling with lupine humor.

"You must try this, Rol. Bionese—Palestrinan, in fact. A little far north for fruitiness. This is dry, a thing to roll along the teeth. Come, boy, drink."

Rol did as he was bidden. All along the heavy table, bottles stood glowing in the light from the tall windows beyond. Spring rain thrashed at the glass, shot through with sunshine. The wine warmed him, a sour thing in the mouth, a taste he had not yet become accustomed to.

"It's bitter."

"To begin with, yes. You must learn to savor the taste, Rol; the best wines demand a little patience, a little knowledge. One does not swill them as though they were beer. They are like life itself; one cannot have sweetness all the time, else it would become cloying." Psellos set down his glass. He ranged up and down the other bottles on the table, a lean figure all in black. His silver eyeteeth gleamed. He looked like a great sable spider done up in velvet and satin and silk. Rol's attention drifted. He edged closer to the great windows, and looked down. In the cobbled yard fifty feet below, Rowen was saddling her black mare. She had thrown back the hood of her cloak, and the rain was shining in her hair so that it was slick as a seal's back. Rol watched her lips move as she talked to the horse.

"A gentleman," Psellos went on, "must have discrimination when it comes to wine; his tastes betray him as surely as do the contents of his library, or the quality of his women. There is the stuff of everyday use"—he lifted a bottle and held it up a moment—"and then there are the finer vintages, to be enjoyed sparingly." He caressed the neck of a bottle whose label was darkened with dust, yellow with age. He strolled to the windows, looked down a second, and smiled. "One cannot expect to continually enjoy the best of what life has to offer. That would be stultifying. There must be bitterness amid the bliss. A man must learn that, if he is to become much of a man at all."

Psellos's curious eyes darkened. "Drink the wine, Rol. Savor the taste. And when you are served up something inferior in your glass, drink it also. Taste everything, but do not forget those times when what you have tasted has been sublime."

When Rol came to himself again he found that tears had run in frozen tracks down the sides of his head, and his eyelashes crackled as he blinked. Daylight again. They were still on the move, the handcart trundling stubbornly onward beneath him, the air thin and cold. A mist hung heavy about him, and out of it shrouded shapes appeared and disappeared like wayward ghosts.

One of those ghosts walked by the side of the handcart, muffled and hooded. A gloved hand gripped his. "You're back! Can you speak?" The shape dropped a scarf from around its face, and it was a girl under all those ragged folds, dark-eyed and sallow-skinned.

"I know you," he said, the cold air clicking in his throat.

Her fingers tightened around his. "The night of the ball; we spent it together." Some color crept into her face. "You don't remember."

"Your name is Rafa. I remember. Why are you here?"

"I did not want to be a slave anymore."

"You were going to be freed. I remember."

"The Queen was going to free me, but she's dead now. This new King will do different things."

Elias Creed appeared out of the mist like an old memory. His badger-striped head was more white than black now. He used a spear as a staff. "You decided to rejoin us, then."

The handcart halted, and Gallico was there, too, a looming giant with green lights that blinked in the mist. "How do you feel?"

"I feel—I—" Rol sat up. Relinquishing Rafa's hand he began picking at the massive bandage on his own. It was loose now, hanging flaccid as a cobweb. He was able to rip it off without undoing any of Giffon's neat knots. Below the stained linen there was his own flesh, yellow-white and smelling of old cheese. He flexed his fingers and studied in some wonder the stump where the ring-finger had been. It was closed over, a ripple of scar—but he could still feel the missing digit move as he opened and closed his fist.

"I knew it!" This was Giffon. He barged between Creed and Gallico and took Rol's hand in his own, face shining. "I knew you could do it, skipper. You're healed. You're going to live."

"I'm glad to hear it," Rol said mildly. He felt slightly absurd sitting there on the handcart, one hand gripped again by the girl Rafa, the other by the boy Giffon. Creed and Gallico beamed at him like a pair of simpletons.

"Get me off this damned cart. My legs need a stretch."

"It's been five days," Elias Creed said. "You've been raving for three of them, a fever like I've never seen. We were all set to dig you a hole here amid the rocks, but Giffon never lost hope. He and the chambermaid—that lovely dark wench—they've been fussing round you day and night, doing things a mother would quail at."

"Rafa can wipe my arse anytime she likes," Gallico said.

"We're maybe eighteen leagues from Myconn, up in the high foothills to the northeast of the Fornivo Pass. There's been no pursuit that I can see."

"Canker is busy with other things," Gallico said.

"Indeed. And just as well. We've gathered quite a mob around us. The column stretches two or three miles; thousands of people, many of them noble. Where in hell they think they're going is anyone's guess."

"We must get back to Ganesh Ka," Rol said. He was leaning on Creed's arm, his legs still rubbery, still remembering what it was to bear his weight. The thin air had him gasping. "How high up are we?"

"Some ten thousand feet," the halftroll said. "The Fornivan Hills rear up pretty steep to the north, but then come together in a kind of plateau—we're on the lip of it now. There's a wide, broken plain of sorts to the south and east of us, until you hit the Myconians themselves; they rise up like a wall, another five thousand feet."

The breath plumed out of his wide nostrils in two jets, and in his chest it rattled through mucus: an awful sound.

"Gallico, I thought you were healed."

"So did I. I told you, it's the cold." The halftroll frowned.

"How far are we from the Ka, you think?"

Gallico's bright eyes narrowed. "As the crow flies, I'd put it at some seventy-five leagues, but not even crows fly over the Myconians in winter. There's the pass at Fornivo, some forty miles southwest of us. It leads through to the Goliad, and is studded with Bionese fortresses. It's the only way across the mountains that I know of—in this part of the world, at least."

"Canker will have thought of that. I'll bet the Fornivo garrison has already come over to him. That's why there's no pursuit; he thinks us trapped."

They trudged along in silence for some time after this, until at last Elias Creed said, "Then what are we to do?"

Rol raised his head, but could see nothing through the caul of mist. "We must find another way through the mountains," he said.

"One cannot simply put one's head down and charge blindly at the Myconians like a bull at a gate," Gallico said.

"Can't one? It's what one will have to do, all the same. Gallico, there must be a way."

"Not for these people." The halftroll gestured to the disparate throng that disappeared into the mist behind them.

"If they were desperate enough to follow your lead out of Myconn, then they're desperate enough to attempt the mountains."

Desperate indeed. At night the straggling column coalesced into an amorphous huddle, like that of herd animals seeking protection amid their fellows. While Gallico and Elias Creed went through the crowds, noting their names and station and physical capabilities, Rol gave a series of little speeches. Short and to the point, they informed the refugees of his plans and gave them three choices. They could follow him over the mountains, they could turn back for Myconn, or they could break off for the southwest and attempt the Fornivan passes, hoping that the garrisons there would not be against them.

As choices went, none of them were particularly appealing, and Rol did not try very hard to woo anyone to his own course. Those who followed him would walk the hardest road, and they would either come to Ganesh Ka in the end, or they would perish along the way. There would be no turning back, and the weak would be abandoned. He made this very clear, and saw blank fear in the faces of all who listened to him. His wounds had made him less pretty than he had been. He was short a finger and part of an ear, and had a white scar that wriggled from one eyebrow into his hairline. He looked older, a fearsome captain of privateers every bit as ruthless as rumor had made him. And his eyes were colder than the white mountains ahead. Many looked upon that face and found themselves quitting the host for fear of what was in those eyes as much as the dangers of the road they would follow.

The host began breaking up the next morning, in small groups and large, by dozens and scores and finally hundreds. They trekked away in solemn companies through the snow, heading southwest, or north. Rol and his friends remained encamped all that day while the desertions went on, and as the night swooped in on them again, there were barely four hundred left out of all those who had followed them into the hills.

"We keep to the valleys, so far as we can," Rol said, warming his hands at the guttering campfire. "We stay as low as the terrain allows. There's forests on the flanks of the mountains, and scrub higher up still; we'll need firewood if we're to survive the nights. The main worry is food. We're still a fair crowd. Did anyone bring provisions out of Myconn with them?"

"All eaten a day or two back," Elias Creed said. "These are city-dwellers. They brought gold and trinkets when they should have packed warm clothing and food."

"There are reindeer herds in the high valleys, or so I've been told," Gallico said. "We have quite a few firearms among us. We must hunt every chance we get, anything from deer to foxes. And if we run short, we'll eat the dead."

He was half smiling, but the group around the campfire looked at him in grim silence. Giffon's eyes were wide as plums in his pinched face, and Rafa had buried her head in her knees. Rol touched her black hair.

"So be it," he said. "Gallico, what's our course?"

"South-southeast."

"You're sure about that?"

"Even here, Rol, I know in which direction lies the sea. There are times, when the wind is in the east, that I think I can even smell it."

"Then your nose is our compass, Gallico, and may it be as sharp as you say it is."

Their daily marches were short, by necessity, as part of each day had to be given over to gathering firewood and hunting for game. Within a few days the company fell into a routine, and within it each of them found some niche to fill. Some preferred to gather firewood, others to trek out from the main body in small groups to hunt, while yet more grubbed for other forms of food in the frozen landscape around them. In the twilit hours after each day's march they foraged like their flint-using ancestors, desperate to recoup some of the day's expended energy. They collected tens of thousands of pinecones, roasted them in the embers of their fires, and ate the nuts within. They tapped silver birch, while those still grew about them, and heated the sap with water to make a sweet, hot drink for the weaker among them. They dug under the snow for any form of tuber they could find, and all went in the communal pots. They set overnight snares for rabbits and martens and any other beast with warm blood that might chance by, and the hunting-parties brought down a family of elk, which fed them all for three days.

But it was not enough to keep the pinch of hunger out of their bellies. The flesh began to melt from them, and the cold dug deeper into their marrow. Within a week, they had the first deaths, from cold and exposure. They stripped the dead of all their clothing, though they were not yet hungry enough to prey on the meat of the corpses themselves.

The company began to ascend the flanks of the mountains proper, and around them the thick pine woods receded like the ebbing tide of a quiet sea. Firewood became harder to come by, and often the campfires puttered out in the dark hours whilst around them hundreds lay in chaste embraces and shared their body's warmth for want of something better.

Two weeks. Every morning there were more stiffened corpses amid the huddled crowd. The cold intensified, though mercifully the days remained calm and clear, snow blowing in powdery banners from the peaks of the mountains, but down below a windless silence, an abeyance of life. They began to dream about food, and it was discussed endlessly round the fragile campfires. The splendor of past dinners, the constitution of ideal menus, the listing of favorite delicacies. Their mouths watered on memories.

Some went blind from the glare of the sunlit snow. They tore strips of cloth from their thinner clothing and tied them about their eyes, staring out at that terrible whiteness through frayed silk or cotton or linen, stumbling myopically on numb feet. Those among them who prided themselves on their skill at stalking no longer had the strength to fare far afield in search of game. Gallico alone continued to hunt most nights, and it was rare he did not bring in a deer in the morning, its neck broken and dangling. As they climbed higher they dared not shoot the arquebuses anyway for fear of bringing down an avalanche on their heads. Some resisted this stricture, until

Gallico rounded on them, eyes blazing amethyst, gaunt flesh drawn back from his great fangs. What game he brought back was sliced up and shared out with the meticulous care a miser might show to his hoard of gold. If they had no wood, the meat was eaten raw, bloody gobbets washed down with handfuls of snow.

A remarkable stoicism pervaded them. Though there might be arguments over the sharing out of food, in the main the Bionese accepted their meager portions with good grace. They were a hardy people, Rol realized. He had seen this in their soldiery, but he realized now that it pertained to all, old and young, male and female.

Of course, many of those who had followed him thus far were not Bionese at all, but, like Rafa, were foreign slaves fleeing their new master back in Myconn. These, too, were uncomplaining folk, and they trusted Gallico implicitly, for in the halftroll they sensed a great compassion for their lot in life. In the beginning, the company was divided along the lines of slave and free, but as time went on these distinctions became forgotten, and nobleman huddled up beside thrall, the distinctions of their former lives forgotten. The only differences now were between the weak and the strong, those who could stay with the column and those who were destined to fall by the wayside.

Three weeks. The dead continued to slough off from the living, their corpses turning up every morning, stripped and stiff as wood. Many of these bodies now were carved up in the dark hours of the night, and each dawn lay eviscerated, whittled down to the bone, barely human at all. None admitted to doing it, but nearly all partook of this ghastly sacrament. The anonymous meat was passed around the campfires and eaten without comment. Rol had his share of it, as had Creed, Giffon, and Rafa, but oddly enough Gallico refused to partake with them. "You must eat, and keep your strength," Giffon told him, but the halftroll smiled and set his massive clawed hand on the boy's shoulder. "I have more meat than most on my bones; my body can eat itself for a while yet."

Four weeks. The weather broke at last, and the wind picked up through the peaks, the stars crowded out of the sky by a blank furious whiteout of hurling snow. The company went to ground in the sparse shelter of some contorted spruce and juniper and squatted there hour after hour as the snow piled up around them, finally muffling all in a merciful white roof that gathered inch upon inch as the hours went on, and lengthened into a day, then two. At first they took turns sitting on the outside of the tight-packed circle, for those unfortunates had it worst. But as more and more of these died, their corpses were propped up as a kind of horrible windbreak behind which the living sheltered and shivered. Drifts built up around them, and finally covered them.

They were entombed, and within their white sepulchre they feasted on the dead openly and without shame, fighting beyond rationality to keep the life in their gnawed-down souls. Some staggered out into the blizzard to end it all, hoping to find death in a place where their corpses would be left in peace, but most died in silent surprise, or drifted off into a warm sleep and left the world with meaningless smiles on their gray faces. The world slowed. Their cocoon of snow became a small, fetid space of numbing cold and butchery, a dwindling circle of faces in which only the glitter of the eyes gave any clue of life remaining. They were five days like this.

The wind fell, and they tunneled their way out of their white tomb to find a barren world in which all color had disappeared except for the violent, cerulean blue of the sky above them. Waist-deep in snow, many gave up then and there, and crawled back into the blue-dark of the cave that had built up around their bodies in the preceding days. Others stared blankly at the pitiless mountains all around, knowing they would never walk out of this place, never see grass again or hear running water. Their hearts still beat, their eyes still blinked, and the blood still pushed its stubborn way through their veins, but they were dead men all the same. The Myconians had killed them.

Gallico took Rol aside while the others crawled about the blank landscape like old men. "They are all going to die, Rol, unless we do something."

Their eyes met in perfect understanding. "It cannot be everyone," Rol said. "And it must be done discreetly. We'll make a day's march, and those who are still with us at the end of it shall partake."

"That's consigning half of them to death."

"It can't be all of them, Gallico; that would be our own end."

The halftroll considered, then nodded at last. Broad though his shoulders were, his head appeared too large for them, and his face was a mere fanged skull with green skin stretched taut across it. Only in the eyes was there any remnant of the humanity that Rol knew still bulked large in Gallico's heart.

"How far is left, do you think?" Rol asked.

"My nose is not what it was," Gallico said with a wry smile, "but we're over the spine of the mountains. I smell trees below, a whole forest of them. Another week or two, and we'll be in the Ganesh Highlands. Remember them, Rol?"

"How could I forget?"

"It was only a year ago, or a little more."

"Is that all? It seems like a different age of the world."

They bullied and cajoled and cursed the survivors of the company to their feet, and Gallico led the way, burrowing through the drifts and forging a passage for those who came behind.

The halftroll carried Giffon on his back, for the boy could no longer walk, and Rol and Creed took it in turns to carry Rafa. The chambermaid was in a bad way, with frostbite in pale patches on her face and her feet blackened with it. The less fortunate had to make their own way in the furrow that Gallico's great body carved through the drifts, and when Rol looked back later that day, he saw the black shapes of their bodies dotting the snow like drops of ink on a blank page. They were above him now; the company was indeed descending.

That night he took Fleam and nicked a vein in his wrist, then one in Gallico's. One by one those who were still able came to suck upon their blood, a few drops each, no more. Fewer than a hundred of them were still alive, but by the time it was over both he and Gallico were barely conscious. Someone had found enough wood for a single, solitary campfire, and they were laid down beside it whilst Creed, Giffon, and Rafa shared the meager heat of their bodies under piles of dead men's clothes, the five of them in a tangled heap, their hearts beating together and the welcome flames flickering across their faces.

In the night, Rol rose without disturbing his fellow sleepers, his body as light as a breeze-borne scrap of thistledown. All around him the savage heights of the Myconians dreamed placidly under their mantles of snow, and above them the stars glittered bright and blue, windows to another world. He stood in some indeterminate space, looking down on the sleepers below with serene detachment.

"I died," he said, wondering.

"Not dead, but dying," a voice said. "Each day you leave behind more of this husk you inhabit, and come closer to what is at the heart of your existence." The speaker was a dark shape, no more, an impenetrable shadow in which two green lights burned for eyes—like Gallico's eyes, but with none of the halftroll's compassion. No humanity.

"What are you?" Rol whispered.

"The last remnant of an older world. I am part of your conception. You and I both are only pieces of a bigger plan which even I cannot foresee entirely. You are my son, the child of my blood. I have remained upon this earth far beyond my time, waiting out uncounted centuries merely to see you born. That was my doom."

"Who are you?" Rol repeated.

"What's in a name? At one time I was called Cambrius Orr. In this age of the world I am known differently. Men call me the Mage-King. You are my son, blood of my blood, but it was not I who brought you into being."

"Then who did?"

"Perhaps it was Umer herself. Perhaps Ran. I don't know. I know more of the world's history than any other thing now living, and I do not have the answer to that question."

"Perhaps it was God."

"There is no God. He has forsaken us. There is no heaven, and there is no hell except that which we make for ourselves here on earth. I know only that you were brought into this life for a purpose. And this: there is nothing human in you, nothing at all."

"I'm a man; look at me. I—"

"I don't know the full story of your heritage, and if I do not, then no one does. But I can smell your blood. Look at your hand."

Rol did so. His scarred hand, a mark put there by something that might have been Ran himself, god of storms, ship-killer. The lines that whorled upon his palm seemed more prominent now, and more than ever he thought that there was a purpose to their sinuous geometry.

"It was put there for a purpose, like everything else. One day soon you will read it clearly, and when you do, it shall show you where to go. These beggars in the snow, those beggars of the sea who await you; they are all part of it. It will come to you, in time."

Rol raised his head. "I don't want any of this."

"No matter. It is your fate, and cannot be outrun."

A strung-out, staggering company, they trudged on, and about them the air began to lose the thin gasp of the high places. The trees returned, dark forests of silent pine and spruce and fir. The company were walking downhill, always downhill, back into color and life and a world they had thought lost forever. But it was too late for many.

They buried Rafa under a cairn of stones just below the snow-line, and when they had clicked the last rock on top of her somber marker, the rain came sweeping in from the east to drench them. Not snow, rain—which they stood shivering under and let run in and out of their mouths like simpletons.

Simpletons, and starveling scarecrows. Despite Rol and Gallico's gift of blood, they continued to die in ones and twos. By the time they finally felt green grass underfoot there were barely four score of them left. They were in the Ganesh Highlands, scant leagues away from Ganesh Ka itself, and they had crossed the Myconian Mountains in a little over six weeks.

Nineteen

THE BEGGARS OF THE SEA

"IT'S STILL THERE," GIFFON BREATHED, AND HIS RAW knuckles whitened on the staff.

"Did you think it was going to drift away into the Reach?" Gallico asked. His eyes flickered, embers of old humor.

"It just seems so long. So much in between."

They stood and stared at Ganesh Ka's towers looming up out of the morning, and all around them rose the scent of juniper, and thyme bruised by their feet. Rol's eyes stung and smarted at the sight. If he called any place in the world his home, it was this. He knew that now.

"I see a ship, out to the northeast," Creed said, voice cracking. "Ran's arse, it's the *Revenant.* Rol, I see the *Revenant.*"

They stood transfixed, their eyes hunting out the blue horizon. It was too far away to tell, but, "Yes. It's the *Revenant,*" Rol said.

"So Artimion hasn't gotten her sunk yet," Gallico said.

Behind them the rest of the company was gathering in a ragged, stumbling band and staring east in their turn. Rol turned and surveyed them. Runaway slaves, Bionese soldiers and freemen, common criminals. Once they had all been inhabitants and citizens of the Imperial Capital. Now they looked like nothing so much as a crowd of haggard, malodorous beggars.

"Where is it?" one demanded. "Where is this city of yours?"

"Hidden in the rocks. The pillars of stone you see down there are not natural; they're the towers of Ganesh Ka. I wish you joy of the sight; we have accomplished the crossing of the mountains."

The man wiped his eyes with a black-nailed hand. His nose had been lost to frostbite but his eyes were clear. "Will they feed us there?"

"As much as you can eat. We're all brothers now, vagabonds of the sea."

"Aye. Until the new King sends his ships against us."

Rol and Gallico exchanged glances. It was not something they had given much thought to, but now that it seemed they were not to die, after all, the knowledge of Canker's hostility raised inevitable questions in their minds.

"The prevailing winds will be blowing right in the teeth of any ship trying to round Windhaw Island from the west, this time of year," Gallico said. "And it's by ship they must come; there's no bringing an army over the road we've just followed."

"Have they ships to send?" Rol wondered.

"Canker rules all of Bionar by now. He has no one afloat to contend with save us."

"So we must rely on the mercy of the wind."

"And Ran. He knows all that goes on upon the face of the waters."

It was Creed who led the company over the ruined boundary wall of the Ka, for Rol and Gallico were too exhausted to do anything else but stumble blindly after the man in front. They hardly noticed the green-tipped trees, the primroses and snowdrops sprinkling the ground at their feet. Spring was almost upon them, and the air here down by the sea seemed incredibly warm after the mountains. It was not much more than a year since Rol, Gallico, and Creed had last come this way together, the skin of their faces still peeled and blistered from the heat of the Gorthor Flats.

"I'm never walking anywhere again," Gallico mumbled. "It's the sea for me now; blessed Ussa shall bear me everywhere I wish to go."

"Amen," Rol said.

At the broken gate of Ganesh Ka there was a troop of Miriam's musketeers, plainly taken aback by the stricken mob they saw shambling down out of the hills toward them. In the last mile or two Rol and his companions had accrued a swarm of the Ka's inhabitants who had been working in the upland fields, or with the logging camps, and these folk were now bearing on their shoulders those of the company for whom this final mile had proved too much. Heads lolling, these unfortunates were beyond caring if they should ever eat or sleep or bear their own weight again.

Rol heard his name called, and that of Gallico, spreading in whispers and hoarse shouts before them. More people were streaming out of the towers, coming up from the sea in crowds. He had not thought the Ka contained so many. They pressed around, yelling, cheering, waving their arms. Creed tried to warn them back, but he was engulfed by people who clapped him on the shoulders and laughed out his name. The company staggered to a halt. Rol grasped Giffon's shoulder. He and the boy helped each other remain upright as they were buffeted by the misplaced goodwill of those around them.

Gallico's good humor evaporated. "Get out of the fucking way! Can't you see these people are dead on their feet? Make a lane there! You, Sorios, get word to Artimion and Miriam. We need food for these people. Get the goddamned spits turning. Lend a hand there, you damn fools."

Somehow they made it down to the stepped tunnel leading to the square, the bright day cut off and torchlight taking its place. By then almost every soul who had made it over the mountains had a pair of helpers to prop him up, and around Gallico half a dozen vied for the honor. In the massive hollowed cavern Rol and his fellow travelers were at last allowed to sink to the ground, whilst people ran to and fro seeking out blankets for them, jugs of wine, barley-bannock, honey, goat's cheese, and anything else they could get their hands on. Within the square itself, the raised stone hearths were set blazing and the heat mounted. It seemed suffocating after the weeks out in the open. The travelers snatched greedily at any food offered to them, only to become sick after a few mouthfuls. Their stomachs had shrunk, and no longer knew what to make of civilized fare.

A raucous cacophony of voices rose round them. Questions flailed through the air. People pressed clothing upon them. Some of the women took it upon themselves to try and wash their faces. One large matron held Giffon between her ample breasts and spooned soup into his mouth. It dribbled down his chin. He was saying something, but it was lost in the hubbub.

"Out of my bloody way." Esmer pushed through the crowd. She stared at Rol unsmilingly a second, then knelt beside him, black hair swinging in greasy plaits. "Well, Captain, you have come home again, I find."

"Home, Esmer."

She ran a hand over his face like a man testing the muscle-tone of a horse. "What in the world have you been doing to yourself?"

The press, the heat, the noise were too much for him. Something like a snarl flitted across Rol's face. He stood up, leaning on Esmer's sturdy shoulder. As she tried to rise with him he pushed her down again.

"No. Leave me be."

He shoved Elias flat as the dark man tried to rise also, exchanged a rueful smile with Gallico, and then made off for the exit to the square—a tall, linteled doorway that led toward the seafront.

It took him some time, but he had learned patience of late, and he was able to pause and rest every so often without chafing too much at the delay. People went past him in bustling crowds. He hitched up the old sea-cloak some nameless benefactor had given him, and covered his face. He saw Miriam stride by like a warrior queen, russet hair flaming behind her and musketeers trailing in her wake. Ganesh Ka had been stirred into something near frenzy by their return. It seemed to Rol absurd, and almost unbearable after the open spaces of the high country. He tacked away from the crowds, anonymous under his hood.

The ship-cavern at last, and at the far end of it the three tall sea gates through which light still flooded to kindle the water eddying round the docks. Rol breathed in the smell. After the sterile mountains, this barrage of stinks assaulted his senses. Old fish, tar, wet wood, salt, and a hundred other odors clamoring for his attention. There were several ships tied up at the quays, and with a leap of his heart, Rol recognized the sleek lines of the *Astraros*. He made his way to her gangplank and walked aboard, letting fall his cloak. The xebec seemed forlorn and deserted, and the ship-cavern itself was oddly untenanted. The entire population of the Ka, it seemed, was converging on the square to view the prodigals. Well, that was just fine.

Rol leaned against the bulwark and knotted an arm in the larboard mainmast shrouds. The tarred rope seemed to fit his hand somehow, and under his feet the minute movement of the ship upon the water brought peace to his mind.

Footsteps on the planking. He opened his eyes in time to find himself falling over, but was caught by a strong pair of arms before his face hit the deck. The arms set him down gently on his back and he found himself looking up at a bearded face that seemed oddly familiar.

"I know you."

"Yes, you do. Stay here. I'll be back." The man left him, cushioning his head upon a coil of rope. Rol lay there, content to stare up at the rigging lines of the *Astraros,* and the roof of the cavern above with the writhing bright snakes of water-shadow playing upon it.

The man returned, and set a hand under Rol's head, raising it. "Drink this."

A leather nozzle was against his lips. Rol put his lips about it as though it were a teat, and wine was squirted into his mouth, cold and warming at the same time. He swallowed it down: acrid, resinous wine from the shores of the Inner Reach. It was rough laborer's drink, the kind ten thousand small-holders made for themselves up and down the southern seas, and it seemed to Rol in that moment that he had never tasted better.

The wineskin was taken away. Rol was propped up and a flat barley-bannock was placed in his hands. "Eat."

He broke the bread, and took a chunk in his mouth. As he swallowed, he remembered the face that was smiling at him.

"You're Aveh, the carpenter."

"Welcome home, Captain. You look like you have traveled a hard road."

Rol ate more bannock. It seemed to be swelling in his meager stomach. He coughed, and Aveh set the wineskin to his mouth again, poured in another stream of the brown liquid. Rol swallowed it down, and felt the warmth of the humble stuff course through his innards.

"The mountains. We came over them. Thef got the *Astraros* home, then. I'm glad."

"Yes. We put in almost seven weeks ago. They've all gone to the square to see you. I was left alone here, as harbor watch."

"Alone? You have your son. Where is he?"

Aveh's face clouded. "My son is dead, Captain."

Something sank in Rol's heart. "How?"

"A Bionari cruiser chased us past Windhaw, firing its chasers as it pursued. It could not catch us, but a lucky shot came aboard."

"I'm sorry, Aveh."

"These things happen. It's the way of this world."

"This world is a filthy sty."

The carpenter had a strange look in his eyes—not sorrow, not anger. It was a kind of judicial detachment. "Perhaps it is," he said.

Aveh helped Rol below, and he tumbled into the hanging cot of the xebec's stern-cabin, dead to the world, his travel-stained clothes still wrapped about his bony limbs and Fleam cradled in his arms. For a while there was nothing, only a darkness without dreams. Black sleep, and within it the slow repair of his blood-starved muscles and overworked bones.

Rol slept the clock around, and when he woke, he washed himself in a bowl of fresh water brought into the cabin by Aveh. The old carpenter would have left him to his ablutions, but Rol asked him to stay while he washed and changed into some of his own clothes, left in the cabin since he had turned the ship over to Thef Gaudo, off Arbion. It seemed a long time ago, but it was only a matter of months. Now, back on board the xebec, it seemed that his sojourn in Bionar must be only some form of unquiet dream, less real than the memory of capturing this ship, of sailing the *Revenant,* of climbing through the slave-hold that once had festered here below his very feet, and seeing Aveh's simpleminded son smiling at him through the filth and manacles, the degradation wrought upon him by men simply trying to turn a profit.

The world was indeed a sty, and mankind a herd of pigs rooting through it. Rol sat on the edge of the swinging cot with the water still dripping from his face and stared at the stump on his right hand where his invisible finger still ached and wriggled. This was not the triumphant homecoming he had imagined.

"We have *Osprey* and *Skua* docked at the moment, after barren runs to the east of the Reach," Aveh said. "Artimion cruises two or three weeks at a time, then puts in for a few days to give the crew a run ashore. He's chased off a couple of Bionari sloops, but has seen nothing big since you left. A longboat has just put in from the *Revenant*. I think Artimion has sent some news. The ship is in peak condition; I've worked upon her myself. It's fine timber, that black teak that makes her hull. I doubt I've seen better."

Rol's clothes hung on him like sacks. He could make thumb and forefinger meet about his forearm, and had made a fresh hole in his belt with Fleam's keen point to stop his breeches from sliding down his hips.

"What time of day is it?"

"Past noon."

"And what's everybody doing?"

The carpenter smiled. "They're trying to struggle along, Captain, same as usual."

"Aveh, if I had not taken this ship, your son might still be alive. A slave, but alive."

"You cannot know that; no man alive can. You did the right thing at the time. That's all anyone can do."

Some kind of foreboding was upon Rol. It was as oppressive as anything he had ever known.

"Is it enough, you think, just trying to do the right thing?"

"It's more than enough."

"I was brought up to think of ordinary men as cattle, not worthy of consideration. Their lives and deaths were without meaning or significance. How can it be otherwise, in a world where death ends everything? Why do the right thing, if the wrong thing is easier, and in the end no one is made to pay for their misdeeds?"

"I think some men—good men—will always do the right thing, Captain; or at least they will wish they had. Consideration of life or death does not come into it, not in the day-to-day business of their lives."

"I am not a good man, Aveh," Rol choked, remembering. Rowen's face on the battlefield at Myconn. Rafa's body with the stones piling up upon it. Those men and boys he had had blown from the guns of the *Revenant*—out of anger, and because it was simply in his power. In his travels he had met with death many times, but now the collective weight of all those killings seemed to hang leaden about his heart.

"Then try to be better," the carpenter said. He laid a hand on Rol's shoulder for a moment, and then got up and left.

Rol wiped his face, nodding.

The febrile tumult of the day before seemed to have cooled. Men and women greeted Rol as though he had never been away. They told him it was good to have him back, and by their eyes they meant it. There was not the same joyous welcome that they gave to Gallico, or even to Elias Creed; it was a subdued reception, something else. Rol realized with a flash of insight that they looked upon him with hope. They did not love him, but he reassured them somehow. He had no idea how this could have happened, but accepted it without question.

He made his slow, painful way through the subterranean passages of the Ka, up into the light aboveground, until there was blue sky above him and the soaring towers of the city reared up against it, serene and eternal. A cool air was blowing, and as he sniffed at it, looking out to sea, part of him registered that it had backed round. The easterlies had faded, and in their place there came a cold north wind off the Winterpack at the top of the world. A fair breeze to clear Windhaw. He felt the chill of it steal into his bones.

People walked by him in knots and ribbons. Farmers on their way to the lower fields, woodsmen out to tend the charcoal-kilns. Grubby children following their mothers with halloos and cries. He nodded at them, accepting their stares and their greetings, some murmured, some shouted. For the first time in his life he felt he fitted someplace. He had earned his right to be here.

He walked on, and climbed one of the Ka's crumbling cyclopean ramparts, sitting atop it like a conqueror. He had a view of the sea to the east, a wall of blue so intense and bright it watered the eyes to look upon it. In the beginning, it was said, the sea was the first thing that had come into being, a life to itself in the yawning gulf below the stars. And his grandfather had told him it would be there at the end, when all other things would be taken to its depths, to sink into the darkness there.

"I found you," a woman's voice said, and he started, lost in his own imaginings. Turning, he saw Esmer looking up at him.

"You found me," he said.

She climbed up beside him and took a seat on the mustard-pale stone. In the clear winter sun he saw the lines about her nose and mouth. She was sloe-eyed, smelling of sweat and woodsmoke, and her woolen robe was only slightly darker than the waves that rolled to the horizon.

"I hear you were in love with your sister," she said.

"I heard that too."

"Gallico told me. It must be true, then."

Rol smiled. "Gallico always tells the truth."

Esmer chewed the end of one of her black braids. "I do not love you," she said.

"I know," Rol retorted, surprised.

"Just so we understand. I'm not some fresh-faced girl, and as it happens, you're not a youngster yourself anymore." She took his hand, speaking through her white teeth with the braid of hair still hanging from them. "But it's good to have someone, now and then," she went on. "We all need someone. Because there's the here and now, and that's all. We take what we can from the world, before the world gets what it wants from us." She paused. "Memories are only poison."

Rol set an arm about her strong shoulders. "Some memories," he said.

Chilled through and through by the keen norther, Rol and Esmer helped each other down below again. Those he had brought over the mountains were still in the square, eating, sleeping, staring into the cooking fires with bemused looks on their faces. As he entered the firelit cavern they turned toward him, and he saw the same thing in their eyes. All these people were his now. They looked to him for a direction, and for some kind of protection. He could give them neither of those, he was sure. But that no longer meant he would not try.

Even Miriam looked at him differently. There was a new appraisal in her glance as he joined his friends at one of the fire-pits and was handed a cup of wine by Gallico. Miriam and Esmer measured each other a moment before the dark-haired woman left. "I've work to do," Esmer said. "Unlike some. Later, Cortishane."

Miriam leaned on her musket and shook her hair out of her face. "You've been having adventures, it seems, Cortishane. Fighting wars and making kings."

Rol drank his wine. Gallico was reclining on one elbow, eyes glimmering in the flame-light. Giffon sat leaning against his huge bulk, head down, and Elias Creed stood to one side like a stripe-bearded scarecrow. There was something in the air among them, some knowledge hovering.

"What's happened?" Rol asked.

They looked amongst themselves and over their shoulders, like people unwilling to share a secret. Finally, Miriam spoke.

"You arrived in good time. Artimion sent in word this morning. There are ships out to the north, a large convoy. They may be Mercanters, they may not. He's putting farther out from the coast to take a look. In the meantime, we are to discreetly make all ships in the Ka ready for sea."

Rol closed his eyes.

"It'll be a Mercanter convoy," Gallico said gruffly. "The wind this time of year . . ." He trailed off, convincing not even himself.

"The wind has changed," Rol said. "It's fair for the Reach now. Canker knows where we are. He's finishing the job."

"What must we do?" Miriam asked him. Looking into her face, Rol saw fear there for the first time since he had known her. For himself, he felt only a kind of dull hopelessness. It was not over. There would be no end to it.

"We must evacuate the Ka," he said at last, hating the words as he said them, hating himself as he surveyed the motley, vagabond crowd about the cooking-fires who believed themselves safe at last.

"We don't have enough ships," Creed said, tugging at his beard, his cheekbones sharp angles planed by the firelight.

"We'll get out those we can. The rest must take to the mountains, like last time."

Giffon groaned wordlessly and Gallico set a hand on the boy's head.

"Miriam, I leave it to you," Rol said. "This word will spread soon enough, and when it does there will be panic. You know better than I what has to be done. I make only one stipulation."

She stared at him.

"The people we took from the slaver, and those who have come over the mountains with me, they shall go into the ships."

"Indeed! And why should—"

"They've suffered enough, Miriam."

After a moment, she nodded. "Very well. Gallico, if those are men-of-war out there, then how long do we have?"

"I don't know." The halftroll flapped one taloned hand. "I haven't so much as been outside to sniff the wind." He spoke to Rol. "We must get out to the *Revenant.*"

"We'll take a cutter," Rol agreed. "There's one tied up next to the *Astraros.* But you're not coming out, Gallico."

"What? Why not?"

"You must assume command of the *Astraros* from Thef and start taking on passengers as soon as she's outfitted for sea. As soon as you've taken on board as many as you can, bring her out and rendezvous with the *Revenant.*"

"No, Rol," Gallico said quietly. "I go with the *Revenant.* It may be we'll have to tangle with these men-of-war, if that's what they are. You need every able officer you can cram on board. Thef can handle the xebec; all she has to do is show a clean pair of heels, after all."

"What about Artimion? He commands the *Revenant* now," Miriam said indignantly.

"She's my ship," Rol told her. "And my crew. Artimion must come back to shore and look after the Ka; that's his command, where he can do the most good. This is not bloody-mindedness, Miriam. There's no time for that now."

Miriam finally nodded.

"I'm going to write out orders for Thef. Miriam, what other ships are in or close by?"

"Jan Timian's *Skua,* and Marveyus Gan's *Osprey.* That's all."

"I'll write orders for them, too, then. We must get as many aboard as possible. If this is Canker's doing, this fleet, then he will have embarked an army with it. I know him. He'll send regiments ashore and scour every inch of this coast."

"What's he doing it for?" Miriam asked. Her face was white as sailcloth.

"He's looking for me, Miriam. I am half brother to the last legitimate ruler of Bionar; a tenuous connection, but it's there all the same. He'll sleep better at night with me dead and Ganesh Ka destroyed."

"The people must make for the hills at once," Miriam said, shocked.

The little group stood silent for a while, staring into the fire-pit before them.

"This is the end, then," Elias Creed said at last. "The Ka is finished. We cannot fight a fleet."

"This place has been here a long time," Rol told them. "Even if they bombarded it for a month, they'd barely make a dent in the stone. No, the city itself will endure, but our tenure of it is over. We must look for someplace else to lay our heads."

"And where will that be?" Miriam asked.

"I will find a place," Rol said calmly. He scratched the itching palm of his left hand, where Ran's Mark burned in folds of flesh. He knew now why it had been set there. To lead them to a new beginning.

Twenty

THE BLACK SHIP

THE BREEZE HAD VEERED ROUND TO EAST-SOUTHEAST and was still freshening, kicking up whitecaps on the waves, a half-fathom swell that set the heavy cutter to pitching like a playful cart-horse. They had hoisted the lugsail, stowed the oars, and were now making a good seven knots or so with the wind on the starboard quarter. Rol sat at the tiller, drenched and grinning, whilst Elias Creed stood by the single mast, clinging to a halliard and peering north. In the bottom of the boat, Giffon was bailing with a wooden pail, his face as green as the translucent swells around them. He was always sick when first he went back to sea after an absence.

Gallico bent to peer at the brass compass between his feet. "Nor'-nor'west by south," he said. "That'll do just fine. Gods in heaven, but it's good to be back in a boat!"

"It's like coming back from the dead," Elias Creed said. And then: "Sail ho! I see the *Revenant,* or her twin. She's under topsails and jib, one point off the larboard bow. Look at that bow wave! Artimion is giving her the wind."

Cold sea-spray came aboard, lit up by the westering sun into a shower of yellow sparks. Rol wiped his face, feeling the new angles upon it, the scars that had not been there before. His youth was gone now. There was no trace left of the fresh-faced boy who had one night knocked on the door of Psellos's Tower in Ascari. But he still had no idea what that boy had become.

"Rol," Creed said, and his voice was quite changed. "Look north."

Rol gave over the tiller to Gallico and made his way forward, ducking under the drum-taut sail. The horizon was a ragged line of white and dark, waves coursing along it like the teeth of a saw, their heads whipped to white foam by the brisk wind. The *Revenant* was less than a league away now, but more distant, to larboard, there was a line of white nicks on the horizon that were not waves. Rol counted over two dozen of them, though one could not be accurate at this distance and in this sea. The sun was sinking rapidly, and the western horizon was a clear, blushed arc of color, dark as wine, with a dying light brimming over the topmost peaks of the mountains. Rol wiped salt-spray from his face. "Big vessels. I can see their courses on the rise. Ship-rigged too. Those are men-of-war, Elias."

They had all expected it, but deep down some irrational part of them had hoped it might yet be a merchant convoy.

"Canker has been busy," Elias said, eyes dark as the shad-owed flanks of the mountains in the west.

"Yes. He is a resourceful man."

They had to wave and halloo like fools before the *Revenant* no-ticed them and backed topsails to let the cutter clunk along-side. By that time, the ship's company had recognized them, and were cheering up and down her decks. They were shouting Gallico's name, and Creed's, and a few yelled *"The skipper!"* too.

Rol hauled himself up his ship's side, aided by the man-ropes they sent down for him. When he stood on the *Revenant*'s deck his head was swimming slightly, and his biceps burned. He was a long way from hale; the mark the mountains had set upon him would take time to erase. John Imbro, Fell Amertaz, little rat-faced Kier the carpenter, and two dozen others; they left their posts and came crowding around as Gallico, Creed, and Giffon climbed up from the cutter in turn, leaving the pitching craft made fast fore and aft to the *Revenant*'s side. As they came aboard, the grinning seamen slapped and manhan-dled them as if to make sure they were real. Rol looked aft, and saw Artimion standing at the quarterdeck rail. If he was sur-prised at this visitation, he concealed it, and he stood as im-passive as a ship's captain should, looking down on the little pantomime below. Rol made his way through the cloud of laughing mariners and climbed the steep steps aft. He had to pause at their top, breathing hard. He offered Artimion his hand, and after a brief moment the black man shook it, then bent his head to peer at the mutilated limb he held.

"You've been through the wars," he said.

"That I have."

"Come below. We can talk there."

The familiar cabin, one of the most beautiful spaces Rol had ever inhabited. Artimion had changed very little. He took the captain's chair, his back to the stern windows so that his face was hid by shadow, and Rol had the light of the sunset in his eyes.

"You want your ship back," Artimion said.

"Yes, I do."

"Fine; it's yours. It was only a loan, after all." Artimion's face was impossible to read.

"The sea air has done you good," Rol told him. "I can't hear your lungs wheezing anymore."

Artimion inclined his head. "You, on the other hand, look

more dead than alive. Perhaps you could tell me what you've been up to, and if it is connected with the doom of Ganesh Ka, which is beating up into the wind as we speak."

He was coldly angry, Rol realized. He blames me.

"The rebel Queen, Rowen, is dead, her armies broken and destroyed. I killed Bar Asfal with my own hands, which, as it happens, was the final thing your old friend Canker needed to hatch out his plans. He is now King of Bionar, and it is he who has sent out this fleet to destroy us." Looking at Artimion's face, Rol added, "Yes, it came as quite a surprise to us too."

"How did you get back to the Ka?"

"Over the Myconians."

"How long—"

"Canker has had a little under two months. Ample time to collect up a fleet and send it south."

Artimion leaned back in his chair and stared at the deckhead above. "We must abandon the Ka," he said, his voice a choked whisper.

"Miriam has it in hand. Now tell me of this fleet. What do you know?"

Artimion collected himself with a visible effort. "They fly the saffron and black of Bionar in the main, but some of them have Mercanter pennants also."

"Merchantmen, in a fighting fleet?"

The black man leaned forward. "No. They are all warships. It would seem the Mercanters have got themselves a navy, and are in league with our old friend Canker."

Rol digested this. His turn to be shocked. "We must stop trying to outdo each other with our surprises," he said to Artimion. The black man smiled.

"You know what it means, Cortishane?" He rose, and from the gimballed jug slung from one bulkhead he poured them clay cups of wine. Rol sipped without replying.

"It means we're finished, all the inhabitants of the Ka. If the

Mercanters have outfitted warships against us then there is truly no place left to run, for there is not a kingdom in the world that would defy them to harbor us. Ganesh Ka was the last sanctuary." Artimion tossed back his wine. "We are floating dead men."

Rol watched him. Canker's treachery had hit him hard. "It would seem there is less honor among thieves than we thought," he said.

"I never thought Canker to be some paragon of honesty, but I misread the scale of his ambition."

"So did I," Rol admitted. "So did everyone."

"With a new regime in Bionar as our ally, we would have been secure, Rol. I did what I thought was best for us all."

Rol nodded. "I know you did. I know that now."

Artimion raised his glass in salute, eyes glinting. "You may have brought our doom upon us, Cortishane, but it was I who sent you out looking for it."

"Yes. Between us, we did quite a job of it."

They watched each other a moment, as if registering the face of a stranger. Then Artimion drained his wine.

"I am needed ashore," he said. "You must bring in the *Revenant,* take on as many as you can, and get them out of here. I don't know where, or how, but you must fill up every boat that will float and get them away. This wind is going to start backing soon, I can feel it. By morning, that fleet will have it on the beam, and lee shore or no, they will be able to creep south and land their marines. The Ka has one more day, two at most. Then it will be sacked."

"Artimion, there are thousands in the city. If the ships can take off seven or eight hundred, we'll be lucky. What of the rest?"

"I will lead them across the hills into the Goliad," Artimion said. He peered into his empty cup, and nodded as though reassuring himself.

"Across the Gorthor Flats? That's madness."

"Have you other suggestions, Cortishane?"

They looked at each other. Artimion's question was genuine.

"No, I suppose I haven't. But they'll die there, Artimion; I know."

"Some will make it. The hardiest. Many will die. But if they stay where they are, all will die. Simple choices, Rol, make for simple decisions."

"That much is true. What if I told you that I may know of another place, a sanctuary where we can all be safe?"

"I would say, lead me to it—what do you think? We've no time for rhetoric." Artimion raised his voice. "Generro! Pass the word for the bosun!"

Young Generro, he of the pretty face and long arms, put his head in at the door, said, "Aye, sir," grinned at Rol, and then withdrew. A minute later Fell Amertaz's sinister, competent face took his place. "Sir?"

"Set course for the Ka, all plain sail. Drop anchor outside the seawall and then set down all boats."

Amertaz hesitated, looked at Rol, then nodded. "Aye aye, sir, course for Ganesh Ka, set down boats."

"My last order as the *Revenant*'s captain, I promise you," Artimion said with a battered smile.

"It's all right. I'm not as precious as I once was."

"You spoke of a sanctuary. Was that wishful thinking, a play with words, or is there something to it? We don't have the time to—"

Rol raised his left hand, palm toward Artimion's face. "What do you see?"

"A scar, a mark. Some call it the Mark of Ran. Superstition."

"It is a map."

"I see no map."

"I do. This is a sea-course, based on the stars. I see

Quintillion there, as plain as I see your face. Artimion, I believe this mark was made on me for a purpose. I intend to follow it with this ship, and any other ship that'll come with me."

Artimion grasped Rol's hand in his own blunt fingers and stared intently at the lines and whorls that were etched thereon. "I see nothing," he said.

"Trust me, it's there."

"What in hell are you, Cortishane? What are you doing among us?"

"I'm going to try and save these people."

"There was a time when you didn't give a damn about these people."

Rol nodded. "That was true, once. But no longer. As I said, you will have to trust me."

Artimion dropped Rol's hand. "It was bad, in Bionar. I can see it on your face, and not just in the scars."

"It was bad. It was war, as it is fought by great nations, without pity or honor. Great wheels rolling, and the little people crushed beneath them. Canker can keep his kingdom. I will never go back."

"How did this rebel Queen meet her end—your sister?"

"Half sister," Rol corrected quickly. Orders were being shouted up on deck, and within the stern cabin the light moved round as the ship fell off before the wind, prior to coming round. Shadow grew in the space about them, and beyond the stern-windows the sunset was red on the surface of the sea.

"I did not see her die. Gallico, he watched. He saw it." Rol's face burned at the memory.

"Canker was right," Artimion said. "You did love her."

"I loved an idea, a memory." Rol was unable to keep the bitterness out of his voice. "When it came to it, I was glad enough just to get away from her alive."

Artimion gestured to the scarred hand he had scrutinized a moment before. "Perhaps you are being saved for greater things."

"I hope not, Artimion." Then Rol turned on his heel and left the cabin. He stumbled along the dark companionway to the waist of the ship, wiping his eyes in angry bafflement.

The *Revenant* took the wind on the larboard beam. Rol assumed his accustomed place by the ship's wheel. Old Morcam, the quartermaster, was steering, along with one of his mates. His eyes gave Rol a rare flicker of goodwill.

"Nice to have you back, skipper," he said out of the corner of his mouth, and tilted the spokes a tad, keeping the sharply braced yards just this side of shivering.

"It's good to be back, Morcam," Rol said.

A ship's gun fired, faint in the teeth of the wind. Rol stared aft.

"Signal gun," Morcam said. "They do it every time they change tack. Not bad sailing, for a Bionese bunch of bastards."

Rol wondered what Morcam would make of the Bionese bastards he had brought over the mountains. He intended to have them board this very ship. They were his responsibility, after all.

The quarterdeck became somewhat crowded as Gallico, Creed, and Giffon joined him about the wheel. Artimion came on deck as they were preparing to anchor two cables from the tawny seawalls of Ganesh Ka. He bore a canvas seabag, and had buckled a rapier at his waist. It was almost dark by then, and a heavy blueness had settled over the water, broken by the flash of foam on the wave crests. They dropped anchor in fifteen fathoms. The *Revenant* slowed and her stern began to come around as the wind worked on her, but the anchor held. Rol looked up at the yards. All sails had been furled in the bunt, and the topmen were clambering down the shrouds, more subdued than he had ever seen them.

"All hands," he called. "Prepare to lower boats from the yardarms. Gallico, take command." He turned to Artimion. "I'll come ashore with you in the cutter."

The inner harbor of the Ka was crowded with small-craft. Fishing smacks, longboats, open-decked cutters and launches— every vessel, great and humble, that could float. Skiffs and row-boats were ferrying folk out to them, so overcrowded there was barely space to man the oars. As night swooped down on them from the mountains, torches flared and flickered in the boats, their light shattered in the choppy water of the harbor.

Creed was at the tiller of the cutter, eight good men at the oars. In the darkness his face was unreadable. "Elias," Rol said. "Once we dock, take a couple of the crew and start loading the folk from Myconn on the *Revenant.* Then the slaves we took out of the *Astraros,* as many as you can track down. Pile them in. We'll worry about provisioning later."

"We may as well grab some provisions while we're at it," Creed said. "Look at the stuff on those vessels; they've broken open the foodstores."

"Bad news travels fast."

Inside the ship-cavern there was a roaring chaos. Crowds milled about the wharves by torchlight, pleading for spaces on the boats, fighting for a place at an oar, scrambling for casks of provisions. Many were already drunk. The crew of the cutter had to physically beat people from the gunwales of their craft. Splashes as people were pushed into the water. Women screaming.

"Issue pistols," Rol said.

The cutter thumped against the stone of the wharf, and

Artimion leaped over the side onto the docks. He punched a man flat, and his roar echoed off the roof of the cavern.

"Back away there, you miserable bastards!" His eyes gleamed bright as glass beads, reminding Rol that in Artimion, too, there was some of the Blood. Men retreated from his face, angry and ashamed and afraid.

"It's every man for himself now!" a wild-eyed fellow shrieked.

Artimion drew his rapier and ran the man through, then raised the bloody blade and brandished it at the crowd. "Get back from the wharves, or by Ussa's mane, I'll start killing you. We will have order here, by the gods!"

Creed spat over the stern of the cutter. "That spell at sea really did him a power of good," he said to Rol.

"Two men stay in the boat, Elias, pistols cocked. Don't moor her; stay a few yards off the wharf. They're to shoot anyone who tries to swim aboard."

"It's like that, is it?" Creed asked.

"It's like that." Rol gripped Creed's shoulder and looked back at the sea gates. "The rest of the ship's boats will be arriving soon. Same goes for them."

"Poor bastards," Elias said, surveying the mob at the seafront. Artimion had cleared them away from the water and was haranguing their ranks in a voice of brass. The blood had slid down the blade of his sword to stripe the back of his hand. He had them cowed; they were listening to him with desperate eagerness now, trying to squeeze any mote of hope they could out of his words. From their midst stepped a half dozen of Miriam's musketeers, faces white with fear.

Rol took his master-at-arms, Quirion, and four other sailors ashore, all armed with pistols and cutlasses and capable of intimidating their way through the most truculent of crowds. Creed took two more with him. They nodded at each other, and then forged uphill, ignoring the questions and accusations

that were flung at them. Rol drew Fleam, and the cold light of
the scimitar's blade was enough to clear a path for him, though
his withered muscles were barely able to raise the weapon. He
peered back once and saw that by some miracle Artimion had
dispersed the crowds somewhat. The looting of the store-
houses went on at the back of the ship-cavern, though, and it
was galling to see all that precious gear strewn upon the quays
and trampled underfoot. He hoped Miriam had put a strong
guard on the powder-arsenal, or else Canker's fleet might find
its job done for it before it arrived.

"You know the tower you're looking for?" Rol asked Creed.

"It's not far off the square. Nearly all the slaves were billeted
there."

"Go to it, Elias, and don't let them bring too much baggage.
If anyone disputes your passage, shoot them."

Creed raised the pistol-barrel to his temple in mock salute.
He looked profoundly unhappy.

"And Elias, if you see Esmer, bring her with you. Get her on
a boat."

"I'll try, Rol." Face set, Creed stalked off briskly enough, ac-
companied by Gil Whistram and Harry Dade—good, sound
men.

The square was full of quarreling and arguing people. The
cooking-fires were burning low, and that added to the hellish
unreality of the scene. The refugees who had followed him out
of Myconn had drawn themselves up in a corner like a ragged
band of fearful children. Strangers here, they did not know
what to make of this rancorous uproar; perhaps it was a nor-
mal occurrence. Rol saw relief in their eyes as he strode up to
them.

"On your feet," he said brusquely. "There's no time to talk.
You have to come with me. We're putting to sea."

Incomprehension, panic. Rol turned to Quirion. "Get them
up, and herd them down to the quays. Keep them together."

The master-at-arms looked both startled and dubious. Rol grasped his arm. "*Do it,* Quirion. Don't fuck around."

They herded the emaciated, ragged band together like wolves hounding sheep. There was no time for gentleness or explanation; that would have garnered too much attention from the others in the square. Blows were exchanged, people knocked to their knees. Rol saw blood glisten scarlet in the firelight. "What are you doing to us?" someone wailed.

"Get on your feet," he snapped, and hauled a rail-thin woman off the floor. "Follow my shipmates. Trust me."

Trust me. The ghost of Michal Psellos must be laughing now.

Someone at his elbow. So tense was he that he raised Fleam. Aveh, the carpenter. "Shouldn't you be on the *Astraros?*" he asked the man irritably.

"I was off at the northern stores with a working-party. Miriam is handing out food and weapons. Captain, Bionese marines have been sighted up the coast, two or three full regiments. A shepherd-boy brought the news only an hour ago. Miriam sent me to find you."

"Gods in heaven," Rol said. "How far?"

"Five, six leagues. They're marching in the dark, in unfamiliar country, but they'll be here before morning." Aveh looked at the brutal work in hand and asked, "Do you need some help?"

Rol lifted a crying teenage girl off the ground; even to his weakened muscles she felt light as a bundle of rags. He handed her to Aveh and she buried her face in the carpenter's shoulder. "Yes. Help me. We must get these people down to the docks."

Quirion, Rol's hardened master-at-arms, had been a privateer most of his life, and before that a sell-sword for Augsmark, Auxierre, half the kingdoms in the Mamertine League. Now he held a skull-faced, sexless child to his breast with one arm and in the other he brandished a ship's pistol.

His eyes were full of incredulous rage. "What happened to these people?"

"Never mind," Rol snapped. "Keep them moving."

They made their tortuous way back down to the ship-cavern—a stop-start, infuriating, exhausting half-mile odyssey. Their progress was punctuated by bursts of violence, brandished pistols, Quirion kicking his way forward to the front of the line. Rol's strength began to fail him, and his knees buckled. Aveh's fingers fastened on his bicep and raised him up again. The carpenter was immensely strong, but he could not bear all of Rol's weight on his one free arm. The press of bodies grew intense. Someone took Rol's other arm and kept him from falling. It was Esmer, narrow-eyed and fierce as a cat. "Keep your damn feet on the floor!" she shouted at him, braids flying.

The wharves were packed again. Artimion had disappeared, and all order had vanished. The bigger ships of the Ka, the *Skua,* the *Osprey*—both flush-decked brigs—and the *Astraros,* had slipped their moorings and were being towed out to the open water of the harbor by their ship's boats. Their decks were crammed with people and around them the water was stubbled with the bobbing heads of dozens more, desperate to climb aboard. The *Revenant*'s heavy cutter was still there, and all the other boats of the ship; light cutter, launch, and captain's skiff. Their crews were clubbing people from the gunwales with their oars. Elias Creed stood on the lip of the quay with a naked cutlass, eyes blazing, blood trickling from a gash at the side of his mouth.

Rol struggled to his side through the mob. "Load the boats!" he yelled. There were bodies at his feet, but he did not look down. "Get as many as you can aboard without swamping them."

The ex-convict nodded. "Rol, I only found a couple of dozen. The rest—" He gestured helplessly at the faces of the crowd.

"I know, Elias. We did our best. Get them aboard now."

They filed the Bionese refugees aboard the boats through a gauntlet of the ship's company, hardened mariners not afraid to use their weapons. Some had wives in the Ka, children lost somewhere beyond that howling mob, but they stood to their posts and held back the desperate throng at sword- and pistol-point. People spat in their faces, threw stones, cursed them, and vowed revenge.

Rol was the last to leave the quay. He clambered aboard the heavy cutter and pushed her off from the stone with his boot. Someone tried to leap past him and Fleam flicked up without his will to slash the unfortunate open from crotch to breast-bone. The corpse splashed into the water. A cry went up. A stone swooped past his head. In his fist, Fleam quivered in pleasure, and he sheathed the scimitar with revulsion.

The cutter was low in the water, the crew barely able to ship their oars for the mass of people cowering within. The sailors used them like giant paddles instead, and slowly drew away from the wharves. Musket-shots, echoing off the cavern walls. People wailed and shouted and fell tumbling from the wharves and fought one another in the water. Some threw torches at the departing boats.

The cutter was paddled out of the ship-cavern, into the harbor with its mighty encircling arms of stone. Rol looked up to see the stars overhead, a sliver of moon. The tide was still just on the ebb, and it took their keel, slid them quietly along with the plash of the oars. The water around them was thick with small-craft of all sizes and rigs, and ahead the yards of the three ships stood stark against the paler stone. The noise died away. No one spoke in the boat.

Twenty-one

THE MARK OF RAN

A RAT-TAG FLOTILLA, THEY ANCHORED TOGETHER around the *Revenant* and transferred their wretched cargoes to the larger vessels. Rol came aboard to find Gallico standing on the starboard gangway, his face a desolation.

"Is this all?" he asked. "You must go back for more."

The Revenants rigged tackles to the yardarms and began hauling the weaker occupants of the boats aboard like sacks of grain. "There's no going back," Rol said. "We barely made it away afloat."

"I'll go back. Let me take the cutters in again, Rol. We have space for more."

"No. Gallico, that place is not Ganesh Ka anymore. It belongs to a maddened mob. You take the boats back in and they'll sink them under you."

"Now, listen—"

"That's an order, Gallico. As soon as the boats are back on the booms we weigh anchor. It's over."

Gallico glared at him with something like hatred in his shining eyes.

"Where's Miriam, Artimion?"

"I don't know. The Bionese have landed up the coast. They're on the march as we speak, whole regiments. We have to get away."

Gallico's great fist came up and grasped the front of Rol's tunic. Gaunt though he was, the strength in the halftroll's arm was startling.

"He's right, Gallico." This was Elias Creed, climbing aboard with his mouth still bloody. "We can do no more. We've saved all we can."

Gallico released Rol. "The wind has backed to east-nor'east," he said formally. "The tide will be on the flood in two turns of the glass."

"Then we must put out to sea as soon as we can, and claw off this coast."

"What course shall I set?" Gallico asked.

"Due south, reefed courses and jib."

"You're the captain," Gallico snapped. And he walked away.

"Let him go," Elias said, as Rol tried to follow. "It's not you. He knows. He just has to get over it."

The small boats surrounding them were already sculling down the coast in an ungainly gaggle, their oars striking up white water from the darkened surface of the sea. The *Astraros,* the *Skua,* and the *Osprey* were making sail. Rol hailed the nearest: Thef Gaudo on the xebec.

"Due south, Thef—pass it on to the brigs!"

"Due south, aye aye—glad you made it, skipper."

"Elias, throw lines to the smaller boats. We'll tow them if they can't keep up."

Aveh and Esmer had joined them at the gangway, looking landward. "I see lights," the carpenter said.

They were springing up all over the shoreline, disembodied in the dark, some larger than others.

"They're burning the place," Esmer said, astonished. "Is it the Bionese? Have they arrived already?"

They watched, transfixed, as the fires spread. Not in one single wave, but in dozens of discrete glows, licking out of the stone windows that peppered the seaward sides of the towers and the cliffs. It looked almost as though the Hidden City were finally coming to life, lighting up for some unknown celebration, unafraid of watching eyes at last.

"We're burning it," Rol answered him. "We're doing it to ourselves, room by room."

The looming towers were outlines above a saffron blaze now, a bloom of fire. As they watched, there was an incredible mushrooming ball of flame that rose up hundreds of feet, and a second later the air shook with the deep thunder of the explosion. They all ducked instinctively. The ship's company, the refugees on board, all paused to stare, aghast.

"That was the powder-arsenal," Rol said.

"Artimion has lost control," said Creed.

Between them, Aveh the carpenter looked at the vast fireball now rising up to blot out the stars, and merely nodded to himself, as though it confirmed some knowledge he already possessed. Then he hid his eyes with one hand and bowed his head until it rested on the good wood of the ship's side.

Rol and Creed went to the quarterdeck. Gallico was fixed there like a standing stone, and the tears on his face gleamed bright in the light from his eyes.

"There was no going back," Rol said quietly, looking up at the halftroll, this monster he loved as a brother.

"I know," Gallico said.

Rol raised his voice. "Weigh anchor. Morcam, course due south. Lookouts to fore and main. Elias, get those people below."

The crew of the *Revenant* went about their business, and in the white-tipped sea around them the other ships and boats and desperate souls of their little fleet watched the Black Ship unfurl her sails and take wing for the south. On her quarter-deck a tall, gaunt man stood among his friends, and stared at the palm of his hand.

ABOUT THE AUTHOR

PAUL KEARNEY was born and grew up in Northern Ireland. He studied English at Oxford University and lived for several years in both Denmark and the United States. He now lives by the sea in County Down with his wife and two dogs. His other books include the acclaimed *Monarchies of God* sequence.